GHOSTSPEAKER CHRONICLES BOOKS 4-6

PATTY JANSEN

GET FREE EBOOKS

Visit pattyjansen.com
to sign up for Patty's mailing list. You get four series starter
ebooks for free!

FIRE WIZARD

Book 4 of the Ghostspeaker Chronicles

PATTY JANSEN

CHAPTER 1

MAN'S VOICE shouted at the bow of the ship. The sound echoed over the water in the still afternoon air.

Johanna sat up, dazed. She'd been lazing on the sloping covers of the ship's hold, warmed by whatever little winter sunshine made its way over the hill on the western side of the river, and she must have fallen asleep.

She'd been exhausted.

With her overnight trip to the farm of the Guentherite order, she had barely slept the previous night, and after their frantic escape from Florisheim, both the *Lady Sara* and the *Prosperity* had settled into a steady drift down the swollen river. There had been little for the refugees to do except rest.

Until now, that was.

Ko, at the bow, had pulled in the team of sea cows and was directing them to the riverbank. Johanna let herself slide down the sloping cover and went up the front to join him.

They were in a bend in the river, and forest on the high bank had been cleared to make room for . . . yes, what exactly?

Or rather, what had it been?

Because clearly some disaster had happened recently, maybe as recently as last night, judging by the churned earth and the splintered stumps of wood that were still smouldering.

The jumble of broken and shattered buildings stretched over

most of the lower part of the sloping riverbank on the left hand side. A stately house surrounded by vineyards at the top of the hill remained untouched, but every other structure closer to the river was reduced to a pile of smoking rubble.

A blue haze hung low over the ground.

In between the wreckage lay mounds of dirt. There were a couple of carts, torn to shreds, and the body of a horse. Overnight wild animals had ripped part of its belly open, spilling blood and entrails on the blackened ground.

"What is this place?" Johanna asked.

"This is the Guentherite abbot's summer residence," Ko said, his face white. He stared at the scene, his mouth open.

"The place where you were captured?"

"The very place. When you sent us to check on Saardam, we came down the river and saw all this activity here. There were people with boats, and there was a jetty over there."

All that remained were shattered pylons.

"We didn't know what to do so we pulled the boat to the bank, but it was a poor hiding place."

Both riverbanks were too steep for reed beds and there wouldn't have been anywhere for the men to hide.

"I'm guessing it didn't used to look like this."

"There used to be a couple of open sheds with carts." He pointed. "That over there was the caretaker's house, and over there was a large furnace."

Johanna remembered the furnace on the Guentherite brotherhood's farm. "For what?"

"Making iron."

"What do they want all this iron for?"

He shrugged. "They were making it into big blocks and sheets that they stored in a shed over there." But that shed no longer stood upright and Johanna could make out no iron in the rubble.

"Did many people live here?"

He nodded. "At least a hundred. Maybe more. I don't know. We never spent that much time here."

Johanna saw no one, not even dead people.

The two boats drifted towards the remains of the jetty. A

couple of boys came with sticks and ropes to hold the boat off and tie it to the jetty.

"Hello!" someone yelled at the deck of the *Prosperity*. "Hello! Is anyone there? Hello! Do you need help?"

Something moved behind the dead horse. A man rose, leaning on a shovel. He probably climbed out of the grave that he had been digging. He stared wide-eyed at the two ships coming towards the shore. His hair was grey and dirty, his hands were black and he had smeared a black smudge over his face.

"Is he a monk?" Johanna asked. The man wore a drab grey garment that didn't look like a habit.

"Prisoner," Ko said, his voice dark.

"By himself? Why doesn't he run away?"

Ko met her eyes. "Because there is nowhere to run to? The forests around here are not kind. There are bears and wolves. Looking at the horse, the wolves have already been here. There are ghosts, too."

Maybe, but Johanna thought that the worst thing one had to fear in the forest was other people. Sylvan and his bandits roamed these places. She still didn't know for certain who had killed all those people and put them in the ice cellar.

The stories of the two scouts Ko and Willem had been told and retold many times: they had been captured when they went downriver to check on Saardam. They'd been taken to the Guentherite brotherhood's farm where they had been forced to dig black rock out of a deep hole in the mountainside. The hole was close to the river and constantly at risk of flooding, because water seeped through the rock. The monks used the water wheel to scoop it out, but still, the diggers stood in water all day. There had been many different people, mostly young men, mostly from downriver. Some were hapless farmers who had stumbled across one of the brotherhood's projects while going to market or moving their animals. Some were peddlers or merchants travelling on horseback from town to town. They'd found their horses and stock confiscated, their travel clothes removed and replaced with a grey sack-like garment. Others were people whose families owed the brotherhood debts from as far away as Burovia. They all worked in the hole together, and learned to communicate across languages.

It was always dangerous. When the water seeped through the black rock, it absorbed ghosts that had been disturbed by the digging activities. The ghosts would float between the workers, sometimes making them fall asleep on the spot, sometimes making them fight each other.

Once the black rock had been brought to the surface, some of it would be used to light the furnace at the back of the chapel. In the furnace the monks would melt ore that came from upriver by boat, and turn it into iron. Both the bars of iron and the rest of the black rock would be shipped to the Abbot's summer residence along the river, and no one knew what happened to those materials there.

The lonely surviving man walked to the shore with a painful-looking gait and a distinct limp. He called something in a local dialect, waving his hands.

Johanna asked, "Does he want help or does he want us to go away?"

No one could answer that.

Karl, aboard the *Prosperity,* yelled something back at him and the man replied.

"He says we should move on as soon as possible," Karl yelled across the water to Johanna. "He says this is a dangerous place."

"Is there anyone else here?" she yelled back.

He asked the man and the man gave a longer reply, waving his hands and pointing. Karl looked up into the sky, frowning. He asked more questions and the man answered.

Roald said next to her, "He says that a great fire serpent came and burnt the place down."

Yes, that was true, he had spent time at the order. He would be able to understand their dialect.

"He says that the other people all ran into the forest and didn't come back. He says that he can't run because of his leg, so they left him behind."

"Did he say what sort of place this is, what they're making here?"

"No, but he keeps saying that we should leave because the fire serpent will be back."

The man kept looking at the sky.

"What is this fire serpent?"

"The fire serpent was mentioned in the books we read." Roald sounded indignant. "I showed you the pictures."

"But they are mythological creatures."

He gave her a *yes, and?* look.

Johanna remembered the dragons described in the book called *On The Magickal Creatures of the High Lands, the Sea and the Orient* that Roald had borrowed from the Jeromist monastery in Florisheim. There was no time to argue about what was real and what were folk tales. He was unlikely to understand the difference.

Then again, he had also told her that there was a dragon at the Guentherite farm, and that it used to sit on a brother's shoulder warning of bad air. She hadn't seen it when she went there, not that she'd looked for it. People seemed confused about what type of creature was called a dragon.

The conversation between Karl and the old man went on for a bit, and ended when the old man retreated up the riverbank. Short of rowing the dinghy to shore, the passengers couldn't have a closer look, and no one on board showed any inclination of wanting to do that. The women stood holding scarves over their noses. The air smelled of charred meat. They might not see any dead, but evidently the fire dragon had burned a lot of people.

Johanna beckoned for the old man to join the boats, but he seemed scared and not interested in coming on the boats, so they could do nothing except push off again.

The boats slowly drifted downstream while the man stood on the riverbank, watching and leaning on his shovel.

When there was a bend in the river and he vanished from view, Johanna went downstairs and leafed through the book of magical creatures, but it gave her no more information than she already remembered. The book contained a drawing of a dragon, a scaled, snake-like creature with wings that were far too small for it to get off the ground.

While it was said that dragons breathed fire, this particular one looked like a lizard to her with some wings drawn on. She had seen lizards in Lurezia where people kept them as pets. A peddler at the markets had baskets full of them. Some were thin and lithe, others short and fat. He had picked one up and given it to her to hold. She remembered the heavy and smooth feel of the creature as it warmed itself on the palms of her hands. Lizards were harmless, and she was sure that the "dragon" Roald had referred to that was supposed to be at the Guentherite farm was really a lizard. A fire serpent, whatever that was, didn't sound harmless.

Johanna couldn't help thinking that the Guentherite order's digging activities in the ground had upset a lot of bad things.

Necromancy, ghosts released from the ground in such numbers that the water became murky, fire creatures. Evil wizards taking over peaceful lands.

And the boats were drifting on this sick and ghost-infested water, closer and closer to Saardam, where people had no magic, where a Guentherite wizard had taken up residence, and the only useful magic they had was Johanna's ability to see things in wood. The fact that wood burned in fire seemed a cruel coincidence.

CHAPTER 2

WINTER WAS COMING. It was in the crispness of the air, in the whiteness of the dew on the grass, almost but not quite frozen as rime. It was in the steam rising from the river and blowing out of the nostrils of the cows that stood on the riverbank and that raised their heads curiously as the two river boats drifted downstream.

Johanna could feel the winter in her bones. Still, she counted herself lucky that she had a bed to sleep in, and that she didn't have to lie on the floor, or even sit on the deck, covered only by a horse blanket. But even down in the ship's hold in the little cosy room she shared with Roald, it was damp and cold. She'd given the warm blanket to a mother with two young girls—they were asleep in the corner of the room under the stairs, the mother leaning against the wall and the girls with their heads in her lap.

Their cheeks were red, and Johanna hoped that the girls were warmer than she felt. She had mistakenly thought that Roald would keep her warm, but all he did at night was toss and snore and keep her awake, and now she was stiff and cold as well as tired.

When she came up on the deck, the temperature dropped even further. Shivering, she pulled the cloak closer around her. Her breath steamed in the air.

Loesie sat at the bow on the driver's bench, her legs pulled up under her. The rope that held the harnesses of the sea cows hung slack, because the ship had moored at a rickety jetty and the animals were grazing nearer the shore.

"How far do we still have to go?" Her voice sounded loud in that silence.

Loesie let out a gasp. Had she been asleep? She let her feet down from inside the blanket and stuffed them in her old boots.

"There," she said and pointed over the riverbank, between a couple of willow trees.

Squinting through the mist, Johanna tried to make out what Loesie was looking at. A concentration of trees. A few windmills. And on the horizon, the faint outline of a tower.

Saardam. "Is that it?"

"It is. I don't think we should go any further with the boats."

They had discussed this when mooring here last night, that they were not going to take the ships all the way into Saardam because no one knew what they'd find there.

The Nieland vessel lay in the next bay upriver, tied to a couple of trees. The *Prosperity* was both larger and had a larger deck, and it carried most of the refugees. Normally used for storing transport crates, they had planned to use the deck as seating area for Roald and Johanna's official wedding. How trivial that planning now seemed, and why had they been so addled by magic to even consider having the ceremony in Florisheim?

Magic.

She shuddered.

Everything in Florisheim had been steeped with magic. It had affected everyone's decisions.

Some people on the *Prosperity* were early risers, courtesy of the cooks and the former soldiers who had made it on board. Captain Arense, too, already stood on the deck. He was wearing his grey cape. Some children had taken the dinghy ashore and were coming back with a bucket of milk. They chattered with shrill and far too cheerful voices that made Johanna's head hurt. Maybe they'd slept better on board that ship. Maybe they were used to discomfort. Maybe it was because they were children and didn't feel the cold. Everyone had been exhausted. No doubt the coming days would be even more exhausting.

Johanna went down the *Lady Sara*'s gangplank and picked her way across the rotting planks of the jetty. It would be a place where farmers loaded their milk and cheese to take to the markets in Saardam. But judging by the weeds that grew in the cracks of the wood and the grass that pushed through the gaps from underneath, it had been a long time since anyone had used the jetty.

Johanna waded through the grass of the riverbank. It was cold and damp closer to the ground, and remnants of mist trailed over the grass. A couple of willow trees guarded the bank like silent sentinels. In passing, Johanna ran her hand over the weathered trunks, and saw peaceful grazing cows in a brilliant green paddock. At least nothing bad had happened here in recent months.

The rope holding the ship in place had been tied around one of the tree trunks, and the wood did show her a man going out in the dinghy to tie it. He pulled the dinghy up onto a little beach a few steps across, climbed up the bank, dragging the rope through the reeds, and looped it around the trunk.

When Johanna came to the little beach, Captain Arense himself came down the ladder. He pulled the dinghy close and rowed a few strokes to the shore.

"It is getting cold these days, Your Majesty," he said while helping her in.

"It certainly is." She longed to be in a warm room with a roaring fire. Her heart ached when she thought of her father, and that she would soon know whether he was still alive. In a way she feared to find out, because if the news was bad, she would be better off not knowing.

The oars splashed in the calm water.

The dinghy glided across and a moment later clonked into the side of the *Prosperity*'s hull. Captain Arense grabbed the rope ladder and held it down. Johanna clambered up, her hands stiff from the cold.

On the deck, a number of women stood huddled around a camp stove on which stood a huge pot. The little boys that

Johanna had seen carrying the milk sat on the railing, eying the spoon going around and around in the porridge.

It smelled really good.

The door of the cabin opened and Johan Delacoeur stepped onto the deck. He was a tall man and he had to bend to avoid hitting his head against the top of the doorframe. He, too, looked a little the worse for wear, with a giant mud stain on his shirt that he must have acquired in the scramble to get on board.

He nodded when he saw Johanna, but his expression remained guarded. Did he remember how wrong he'd been about the Red Baron and the Baron's son's evil magic? Both his noble mates, Fleuris LaFontaine and Ignatius Hemeldinck had not made it onto either the *Prosperity* or the *Lady Sara*. There was no way of knowing whether they had survived, but Johanna guessed that they were probably with the Baron or staying with their cronies in Florisheim. Maybe they had seen the Baron's evil ways, but she didn't hold out too much hope. She didn't even think that Johan Delacoeur saw the truth. He was just here because of his family and because he happened to be in the camp when the panic broke out and his mates happened to be . . . elsewhere.

Johanna sat on the railing, waiting for the porridge to cook. Johan Delacoeur put his hands in his pockets and remained outside the door to the captain's cabin, looking ruffled and tired.

He yawned. "Pray, why have we stopped in this field?"

"Saardam is just over there." Johanna glanced at the western horizon, where pale sunlight touched the mist-covered meadows.

"Isn't that a reason to keep going?"

Johanna resisted the temptation to roll her eyes.

A woman handed Johanna porridge in a chipped bowl. "Be careful. It's very hot."

Johanna ate as quickly as she could, letting the hot goo make its way to her stomach.

The Shepherd Carolus had also come onto the deck, looking rumpled, unshaven and rubbing his face.

"So, when are we going to continue?" Johan Delacoeur asked the Shepherd. He held his bowl, untouched, as if eating porridge was beneath him.

"I thought you'd heard at the meeting last night that we're leaving the ships here." The Shepherd had been attending a sick child and had not heard all of the discussion last night.

"Ridiculous." Johan muttered under his breath.

The Shepherd gave him a startled and too-innocent look. "Why ridiculous? When the scouts return, they'll tell us how safe it is to go in. We'll be splitting up and going into town dressed as farmers and peddlers so that we don't attract attention."

Johan scoffed. "I'm not going to dress up in rags—"

"Oh, yes, dear, you are." This was his wife, Martine.

One of the younger girls said, "You can always be a pauper for real, like the rest of us."

Johan went red in the face. "I'm going to stay with the ship."

Martine said, "The boys are already doing that. They're much handier with sea cows than you are. We'll do whatever is necessary to go home. Aren't you keen to find out what has become of your sisters?"

He snorted, took a spoon full of porridge, burned his mouth, but ate it anyway, glaring at his wife.

Johanna was beginning to like Martine Delacoeur, who might be of noble birth, but didn't put up with any nonsense. She nodded at Johanna as if she wanted to say *Never mind him, we'll do whatever we want.*

It was a pity they didn't have children.

ONE BY ONE, the fellow travellers came onto the deck, either from the *Prosperity*'s hold or ferried in the dinghy from the *Lady Sara*. There were eighty-two people on both vessels, men and women of all ages, but they were mostly from the middle and upper classes and their households.

The women at the stove doled out porridge, while their daughters climbed the rope ladder down to the water to rinse bowls and spoons because, between the inventories of the two ship kitchens, they didn't have enough of either.

Johanna remained out of the way and only moved to the ladder when Roald had decided to come up. His straw-blond hair was too long and messy and his beard had gotten quite long as well. He looked perfect for disguising himself as peasant.

She thought he looked cute and with pain in her heart remembered how happy he was when gardening or catching frogs, and how much he was unsuited to meetings, speeches and politics. One of the women gave him a bowl, and he ate, quietly and neatly, with a spoon, without slurping and without spilling, while standing next to Johanna, leaning against the railing.

On the deck, the word went around that Saardam was visible from the *Lady Sara*'s position and young Gijsbert and his little friends hoisted each other on top of the cabin to have a look.

They reported that it was really misty. Some blue sky peeped through the mist directly overhead, heralding a sunny day. A flock of geese flew high up there, on their way south for winter. Roald was looking at them, too.

"Winter is coming," he said.

Johanna nodded and touched his hand. He looked tense, unused to sharing his home with so many people. His need to be alone and on the riverbank, looking for birds and frogs, radiated off him.

The young boy Gijsbert called out, "Look, they're back!"

He stood on the roof of the cabin, pointing at the riverbank, where the two scouts that had gone out that morning were wading through the grass back towards the boats.

The captain sent out the dinghy and the two, Dirk and Jan, brothers and the sons of a merchant, were hauled up the ladder. Everyone crowded around them, wanting to know how things were in Saardam and whether their houses were still standing.

"Give them some space and let them eat first," Master Deim said, waving people aside.

The two young men bowed to Johanna and Roald. "Your Majesties, we're back to report what we've seen in Saardam."

"Be at ease, and have some porridge first, while it's warm."

One of the women brought two bowls, which the men cradled in their hands. "It was cold out this morning," Dirk said.

This was followed by a tense silence while he and his brother ate. More and more people gathered on the deck, everyone keen to hear how their families or houses were.

Then Jan, the oldest and tallest of the two began, "When we got to the city gates at first light, there were two guards stationed at the gates, but they allowed us to pass without a glance. We weren't the only ones queued up to get into the city. People, like farmers and monks were all going in and out, most of them carrying things to sell." He went on to say that a lot of houses had been touched by the fire, but there were also many that had not. The destruction was in the middle of town, around the palace, the harbour and the markets. "But even there, some houses have strangely survived. It was almost as if some of the houses were made from stone and couldn't burn. You'd see two houses next to each other, and one would be burnt to cinders while the other was untouched."

"Witchcraft," someone muttered, and people nodded.

A lot of people then wanted to know about their houses in particular and did the brothers see anyone they knew? Master Deim had to call for people to calm down again.

"The only thing we can say for sure is that Joris DeCamp will have to find a new house. There is a queue of people waiting outside the door. It looks like the occupier and his cronies have taken up residence there."

"Is there any sign that they know that we're coming or that the heir to the throne is still alive?" Master Deim asked.

The men shook their heads.

"The guards at the gate are pretty easy," Dirk said. "We spoke to some people on the streets. No one knows anything. And if Alexandre knew that we were coming, he would have put more men at the gates."

True.

"What about the palace?" someone asked, and Johanna wanted to know about this as well.

"Couldn't see anyone there. The gates are shut. The building looks damaged, but no one was there and no one has fixed it yet. The church is completely gone. That area is a wasteland of mud and rubble."

There were gasps at this.

A woman said, "But when we left, though it was badly damaged some of the walls were still standing. They could have put on a new roof."

"None of the occupiers would have been interested in restoring the church," Martine Delacoeur said. Johanna wasn't sure if she had ever gone to church, since most of the nobles were members of the Belaman Church, even if people in Saardam considered those two one and the same.

The Shepherd Carolus was shaking his head, a pained look on his face. He had his parish at a different church, and already knew that his church had been destroyed, too. "It is a monstrous thing. We have never harmed anyone, never encouraged a war, or tried to drive out others. We have always helped people—" He spread his hands.

The Church of the Triune helped *common* people and forbade magic, both things that would disturb the noble classes that ruled much of the low lands.

Dirk said, "It looks like they're building something new where the church used to stand. There's blocks of stone and they're putting down trenches for the foundations."

People talked about what they thought was being built—a new palace, another church—

Johanna asked the scouts if they'd seen evidence of bandits or soldiers.

Jan said, "There are some, but unless a lot of Alexandre's men have left, the occupying army doesn't look very big. They use Saarlanders. We did see some bandits, one with a bear, but it's not like the streets are full of them."

That's because Alexandre uses magic.

At any rate, Johanna judged it safe to proceed with their plan.

She asked the women to pull out all the clothing they had. As coincidence had it, the *Prosperity* had been carrying a shipment of luxury goods when it fled Saardam. Some of its cargo included fabrics. In the previous months, women had used all of the fabrics to make clothes, and those items now looked a little the worse for wear, and perfect for the purpose of disguising as travellers or peddlers.

A few men went ashore and brought back two wheelbarrows with cabbages, eggs and some beetle-ridden dried beans from a nearby barn. One of them said, "It's a sad thing to have to do this, Your Majesty, but I guess the dead have no more use for food and wheelbarrows."

Johanna nodded, sadly, remembering the carnage they had seen at a few places along the river.

They had also collected apples, most of those worm-infested. Johanna told the children to pick out the best ones, and that they could have the rest. Gijsbert, some older boys and a couple of girls bickered over who would get which apple and then went to great efforts to eat around the worms.

The first group of "farmers" left soon after, taken ashore by

Captain Arense. There were five in the group, a father and a son and daughter, and the two brothers who had gone before. One of the young men took one wheelbarrow and bowed to Johanna and Roald on the deck of the *Prosperity*.

Johanna watched them disappear over the path on top of the levee with a feeling of apprehension. The thought that they were doing this for her made her feel sick. She'd been hungry this morning but now she felt so nervous that the porridge she had eaten might make its reappearance any time soon.

What if Alexandre's men knew they were coming and were waiting for them at the city gates? What if none of the people loyal to the royal family were still alive? After all, King Nicholaos hadn't made himself popular with influential people, and the nobles left in Saardam had decided they were better off without the royal family. What if there was nothing left to save? Were all these people risking their lives for nothing?

Not too much later, a group of six left, including Master Deim, Julianna Nieland and Shepherd Carolus. They were dressed in rags, some with burn holes, and their story would be that they came to look for work in Saardam after the destruction of their village.

And so they spread out and left in dribs and drabs, with some people planning to enter the city from the western gate in order to prevent the guards at the gate from getting suspicious.

Everyone would try to find their own family and their own houses. Those who found that impossible would meet at the end of the day at the Brouwer Company's sea cow barn, or, if the barn was no longer there, Master Deim's barn, which was on the next quay.

As the day progressed, the ships emptied of people. Johanna felt drained and slept a bit. Roald wanted to go into the reeds to catch frogs, and was upset that she told him that he could not, so he threw a fishing line over the side of the boat and leaned against the railing, moping. He caught two little fish.

By midday, none of the people had come back yet, so Johanna got changed into the peasant's dress that she had taken from the mill and that had sustained rips during the trek with the bandits. Nellie had since fixed it as best as she could.

Then she helped Roald get changed, too. He fidgeted and wouldn't keep still. She probably got a bit more impatient with him than was warranted. It was impossible to hurry Roald along. He did things at his pace or not at all.

"I don't like this shirt." He pulled at the collar which, to be honest, was a bit tight.

"You have to wear it anyway."

"I don't understand. Why are we leaving?"

"We're going back to the palace." If there was anything left of the palace.

"I don't want to go. I like the boat."

She sighed. In a way, she liked it, too. She liked it that it calmed him to be outside, pottering about near the water, catching frogs. She let her hands fall and looked around the cabin that had been their home for two months. The bed, the cosy desk with the Baron's books still on it. Oops.

There was also the jar that Roald used for holding frogs. She remembered using it to scoop up the frog that had escaped.

"Why are you laughing?"

"I remembered trying to catch that frog."

"Oh, yes, the frog that got out."

It was sad. It was the end of their uncomplicated life.

CHAPTER 4

WHEN JOHANNA and Roald were ready to go, they climbed back onto the deck.

Roald looked quite like an unshaved peasant from a distance. Close up, people would see that his hands were clean and fine, and that his trousers were of a material that was too expensive for a peasant. Even Nellie in her old torn and stained dress no longer looked like a simple maid. And Loesie wore her dark farm dress, but the expression in her grey eyes was chilling. Johan Delacoeur refused to take off his jacket. It was plenty dirty, he said, as if being "dirty" was indicative of peasants. Martine wore one of the dresses that had been made out of the material that had been on board the *Prosperity*. Too fine, really, to make a convincing peasant dress. Johanna hoped that the guards wouldn't notice any of those things.

The six of them were meant to be farmers going to market, and they were to take the last wheelbarrow and cabbages and apples.

They descended to the dinghy and Captain Arense rowed them across.

"Good luck," he said in a grave voice when they were at the beach.

Johanna nodded.

Johan Delacoeur clapped him on the shoulder.

The captain would stay with his ship.

It was worrying to leave the *Lady Sara* behind. Yes, Ko and Willem would stay with the captain, but they were no real defence if someone wanted to take possession of the ships, and if they had no time to rig up the sea cows their only measure of escape—to simply cast off—would only take them into Saardam, where their problems might be worse than the ones they'd be trying to escape.

They distributed the farm produce. Johanna got a basket of eggs.

Roald was pretty good at wheelbarrows and pushing it gave him something to do. That was another thing about Roald: when he had something to do, he wouldn't panic and start swaying or squealing.

In this manner, they picked their way up the grassy side of the levee. The *Lady Sara* disappeared from sight. The day had turned sunny, if windy and crisp, and the breeze brought a muddy scent from the nearby lowlands. The trees had lost all their leaves and the wind whistled through the bare branches. The grass had started to yellow.

The group followed the track along the river, occasionally having to divert to avoid muddy areas. Clearly, the water had been high here, too.

They'd been walking for a while when Nellie said, "Wait, is that a horse?"

Johanna looked at the stand of willows where Nellie pointed. Strands of hair blew across her face.

A horse it was, with a brown coat. When Roald whistled, it came clopping through the paddock towards the group.

It was a fine animal, not suitable for the field. Its coat was unkempt, full of thistles and other seeds; it had likely fled the city during the fire. A coach horse, maybe. It had the reins still over its head, and that would have made it very uncomfortable. Not to mention that it was a wonder it hadn't become tangled somewhere. No bit fortunately, or it would have starved to death.

Roald put down the wheelbarrow and coaxed it close enough that he could grab the dangling reins. He lifted the headpiece off. The apple in his hand disappeared with a big crunch.

"What are we supposed to do with a horse?" Nellie asked.

Johanna said, "Take it into town. It belongs to someone there. Maybe we can sell it."

Roald said indignantly, "I found it. It's mine." He tied a piece of rope around the horse's neck.

Johanna guessed it could sleep in the barn, if the barn was still there, but it was one more thing to worry about.

The horse kept shying when Loesie came too close, so Johanna ended up taking the rope and leading it along.

The light was turning golden when the group finally arrived at the gates, which Johanna saw, to both her disappointment and relief, looked no different from when she had left. Wait—there was a difference: one of the towers on the gate flew an unfamiliar flag in blue and white.

Johan Delacoeur was looking at it, too, a frown on his face.

"Do you know the flag?"

He shook his head.

A small number of people were going in and out of the gates, mostly farmers and other folk from out of town. The horse was getting nervous, so Roald put the headpiece back on and Loesie took the wheelbarrow from him while he led it.

They went up onto the bridge over the water.

The horse's hooves went clop, clop, clop on the wood. Some of the farmers leaving the gates gave the animal suspicious looks.

The men at the city gates wore unfamiliar uniforms, but their faces were undeniably Saarlander.

One called, "Halt! Who enters the city?"

"We be wanting to sell cabbages," Loesie said. "Also, we found someone's horse jus' wandering around. It don't look like a farm horse."

The guard eyed the horse and the thistles stuck in the fetlocks. "No, that don't look like a farm horse."

He walked around the group, stopping to examine Johan Delacoeur. "Stole yesself a nice jacket, huh?"

Johan's face went red, but to his credit, he said nothing.

The guard eyed Martine, who held her chin up and glared

back at him. Calling him a traitor would be unhelpful, but she looked like she very much wanted to.

Then he turned to Johanna. She studied the man's face, hard and unemotional. It occurred to her that it might not be his choice to work for Alexandre. Johanna wondered if, facing the same situation, she would be strong enough to stand up to the occupying army, especially if they were threatening her family. Ultimately, life was about survival, and there was no point in picking fights you couldn't hope to win.

The guard snorted and shifted his attention to Roald, who had pulled his hat over his forehead so that people wouldn't see his face. Fortunately, few Saarlanders knew him by sight, and the guard was not one of those people.

Meanwhile, the other guard looked in the wheelbarrow that Loesie had put down. "Harvest hasn't been the best, huh?"

"No, sir," Nellie said. "But we sell what we can spare so's we can buy blankets for the winter." She sounded quite convincing. If anything, Nellie had constantly surprised Johanna with her strength. Only one thing upset her badly: unwanted advances from a man.

The guard snorted.

"All right, into town with you. Excuses about the questions. There's been too many strange characters entering here today."

They started walking again. Johanna's heart was thudding. Strange characters? What had the guards done with those strange characters?

Johan Delacoeur was muttering under his breath. "What does he think he is, suggesting that I *stole* the jacket. This jacket's mine, sir. I paid for it with my own money, and it was made by a clothes maker many times older and wiser than you—"

"Shh," his wife said. "We're inside, that what matters."

"Well, I'll be sending a complaint to—"

"We're inside. Now be quiet."

It seemed that she was the only person who could shut him up, because he did just that, even though he still didn't look happy.

The scouts Dirk and Jan had been right about the lack of damage in this part of town. Nothing much seemed to have changed here. There were normal people in the streets doing normal things and the houses in this part of the city were undamaged.

But guards were on every street corner, keeping an eye on every passerby. People walked past them, not looking at the men. Johanna felt like she and her group had a big sign over their head. She kept wanting to pull the hat further over Roald's face. She hoped the guards had more attention for the horse than for who held the rope, or that they were more interested in Loesie, who didn't look normal at the best of times.

Johan Delacoeur and his wife walked arm in arm behind the others and didn't draw quite as much attention from the guards.

"They're looking at us," Roald said.

"Yes, I know. Just don't look back."

"I don't want them to look at us."

"I can't help that." As soon as she said this, Johanna knew she had made a mistake.

Roald burst out, "I don't want them to!"

The horse sidestepped and tossed its head.

"Shhh!"

Roald's eyes were wide and his breaths were fast. He wasn't going to have a screaming fit, was he? He'd been really tense all day. Heart thudding, she took his hand and placed it on the horse's neck. She pressed his fingers into the warm fur, scratching the horse with him. His skin was sweaty.

She spoke to him in a low voice. "Calm down. Don't look at anyone, don't listen to anyone, don't speak."

He nodded, still looking at the horse.

They continued, slowly at first, but they sped up when Roald calmed. But now Johanna grew nervous. The further into town they went, the more likely it was that someone would recognise her. What would she say?

Next to Johanna, Loesie was looking so much over her shoulder that she bumped the wheelbarrow into a woman carrying a basket.

The woman gave a little squeal and dropped the basket on top of the cabbages in the wheelbarrow. "Oh, watch where you're going with that thing." She was a merchant wife or domestic servant, sturdy, broad, with healthy red cheeks.

"Why blame me? You should watch where you're walking." Loesie picked up the basket and shoved it in the woman's hands.

Her face went red. "You rude little—"

Johan Delacoeur joined the group, and Johanna intervened before he could start with his *Do you know who I am?* tone. "We're very sorry that my friend bumped into you. It's our first time coming to the markets. Which way to go?"

The woman jerked her head. "That way. But if you're going to be this rude, you won't sell much."

She gave Loesie a glare and hurried along.

Johanna had been about to say something to Loesie about not creating a fuss, but closed her mouth again. An expression of horror had come over Loesie's face.

"Anything wrong?" Johanna asked.

"I touched the basket. That's why I ran into her. I saw the basket. I wanted to see what it could tell me."

By the Triune, that was a smart thing to do. Johanna should have thought of doing that herself.

"And? What did you see?"

"A lot of scared people. The usurper lives in a house at the markets. People line up in front of his door begging for him to give them food and clothes. He comes out, wearing pretty clothes, and walks straight past them. There is a man with him, with long dark hair. He also dresses pretty. I've seen him before."

"Octavio Nieland?"

"I don't know who that is."

Johanna forgot that Loesie had only come here to sell cheese and baskets.

Loesie continued, "The men walk across the markets. They're laughing. They're not paying any attention to the poor woman with the bandages on her face. Then Alexandre turns around and sets fire to her. Her clothes catch fire. She screams and rolls around on the ground, but no one helps her. That's what I'm seeing."

"No one helps her?"

Loesie shook her head. "People walk past, but no one stops. People are scared."

Johan Delacoeur said, "Much has changed, even if most of it is invisible."

"I don't like it," his wife said.

No, Johanna didn't like it either. If people were this scared, would they still support the royal family?

GRADUALLY, THE STREETS changed. First they came across sections of paving that had been dug up. Loesie had some trouble pushing the wheelbarrow across and Johanna and Nellie had to help her. Roald took care to guide the horse, and Johan Delacoeur wanted to guide his wife by the arm, but she retorted that she had just spent months navigating a slippery riverbank to get water and do washing, and she was capable of walking herself. At which he muttered something about not having married a fishwife.

Johanna laughed secretly at hearing this exchange. Yes, she liked Martine Delacoeur.

Fences had been removed along both sides of the road. Some houses looked abandoned, and people had removed doors and windows, presumably because they were needed elsewhere.

A bit later, they came past the first houses that showed signs of fire damage, mostly boarded-up windows and peeling paint on doors and window frames.

"Look, there," Nellie said.

A house across the street had lost part of its roof. Blackened beams stuck into the sky. As the scouts had said, the pattern of damage was strange. It had skipped certain houses while affecting others.

There was a gasp from behind. Johanna looked over her

shoulder. Martine Delacoeur stopped in the middle of the street. She covered her mouth with her hands, staring into a side street. Johan's face was unreadable, perhaps a bit paler than usual.

"Your house?" Johanna asked.

She nodded.

"Burnt?"

"No. I don't think so." She walked into the street, first slowly and then faster.

Johanna followed, telling Roald, Loesie and Nellie to wait. She sort-of knew where the Delacoeurs lived, but didn't remember the exact house.

Martine squealed and started running, while Johan followed, muttering. His wife ran up the steps of a house on the right hand side of the street. The house had some broken windows but was mostly still intact.

She tried to open the door, but it was locked. Then she banged on the door. "Lotta, Lotta, we're back!"

After a little while, the door opened and the woman who stood in the opening was obviously not Lotta, because Johanna knew Lotta, a cousin of Nellie's, and this woman was much older than that.

"Well . . ." She looked taken aback.

"What are you doing in our house?" Johan blustered.

"Well . . . I . . ." Her cheeks went red. "We got the house fair and square. It was abandoned."

"Who said you could live here?"

"The house was empty—"

"Because we had to run for our lives. The house was not yours to take."

"The Town Council said—"

"Which Town Council? The one that includes the man who burnt all this down?"

"Well, I . . ."

A man came into the hallway behind her. "Why are you bothering my wife?"

"Bothering? Bothering?" Johan's face had gone red. "You're in my house, that's what."

The man gave him a hard stare. "You're a liar. The real Johan

Delacoeur would never go around dressed up in dirty clothing like that. Go away, man, you're nothing but a simple peasant. In any case, if you really wish to complain, I recommend that you take it up with the regent. He decreed that we need to share available housing."

"The regent . . ." Johan's face grew even redder. "Let me tell you what I think of this *regent*—"

Martine pulled his sleeve. "Shh, darling calm down. We don't want too much trouble."

He whirled around at her. "Trouble? He's in our house and you talk about *trouble?*"

"Just calm down," Martine said. "Guards are coming this way."

"Guards? This is ridiculous. I'll tell them who we are—"

"Come, Johan." She pulled him away from the door, which shut.

"I don't understand you, woman. First we had to come here dressed up like this, then you don't want me to throw these people out of our house. I'll—"

"We'll get them out later. Let's not create a fuss straight away. Think of keeping the king safe."

Johan snorted, but returned to the place where Roald, Loesie and Nellie were, even if he was grumbling and red-faced. Johanna thought she could see tears in Martine's eyes. And so the Delacoeurs were the first people who found themselves homeless. And Martine was right in that they could absolutely not afford a fuss. Probably, too, if many houses had been burnt, there would have been a shortage and of course empty houses would be used if there was no sign of the original owners. Martine suggested that they go to check on her sister's, so the pair of them went off in another direction.

Johanna watched them go with growing apprehension. If the time came, would Johan help her or would he side with the nobles in power? That was the big question. She thought the common people would support her, but without support of at least some nobles, Roald might as well walk to the jail straight away.

She pushed that thought away. "Let's go to the markets first."

Get rid of that horse and the wheelbarrow, and then check what was left of her house.

Johanna didn't like the look on Roald's face. He was staring at his feet, and his lips were twitching.

She went to walk next to him, but didn't dare touch him because that would draw attention. She spoke softly. "We're going to take the horse to the barn and then we're going to my house." If there was still a house to go to.

He didn't reply or react, so she asked, "Are you all right?"

He nodded, stiffly. She didn't think he was all right. He should really be off the street, and soon.

They were now coming to the more badly affected part of town. Several houses along the street were so badly burnt that they were uninhabitable, but houses next door had remained untouched. It was really strange. The smell of fire hung in the street. One fire was smouldering, with wisps of smoke drifting into the street.

"They're still burning houses," Nellie said in a soft voice. Her face had gone white. Her family lived two blocks from here. They should go to check on them, too.

Loesie nodded, still hugging herself.

In the next street, two more houses were burned, also in haphazard fashion. A guard stood in front of one of those houses. Next to him sat a bear on its rump with the forepaws resting on the ground.

The accompanying guard was not a Saarlander. He had dark hair, which he wore loose over his cloak. He stood still, only his eyes moving, following the group down the street.

Whether it was the clopping of the horse's hooves or a foreign smell on the wind, Johanna didn't know, but the bear grunted and heaved itself on all its four paws.

The horse shied and pulled at the reins. Parts of the whites were showing in its eyes.

"Shh." Roald patted the animal's neck. Johanna grabbed the end of the rope, briefly touching Roald's hands. They were clammy and sweaty.

The guard gave the group a penetrating look, as if he knew exactly who they were.

Johanna's heart thudded like crazy. She didn't dare look over her shoulder, but she suspected that he would use a pigeon or some magical thing to warn Alexandre. *Oh, look, the lost prince has been found. He's coming in your direction. Half a dozen soldiers should take care of him.*

She had to force herself to abandon that line of thought.

Closer to the markets, the fire damage became more prominent. Large swathes of houses had been burned, whole streets turned into a wasteland of blackened stone walls and skeleton-like remains of floors and roofs. Nothing was smouldering here.

There were some signs that people were rebuilding, with stacks of bricks and planks of wood, but many ruins lay abandoned, with weeds growing in the formerly neat yards. Where were the people? Wasn't this the street where Master Willems lived? Used to live, she thought with a chill. There was no way he would have survived if he had been home.

The markets were at the end of the street; and it was quite busy here, with people making their way across the blackened ground carrying produce. None of them took any notice of a man in a grey cloak who kneeled on the ground at one of the ruins.

There used to be a small church in that spot, the precursor of the large church in the market place. The grey-cloaked figure buried his face in his hands. Of course it was the Shepherd Carolus and Johanna guessed that the church had been his.

Johanna wanted to go comfort him, but couldn't. They were not supposed to know each other.

Another guard with a bear came into the street walking towards the group. The man noticed the Shepherd and before anyone could do anything, belted Shepherd Carolus from behind. He fell face down in the soot. Johanna stood frozen. What could she do? Help him and risk Roald, or let the Shepherd suffer?

She knew Carolus wouldn't want her to risk herself, but still she couldn't just leave him there. He might be badly hurt. But then he heaved himself onto his hands and knees, coughing. Johanna followed the others to the markets, staring ahead as if she saw things like this every day. Inside, she was crying.

They rounded the street corner and came to the markets. Johanna almost gasped.

Not only was the church gone, but the houses on one side of the marketplace were gone, too. You could see across the area of soot and rubble to the canal that ran at the back of those houses. The grocery store, the inn, the barbershop, the candlemaker's shop were all gone.

The land where the church had stood had been cleared.

Two workers were digging trenches in the muddy ground marked with pegs and pieces of string. It looked like they were building a new large construction, but their toil in the mud resembled a punishment more than it did a real building site.

The roof to the market and weigh house had sagged inwards and the normally open sides had been boarded up. Someone had constructed a new set of weighing scales for market produce, and a roof to protect it from the weather, all of it made out of rubble, but it was a poor construction, nowhere near as solid and pretty as the old weigh house.

The houses on the far side of the markets had mostly survived. They belonged to rich families, were built mostly from stone and had sustained minor damage at the most.

As the two scouts had said, a long row of common citizens waited in front of the undamaged mayor's house. The start of the queue was kept at the bottom of the steps by a pair of long-haired guards in bearskin cloaks. Most of the people in the queue wore several layers of coats and blankets, and some had brought fold-up stools as if knowing they'd stand in that queue all day. Johanna didn't want to stare at them too much, for fear of being recognised.

The curtains were open at the ground floor of the house, and Johanna could see movement inside. Had Alexandre brought a wife and family here?

As for the markets: the meagre number of stalls that occupied the middle of the soot-stained paving was a pale shade of the vibrancy of the marketplace before the fires. Many of the vendors used to come from outside town, and those people would be too scared to come—or dead.

Nellie and Loesie—with the wheelbarrow—led the way

between the stalls and Johanna followed with Roald and the horse, eying the miserable produce for sale. Cabbages and worm-ridden apples everywhere. There were also some potatoes, eggs, carrots and parsnips, but the harvest must have been poor, and if this was going to be enough to feed the people of Saardam then by the Triune, there weren't many people left.

Father.

A chill went through her at the thought of crossing the markets, going to her house to find out the ultimate truth. Which might be joyful, but it could also be really, really terrible. The fact that she was about to find out made her feel ill.

Someone called, "Mistress Johanna!"

Underneath the cover of a stall stood a familiar person: Leo Mustermans, the cheese seller whom she used to visit.

Johanna ran to the stall. "Shh."

He came out from behind the stall and swept her up in a hug. "We all thought you were dead, with the palace burnt down and the *Lady Sara* stolen." He was a lot less chubby than he used to be, and with the fat gone from his cheeks, he looked to have aged ten years. "Oh, look at you!"

"We took the *Lady Sara* to safety."

"And you come back disguised as farmers."

"It's a very long story, but we're hoping that there are still people here who support the royal family."

"You will find plenty. They're battered and bruised and scared, but there are plenty. You do know that the king and queen were both killed, right?"

"I do. But did anyone ever tell you that the crown prince was dead, too?"

"They did. They said he drowned in the harbour and that was why there is no body."

"They were lying. The prince is a very good swimmer."

Leo patted the horse and then met Roald's eyes. His eyes went wide. "Is that. . . ?"

"Oh, you haven't met my husband?"

He gasped. His face went red and he held his hand over his mouth to stop shouting his excitement. But a couple of people around him noticed his reaction and looked at Johanna.

A man said, "Why, that's Miss Brouwer. I'd heard people say that she was dead."

"No, no," his wife said. "Look at the young man."

Roald's face went pale. He let go of the horse's rope. Johanna managed to grab it just in time before the horse could create trouble and draw the attention of the guards.

"Look after the horse," she whispered to him, rather more sharply than she normally would have.

"I don't want to talk to people." It sounded like his teeth were chattering.

"You don't have to. Hold the horse. Let me do the talking."

"It's the prince!" someone called.

"The prince is back."

"The Triune be praised!" said a merchant.

His wife berated him. "Shush and don't say that. Do you want your house burned like Master Pieters?"

More people ran closer to have a look.

Johanna stepped forward so that Roald stood between her and the horse. There were at least twenty people facing her, mostly merchants. Nellie had come to stand next to her. Johanna's back touched Roald's side. He was swaying, the muscles under his sleeves tensing.

"We're farmers selling our produce, and we want to sell a horse." She spoke in a loud voice. Her heart was thudding. Any moment now and the guards would notice the gathering, or Roald would go into panic mode and then they would definitely notice him.

Several people nodded and dropped off. They understood.

"If you want to buy a horse, let this man here know about it." She indicated Leo the cheese seller.

Further nods.

"I'd like to put a bid on that horse," said a man.

Others made agreeing noises. They assured Leo that he'd be hearing from them and went back to their stalls.

"That was a smart thing to do," Leo said.

"I'm sorry about drawing you into this—"

"I'd be honoured, lady. I happen to have become a horse

seller today. Except that looks like a coach horse. You could be in trouble for trying to sell it."

"We found it wandering around outside the city walls. I'm not sure what we should do with it. Roald wants to keep it. He likes horses."

"I'll find a safe stable for it where no one is going to accuse you of stealing."

"Thank you."

"No, thank you. You give us hope."

Johanna didn't know what to say to that. From what she had seen, they needed a whole lot more than just hope.

"We're going to see my house now. Is my father all right?"

"Alive. Don't know about all right, but he's alive."

Johanna breathed out a sigh of relief. "And the house?"

"Still standing." He hesitated. He eyed Roald again. Roald was scratching the horse's ears and the horse was nuzzling his clothes. Roald really did have an extraordinary way with animals.

"Your husband, right?"

"We've shared the bed since the day we arrived in Aroden for help, but found that Aroden had been burned to the ground."

His eyes went wide. "Oh, we'd hoped they would help us, if only we could send out someone to tell them."

"There won't be any help from Aroden. It's up to us."

Then he looked at Johanna and bowed. "Your Majesty. It would be an honour to serve you."

"Shhh. Nothing is official, and if anyone asks, you didn't see us here."

"You're right. I didn't see anyone I haven't met yesterday."

LEO SAID IT WAS no more risky to go to her house than to walk anywhere else. "Which is pretty risky, mind. Those magicians are everywhere, and they know everything. Including about horses. They'll have seen you come in with this animal and they'll want to know what you've done with it. You be very, very careful."

"What about you?"

"I have my way of solving these problems, lady."

They left him to look after the horse and the produce they had brought, and continued to the other side of the markets. The fire had also hit hard here, but had spared pockets of houses. In one such pocket Johanna found her own house. Some of the windows had broken from the heat, and paint had peeled off, but the steps were clean and swept and a glow of light came from within Father's library.

The door was bolted from inside and when Johanna let the knocker fall, quick footsteps approached.

The door first opened a crack. An eye peeked out.

"Koby?" At least Johanna thought it was Koby.

A squeal; then the door opened further. Definitely Koby.

"Mistress Johanna! Quick, come in, come in!"

Johanna went up the steps and was enveloped in a gravy-scented hug.

"Come and look at this, master, Johanna is back!"

The door to the library opened and there was Father. Greyer than she remembered him, and leaning on a walking stick. He wore his favourite jacket but had lost so much weight that it hung off his shoulders like a sack. But he was alive.

Johanna extricated herself from Koby's arms and hugged him tightly. His shoulders were so thin that she could feel the bones through his jacket. His grip was so feeble that she thought her hug would break him.

For a while he could say nothing except, "Oh, oh, oh." Then he recovered a bit. "We thought you were lost. When I couldn't find you in the burning palace . . ." Tears rolled over his cheeks.

Then he looked past her to the others who had come into the hall, where Koby had once again bolted the door.

"Nellie has become a good lady, too, I see, and who is the other young lady?"

"That's Loesie."

"Your basket-selling friend?"

"Yes." She was surprised that he remembered her.

"And the young man?"

"That's a bit of a story. We fled in the *Lady Sara*. Loesie knew how to handle the sea cows. We went upriver to find help, but all we saw along the river was destruction and death. Aroden castle is completely burnt. There is nothing left, so we thought we were the only Saarlanders left—"

"Wait, you said the *Lady Sara*?"

"Yes. It's moored around the river bend just outside the city gates."

"The *Lady Sara* has survived?"

"There might be a small scratch on it somewhere, and we lived in the hold and modified it into a room, but yes—"

"Oh, heavens be praised! I thought I'd lost everything. The *Lady Davida* was burned in the fire and I thought the Brouwer Company was doomed after all the work I put into it my entire life. Oh, you can't possibly understand how happy I am that you're back—" He frowned at Roald. "I think I know who you are, but . . . it can't be. They said you'd drowned."

"King Roald of Saarland," Johanna said.

"Oh," was the only thing he said before he dropped into a stiff bow.

Roald froze. He never seemed to know what to do in situations like this.

I must teach him, Johanna thought. "Come on, Father, that's not necessary. We've travelled with him for months. We need a safe place to stay. He's my husband."

Now Father looked up, his eyes wide. "You . . . Oh, heavens be praised! I thought I'd lost everything. My wife, my daughter, my first and dearest ship." Tears were streaming down his face. "And on top of that . . . you're saying that you married the prince."

"I did. Nellie did the service when we thought that everyone was lost and we couldn't get help at Aroden. It's not official, but it's the most official we could make it."

"Oh, what a day, what a day. There is hope yet for all of us. You must stay here. We have plenty of room in the house. I'll see to it that you get the best room, and that it's clean and that there are fresh sheets and clean clothes. We lost some of our workers. Jan was killed trying to put out the fires." Jan used to look after the garden and fix things in the house. "Adrian went down with the *Lady Davida*. She is still in the place where she sank, burned and all, at the bottom of the harbour. We never found Adrian. And the Hendricksen warehouse burned down. The old man died a few weeks later from the burns. His poor widow has been living in poverty ever since. And so many people have left town. Your family, too, Nellie."

Nellie's eyes widened. "They're alive?"

Johanna felt guilty that she hadn't yet walked past Nellie's house.

"As far as I know, they are, but the house is lost, so they had nowhere to live. They were involved with the church, too. This filth has been punishing people from the Church of the Triune for something they didn't do. You know I was never keen on that church, but they didn't cause the fires. The church did nothing wrong. But far too many people believe what this terrible man says, many of them nobles—"

"Octavio Nieland."

"Yes, he, and many of the other nobles. Alexandre gives them the influence they always wanted and King Nicholaos was unwilling to give them—" He bowed to Roald. "I'm very sorry about your parents, Your Majesty. We will protect you against these evil men."

It was disturbing how he had gone from being a confident man to one hoping for miracles. "You have to tell me about everything that happened here."

"Yes, yes, but first you must hide."

"We're already hidden. We're off the street, the door is shut and—"

Someone dropped the knocker on the wood.

There was a moment of intense silence. Father's eyes widened as he turned to the door, a horrified expression on his face. He put his finger to his lips.

"You must hide *now*," he whispered. "Quick, go upstairs and be very quiet. Don't speak. They must not see you here. They must not hear you."

All right. "Come," Johanna whispered to the others. She led Nellie, Loesie and Roald to the stairs and, on the landing between the two floors, went through the little door that led into the storeroom above Father's office.

"Be very quiet now," she said.

Whereas before the storeroom had been full of spare dinner things, now the room contained a lot of Father's nice dinnerware and the precious treasures brought from other lands during his travels. Why weren't those things in the cabinets in the sitting room anymore?

THEY SAT DOWN on the floor, while in the hallway downstairs, Koby pulled back the bolts that held the door shut.

"No, no," she was saying. "I was just talking to the master. He's in the library waiting for you."

Someone replied, the voice too soft to recognise or make out words.

"What are we doing here?" Roald asked in a too-loud voice. "Hiding? I like playing hide and seek."

"Shh. It's a game. Be very, very quiet now."

He nodded. "I like playing hide and seek. You know I used to play it with—"

"Shhh!"

He giggled, but covered his mouth with his hand so he didn't make any noise.

Like this, he looked like an overgrown child, his eyes bright, innocent to the terrible things people did to each other. She loved him for that simple, unconditional attention that he gave her. Nellie had her lips pursed. Johanna knew that she disapproved of listening to conversations. Loesie lay on her stomach in front of the window, looking into the garden.

Downstairs, the door to Father's library opened and the person, or persons, came inside the hall with the clack-clacking of high-heeled boots on the marble floor, and then the more muffled sound as the visitor walked onto the carpet.

"Good morning, Dirk." It was a dry, male voice that Johanna didn't recognise. One of the proper nobility, judging by the cultured sound of his speech. "It's a very good morning, don't you think?"

"Never since the light of my life was taken from me has there been a good morning."

Whoa, since when did Father speak like that?

There was the sound of a chair being dragged across the mat. "Suit yourself, Dirk. I've brought the contract for signing."

A period of silence. Johanna pictured a man putting a piece of paper on Father's desk.

"What, Dirk, are you not going to sign it?"

And pictured Father pushing the paper back across the desk.

"I would like some time to think about it." She pictured Father giving the man his famous critical look. A glimmer of hope sparked in her that his famous sense of business had not been damaged too much.

"Even more time than you've already had? You're not getting any younger. You might drop dead tomorrow, and then who is going to inherit your wealth? Who is going to run your business?" The arrogant tone of the voice was starting to annoy her. Who was this upstart?

The arrogant voice continued, "Are you going to ruin the life of my sister as well as the lives of your wife and daughter?"

"You vile snake!"

The man laughed. "You can call me whatever you want. The fact is my sister is the only one who has volunteered to share an old man's bed to beget him another heir. And getting heirs was never your strong point, Dirk."

"Shut. Up! Before I wring your skinny neck."

Again that dry laugh. "You're welcome to try. But you're an old man, Dirk, and you know that. This is your last chance. All right, then. I'm reasonable. Have your few days to *think about it*. I'm patient. Lisbeth is patient. You will die long before she. I'll leave you with this document. Just have your secretary bring it up to my office when you've changed your mind." The chair was dragged over the carpet. "Oh, I forgot. Your secretary has been missing."

One more chuckle and he left the room.

The door creaked. High-heeled boots hit the floor in the hall. Koby said something, but her voice was too soft for them to hear what. The man replied, "No, that's not necessary." The front door opened and shut.

Koby dragged the bolt across.

That was when Johanna first dared move.

Lisbeth? Lisbeth LaFontaine? A young woman a few years older than Johanna, a cousin of Fleuris LaFontaine. Hadn't she been married last year? Hadn't her husband died soon after?

And by the missing secretary, did he mean Master Willems?

She met Nellie's eyes, and Nellie, having heard everything, stared back, a puzzled look on her face. "What in the Triune's name is happening in this town?"

Loesie turned to them. "It's the hand of evil."

Johanna swore that there was a haze of white in her eyes when she said that. She shuddered.

She left the storeroom, followed by Roald, Nellie and Loesie. Nellie and Loesie were short enough to be able to walk under the beams, but Roald hit his head twice.

Johanna shielded his head from the last beam, and when she touched the wood, saw some men carrying boxes full of Father's pretty treasures from the sitting room through the little doorway and up the stairs. Johanna recognised the men. They were porters who used to work in the warehouse.

One of the men said, "If they search the house, they'll find all these things."

"The trick is not to let anyone know that this is here, so they won't search for it."

This had to have happened a few days after the fire. Maybe Alexandre's bandits were looting the town. Maybe the council had asked for citizens to hand in their wealth.

In the downstairs hall, the door to the library was open. Father sat slumped in his chair and did not look up, even though he must have heard them come down the stairs.

"Look, why don't we go and help in the kitchen?" Nellie said in a low voice to Loesie.

Loesie and Roald trundled after her. Poor Koby.

Johanna went into the room. Father looked up and sighed. "You heard."

"They're forcing you to get married?" It was hard to believe.

He sighed and nodded. "I need an heir. That much is true."

"No you don't. Not anymore. You have your heir." And hopefully, there would be a new generation at some point.

"But he doesn't know that, and he can't be allowed to find out."

Also true. "That was Auguste LaFontaine?" She remembered him as a small man with a thin, sharp face who never had much good to say about other people.

He nodded. "It's his sister Lisbeth whose life they're trying to ruin. I don't believe for one moment that she volunteered."

"But why? Why her? Why don't you just walk away from his silly proposal and tell them to go somewhere else?"

"It's not as simple as that. The *Lady Davida* was lost in the fire and the *Lady Sara* is missing. The LaFontaine family owns the only shipyard in town that survived the fire. They will build me a new boat, but I have to agree to their conditions, otherwise they won't take the order."

"And their conditions are to marry Lisbeth?"

He nodded and looked down. "To make the filthy LaFontaine family the owner of my business, whatever it's still worth." He spread his hands, let them sink to his sides and shrugged. "It will be worth less every day that I don't have a ship." The light from the fire made the wrinkles in his face show up like canyons. "I can't operate a river trading company without a boat."

"But you have the *Lady Sara* again."

"That's why I won't be signing this." He scrunched the document up into a ball and threw it in the fire. Flames quickly turned their prey into an inferno. Within moments, there was nothing left of the paper.

"Won't that get you into trouble?" Johanna asked.

He gave a wry smile. "If it does, it will have been worth it. I've wanted to do that for a while. Frankly, I think they were disappointed that I didn't die in the fire. People have been looking at me as an example of withstanding the tyrants. But I'm old and tired. I don't know how much longer I could have refused them, and now I don't know how much longer they will stay polite."

"Then we must act quickly."

He held up his hands. "What can we do? There are so few of us and no one wants to risk their family."

"We're going to reclaim our town. We have the rightful king, and we're going to get the people behind us—."

"Reclaim the town? You mean get rid of Alexandre? You can't. Have you seen what he can do? They call him the Fire Wizard. He sets fire to people's houses with a wave of his hand. He's done that to everyone who doesn't agree with him. He'll burn down the whole town before he'll leave."

"I don't think so. He could have burned all of Saardam already if that's what he wants, but I think he wants Saardam reasonably intact—maybe because he needs us as workers, maybe for some other reason. He doesn't want to destroy the town, he wants to control the town."

"That's what tyrants usually want, tormenting poor people to amuse themselves. This man is evil, Johanna, and I don't want you standing up to him, because he will kill you."

"Only you can stand up to him?"

He opened his mouth, spread his hands, closed his mouth again and let his hands fall by his sides. "I just want you to be careful. That's all."

CHAPTER 8

IT WAS TIME for the midday meal, which was being set on the table by Koby and Nellie, while Roald fussed about with tableware and finger bowls.

Koby tried to do it for him, but he wouldn't let her. She apologised, red-cheeked. "Oh, I'm sorry that the prince is doing this work. I couldn't help it."

"Never mind, Koby. Let him help you if he wants to. Thank you."

Father sat down and Johanna took her usual place at the table. Roald looked a bit lost so she waved for him to sit next to her. Johanna noticed that he had flour on his hands.

Nellie would once again eat downstairs, even though it felt strange. "Where is Loesie?"

Koby gave her a sharp look. "You know that girl is a witch, don't you?"

"Yes, I do. She has helped us for months." *And brought us into danger*, but she left that unsaid.

"Witches are dangerous. If nothing else, they're spies from the Belaman Church."

"I assure you, Koby, Loesie is nothing of the sort. She's my friend and she should be here, because with her magic, she will be important in our plans." If, in some way, Johanna could figure out how to get Loesie using her magic.

"As you wish, mistress." Koby left the room.

"Sit down, Roald," Johanna said when the door had closed behind her.

He did, in his usual, nervous, straight-backed manner. Roald and Father looked at each other. Father nodded, perhaps a bit puzzled. People behaved like that around Roald. They didn't quite know what to say, because Roald didn't come across as expecting bows and curtsies and wasn't interested in conversations about trivialities. She would have to work out a way of getting Roald to accept that people wanted to do this, and to get him to react in a way that didn't confuse those people.

She wondered what King Nicholaos and Queen Cygna had done for him, except send him away to the Guentherite brotherhood farm for unruly royals. The memory she had of Roald running after his sister's birthday friends squealing had taken on new meaning. Back then, she'd thought it was fun, but now she understood how distressed he must have been. She put a hand on his knee under the table. The tense muscles in his legs relaxed a little.

"Tell us what has happened here while we were gone," she said to Father.

Father spread the napkin on his lap and took his spoon. His hand shook. He was about to start eating when he stopped and lowered the spoon again.

"They were bad tidings." He scooped up a spoonful of soup. "When I lost you in that hall, the best I could do was try to get home, hoping that you had also made your way there. The whole town was in chaos and people were running for their lives. I found the house undamaged, but you weren't here."

His expression grew distant. "I was too scared to go out again. Bandits with bears were roaming the streets. I'm but an old man and I thought if I went out there and died, you would have no one to come back to. So I chose to be a coward, and hid inside. I also couldn't face sending Koby into that chaos."

He let the soup fall back into the plate. "Many people lost their lives that night. I went out in the morning to look for you. The city was a wasteland. Many houses were still burning. I . . . couldn't find you anywhere. . . ."

He swallowed hard and wiped at his eyes. "Not Master Willems, either. His family's house was gone. The office was still there, but it was damaged, and the sea cow barn had been spared. But the only thing I could see of the *Lady Davida* were the masts sticking out of the water. The bandits and the bears were gone, too, and some people were in the streets trying to help. Octavio Nieland was one of those people. I've never considered him to be helpful, especially not towards common people. But he gave them food, cooked by his housekeeper, even though his own parents and his sister were said to be amongst the people who didn't make it out of the palace."

"Julianna came back with me."

His eyes widened.

"We caught up with her in Florisheim. She and Captain Arense took the *Prosperity* upriver."

"Well, that's . . . good news."

Johanna didn't like the hesitation. "Julianna is all right. You know I never liked her, but she has changed. She was sick, but she came through and has helped me ever since. She knows how Octavio sold himself to the occupiers. She didn't leave immediately after the fires but later, and she left *because* of what Octavio did. Yes, their parents are probably dead."

He nodded, his face drawn. "If we thought the fire was bad, what happened afterwards was even worse. Alexandre and his band of cronies would walk through town proclaiming that he was the king. Whenever people challenged him, asking him where his crown was, he'd just flick his hand at them, and they'd burst into flames. He said he was looking for betrayers, but he seemed to be targeting members of the Church of the Triune and murdering their entire families. The Shepherd Romulus had survived. . . . You know I was never a great supporter of the church, but . . . this was just awful. He had been badly burnt in trying to stop his church burning down. Say whatever you want, but it was a very nice building. The Shepherd begged Alexandre to help the people. Here was this badly wounded man, with blood and gore oozing from his hands and arms, and he was asking help on behalf of *other* people. Then this . . . monster just flicked his hand and set him on fire and he died screaming.

To help him out of his misery, he said, and then he laughed. Johanna, we must do something so that we won't ever have to see anything like that again." The waning light that came in through the window cast his face in sharp relief. He looked old and tired.

"I've heard that Alexandre gave a speech."

"Yes, he did, a few days after the fire. It was full of hatred for the Church of the Triune and how he was bringing the only true church."

"The Belaman Church."

He nodded.

"Their teachings include magic."

"They do. He was rounding up people in the streets and scouting them out for magic, which, of course, very few of us have. The ones who were found to have some magic, he forced in his service—"

"Master Willems?"

"I don't know. I hope he fled with the many people who left in disgust. They were not seen again."

"Many of them came up the river in the *Prosperity*. Maybe they expected to find an ally in Aroden or Baron Uti, but Aroden is even worse off than Saardam, and all Baron Uti ever did for the refugees was to let them wait for things that he'd promised, but never delivered. He gave them land to camp on, but did nothing else. His son is pure evil." She shuddered. "There are things I've watched him do that I won't even talk about."

Father frowned. "Baron Uti's son who was at the ball? Who danced with you?"

"Yes." She shuddered.

"What is going on in Florisheim?"

"I wish I knew, but only the Baron knows that, and the Guentherite order of the Belaman Church. They're doing all kinds of magic. Digging black rock out of the ground, and making iron. Waking up all sorts of ghosts." That seemed to sum it up. "Florisheim is full of ghosts. They're coming down the river, and they listen to no one except magicians."

"You'll understand that magic isn't very popular with us survivors. I'm almost beginning to agree with that church of yours wanting to ban it. That's me speaking, a merchant, one of those who married into a magical family."

Johanna shook her head. "Banning it is not the answer. People still have magic, even if it's fairly rare in Saardam. We will need to use magic if we are to get rid of Alexandre."

He met her eyes, the look in them full of concern. "You really think you can do this, don't you?"

"Not me alone." If only she could find someone to help her. The Baroness Viktoriya called Alexandre a little man, but he had obviously struck fear in the heart of the people of Saardam before they could find out that he was little.

"Do you know anything about him?" Father asked. "He did come across the river from Florisheim, didn't he?"

Johanna nodded. "Alexandre Trebuchet is an ex-resident of the Guentherite brotherhood's farm in Burovia across the river from Florisheim," Johanna explained. "A lot of princes spend time on the farm."

"It's said that he's a cousin of King Leopold of Burovia."

"He is, but I don't think that the king has anything to do with this."

"I don't know. I've always heard that Gelre or Burovia didn't like the influence that the Church of the Triune was holding over Saardam. Apparently, Alexandre came under cover on the Burovian ship that brought the prince back."

"What about all the soldiers that Alexandre brought?"

"The ones with the bears? They are Estlander. They dress in woodland gear, but I've heard them talk, and they're Estlander, from just across the border, most of them."

"They're mercenaries?" That was interesting. Johan Delacoeur said that this wasn't done, that a good military campaign did not rely on hired troops. It brought the interesting possibility that these men with their bears could be *bought*, if enough money could be found. And if what Father said was true, and they came from Estland, maybe the name Sara Aroden—Johanna's mother—would mean something to them.

Roald had been sitting through all this while watching silently. Now he said, "I'm not afraid of that man. He is mean to animals."

Father gave him a strange look. "Animals?"

"He whips the horses and I've seen him kick a dog."

Father frowned. "Um . . ." He met Johanna's eyes.

"When Roald was in Burovia, he worked at the farm where Alexandre lived." Johanna patted Roald's hand under the table. It felt sweaty.

"Oh," Father said. "So Your Majesty is familiar with the reasons why this man occupied our city?"

Roald gave him a blank look, but under the table his hand gripped Johanna's. He didn't "do" reasons, at least not ones that required understanding people.

"No one knows what Alexandre wants," Johanna said. Well, the Baron or Kylian would know, but they weren't going to share.

Koby came into the room and Johanna suggested that Roald go upstairs to get changed and freshen up. Koby showed him upstairs, while Johanna went with Father into the library.

"What is actually wrong with him?" Father asked. "He doesn't strike me as dumb, but something is not right."

"He doesn't like people."

Father laughed at this.

"No, I mean, for real. He doesn't know how to talk to people. He's fine with animals, and he knows everything about them and about history and about the Burovian king's family tree, and he knows about birds and frogs and dragons."

"Dragons?" Father laughed. "They're not real."

"That doesn't matter to him. It's written in a book, so it's real to him. You name it, he knows about it. But he's bad at talking to people."

"So, even his stay at the farm hasn't cured him?"

Johanna shook her head, feeling a bit uneasy and even annoyed at the word *cured*. Roald wasn't sick. He was just a bit strange.

"Could he rule?"

"By himself? No. He would probably just ignore everybody and potter about the rose garden every day."

"Does he know that this is all about him?"

"I think he does." But sadly, Roald couldn't do much to help retake Saardam for his family. If anything, he would need to stay inside a lot and he would get bored. There weren't even any ponds to collect frogs here. There was Father's library, of course. Although it mostly held books about strange lands and their spices.

"What are you going to do when your first child is born and is afflicted with the same condition?"

"Roald's father wasn't afflicted with the condition. And neither was Celine."

"King Nicholaos was odd, in the way that he spent all his money on the church. If Alexandre came here to loot the Carmine coffers, he must have been sorely disappointed."

Johanna felt chilled. "I thought you wanted me to marry Roald."

"That was when the king assured me that his son was cured."

Johanna's cheeks flushed with anger. "Father, I think the only thing that was wrong with King Nicholaos was that he truly didn't care about his son. Maybe he was ashamed of him. Well, I'm not ashamed to say that I care for him."

"No, but this does make the situation more difficult."

"Different, not more difficult. We will do the work for Roald. He just takes up the position, and we help him with what he needs to say."

"I hope so, Johanna. It's not a kind of position I would prefer to be in, considering the evil of the man we're facing. He's not going to be polite because Roald is not quite normal or you're a nice girl. I've seen him burn people to death, both men and women. He has no morals and no serious rivals. You would need a magician to defeat him." His eyes met Johanna's, as if he knew that they were lacking in the magician department.

If only Loesie were a bit more cooperative. Johanna understood why she was hesitant to use her magic, but would she still refuse to help if there was no one else? If it meant Alexandre would win?

After Johanna had said goodnight to Father, she went down into the basement to find Loesie.

But Loesie was not at the table in the kitchen. She was not in any of the servants' rooms. Johanna asked Nellie, who sat combing her hair on her bed, but she hadn't seen Loesie since they had shared the meal in the kitchen.

Koby came into the hallway from the laundry, her cheeks red from the cold.

"The witch?" she said when Johanna asked. "She left. She says she knows when she isn't welcome."

"Left?" Where to?

"Yes, out the door."

"Oh, that is nonsense," Johanna said. "She sat at the table at Duke Lothar's castle."

After all this time together, she had to admit that she still didn't understand why Loesie would go like this. At first she had thought it was because of the spell, but she was beginning to think that this was just Loesie.

Loesie didn't *want* to be included, just so that she could go on complaining that she wasn't included.

Great. Now what?

Then another thought: the sea cow barn. She had told the other people from the *Prosperity* to meet there if any of them found themselves without family and without a home.

Not only should she check the barn for them, but it was probably where Loesie would be. She often used to sleep there when she came to the markets with her grandma, too.

CHAPTER 9

J OHANNA WAS so tired that she felt she could sleep for a
week, but she dressed in her outdoor clothes and dragged
her weary limbs back into the cold to look for Loesie.

An icy wind had come up that whipped leaves through
the street and prised its cold fingers through the gaps in her
clothing. Johanna pulled both sides of her cloak together, shivering, wishing she could be inside by the fire.

And yet, despite the destruction and misery that people
obviously suffered here, she was glad that she was in Saardam
and no longer in a wet field in Florisheim. The combination of
rising water and the coming winter would have been utterly
miserable. The nosy baroness would have made things worse.
Now that she looked back on it, the baroness had been trying to
pull Johanna and Roald into her influence. The woman *had* to
know at least some of the things that her son was up to.

Now if only she could understand why Loesie kept running
away.

The markets lay deserted in the gathering darkness, the
produce sold or brought inside, the stallholders gone home. The
only house where there was light behind the windows was the
mayor's, but the queues had gone, even if people in those queues
had left little markers—a piece of wood or stone with a name
scrawled across it—to remind others of their position.

She walked across the open wasteland of the markets, where the cloth covering the few meagre stalls flapped in the squally breeze.

During the day, she hadn't noticed that in one of the side streets so many houses had been destroyed that it offered a view of the palace gates. Curious, Johanna turned into the street.

On the night of the ball, she had gone through the main gate with Father in the coach to line up in the forecourt at the bottom of the palace steps. She remembered all the noble women in pretty dresses tut-tutting about her presence. This was also where, after the ball, she had last seen Octavio Nieland looking for his parents and palace guards corralling people into coaches. Panicked horses. Creatures made out of fire gambolling over the city's roofs. In the dying daylight, there was no sign of the many bodies that had littered the ground. No sign of the broken coaches and the dead horses.

The gates were closed and held shut with a chain. Johanna pushed, but there was a sturdy lock on the chain.

She peered through the bars. Most of the building was made of stone, and stood far enough away from the rest of town to have remained untouched by the inferno that had flattened the houses around it.

To the right, Queen Cygna's rose garden had been desecrated, the wall broken, the statue of the Triune taken away. There were still drag marks over the ground.

At the palace itself, there were signs that repairs were underway. Johanna didn't remember that the doors were blue—in fact, she was sure they used to be carmine red.

Some stacks of new stones stood to the side of the steps, but piles of leaves had collected between them, so clearly Alexandre had put his efforts into other projects.

It's ours.

No matter the state of the palace, Roald should live in it. This building belonged to Roald and this filthy man did not have the right to touch it, not even to paint the doors blue. She and Roald would live in the palace again, and the children would hold parties in the rose garden, *with* the statue of the Triune.

She clutched the bars of the gate until the metal became too cold for her hands. Then she continued through the ruined streets to the harbour.

The Brouwer Company office on the southern end of the quay had sustained limited damage in the fire, but Father had money and people who would work for him and the roof had since been repaired.

All the buildings on the western side of the harbour had not been so lucky. Most were no more than soot-stained ruins, barely recognisable shells of their former selves. Stacks of bricks stood on the quay, and the foundations for a couple of walls had been built. By the way the walls surrounded an entire block where there used to be two or three buildings, Johanna judged that this was more than a simple rebuilding of the warehouses that used to stand here. The builders had also taken blocks out of the quay and dug out a mooring area set back from the quay wall. Stacks of stone blocks stood on either side. They had pulled up much of the quay's paving as well. What was going on here?

A pocket of the buildings on the eastern side of the harbour still stood, including, by stroke of luck, the king's armoury. The fact that it hadn't exploded was probably responsible for the relatively high survival rate of buildings in this area.

The Brouwer Company's sea-cow barn, two warehouses down from the armoury, had also been spared most of the destruction. Some of the roof tiles had come off and lay haphazardly on the lower roof. One of the doors had blown off its hinges and the other had a big burnt patch in one corner. The roof would leak and the weather would have played havoc with the harnesses and tools stored inside, but the main building was still intact. Without either the *Lady Sara* or *Lady Davida* moored in front, it looked empty.

Johanna walked quickly along the quay and remembered the warehouse next to the barn where she had seen the mysterious men on the evening before the fire.

It was completely empty. Untouched by fire, and empty.

She wasn't sure what to make of that. Who would have had time and ships to empty an entire warehouse after a disaster? What had been in it that needed to be taken away?

A couple of people stood in front of the sea cow barn, huddling in their cloaks.

These were the people from the *Prosperity* who had returned to their houses and found them destroyed and had no other place to go.

She half-expected the Delacoeurs to be there, but they must have found room at Martine's sister's house.

The refugees were a few young men, and Julianna Nieland, who called out, "There she is!" when Johanna came closer.

"Oh, Julianna!"

Johanna took her hands. They were icy cold.

"I can't go back to my brother," Julianna cried. "I can't stay with any of my family because they will tell him. They're all afraid of him, and I know he makes them do awful things. I don't know what to do. I truly don't."

"I think you should all go back to the *Lady Sara*," Johanna said.

One of the men spoke up. "We most certainly will not, lady. We will stay here with you and fight."

"But we're not fighting anything yet. What use are you going to be when you're cold, hungry and ill? It's almost winter and houses are scarce. You can't sleep here." They could, possibly, sleep in her house. There were several rooms in the attic as well as downstairs in the servants' quarters that were not in use. Julianna could, at the very least, sleep in the spare room on the top floor.

But the LaFontaine family might drop in and find out about these houseguests, and that would be terrible for all concerned. "For now, it would be best if you went back to the *Prosperity*, at least for tonight."

"In the dark?" one of the men said. His name was Jakob, Johanna remembered, and he was the son of a baker.

"The most important thing is that no one discovers that we're back." But she felt horrible about her own safe house and nice bed. "You can sleep in the barn." But the roof leaked.

"I know a better place where we can stay for the night," another young man said. "It will smell of horses, but it will be dry."

That was likely to be in the east harbour, where the newer warehouses stood. There was a horse stable in that area. She nodded agreement. "I'll send someone if we have something better for you."

They said that they would wait, but as the group walked down the quay, Julianna looked so forlorn that Johanna resolved to find a place for her as soon as she could.

She went inside the barn. It took a while for her eyes to get used to the intense darkness, but a crawling sensation crept over her skin. There was magic in the air. She had felt it when coming into town, too. Since when could she feel the presence of magic?

When her eyes had adjusted to the darkness, she found Loesie, as expected, huddled in her usual spot under the tool bench. She had found a disgusting blanket and had lit a small fire in a fire pot that definitely didn't belong to Johanna's father.

Loesie said nothing and Johanna sat down in the straw next to her. The ground was slightly damp, courtesy of the hole in the roof. The air smelled of stale smoke. It was strange to see the water so still, without the occasional snort or flipper from the sea cows breaking the surface. She hoped that the animals belonging in the *Lady Davida's* team had been able to get away and had returned to their wild lives in the ocean.

Loesie came to sit next to her, silent and ghostlike. She was not as thin as she had been when they arrived at Duke Lothar's castle, but still didn't look healthy.

"What are you doing here? Why did you disappear?"

"You know I've always said that I don't belong with all the finery and the pretty houses and pretty dresses."

"But you're my friend. You were with us in the duke's castle. You sat at his table."

"Yes, but I had no choice. I don't like all the pretty things. I'm not pretty and all that stuff makes me nervous."

Yes, Loesie was right. She had always been like this. She loved to point out that she was different. She enjoyed being called a witch and scaring boys. That was why Johanna liked her. Maybe she should just accept it. "At least stay here and come to the house for decent meals."

"That cook doesn't like me."

No, Koby didn't, and Johanna understood why, but still didn't like it. "We'll get the roof fixed for you." It was a lame promise because there was so much that needed doing first, and Loesie continued to say nothing.

Johanna wished she could bring back Loesie's family. She used to talk about "my ma" and laughed at her mother who was silly and didn't know anything about magic. Similarly with Annette, the girl who lived next door and who, according to Loesie, was easily impressed, very girly and gullible. Loesie poked fun at them. The neighbours weren't family, but up there in the little pocket of land where the Rede River branched off from the Saar River, they might as well be, because there were no other farms for miles.

And Loesie was sad and lonely. She could no longer use her magic for fun because magic had suddenly become dangerous, and she wasn't suited to playing games of influence and power.

Johanna didn't know how to help her.

She was about to get up when Loesie said, "It was really kind of you to take me all the way up the river. I got to see a castle and wear fancy dresses and see real magic." Never mind that it hadn't been a leisurely trip and it was not as if they'd had any choice. "You're one of the few people who are decent to me and you've done for me what I don't deserve."

"I think you do. I think you're lonely and you want people around you more than you let out." And it must be terrible for her to have lost her entire family.

"No, I don't."

The intensity in her expression chilled Johanna. She shivered and clamped her arms around herself.

"When I came to the markets that day, I knew that this was about to happen. Well, not exactly this, but I knew that something was going to happen. I knew that the baron's son was behind it. I saw him crossing the river on a water horse. He came to the farm and bought dinner from my grandpa. The neighbour's daughter Annette fancied him. I was jealous and tried to scare her. But he . . . did bad things to her."

"Did you see that?"

"The wood told me. Annette was a beautiful untouched

young woman. He threw her in the grass and defiled her. You remember that woman's scream you heard in the basket I gave you? That was her voice. When he finished with her, and she lay broken and crying in the mud, he changed her into a tree, and then he tried to do the same with me. He only kissed me, he didn't do any of the other stuff he did to Annette. But the kiss took my voice right away. And he changed my family into trees, too. He said I had to stay on the farm, but I got some magic on me, so I got away. The spell he put on me was with me the whole way."

"The only thing he did was kiss you?" Johanna felt sick.

"Yes. Proper kissing, on the mouth."

"Did you feel anything after he did that?"

Loesie gave her a wide-eyed look. "Well, yeah. I was jealous of Annette, because he fancied her. He was the biggest spunk that had ever set foot on our farm, so when he came up and kissed me, I felt all sorts of things that city folk say is inappropriate for a woman to feel. But he could have ripped the clothes off me and I wouldn't have said a peep."

The blood rose to Johanna's cheeks. She didn't quite ask for that frank an admission. "I meant did you feel the spell when he kissed you?"

By the Triune, could *she* have been betraying Roald from the moment she left the palace? Was that how Sylvan had known where she was? Hadn't he said something about feeling magic in the air? She'd thought he was talking about Loesie.

"Only that I couldn't speak. All the other stuff, like that I had fits, only came later."

Johanna's stomach roiled.

She tried to remember the night that she'd had dinner with Kylian in the Guentherite farmhouse. She had seen him try to perform necromancy. Why hadn't she refused his hospitality? What actually happened after dinner? And why didn't she remember? Had he kissed her again? Had he done "other things"?

Loesie continued, but Johanna only heard her through the roaring of blood in her ears. "While we were travelling, the spell he had put on me was getting worse and worse. Then we got to the duke's castle and he and you broke the spell but I still couldn't tell you. Every time I wanted to, I thought of something else. Because part of him was still inside me. Still is. That's why I can't sleep in your pretty house with your nice family. That's why I don't want to have anything to do with magic, and why I can't be your court magician. Why I tried to kill myself. I'm afraid I'll betray you. Maybe I already have."

"You said *part of him is inside me.* What do you mean? Did he . . . did he make you with child?"

"No. I said, far as I know, he didn't touch me in that way."

As far as you know? Johanna nodded, trying to look merely interested, trying her best to swallow down sickness. "Why can you tell me only now?"

"I don't know. Maybe we're far enough away from him that he doesn't have influence over me anymore. Maybe something else has changed. Maybe now that you're here close to his friend the Fire Wizard, he doesn't need me anymore."

All of a sudden Johanna could no longer listen or sit still. She ran out of the barn. Stood on the quay not knowing where to go or what to do. Her stomach roiled. She was dizzy. Her mouth flooded with saliva. She was going to be sick, or faint, or both.

Be sick first. She dropped to her knees and vomited, with great gasps. Again and again until there was nothing left inside her, but she dry-retched and couldn't breathe. She saw black spots in her vision. She was going to die.

"That's how it started with me, too," Loesie commented behind her.

Well, that's very helpful, thanks.

Johanna felt better after that. Come to think of it, she'd felt a bit off the last few days. She had probably caught something.

JOHANNA WALKED home in the dark. She didn't see any guards, but there were some people in the street in front of the house so she felt her way through the back yard and came into the entrance to the back of the house. Koby sat in the kitchen, talking to a young man who had to be the new groundsman.

Koby's eyes widened. "Oh my goodness, Mistress Johanna, what have you done to yourself?"

Johanna looked down. Her dress had acquired black smudges and her hands were black, too. With the heat of the fire and the smell of cooking, it was stuffy in the kitchen and her dizziness returned.

"I . . . didn't feel so well," Johanna managed to say before collapsing in a chair. Black spots danced in her vision.

"Oh no, certainly, I can see that. Let us take those dirty things off and get you tucked into bed."

"Where is Roald?" Johanna asked weakly. She let Koby take off her cloak.

"He was in the library the last time I saw him."

Of course, where else?

The young man said, "I'll let him know that you're back. Your father was a little bit worried, and the prince got worried, too. Your father said you should not have gone out alone, and I agree. It's not safe on the streets at night."

"Nothing about what we will be doing is going to be safe."

"Maybe not, but make it as safe as possible, mistress."

He left the kitchen.

"What is his name again?" Johanna asked.

"Sebastian. I thought you'd been introduced."

"Have I?" She didn't remember. Her head felt so woolly. She pressed her hands to her face.

"Where did you go at this time of the day, mistress?"

"I went to the barn. We had agreed to meet people whose houses had been burned and had nowhere to stay there. I talked to Loesie." The full horror of what Loesie had said came back to her.

"You didn't see Nellie?"

"No. Was I supposed to?"

"She went to see her family."

"Are they all right?"

"Alive, yes, but not all right. Their house was burned and her father was injured and he's very sick. Probably won't make it through the winter."

Poor Nellie. "But she will come back here, won't she?"

"I assume she will be back tomorrow. But come on now. Do you want some bread before going to bed? I made it fresh."

Johanna shook her head. Normally she loved the warm bread, but right now, she thought she was going to be sick again.

"You do look very pale, mistress. You're not going to catch an illness, are you?"

"I don't know. I think I caught something."

"Let's take you to bed, then. Come on, let me take your arm."

Koby helped Johanna up. Now that she was used to the stuffy air, she felt fine, if very tired. They walked through the basement hallway, up the stairs to the ground floor. The sound of male voices drifted from the library.

". . . and Rinius has written a few more works, which are extremely rare," Father was saying.

Roald said, "I have read his *Theories of The Skies* in the

monastery's library. It was a poor copy, but it's the only place I have ever seen one."

"Is it really as controversial as they say?"

"It's a very interesting book. Rinius claims that . . ."

At least it sounded like Roald had found someone to talk to.

Koby led her up the stairs.

Johanna turned left, but Koby pulled her to the right. "This way, mistress. Your father said that you should have his room."

"But . . ." That was embarrassing. Her room was big enough for two.

"There is a big bed in the room, and it's safer, at the back of the house."

That was true.

So they entered the room that had been her parents' sanctuary. It felt somehow wrong, but Johanna didn't have the energy to protest.

Koby took off the disgusting dress, and brought a bowl of water for Johanna to wash with. She wet the cloth and wrung it out. When the wet cloth touched her skin, Johanna shivered deep into her bones. Yes, she was definitely not well. Sleep in a warm bed would hopefully sort that out.

Koby also brought her nightgown and then left her with the words, "I will let the men know that you're up here and sleeping." She was at the door, about to leave the room when she hesitated and turned around. "Do you think that your being unwell means that we will have a little pair of feet running around this house soon?"

"No, I . . ." Johanna was going to say that she didn't think so, but by the Triune, it could be.

Right now that she had decided that it was probably better if the children stayed away until Alexandre was gone, the city was safe and the palace rebuilt, Roald officially crowned and the two of them officially married.

But children didn't wait for that sort of thing just because you wanted them to.

Koby smiled and shut the door.

Johanna lay in the big bed in the somewhat unfamiliar room staring at the ceiling. She put her hands over her lower stomach that felt, if anything, bloated and painful. Just like if she'd eaten something disagreeable.

No, she was probably sick. She had managed to go all the way to Florisheim and stay at the river camp without once being sick. Plenty of people had gotten sick there. She was just a bit late catching up.

But . . .

It worried her.

She worried about what Loesie had said. It had been Kylian who had struck Loesie mute, Kylian who had killed her family; Kylian, who had danced with Johanna at the ball. Who had kissed her. Whom she had witnessed performing an incomplete necromancy. Who had shared dinner with her in the Guentherite Brotherhood's monastery. Forced her to stay. Forced her to . . .

She was still unsure just exactly what had happened at that time in between finishing dinner and waking up on the floor when the others came to rescue her. She feared what had happened.

So many questions.

So many fears and uncertainties.

So much magic.

Roald came into the room later. Maybe Johanna had dozed a bit, or maybe she hadn't. Father was in the hallway with him, holding the candle.

"In there," he was saying. "I hear that she wasn't feeling well."

The door shut and footsteps came across the floor.

"You're feeling sick. I won't look at you today. I'm being very quiet so that you can sleep."

"Thank you, Roald," she said.

The bed moved when he lay down, and soon after, he started snoring.

Johanna still couldn't sleep. She worried and tossed and turned.

JOHANNA MUST HAVE DOZED BRIEFLY, because all of a sudden,

she woke up. Morning light came in between the curtains and the sound of voices drifted up from the hall. It was Nellie, who must have returned from her family, and someone she didn't recognise.

Johanna thought she could hear her name being mentioned. She tiptoed from the bed. Whoa, it was cold. Koby had laid out a clean dress on the bench before the dressing table. She pulled it on. The coldness of the fabric made her shiver, so she didn't think that she was quite recovered yet. Better spend some time resting by the fire today.

In the hall she found Nellie talking to a woman she remembered vaguely as having been active in the church. As soon as the woman saw Johanna, she said, "Oh!" and she dropped into a curtsy.

Well, that was embarrassing. Johanna still felt a bit uncertain on her feet. Her hair was uncombed and her dress was warm and comfortable but not the best. She wasn't fitted out to play Queen.

"There were rumours that you had made it back with the prince. Is . . . he here as well?"

"Still asleep," Johanna said.

"We've been waiting for this opportunity. Waiting for someone to tell us that not all is lost, and that we don't need to live under this tyrant and his evil church."

"I'm afraid I don't remember your name."

"Oh, I'm sorry. I'm Greetje, Your Majesty. Greetje Porter."

Oh yes, from the family that owned the grocery store. They were a customer of Father's but Johanna had always dealt with their warehouse manager.

"Please come into the kitchen where it's warm," Koby said. "It's a most nasty cold day."

They went down the stairs into the low-ceilinged basement. The servants' rooms were on both sides, many of them empty. Nellie had quickly made her room a little home again, complete with a little vase of rose hips from the garden.

The kitchen was warm. A hearty fire burned in the hearth and a pan of soup bubbled on the stove. The air smelled of baking bread.

The smell still made Johanna feel a bit queasy although she couldn't work out if that was because she felt sick or was hungry.

They sat down around the table—sturdy and made of rough wood—and Koby poured tea.

"It's like this, Your Majesty," Greetje began. She self-consciously tucked a strand of hair in her bonnet. "When those monsters took over our city, they cowardly went for the weakest and easiest targets: people from the church. They burnt the buildings, sometimes with the Shepherds still inside. Old Shepherd Darius from the church in East End they tied to the altar and then they set fire to the building." She shuddered and stared at her tea. "As if that wasn't enough, they came after the rest of us, everyone who had involvement with the church. I don't know how they knew who these people were, other than that people like Octavio Nieland or the other nobles told them. They'd always spoken up against the church. So a lot of us hid in the cellars and the warehouses. We took things from houses where we knew that all the inhabitants were dead and they would no longer need their possessions. We didn't like doing it, but we begged the Holy Spirit for forgiveness. We had to be careful because the guards and their bears were also looting people's possessions. They were putting gold and other precious things on barges that were taken up the river. Taking all the wealth from the citizens—"

"What about the palace? I noticed they were rebuilding it."

"The tyrant wants to restore the palace, so he's left it as is, except for the main hall which he has already started repairing. But I've heard that he's finding it hard to get people to do the work."

"That's because most workers were commoners and are supporters of the Church of the Triune."

"They *were* supporters of the Church of the Triune." Her expression was grave.

An unspoken horror went between them: these people were dead.

"How many died?"

"We don't know. Hundreds, at least. It was a good thing that, when the fires broke out, not many people had gone to bed yet.

When it became clear that they were after church people, we hid in cellars and warehouses. But still many were found and killed by Alexandre's men in the days after the fires."

"Are any church people still left?"

"There are. We have services in different places every couple of days. Not on a regular day, because that would make them suspicious, and we meet somewhere else every time. We have a new Shepherd. Shepherd Victor. You might know him." She smiled. "We would be most honoured if you could visit us and take prayer with us."

"Yes, I would."

"What about the most important patron of the church?"

It took Johanna a few seconds to figure out that she was talking about Roald, because he didn't strike her as being very supportive of the church. In fact, she didn't think she had ever heard him talk about the church. Strange that he should be "the most important patron". "Maybe he can come. If it's safe."

"Both of you would be most welcome. We've been looking for a sign of hope. I do believe this is it." She took Johanna's hands. Her hands were still cold from outside. "There is a service on tomorrow night. I will send one of the boys along to pick you up."

When Greetje was gone, Koby started making breakfast and Roald came blundering down the stairs.

"Where is breakfast in this house?"

"You're in the right place. Just wait until I make some new tea. And I do believe that the bread is done." Koby gave him a thick slice of bread just out of the oven that still steamed and absorbed the butter like a sponge.

He started eating, dripping butter and jam down his chin.

He hadn't shaved for a number of days, but Johanna decided that the reddish beard made him look more serious. He looked tired, they all were.

Koby put a slice of bread in front of her. Johanna didn't feel like eating, but she picked at it a bit, because Koby was shooting her you-must-eat daggers. The jam made it better, though. Much better.

Meanwhile, Roald asked Koby questions about making

bread, and as it turned out, he had some experience. "If we did something the abbot didn't like, he would make us work in the laundry or the kitchens. I didn't like the laundry, but the kitchens were all right."

"Your Majesty, that's scandalous. Did you do that many naughty things?"

"Once I said that I thought their statue of the Triune in the chapel was wrong. Once I told a brother to stop hitting a horse. Once I told the brother that his wine was off and he made it wrong, once . . ." He counted on his fingers.

Koby laughed. "You were quite the rascal, then."

"They were unfair. The work I did was fair. The horse didn't ask to be hit, and a horse doesn't know why you hit it. The bad wine was his own fault."

Johanna reminded herself to never do anything stupid in Roald's presence, because he would remember and recount it until the end of his days.

Koby completely relaxed in his presence, and showed him her baking tray and other utensils with flour-covered hands.

Nellie announced that she had work to do, and Johanna remained at the table, clutching her cup and gradually finishing her bread.

It worried her that Greetje had so easily found out that she and Roald were back. It meant that Alexandre would find out soon enough, too. It meant that they would have to move quickly. Visit that church service and the people who gathered there. Have some sort of ceremony to make Roald's assumption of the throne official.

That gesture would be infinitely improved if she could get the crown and staff from their hiding places. Unless Alexandre had combed the palace, she was the only person who knew where they were.

But she was tired, so incredibly cold and tired.

CHAPTER 11

TRUE TO GREETJE'S word, a boy came to the house the next morning with the message that tonight's service would be held in a boatshed in East Harbour.

Johanna didn't see him. She was resting upstairs, as she had done for much of the previous day, and only came downstairs when he returned to accompany them to the secret location of the church service.

She had eaten a bit, but still felt really tired and not quite steady on her feet.

Roald and Father were in the hall. They had spent most of the day in the library. Father looked bright, if thin and a lot greyer than he had been when she left, and he was talking in a lively manner.

He had given Roald the heavy cloak that he used when going out on the boats.

When Johanna frowned at it, he said, "I have no more boats to use it on, and I'm getting too old for that sort of thing anyway. I'm getting out of the way. It's time for the young generation to take over."

He looked lonely and sad. He had always been such a proud man, at the top of his business when all this happened, and now he was reduced to having to give away his business to a rival family in order to be able to continue it. Once Johanna had dreamt of running the Brouwer Company, but even if Father could get a new ship soon and the *Lady Sara* could resume the river trade—and to be honest, what towns were left that were in a position to resume buying luxury items?—she would be too busy helping Roald.

She hugged him.

Johanna and Roald followed Nellie and the boy out into the night. His name was Pieter, he said proudly, and he was thirteen years old. He delivered messages for the church because, "I'm so small, and the guards think that I'm a kid so they never stop me." His voice sounded very young.

Clouds hung low over the city, and an occasional squall would whip cold drops of rain into Johanna's face.

Pieter carried a storm lamp and led them through alleys and back streets so that they avoided most of the spots where the guards often patrolled. He knew exactly where they went and what routes they took. Once they saw two men with a storm light, but otherwise, the night belonged to the wind and rain.

East Harbour was an area where large warehouses lined the waterfront. Most of those were fairly new and purpose-built, so that they could handle the larger vessels. This was where the large ocean ships docked and where much of the imported wares were stored before they were either sold in town or carried upriver by riverboats such as the *Lady Sara*.

It was not a place for river ships or sea cows, because that trade was much older and took place in the main harbour.

It was extremely dark and deserted in this part of town since few people lived here, even before the fires. The seafaring ships bobbed on their moorings. The water was rough, even in this sheltered area, and waves slapped against hulls and seawalls.

The boatshed was at the end of the quay where the pier jutted into the murky waters. A faint glow in the dark indicated the presence of the lighthouse, although the structure itself blended into the darkness.

They walked along the back of the shed in single file, hair and clothing flapping in the wind. Then Pieter stopped and knocked four times at a wooden warehouse door. He said in a clear voice, "The Triune is our Saviour."

The door opened a crack, revealing the faint glow of a storm light against the rough bricks of the warehouse wall.

"I've brought them," Pieter said.

A man said, "Quick, come in. It's awful out there."

The door of the shed opened further and Nellie led Johanna and Roald inside.

To Johanna's great surprise, the ground floor of the warehouse was packed. In the low light of a few storm lamps hanging on wall hooks or hoists that were normally used to haul goods to the upper floors of the warehouse, it was hard to see who all these people were. The cranes and wooden beams cast odd shadows over the crowd, but there had to be at least a hundred people gathered here. They shuffled aside to make a path for the newcomers to the back wall of the warehouse.

Here, a storm lantern stood on a table. Someone had found a smudged, formerly white tablecloth on which stood a candle in a half-burnt candle holder that Johanna recognised as having stood on the altar in the big church.

The candle was tallow wax and smoked more than it burned. Its rancid smell spread through the shed despite the draughty air. Behind the candle against the wall leaned a framed painting that depicted the Triune: a man with a twisted body that had three heads: an old man with a beard, a salivating dog and a wraith-like figure.

Johanna folded her hands and bowed her head in a moment of reflection. Next to her, Roald stood as frozen, staring at all those people who were whispering about him. He had stuffed his hands deep in his pockets. He looked awkward and nervous.

Johanna touched him on the shoulder, but he didn't react.

People started pointing and murmuring. She could almost hear the voices. *Is that him? He doesn't look as crazy as they said he was.*

The light from the storm lamps lit the crowd from behind, gilding hats, bonnets and scarves and the puffs of mist from their breathing. Some people had no winter clothing, and they came dressed in improvised capes made from horse blankets. Some people hid their faces in hoods and shawls. Some were injured. She spotted a couple of people with bandaged hands and one man at the front had weeping injuries on one side of his face. It looked red and swollen and painful. But his face was set in a determined expression.

Nellie's mother was there, and she recognised some people from shops and the markets.

Greetje came out from between the people. "Oh, I'm so happy that you're here."

She hugged Johanna and curtsied to Roald.

Then she faced the crowd and said, "I present to you, His Excellency Crown Prince Roald of Saarland and his Consort, Johanna Brouwer."

A few people cheered. Others clapped, but most watched in silence. Whether that was because they had to stay hidden or because they didn't know what to think of Roald, Johanna didn't know.

Greetje went on to tell the people about Johanna and Roald's escape to Florisheim. Again, most remained silent. Johanna had forgotten the sort of rumours that circulated amongst the townsfolk about Roald. Probably the "idiot" view was quite strong, and they would see by the way he fidgeted that Roald wasn't, and would never be, a "normal" king who gave speeches and held balls. Seeing him potter about the rose garden was about as normal as he would ever get.

This was the part where Johanna would have to stand up and take control, but the very thought made her feel sick. Seeing all these tired faces of people who had lived through hell, she wouldn't be surprised if they refused to listen to her.

But when Greetje asked, she told their story, leaving out everything about Loesie.

" 'Tis an evil world indeed," a man declared when she finished.

Others murmured agreement. Some wanted to know if they'd had church services while they were in Florisheim, and Johanna told them about Shepherd Carolus and that some of the nobles in the group, especially the women, supported the church. That made her remember Julianna Nieland and the young men who had presumably made their way back to the *Prosperity* but needed places to stay.

"We have in our group some people who have come back and found all their possessions burned and relatives killed. Some of these people need places to stay. I'm sure that they will work for their keep."

A man wanted to know, "Do you have someone who can write neatly without mistakes?"

"Julianna Nieland."

Some gasps went up in the audience.

A woman said, "Certainly we can't have the traitor's sister in our midst? She wouldn't go against her own brother?"

"She saw what her brother did to the people of Saardam and she fled because of his actions. She could go back to his house if she wanted, but instead she has chosen to keep away from him. She sees the evil in him. She is brave but has no place to sleep."

"But then she can sleep in our house," said a clear, young male voice. Someone had just entered and was making his way through the crowd. People stepped aside for him, and bowed.

Johanna assumed this was the Shepherd Victor.

A figure in a long hooded cloak dissolved from the crowd and came to the table-turned-altar. The garment was dark on colour, brown or black, and he held it tied with a simple rope. His face was invisible in the shadow of the hood, but he reached up and pushed the hood down.

"It is a great pleasure to welcome Your Majesty in the house of the Triune—" He froze. "Mistress Johanna!"

"Master Willems!"

Johanna stared at the young man. She'd known that Shepherd Victor was not his real name, but she had expected him to be some senior member of the church.

He came to her, his eyes shining. He took her hand and dropped to one knee. "Oh, I am so glad to see you safe and well, and about to become the queen, too. I listened to rumours and prayed and dreamed, and hoped that someone would bring news of your survival."

He had listened to the wind, she was sure, but he still continued the Church line that magic didn't exist.

"I presume you have met my wife, Greetje?"

"I met her, but I didn't know that she was your wife."

"We married after the fire. We are trying to continue life as normal as we can, to have marriages, to baptise children and hold funerals. We've had far too many of those lately. We can use some good news."

"Your parents?"

His face fell. "Died in the fire."

"Oh, I'm so sorry."

"Everyone of us has a story of loss and pain to tell. We've been trying to keep people's hopes up by holding weddings. Maybe now that you have returned, we should have a very short ceremony that we all confirm our love for each other, and that we will help each other. Let us start with the service."

People fell quiet. Johanna took Roald's hand and drew him into the audience where the people at the front made room for them.

The ceremony was simple and short. Master Willems spoke about hope and new life, new relationships. He likened the group, this little seed of resistance, to a blade of grass pushing through the snow after winter.

People prayed. Happy tears rolled over many cheeks.

At the end, the Shepherd asked Johanna and Roald to come forwards and to state officially that they were husband and wife, and that the marriage service had been conducted before a member of the church. Johanna said that it had, and that, when the hard times were over, there would be an official celebration.

"Certainly that will be a celebration of the firstborn prince or princess," a woman said.

Others agreed.

"If you were married a few months ago, we should certainly have an heir by summer," a woman said.

Johanna smiled politely but felt miserable inside.

More people gathered around and Johanna asked about people she knew, like the families of the ship's boys.

In turn, people wanted to know about survivors who had been to Florisheim with Johanna. Most of the names she mentioned met with snorts and scoffs. Of Fleuris LaFontaine someone said that it was better that he stayed there. "Never good for anything except bossing people around and complaining that the work wasn't done good enough. He would go and explain how it was done. He's never done anything himself."

The only person who met with any kind of approval was Master Deim.

"He's a decent sort," a man said. "But I thought he was from Florisheim or has family there."

"He does, but his sister-in-law is a Saarlander." Johanna remembered the picture above the hearth and the woman's awkward pledge of loyalty.

Then the meeting was over and people started filing out of the shed in small groups so as not to draw attention. In the end just Master Willems, Greetje, Nellie, Roald and Johanna were left in the coldness of the empty warehouse.

Johanna held Roald's arm and faced Master Willems, who held Greetje's arm. She was shivering in the cold.

"We are always in the last group to leave," Master Willems said. "We turn off the lights and make the room look like the meeting never happened."

Nellie had already started sweeping dust over the floor.

"It's very good to see that you have survived," Johanna said. "But I don't understand. Father says that you've gone missing."

"He knows where I am, but that I've gone missing is the story we tell everyone. After the burning of the city, it soon became clear that Alexandre and his louts were after members of the church. That's how they got my family."

And that might be why the LaFontaine nephew had mocked about Master Willems having gone missing. He knew that Father had something to hide, because if Master Willems had really gone missing, Father would have appointed a different accountant long ago.

"I'm so sorry about your family."

He pressed his lips together. "I'm learning to move forward."

"You knew that the trouble was coming for us, didn't you? You had seen it on the wind."

"They were omens."

"Would you deny your gift, even now?"

His expression closed. "I do not speak of that thing. The

Triune teaches that it is not a good thing." Even now, he could not say the word *magic*.

"I understand, but I don't think it's wise. Are we going to face Alexandre wielding prayer books while he mows us down with magic fire?"

He gave her a sharp look.

"He will come for us, and he will kill us all if we give him a chance."

"We will stay out of his way until we are so numerous that he can't fight all of us at once. He thinks we are weak and scared. The numbers of Estlanders he employs has already gone down a lot. By the time we are strong, he will have too few trusted men to fight us."

"He's recruiting people in the city."

"Only those who are easily swayed by power will come to him. The rest will not betray their family and friends."

Johanna wasn't so sure about that. If people were desperate enough, they would do anything.

Then they discussed what should be done next.

Master Willems said, "In a time like this, we cannot do much without a strong leader. The prince must assume the throne. We must hold a coronation ceremony and we must make a temporary palace."

Johanna agreed and guessed that her father's house would have to fulfil that function, although Roald would probably never satisfy the description *strong leader*. "We may be able to hold a proper coronation ceremony."

"The crown and staff were lost when the king and queen were killed," Master Willems said, gravely.

"I know. I saw the bodies in the palace. I picked up the crown and the staff and hid them."

He stared at her, open-mouthed. "You know where they are?"

"In the same place I left them, unless you've seen Alexandre wear those things."

"No, we haven't. Alexandre declares himself the regent but he never wears the crown and never carries the staff. We thought that meant the crown must have been lost."

"Mind you, they might still have been lost, but it looks like most of the palace still stands. There is a good chance that the crown and staff are still where I hid them. Alexandre hasn't done much to fix the palace up?"

He shook his head. "Most of the roof has fallen in. He can't find people to fix it."

Greetje started laughing at this, and Johanna guessed that this was one of the ways that the citizens protested against the tyrant.

"We could retrieve them and have the proper ceremony."

Master Willems' eyes shone. "That would be a slap in his face."

"We could get in through the rose garden. There is a hedge in the rose garden that surrounds a wall that's not very high and shouldn't be too hard to climb."

CHAPTER 12

MOST OF THE next day, Johanna sat in the kitchen because an icy wind had come up and there was not enough wood to heat the entire house. Father stayed in the library where, thanks to the high ceiling, it was much colder despite the fire. He said, "You young people should talk amongst yourselves."

Johanna told him not to be silly and join them, but he said that he expected a visit from Auguste LaFontaine and that the LaFontaines should not find out about his houseguests.

Which was true.

But the LaFontaine cousin stayed away, probably because of the weather. Father took his tea in the library. Roald had moved a chair from the cold formal sitting room into the kitchen, where it had stood in the corner for many years. It was a strange thing, made from some kind of twig, much thinner and smoother than willow twigs. She used to love it when she was little, because the wood would show her a large river flowing between steep rocks covered in green. It was a landscape she had never seen before or since.

She didn't know how Father had obtained the chair, but since it weighed a lot less than the traditional furniture, it had been easy for Roald to carry downstairs. He sat there now, reading a book with his feet on a footstool and the glow from the fire gilding his trousers and slippers.

The rain had turned to snow at midmorning, but the darkness was never dispelled from the house.

At some time in the afternoon came the sound of footsteps from the back yard, the kitchen door opened and Greetje came in.

"Cold out there," she said while unwrapping the shawl from her head and shaking out the snowflakes. She stood by the fire, warming her hands. Roald was deeply engrossed in a book and never looked up.

"The boys like the idea of getting the crown and staff," Greetje said, rubbing her hands. "Bert says that there is a new moon in two weeks and it might be good to break into the palace then."

"That sounds like a good idea. Could you find a couple of volunteers to come with me?"

"By the Triune, you're not planning to go yourself?"

"Who else knows where the crown and staff are?"

"You can give directions."

"I don't remember exact details. I can tell on sight once I see the room, but I don't know the palace well enough to give the men precise directions."

Greetje gave her a horrified look. "But you're the consort. You can't possibly—"

"I'm also the only person who knows where I put the crown."

She still didn't look convinced. "By the Triune, the boys are not going to like this. My husband told me to not let you go out more than necessary. He said we will come and guide you. It's tricky enough simply walking the streets. The guards walk certain patterns. If they see you, they will sometimes stop you for a stupid reason and ask you questions to make you angry. They're trying to find an excuse to make you dependent on Alexandre. If you protest too much, he sets your house on fire. He's an evil man, possessed by the Lord of Fire. He just flicks his hand at a house and it burns."

And none of these people with powerful magic wanted to help her. Instead she was left to fight magic with virtually no magic of her own. With a church that denied the existence of magic. They didn't need more people; they needed more useful people.

"Do you want some tea?" Koby asked.

"Well, I . . ." Greetje hesitated. "Oh, why not."

It was warm in the kitchen. Koby had a pan of hot water on the stove for the washing, and after Greetje accepted the tea she took off her coat.

Underneath, she wore a dark dress of thick fabric that looked like it had once made up curtains in a house of a well-off family.

She laughed when she noticed Johanna staring at it. "The dress is a bit odd, I admit, but I had to make something that would accommodate my condition." She joined her hands and pushed down the fabric under her belly. It showed a clear swelling.

Johanna stared. "These are poor times to be having a child."

"The times are as good or bad as you make them. Times may be hard, but there is nothing I can change about them. These hard times are when I got married, and I'm not letting that stand in the way of having a family." She sipped from her tea.

Koby picked up the pan and carried it, steaming and all, into the laundry, leaving Johanna and Greetje at the table. Roald was still reading. Had he even noticed that they had a visitor and were talking about retrieving the symbols of his family?

Johanna played with her cup, looking at Greetje from the corner of her eye. "How do you know . . . that you're going to be having a child? Like, in the very beginning?"

"Well, you don't bleed, of course. You start to feel strange sometimes. Puffy, or full, or sick sometimes, and you can faint, but that hasn't happened to me. And then you notice that nothing fits anymore so you have to get special dresses."

"Do you feel the child move inside you?"

"Yes, but that's not until later. Why are you asking? Are you. . . ?"

"I don't know." And she truly didn't. With all the things that had been going on, Johanna couldn't remember when she had last bled. She remembered the last time she'd been disappointed about it, but she thought there had been another time. In which

case it was probably much too early to tell, and in which case . . .
no, she wasn't going to think about what happened in the Guentherite farmhouse with Kylian. She pushed down her unease. She
asked, "How long did you notice this after you were married?"

"It didn't take me long at all. We were married and that night
he took me to bed and I never bled since."

Johanna gritted her teeth. For some people, it was so easy. "It
took Queen Cygna a number of years."

"That's true. Maybe it's a royal family thing."

Maybe, too, people who weren't entirely normal couldn't
have children. She'd heard of some people called simple or idiots,
but none she knew of had ever had children.

She shuddered.

Which was worse: that she never had a child, that the child
was afflicted with the same condition as Roald, or, heaven forbid,
that Kylian had bewitched her, had his way with her and the
child was his?

Blood rose to her cheeks.

All of a sudden, it was too hot and stuffy in the kitchen. She
rose so quickly that her chair almost fell over. She ran out of the
kitchen, through the laundry, past Koby who was scrubbing
clothes in the big wash tub, and out the back door.

"Mistress Johanna!" Koby protested.

Johanna stopped, panting in the back courtyard where the
neat garden was brown for winter. A drift of fat snowflakes fell
from the sky.

She hugged herself against the cold. The snow melted where
it hit her arms. Her stomach was churning. Shooting pains went
through her breasts. They felt as hard as rocks. Those were all
signs, weren't they?

Koby came out into the snow. "Mistress? What are you doing
out here?"

"I just . . . couldn't breathe in there."

"It's cold and wet out here. Come inside." She put an arm on
Johanna's shoulder, guiding her back into the kitchen.

Greetje raised her eyebrows.

"I'm not very well," Johanna said.

Greetje and Koby exchanged a knowing look.

Koby said, "Not to be jumping to conclusions too quickly, mistress, but I think there is a good chance that we'll have the patter of little feet in summer."

Roald looked up with a huh–what? expression.

"And there we have the father to be."

Roald frowned at her. He looked genuinely puzzled, as if he didn't think that all those nights that she had sat astride him would have any consequences. There had been so many of those nights.

Of course any child she had was his. Any other possibility was simply put into her head by magic. They wanted her to feel uncertain.

She was not going to let her mind wander down silly winding tracks. If there was going to be a prince or princess, he or she was of Carmine blood.

A FEW DAYS later Johanna went to another Church service, this time at someone's house at the very edge of the city. Greetje had drummed up more volunteers for her trip to the palace than she needed. She'd hoped to get two or three men, but she ended up with eight.

Some of the men were adamant that she should not go. "You're the Queen. If we lose you, our efforts at resisting Alexandre will have been for nothing."

"I know where these things are. I know the palace better than any of you. I can't let you go inside without a guide. You might get lost."

The men were all warehouse workers and shipbuilders and carpenters. None of them had ever set foot inside the palace, so they reluctantly had to agree to let her come.

They worked out a plan. They would do it on the night of the next new moon. A couple of men would hide a ladder in the reeds along the river on the outside the palace garden. They would climb in through the Queen's rose garden and then through the garden room and the big ballroom, into the royal family's living quarters.

"That is, if the palace hasn't been looted," Greetje said.

Johanna hoped not, and the signs were good. The only one who would have looted the palace would be Alexandre.

She did wonder why he didn't live in the palace, especially because, since there was such a shortage of housing, it seemed silly to leave such a large building vacant.

The day after, Auguste LaFontaine came back to the house. Johanna didn't see him come in, but Koby told her that he was upstairs when Johanna came back from the markets. She had been trying to buy some fabric because a couple more days of feeling weird and sometimes near fainting convinced her that Koby was probably right, and she intended to ask Nellie to make a dress for her. Except she had come back empty-handed, because everyone had bought all available fabric for the winter.

Voices drifted through the house from the hall when she came into the kitchen. The conversation didn't sound friendly. Koby put her finger to her lips.

Johanna quietly sneaked up the stairs to the point where the steps switched back in the other direction and she would be in view of the people in the hall.

An arrogant-sounding voice said, "I've given you enough time to think about it. I don't want to talk or negotiate about it again. You either sign that agreement and lead a happy life or you don't and we'll take your business from you when you're dead."

Father said, "You'll get it anyway. This document is an instrument of blackmail."

"You dare to be rude to me? You, an old man with no friends and no children?"

Johanna cringed. *Father, we don't have time for this.*

"I've thought about your proposition, and I do not want to accept it. I understood that this choice was up to me."

"Do you really choose to let your business die through a lack of ships?"

"I'll replace the ship. I'll carry on. If, when the time comes, I have not located any of my or my former wife's family, I will pick a loyal employee and give the company to him."

The man made sputtering noises. "Yes, well, don't ask for our help ever again."

"I never asked for help in the first place. I listened to your proposal because I thought it might work, but I've decided that it won't."

"Well then," Auguste scoffed. "Well . . . good luck. Because you'll need it."

There were footsteps in the hall. The door opened and slammed shut.

Johanna ran up the stairs. Father stood in the hallway, bolting the front door. He turned around and smiled when his eyes met Johanna's.

"Why did you do that, Father?"

"Because I'm not going to crawl at their feet anymore. Having you here means that I don't have to do that. I was never much at ease with the idea of taking such a young woman as wife either, and it would have been a terrible thing for all concerned."

"Oh, Father." She hugged him.

She liked how he was proud and didn't give in to pressure—had he ever given in to pressure in his life?—but it would draw attention from Alexandre. He might investigate or keep a close eye on Father, because Father was supposed to be widowed, lonely and unhappy. If he was none of those things, it would arouse suspicion.

This meant that any action against Alexandre would have to come sooner rather than later.

A T NIGHT, Johanna worried. Their group was small and disorganised, and had no magicians. Alexandre controlled the guards, of which there were fewer than before, but still more than enough to wipe their entire group off the world. The Church followers weren't ready for a conflict and it seemed that they were headed for one.

She sat in the kitchen until everyone else had gone to bed, listening to the wind whistle around the corners and gutters.

She should go to sleep, but in the past few days she had slept so much that she wasn't tired. But it was getting cold in this kitchen, so she picked up the candle and carried it upstairs. Roald lay on his stomach, his face squished in the pillow and turned to her. His breathing was soft and regular.

She pulled her dress over her head and lifted her underdress to look at her pale body in the mirror. The skin over her breasts was tight and the tissue underneath felt like a bag filled with beans. It was sore at the slightest touch of her fingertips. They seemed larger. Definitely more filled. She slid her hand over her stomach and then puffed it out to make it seem more round.

By the Triune, it was an unfortunate thing to happen right now. And scary, too. Maybe Greetje was all upbeat about it, but Mother had died while carrying a brother or sister for her. Father had told her that when it became clear that Mother was expecting Johanna, she had signed her will, mainly to, in the event of her death, keep the Aroden family from claiming a part of the Brouwer Company.

Johanna should go and see a lawyer.

Maybe.

Maybe in a day or two, it would all prove to be a false alarm and she would have worried for nothing. Or hoped for nothing, she didn't know which.

They had a revolution to fight and a tyrant to drive from the city. There was no time for sickness and babies.

She let the nightdress fall and climbed into bed. Then she blew out the candle.

In the darkness, Roald said, "You were looking at yourself."

She hadn't realised he was awake.

He slid a hand over her side and up to her breast.

"Ow."

He withdrew. "That hurts?"

"Yes. It's nothing to do with you. It's just . . . sore." She thought for a while, and then decided what the heck. "Roald, I think I'm having a child."

He took quite a while to process that. She expected questions about how that worked, but then she remembered that he had read books about human anatomy and probably knew better than anyone how that worked.

"Like the cows," he said in a matter-of-fact way.

"I suppose." She was a bit miffed to be compared with a cow, but if that made him happy . . .

"I used to have to get up at night and check on the cows when they were calving. Sometimes there was one where the calf was stuck, and I'd have to put my hand in and push it right. It was messy. The calf used to come out covered in a blue-white sac, with blood and water. Like that?"

"Well . . ." *Thanks, Roald, for the detail I didn't need to know.* "I suppose so." By the Triune, now she felt ill again.

"That's all right." He sounded very confident. "I can help." He slid his hand down her side and between her legs. "It comes out here."

"Thank you, Roald, but—oh!" That whole area was sensitive, in a good way.

"Does that hurt, too?"

"No. It feels . . . good."

"Do you want me to look at you?"

"Well, I . . ." She wasn't sure. Didn't they always say to be really careful in the beginning? But then, didn't she want this to be a false alarm? Maybe she was just panicking and felt this way because her bleeding was really late. Maybe it would get the bleeding started. She lifted her leg over him.

Normally, she would be a bit sore when he went inside her, but this time, the waves of pleasure hit her almost straight away, and twice more immediately afterwards. When he finished and she lay in the warm hollow against his body, the entire bottom half of her body was throbbing and glowing. There was no doubt left in her mind that she was with child.

This became even more clear the next morning when she ate two healthy slices of Koby's bread and then had to run outside to empty her stomach. No one saw her do that—it was a terrible thing because people went hungry in town, and the bread was very good.

It had snowed overnight and Johanna used her wooden shoe to push snow over the patch so that hopefully no one would notice. But when she was inside, of course, she felt hungry again. She didn't dare eat, but that made her feel even sicker and she vomited again, in the washbowl upstairs, because there wasn't anywhere else to do it. She stood there, awkwardly holding the porcelain washbowl with a smelly puddle of brown in the bottom, wondering how to discreetly get rid of it, when Nellie came in.

"Oh, oh, Mistress Johanna. Give that to me and go to bed. You need lots of rest in your condition."

Johanna protested weakly that she was hungry but Nellie wouldn't have a bar of it, and so she lay in bed again, sick and hungry, her whole body throbbing.

This was the bed where her mother had lain in the same condition, the bed where Johanna had been born and where, two years later, her mother had died while carrying a brother or sister. Unless something dramatic happened and they could defeat Alexandre, Johanna might do most of those same things here.

Johanna tried some water, but that came back out straight away, so she got dressed and went downstairs and convinced Koby that she needed something to eat that wasn't bread because her stomach didn't like it. Koby gave her some cheese and that made her feel much better.

So much better, in fact, that she went back to worrying about how to deal with the fact that the band of Church followers would soon face Alexandre and they were nowhere near ready.

Failing a magician, they needed all the people they could recruit to the cause, and something needed to be done about this soon.

In the afternoon, when Nellie would let her leave the house, she went to see the cheese seller Leo at the markets, but found the market place infested with guards. They walked between the stalls looking at produce, looking at people, talking to people. They were mostly traitors: Saarlander men in the employ of the occupying force. They wore blue uniforms, some with shiny buttons, but most of the jackets looked a little the worse for wear. Johanna wondered where they had come from and who had worn them previously.

A couple stood around a man who was said to have stolen an apple. He was crying about not having enough to eat and having lost everything and the guards threatened to take off his shirt and beat him.

Really, they would do that?

In Saardam, they'd risen above such barbaric processes long ago. That just went to show that *the veneer of civilisation is thin*, one of the things Master Deim loved to say.

Johanna very much wanted to tell those arrogant young men in their new suits that this wasn't how Saarlanders treated each other, but had to keep walking because she couldn't afford to get involved. They might recognise her. They would report her to Alexandre or Octavio Nieland.

Leo was at the usual table with his cheeses. Not as many as before the fires, Johanna noticed. He raised his eyebrows at

Johanna and made all sorts of hand gestures that probably meant that she had better not talk about anything that she didn't want anyone else to hear. So she told him that she was interested in buying a horse.

His face cleared up. "Oh, you must have heard about the horse that I bought from a group of travellers."

"I was going to put a bid on that horse," said the farmer in the next stall.

"No, I," said the stallholder across the aisle.

About ten people said they were interested in the horse, and Leo was trying to tell everyone where they could view this horse, when a guard turned up.

He stopped at Leo's stall and asked him a question that Johanna couldn't hear. Leo replied something about having found the horse wandering around.

"If it's found to be an escaped coach horse, you will be charged with theft."

"I didn't steal anything. I bought it, fair and square."

"The horse trade is not your normal business."

"Then am I not allowed to earn some extra money and help a fellow out?"

Johanna rounded to corner of the aisle and stopped, heart thudding. The voices of Leo and the guard drifted on the wind, but she couldn't figure out what they said.

"That particular low-life of a man does that all the time," a merchant wife said to Johanna, while jerking her head in the direction of the guard. "Joined this tyrant as soon as he started calling for local volunteers. He was always a funny character, but I never thought he'd betray us."

"I always said he would," added another stallholder. "He's a weaselly little man who likes to pretend he's more than he is, grovelling for this tyrant and Octavio Nieland."

Johanna managed to get them to tell her where Leo's warehouse was and then she continued on her way.

CHAPTER 14

BEFORE JOHANNA had left the markets, there was a to-do at the mayor's house. While she had talked to Leo, more people had gathered in front of the house, kept away from the steps that led up to the front door by a handful of guards.

The door to the house and a third guard came out, holding a trumpet with blue tassels. Some people cheered, others called out, holding out their hands like beggars.

The man stopped right in front of the railing at the top of the steps and faced the crowd. He put the trumpet to his mouth and played a fanfare, loud and clear. The sound echoed over the square

The door opened again and a man dressed in blue appeared on the top of the steps. Blue cape, blue trousers, blue jacket and a white shirt with excessive ruffles. He was thin and wore his honey-coloured hair in a ponytail that stuck out from under his wide-brimmed hat. His boots were of the thick-soled type that made the wearer appear taller, black and polished with shiny buckles.

While he stood at the top of the stairs surveying the crowd, another two men came out of the door, each carrying one end of a box that looked like a travel chest. They manoeuvred this thing down the stairs and set it on the ground before the line of people.

The man in blue, whom Johanna had never seen but assumed was Alexandre Trebuchet, came down the stairs in an effortless glide.

The people in the queue called out to him.

"Please, lord, help an old woman."

"Please, lord, my children are sick and we have no house."

"Please, we need wood for the fire."

Alexandre simply walked past them without looking, his chin in the air, ignoring all their calls. A couple of men followed him, all dressed in finery. One of those men was Octavio Nieland. He and another man went to the box and stood next to it, crossing their arms over their chests. A lot of people in that line were looking at the box with wide eyes.

Johanna pulled the hood of the cloak further over her face and retreated further into the nearby stall. It sold eggs and pears, dried beans and flour. She hoped no one would recognise her.

Alexandre and his men walked along the perimeter of the markets past the boarded up weigh house and the makeshift replacement, past the ruins of the house on the corner, to the empty block where the church had stood.

One of the men produced a roll of paper, which he unrolled and held up for Alexandre to see.

"It be bad news, what that man is doing," said the stallholder, a short woman whose well-fed appearance showed no signs of hardship.

"I assume he's rebuilding the church?"

"That, he is," a man said, presumably her husband. "I've not seen the plans myself, but I hear from my cousin who is a carpenter that it's quite a monstrous thing he's building. That other man over there is Charles DeLuc from Burovia." Johanna presumed that he meant the dark-haired man who was pointing at the plans. "He's known for designing ridiculously expensive buildings."

The farmer in the next stall laughed. "That thing will take so much stone, the ground is too soft for it. It will sink sideways before they ever get to put the roof on it."

A few others agreed with this and went on to debate whether the new church would be more elaborate than the old church; and since that church had been made of wood, it had to be.

Johanna asked, "Do any of you know what that thing is they're building in the harbour?"

"No, lady, not a clue, but they're working hard at it. There's a full team of men turning up there every morning. They get every single brick the brickmakers can produce that we haven't already managed to get. He's using his own men to build it and they don't come into town and don't talk to anyone else."

"I think it's some kind of oven for making bricks," another man said.

"I think it's for building ships," said the farmer. "Why else would they build it in that place?"

Johanna was reminded of the strange activities going on at the Guentherite Brotherhood's farm. The hole in the ground and the black rock that was taken out. And the stranger activities at the Abbott's summer residence.

She asked, "Have you seen any ships bringing in iron?"

There were headshakes at this. "Why iron?"

"We saw similar strange things being built all along the river. Mostly there are monks of the Guentherite order involved. They dig holes in the ground, take out black rock and make iron. No one knows why."

The stallholder's wife said, "There were some monks here in autumn, but they left a few weeks ago. We thought it was to do with their church. People were saying that the Belaman Church got angry with the Church of the Triune and the Holy Father said that the Church of the Triune broke church teachings and banished them."

"Yeah, I heard that, too," said the man in the next stall.

That part of the rumours was true. The Belaman Church encouraged magic. Were they going to take their ghosts, black rock and iron into Saardam? Were they performing necromancy?

She shivered.

All the construction works along the river were part of a plan. She wondered what had gone wrong at the Abbot's summer residence and how much that had delayed their construction.

Something evil was being created and should be stopped. Alexandre should *not* build a church here, in the place where she used to come most days for the Shepherd Romulus' service. Where the wooden pews told her their stories, and where on most mornings, the Shepherd could be seen teaching children and giving poor families food and clothing.

Alexandre and his party had walked around the bare and muddy building site and come back to the house, where Octavio and the other man still stood on either side of the chest.

The people in the queue again started yelling their pleas at him.

An old woman fell to her knees. "Please, my son is ill and I have no way to feed him. Please, lord, have mercy."

Johanna had to look away. It was embarrassing to see citizens lower themselves to this level.

Alexandre walked past the row. At the bottom of the stairs, he said something to one of his guard companions. The man went to Octavio. He said something, bowed and Octavio opened the lid. He lifted out a bag that looked like it contained potatoes.

He gave it to the guard, who put this on the ground in between the chest and the row of waiting people. As soon as he stepped back, a number of the closest people in the queue ran for it. Two men reached the bag at the same time and were pulling both ends. A woman was hitting one of the men on the head. The queue dissolved. Everyone was screaming. People gathered to watch, blocking Johanna's view. Eventually one of the men came out of the melee carrying the bag on his shoulder.

Alexandre stood at the top of the stairs, watching the spectacle. He nodded.

Octavio gave the soldier another bag, which he placed at a different spot. The process repeated, and so it went on a few times before the chest was empty and two soldiers carried it back up the stairs and inside the house.

Alexandre followed the men inside and the door shut.

Johanna felt sick. That was the worst, most revolting treatment of unfortunate people she had seen in her life, and Octavio was just doing the man's bidding. Why?

The beggars in the queue went back to their places, except the ones who had scored gifts. They gathered in a group to compare their loot.

Johanna met the eyes of a man in the queue. She had seen him before. His name was Joseph and he used to work in the Nieland warehouse. As she emerged from between the market stalls and crossed to the queue, he looked down, as if ashamed for taking part in this spectacle.

"Why do you beg him for help?" Johanna asked. "He's just doing this to make you dependent on him and make you look like a dumbwit."

"I'd rather be a dumbwit than dead, lady. Our houses were burnt and we have no food. What else are we supposed to do?"

"Maintain your pride."

"We can't eat pride. He gives us food every day, or we wouldn't stand here waiting. We're not grateful and don't bow to him. We just prefer to eat and not starve."

"So what if I said that you could get work somewhere and you'd be paid an honest wage for what you earned? And that you could use it to buy your own food?"

He laughed. "You mean a job, miss? There are no more jobs. The shops are gone and the merchants are gone. The warehouses are all empty. You don't see any of that in your rich house, lady, but that's the way it is for most of us."

Many in the queue had gathered around. Most of them wore many layers of clothes, no doubt a fair few stolen.

"Do you sit here all night?"

"Most of us have nowhere else to go."

"Many of the warehouses are abandoned. Why don't you go in there?"

"And run foul of the bears? No, thank you. We're weak, and most of us injured."

"If there are no jobs, can you make your own jobs?"

"You're dreaming, mistress. How can we make our own jobs?"

"What needs to be done most in this city?"

The looked at her, puzzled.

"We need to fix all the houses," a young woman at his back said.

"Precisely. So we fix up houses that are abandoned. We don't want another fire and we don't have much wood, so we build them from stone."

The man laughed. "Someone needs to pay for the stone."

"We make bricks from clay. There is a lot of clay around. There are brick pits. Any of you know how to make bricks?"

A few hands went up, hesitantly.

He still didn't seem to be convinced. "But what about food?"

"I know where to find food. It's not going to be wonderful, but you can survive through winter. There are many farms upriver that lie abandoned. The farmers were killed and the cows are walking free, the barns are full of hay and the orchards full of apples. None of it is good quality, but it will get you through winter. Instead of begging, you could go out there, work the farms and make the bricks. We will ship them into town."

"But winter is coming."

"Especially now that winter is coming. You don't want to rely on this man's handouts anymore. Because one day, he will ask you to do something for the food, and it's not going to be anything nice."

He gave her a dubious look. Oh, yes, she forgot that some of the townsfolk looked down on farmers. Loesie knew all about that.

The young woman's eyes were wide. "I understand what she wants. There's a lot of folk in the country who won't be needing their houses anymore. We fix up the houses and they're ours."

"They're farms, Dora."

"But they're safe and dry."

"That's exactly what I mean," Johanna said. "You don't need this foul man's handouts or his help. If you go upriver, you'll find two of our ships moored at a jetty. Tell the men who are with those ships what you're doing. They'll help you."

"Alexandre will come after us and kill us."

"If there are enough of you, let him try. I think he's got enough trouble keeping people in town in line. Also, most of his guards are Estlander mercenaries. They can be bought. Find out what their currency is."

There were some alarmed looks at this.

The man who had scored the potato bag had returned with wood and was now trying to make a fire. A few others helped him. A woman brought a pot and set about setting it up on piles of rubble and cooking. From the way others helped, she deduced that the people shared the spoils of Alexandre's donations and she didn't quite understand why the fight had been necessary.

"Who are you, lady?" the young woman Dora asked.

"I know who she is," Joseph said, but the others shushed him.

He whispered in Dora's ear. Her eyes widened, and she curtsied.

Joseph muttered, "Don't do that. Guards are watching." Then to Johanna, "You better move, mistress."

Johanna did. She was glad to see that when she walked away, a number of people picked up their blankets and left the queue.

"LOOK," ROALD SAID when he sat down at the dinner table a few days later. He produced a sheet of paper with a drawing of some magical creature on it. The thing looked like a snake, but it had wings. He had drawn exquisite scales and featherless, leathery wings. "This is a fire dragon. It is a magical creature of the east."

Father took the drawing from him, put in his eyeglass and studied it. "You say this creature was at the site of the Guentherite Abbot's summer residence?"

"I didn't actually see it, but they did."

Johanna said, "There was only one man who said he'd seen it, and there were no other witnesses. He could have seen anything." Seriously, did they have to talk about this now? Were there no more important things to discuss?

"He said a fire dragon," Roald said. "I was there, I heard it."

"Yes, but how would he know what a fire dragon looked like if he'd never seen one before?"

Roald frowned at her. "It's in the book I read."

"What if he hasn't read the book?"

He frowned in a how-can-he-not-have-read-the-book way.

Father said, "The fire dragons are said to have been brought by the eastern traders sometimes. I've never seen any, but I've met eastern traders. I bought the chair that you've been using in the kitchen off them. There are many rumours that they want to come here and conduct trade with us. They wouldn't attack us with fire dragons if they wanted to trade."

That was true; and for all the talk there had been about eastern traders, one had yet to turn up.

"Do they have books?" Roald asked.

"I suspect they do, but we probably won't be able to read them."

Johanna heaved a sigh. She didn't have the patience for this type of discussion right now, so she changed the subject. "Well, we're going into the palace tonight to retrieve your father's crown and staff."

Father gave her a sharp look. "Are you sure you're not going to run into any patrols?"

"No, but I'm the only one who knows where they are."

"It's dangerous, Johanna."

"I know, but without the crown we have no king."

She looked at Roald, but it was pointless getting angry at him. It was not as if he would be any use if he came anyway. He would be more likely to give them away. Let him play with his dragons.

He had the book open on the table next to him, running his finger along the line as he read. "It says that fire dragons are not always dangerous."

"If any eastern traders had come up the river, we would have seen them," she said, sounding more frustrated than she should. "Whatever happened at the Guentherite Abbot's summer residence, it was a not a fire dragon. It could have been something magical, but I think it's more likely that one of their mysterious machines caught fire. If the black rock burns so well, it might have made quite a show."

"But he said it was a fire dragon," Roald protested.

"He might have been wrong. He might have heard about fire dragons and might have thought that this was one."

Arguing about it was doubly pointless. Roald did not understand the concept of lies or untruths.

"Anyway, I have to go." Johanna rose from the table and gave

Father a kiss at the top of his forehead. "Don't look so worried. I'll be back."

Johanna went upstairs. Earlier in the week, she had found some of Father's old work clothes in the wardrobe in the hallway. The trousers were too big but she tied them with a rope. The jacket was also too big, and heavy, but it was warm. She wound a scarf around her neck and pulled one section over her nose and mouth and another across her forehead before putting on the cloak and pulling the hood up. The mirror showed her a figure of undetermined gender, with just the eyes showing in the shadow of the cloak.

Like this, she went downstairs where she found her boots. Father and Roald's voices drifted from the dining room. They were still talking about dragons.

Johanna went down to the basement and out through the back door. It was just as well that they had chosen the night of the new moon, because it was completely cloudless. The night was still and there would probably be frost tonight.

Johanna saw no guards, no soldiers and no sign of life except a cat that gave her a fright when it ran off from a dark spot close to her with a protesting *mrrreeeooow!*

The party of helpers waited at the boatshed in East Harbour where Johanna had first been to the service. There were nine of them, including Master Willems, who had insisted on coming. They all wore dark clothing and head coverings and in the darkness, they were all just shapes and Johanna couldn't begin to distinguish who was who. They had three storm lamps, but they met in darkness to save oil for when they were in the palace.

They decided to split up because that would draw less attention. Master Willems went with Johanna's group. Apparently, some other men had already taken the ladder to a nearby hiding place and needed to retrieve it. They also had two storm lights which they would light once they were inside the palace garden.

They left the warehouse, walking quietly through East Harbour so as not to draw the attention of the guard patrols with the bears. They saw a patrol once, but at a distance.

The palace lay on a little rise directly along the river. The gardens, including the Queen's rose garden, ran between the hillock and along the riverbank. It had its own jetty for small riverboats. A path led from the western pier of the main harbour along the bottom of the seawall. During storm tides, the water would be lapping at the stone, but normally there was a muddy beach where boys would cast out fishing lines and search for crabs and worms to use as bait. A few floating fishing sheds bobbed on their moorings. Nets hung on drying racks. The mud breathed a salty tang that came with the brackish water.

Johanna followed the men in her group along the soft and slippery ground until they came to the back of the wall that surrounded the palace garden. The rest of the group were already waiting there. They had retrieved the ladder.

A man placed it against the wall and climbed on top. He looked around and came back down again.

"The land on the other side is higher than on this side. There are some bushes, and I think we can just jump into them and won't need to use the ladder."

Johanna nodded. She already knew this. Kylian had done that on the night of the fires.

The first men climbed over.

When Johanna's turn came, they wanted to help her, but months of climbing up and down that ladder into the *Lady Sara*'s hold had made her an expert in climbing ladders. She was on the wall in no time, and lowered herself into the leafless branches of the hedge that did not look like a hedge anymore.

The rose garden was a riot of unkempt shrubs. The lawn had not been cut for months and the dead grass lay like a mat on the ground. The fountain was dry, the basin cracked, and the large statue of the Triune was gone. Deep gouges in the grass showed where it had been dragged away. Someone had vandalised the Queen's benches.

She remembered sitting here with Kylian while he remarked how ugly the statue was. Back then, she had thought he was saying these things just to get a reaction out of her, but it turned out that his plans were much more sinister than that.

The men lit the storm lanterns and ran in single file towards the palace, where the smashed windows of the garden room reflected the glow from the storm lamps like jagged shards in the night.

At the bottom of the garden steps, the grass had been dug up. There were two longitudinal mounds of dirt, and both grew a selection of weeds and daisies.

Someone had placed a stone tile on each mound and had written something on it.

Johanna stopped.

"Come on, keep going," one of the men whispered.

"Come over here with the light," she said.

He did.

The inscription on both stones was simple and crudely scratched by someone who clearly wasn't a stonemason. The closest one said, *Queen Cygna Gunhilde Savorsen Carmine* and the other one *King Nicholaos Carmine de Lacoeur van Leeuwen*.

Johanna knelt, and next to her, Master Willems did the same.

"By the love of the Triune, we pray for salvation," he said. "We pray for our king and queen and that they have been delivered from this cruel world and look upon us with smiles. We pray that the only rightful house will return to the throne and that our actions will help."

He rose, and Johanna did the same. He took her hand. They stood for a while, looking at the graves of their king and queen.

Johanna was glad that someone had been here to bury them. In her heart she knew: this would once again be a beautiful, peaceful garden. The statue of the Triune would be found and brought back. The fountain would be fixed. The graves would have proper headstones and flowers. There would be roses all around, and swans in the pond. Lots of swans.

"Come on," one of the men said. "We need to go. I don't want to be caught here."

After one last look, Johanna followed the others up the steps to the garden room.

CHAPTER 16

THE AIR IN the palace was cold and damp. The cloying scent of stale smoke crept through the layers of Johanna's shawl.

Thick layers of dust had accumulated on the floor in the garden room and spiders had covered walls, ceilings and furniture in their silky webs, as if the room had lain abandoned since that night. Glass from the broken windows littered the floor and crunched underfoot. Curtains were stained from being exposed to the weather and ripped to shreds from catching on the shards of glass. All the fine vases that had stood along both sides of the room had been smashed. Some of the doors into the hall had deep gouges, as if someone had taken to the wood with an axe. Johanna remembered hiding here while the people in the hall next door were ruthlessly murdered.

Shards of glass and pottery lay scattered across Celine's grave. One of the young men stopped to read the inscription in the marble slab.

"Across there," Johanna whispered, pointing at the dark entrance to the ballroom. Master Willems went first, carrying the light. But he stopped suddenly a few steps into the room and muttered, "By the Holy Ghost."

Johanna looked past him. While someone had buried the king and queen in the garden, many of the nobles in the ballroom had not been so lucky. In between the jumble of ruined tables, rotting tablecloths and shards of glass, she counted at least five skeletons, some still with scraps of silk clothing attached. Here, too, spiders had woven the dreadful scene into an ethereal tableau.

"By the Triune," one of the men said. "I didn't know there were that many spiders in the world."

Johanna drew the shawl up over her nose, even though the cold stifled whatever smell still lingered after all this time. She felt sick.

They walked across the ballroom in single file. Johanna followed Master Willems with the light, picking his way through the rubble. The thick layer of dust on the floor muffled their footsteps.

In the far corner, the roof to the main hall had caved in and starlight peeped through the gaps between the broken rafters.

They left the ballroom through the main doors into the foyer. The doors to the palace forecourt were shut, as Johanna had already seen from outside. The foyer to the main hall was the only place where there had been some attempt at cleaning up. All the rubble and mess had been swept into a heap. A wheelbarrow still stood here, half full, with a shovel on the ground next to it, as if the workmen had been called away and never returned.

This was where Johanna had stood looking out over the city, seeing the creatures made of fire. This was where panic had struck the attendants of the ball. This place was a tomb, a shrine to that terrible day.

"I don't like this place," one of the men said.

"Keep yer mouth shut and keep going," someone else said.

But Johanna agreed with the first man. There was something about this place that gave her the shivers. She kept looking over her shoulders, expecting . . . she didn't know what. Something magical. A bear, a fire demon, a ghost. So many people had died a violent death on the steps outside, in this room and the ballroom.

"This way." She had to clamp her jaws to stop her teeth chattering.

Master Willems led the party into the corridor to the right that went to the king and queen's private quarters. The storm light cast long shadows over the walls that moved and danced as they walked. This part of the palace was not as dusty and hadn't been exposed to the weather. They passed a few doors. Some of the rooms had been emptied, but all the pretty furniture still stood in the hallway, now covered in dusty spider webs, waiting for the people who were going to take the loot, but who had never returned. Or who had, judging by a pair of shoes with cloth-covered bones attached, never left.

The air here was dry, but laced with the foulness of death. Things skittered in the dark beyond the reach of the lantern's light.

Johanna stopped at the entrance to a larger room. "This is the room where I found them."

Master Willems went to the door and held the light inside.

The room seemed untouched except for the fact that the bodies were gone. The couch still stood where it had before, as did the table, both covered in dust and spider webs. In her mind, Johanna could still see the crown where it had rolled under the table. And the staff that had been caught under the king's body. She'd had to roll him on his back to retrieve it. She remembered the mess of the gaping wound in his stomach. The carpet was dusty and smudged. Were those dark stains dried blood?

She shivered.

"In here?" Master Willems asked.

"No. This is where they were killed. I hid the crown and staff a few doors down. There is a broom cupboard." She spoke softly, but her voice sounded loud in her ears.

"Let's go then. I really don't like it here."

A bit further down the hall, Johanna found the broom cupboard, untouched. She reached up the top shelf where she couldn't see and under a pile of cleaning cloths, her hands found both crown and staff, where she had put them.

As she lifted the crown off the shelf, its weight heavy in her hands, the enormous sense of importance washed over her. It was only a piece of metal, but it symbolised the hope of all Saar-landers. The staff was a piece of wood with a gold tip in the shape of a lion's head with jewels for eyes. It was beautifully made, but she knew for sure that the jewellery made by Lurezian master smiths these days was more intricate. Yet the wood showed her images of the great hall full of nobles in their finery, bowing as the king entered. She carried the pride of the Carmine House in her hands.

She turned to the others, holding out both precious items.

"Heaven be praised," Master Willems said.

A breeze wafted through the corridor, making the flame in the lamp flap. Johanna's skin pricked.

She peered into the darkness at the far end of the corridor. "Why is it so windy?"

"There are probably some doors open," one of the men said. He sounded as uneasy as Johanna felt.

The night had been cloudless and still, not the type of weather for a breeze.

Johanna had an awful feeling that they were about to find out why Alexandre had not done anything with the palace and why he didn't live here, why people had left a wheelbarrow and a shovel and had gotten no further than a cursory tidy-up of the hall and had never collected the precious furniture.

"Quick, let's get out of here," Master Willems said. He was looking over his shoulder, his eyes wide. What had he seen on that breeze?

One of the men took off his jacket and Johanna rolled the crown and staff inside. She pulled a folded cloth from the broom cupboard, which turned out to be an old sheet, tied it around the precious loot, and tied that around her waist.

They left quickly, the same way they had come. Through the corridor, the foyer, through the hall and into the ballroom. Master Willems walked at the front, but the flapping flame from the storm lamp barely produced enough light for Johanna to see. It was as if a darkness had descended on the air that took away any light and a cold had crept into the building that settled in her bones.

Master Willems stopped abruptly at the door into the garden room.

"Someone out there," he whispered.

Johanna peered into the room, but saw nothing except broken vases and furniture covered in spider webs.

There was a small sound, a snort or grumble, made by a human or large animal.

Master Willems slid the covers over the light's windows, plunging the room into total darkness.

Johanna stood still for a while, staring into the night, waiting for her eyes to see where a human couldn't possibly see, listening, holding her breath and trying to hear over the thudding of her heart. The sound came again from somewhere in the darkness: the growl of some sort of animal, like a dog, or a bear.

"What's that?" someone whispered.

"It may be a good idea to split up," Master Willems said, not answering the question.

"What did you see in that breeze?" Johanna asked him.

"What do you mean?"

Johanna would have hit him if only she could see where he was. This ridiculous Church decree that there was no magic would have to change. It was stupid beyond belief.

He continued, "Look, why don't you go straight for home with the young boys. They'll help you over the wall and will take you to safety."

"What about you?"

"We'll go . . . the other way and keep them busy. Whatever 'they' are."

"No. There is a magical thing in the palace somewhere. We need to stay together to have any hope of defeating it."

"Go, Mistress Johanna. Please."

"Do you know what it is?"

"Go!"

At that moment a loud crack echoed through the room. The paving in the garden room split open and shafts of light blazed from under the ground. Tiles and bits of stone flew everywhere. One or two of the men used some words that they would normally never dream of using in front of a woman.

Master Willems screamed, "Go, go!"

Johanna got caught up between the men in their scramble to the wall of the room, ironically to the very place where Johanna had stood while the nobles in the ballroom were being slaughtered.

Only Master Willems remained in his position, now backlit by the eerie glow that spilled from the hole in the ground. "Go home, Mistress Johanna! Go home now!"

Standing there, in between the shivering men with chattering teeth and with her back pressed against the wall, Johanna realised several things. It was Celine's grave that had burst open, and judging by his behaviour, Master Willems knew a lot more about magic and this phenomenon than he was prepared to talk about.

Something rose out of the hole in the ground: a human shape made of glowing mist.

"It's the ghost!" a man's voice squeaked behind her.

Master Willems stood with his arms spread, chanting in a booming voice. "Begone with you, spawn of the Lord of Fire. Begone, begone, return to the depths of evil. Let the Holy Spirit smite you."

Pale and ethereal, the ghost radiated soft light. Her hair flowed over her shoulders like a waterfall. The ruffles on her dress oozed glowing mist. The pale skin on her arms glowed almost too brightly to look at. She turned her head so that Johanna could see her face.

"It's Princess Celine," a man gasped behind Johanna.

Indeed, the woman looked like she had walked off the painting of the princess that used to hang in the church, complete with the yellow dress.

Master Willems continued chanting. "The holy Triune will banish you from all the known lands . . ."

One of the young men said, "They said she haunted the palace. Why didn't I believe them?"

"Because we don't believe in ghosts?" squeaked another.

"That looks pretty real to me."

The ghosts Johanna had seen on her travels through the forest did not interact with living people. The merely repeated scenes from their lives like echoes of memories, and would never deviate from those actions. The only apparitions that interacted with the living were the partially-resurrected beings that were the result of Kylian's botched attempts at necromancy.

Her suspicions had been right: King Nicholaos had paid Kylian to perform a necromancy on his daughter because he judged his son inadequate for the throne. Kylian, despite his boasting otherwise, could not perform a full necromancy and, having seen Kylian's half-hearted results, the king might have demanded that money or favours paid for bringing Celine back to life be returned. So Kylian and his father had sent a magician to keep this annoying little king silent.

Master Willems had appeared to have temporarily run out of words. He stood, panting, facing the apparition.

"Master Willems, be careful. That's no ordinary ghost."

"Is there such thing as an ordinary ghost?" a frightened voice said behind her.

The apparition turned to Johanna.

She spoke in a voice colder than the night. "You are a usurper. You cannot leave this place with the objects that are the symbol of my father's reign."

Master Willems yelled, "Begone, spawn of evil! You are not our beloved princess. You have no right to speak to our lady Consort like this."

The apparition took no notice of Master Willems' chanting, but continued to look at Johanna. "You're not fleeing, worm?"

"I'm not defeated that easily. The Carmine House will survive through King Roald and his heir."

"You lie!" An icy wind whirled through the room, lifting up dust and blowing it into Johanna's face.

"Begone—" Master Willems staggered back, yelling. "No, no, no!" He clamped both his hands over his face. The storm lamp crashed on the floor. Precious oil ran out of the reservoir.

"No, no, no, no!"

The cold breeze whirled up dust around him, tormenting him with images. The ghost spun threads around him, encasing him in a glowing cocoon. She was going to draw him into the grave.

Johanna groped along the ground at her feet and the wall at her back for something to use as a weapon. She found nothing except shards of pottery.

Wait—the King's staff. She dug in the sheet that she had knotted around her waist. The handle of the staff was made of wood. She pulled it out of the folds of fabric and held it before her. The wooden handle showed Johanna images of the great hall full of people cheering for the king. People who supported the royal family, nobles and commoners alike. People who were the *hope* of the kingdom.

She sprang forward, brandishing the staff. "Leave him alone. He's done nothing to hurt you."

The apparition let out a low hiss. "He's but a gibbering priest, denying his gifts."

"He's a good man and he's got nothing to do with this fight."

The ghost laughed, a horrible, wheezy sound that made Johanna's hair stand on end.

"He's got *everything* to do with the fight. It's his stupid church that my father ruined himself for that is the very cause of this fight."

Did the apparition fear the wood? Johanna took a step closer to the grave, holding out the staff's glittering gold tip.

The apparition gave another hiss, but didn't come closer.

She reached Master Willems who sat crouched on the ground, surrounded by the ghostly glow. The cocoon shook with his shivering. Johanna poked the glowing substance with the golden end of the staff. A spark zapped across the room. Then she remembered how Loesie had made a similar apparition disappear with nothing more than a willow sapling. She turned the staff around and poked the material with the wood. The cocoon parted briefly but closed back up.

The ghostly Celine reached out gnarled hands to the staff. "Give that. It's mine. It's mine."

The voice rasped and hissed, even less human than before.

Johanna plunged the handle of staff into the glowing cocoon. Glowing mist leaked from the ghost and wrapped around her hands. It was cold as the coldest of winter frost. It bit into her hands and made them numb. She yanked the staff free, shattering the cocoon into little pieces.

The ghost reached out. "Give it, give it. It's mine."

"Come and get it." She pushed Master Willems with her foot, whispering, "Come on, get up."

If only she could the apparition to touch the staff.

Master Willems groaned.

"Get up, quickly." If her previous experience was anything to go by, the apparition would change into a giant spider very soon. That also explained the abundance of spider webs in this room.

"You'll regret taunting me." Already, her voice grew raspier.

"We'll see. Come and get it."

"What are you doing?" One of the men squealed. "It will come for us now."

Johanna walked backwards, carefully so as not to trip over debris on the floor.

The ghost floated out of the grave, ignoring Master Willems who still sat on his knees, whimpering, past the shards of one of the Queen's large vases.

Behind her, the men scrambled out of the door and ran into the ballroom.

But then a different, harsh male voice echoed through that room. It sounded like Alexandre's guards had come in. There were sounds of a scuffle behind her and then a man said something in a foreign language. Burovian, Johanna thought.

The ghost hissed. It spewed a glowing thread of silk across the room.

The man yelled. Johanna couldn't see if he had been hit.

More people ran in. There was yelling and shouting. The ghost produced a sibilant hiss that made the hair on Johanna's neck stand up. The shape of Celine disintegrated into strands of mist that glowed and separated and re-formed. They grew into long limbs with long bristles. The arms and legs melted into a round body. The spider spewed glowing silk at the men like a fisherman casts a net.

Johanna lifted the staff holding it by the golden head, and waved it through the room. Threads of silk collected on the wood. They melted into dripping strands of light.

A couple of men had been caught in the strands and lay caught in cocoons on the ground. Johanna had no idea if these men were hers or Alexandre's. She waved the staff in great arcs.

Magic light flew in globs around the room. It leaked down her hands and the front of her dress.

More men came into the room, and the spider was so occupied with these new people that Johanna got close. She lifted the staff and drove the wooden handle through the spider's head. It met little resistance, but the glowing mist attached to the wood. For a moment, the spider froze. Then she yanked the staff free.

The spider shattered into hundreds of little glowing pieces. They flew through the air and bounced off the ceiling and tumbled on the ground, where they slowly dimmed.

The room returned to darkness. Johanna stood there still holding the staff, panting.

Then there came the sound of footsteps of hard boots on the stone floor. A small flame appeared in the shape of a fish with a long flowing tail and delicate scales, swimming in the air. Johanna knew only one person who could do this.

Alexandre.

He had seen all the magic that she had just performed.

CHAPTER 17

JOHANNA STUMBLED away from the grave and pressed herself against the wall. It was so dark in the room that she could only see that little fish made of flames that gambolled through the air. It was a thing of mesmerising beauty, if dangerous.

She became aware of a glow of light from below: the front of her dress glowed with magic. She drew her cape over the spot to conceal it, but there were glowing spots on her hands, too, and goodness knew where else.

She had no idea where the others were. Some men had escaped into the ballroom, she hoped. Master Willems might have been smart enough to crawl to the side of the room. She clutched the wooden handle of the king's staff, doing her best to keep her breathing as quiet as possible.

The sound of footsteps from Alexandre's high-heeled boots echoed in the empty room. Johanna couldn't see him, but she felt his presence like a burning beacon. Why had the baroness ever said that Alexandre was a weak magician? Why had she ever thought that she could defeat him with a band of followers whose only weapons were their prayer books? Why did no magician want to help her? Master Willems, Loesie, Magda, all of them had refused.

She waited.

The little fire fish frolicked through the air, lighting up different parts of the room. The orange glow lit the rubble-strewn ground, where dust and broken glass revealed no signs of magic. Then it came to the middle of the room where the slab of stone that covered Celine's grave had split open. Jagged shards of stone pointed up at the ceiling. Sprays of dry earth had been cast over the floor. The grave itself was a jagged hole.

Alexandre stopped at the edge of the grave. The little fish-light frolicked around him. He wore well-polished high-heeled boots with shiny buckles, velvet trousers and a knee-length coat. A sand-coloured ponytail hung over his back.

"Hmmm," he said, and then he said something in a foreign language. His voice was cultured and sounded sharp and arrogant.

A gruff voice responded at the door to the ballroom.

Johanna looked for ways to escape. She had to get out of here before they discovered her. She was probably leaking magic and no matter how well she hid, they would discover her before they discovered the others.

But getting out required first getting past the grave. The room was narrow, with glass doors all along the left-hand side. Johanna stood against the right-hand wall, which had doors into the ballroom. She could try to sneak along the wall to the very end, where the short wall of the room consisted of glass doors. Or she could try to sneak back through the ballroom, but she had no light and, short of the palace foyer—where the doors were locked—and the forecourt—where the gates were locked as well—she knew no way of getting out of the palace.

So she took a step forward, feeling her way along the wall. Another step, and she felt the warm presence of one of the boys. She poked him and he also moved along the wall.

With every step Johanna took, she watched Alexandre. There was some sort of commotion at the far end of the room. Men spoke in foreign voices. Someone came in carrying a bright torch. By its light, Johanna could make out the silhouettes of three men in hairy cloaks. Also clearly visible were a group of people in dark clothing against the wall. Those were some of the men in her group.

Immediately, Alexandre's guards sprang into action with a lot of yelling and shouting.

Johanna pushed the man in front of her. *Hurry up, hurry up.* They made their way along the wall as fast as they dared, while one of the young men at the back screamed obscenities at Alexandre.

Johanna cringed, but a good effect of his action was that Alexandre and his fish left the area near the grave and went back to the door.

"Run," Johanna whispered to the man in front of her. She would not let the young man who was brave enough to call Alexandre names draw the tyrant's anger in vain.

They ran. Well, it wasn't a proper run, but more a fast shuffle along the wall, avoiding the pillars that supported the roof and unspecified debris that had lain there since the night that the city burned. Johanna didn't want to think about what all the things were that she kicked, trod on and crunched under her feet.

The shouting behind her intensified.

They reached the far end of the room where the glass wall came around to meet the inner wall. The first door was miraculously still intact. It also wouldn't open.

"Smash the glass," Johanna said.

"They'll hear us."

Johanna looked over her shoulder, where a couple of men with torches were coming in their direction. "That doesn't matter. Quick."

The young man kicked. Glass shattered. His mate helped him kick the glass shards out of the frame.

"Come, mistress, you first." He helped Johanna through the hole and then climbed through himself. His mate followed. His clothes caught and fabric ripped. The glow from the torches was getting stronger. By its light, she recognised the faces of the two young men with her. They were Bart and Simon, sons of the merchant Jan Hendricksen, who had not survived the fires.

"This way," Johanna said, starting down the stairs into the garden. She had inserted the staff back into the sheet around her waist.

"We're not waiting for the others?" Simon said.

"We need to get the mistress out," his brother said.

"I don't like leaving them. I didn't even see where they went."

"Outside, I hope. Come on, the Shepherd said that the most important thing is that the mistress is safe."

Johanna followed the brothers down the stairs into the darkness of the garden, past the graves of the King and Queen.

She understood why Master Willems would have instructed them in this way, but didn't like to be considered worth more than the other people. *She* didn't like the idea of running away, especially when Master Willems was still inside.

They ran in single file across the dirt-covered pavement. Sounds of a struggle drifted on the wind.

Johanna looked over her shoulder, but it was far too dark to make out anything except the glow of three lanterns bobbing as the men carrying them ran through the garden.

Johanna and the brothers reached the circular area with the benches around the empty fountain with the empty pedestal in the middle. They ran along the basin's edge, through the bushes to the garden wall. Bart climbed into the hedge and to the top of the wall. He cursed.

"What?" Simon said.

"Ladder is gone."

Simon cursed as well and then apologised. "Sorry, lady."

"I'll jump," Bart said. "It's not far."

He disappeared. Simon clambered onto the wall using the bushed, and then he helped Johanna up. It was very dark and she couldn't see where she was putting her hands and feet. Branches scratched her. The stone of the wall was cold and slippery and her fingers were fast losing sensation.

But finally Johanna sat atop the wall, balancing with one leg on either side. It was awfully dark down there on the other side of the wall.

"Jump, mistress," Bart said.

Simon jumped off and vanished into the darkness. "Come on, mistress, we'll catch you."

The lights in the garden had come much closer. Men yelled out in foreign voices and spread out to search for the escapees.

Alexandre himself was coming into the garden with a creature of fire leaping next to him, a long-bodied creature, like a stoat or an otter.

Johanna jumped into the dark void.

Hands tried to catch her, but the young men couldn't support her weight and she fell hard and awkwardly on her side. The tide had come up and the beach was covered in briny water which seeped into her dress.

"Are you all right, mistress?"

Johanna scrambled to her feet. Icy cold fabric stuck to her legs. "I think so."

She took a step. Ow, her ankle. She fell against Simon.

"You're sure?" Simon asked, holding her arm.

"Just don't go too fast."

As fast as they could, they walked across the muddy beach along the water. By the light from the lighthouse Johanna saw the ladder bobbing on the waves. There was now a lot of noise on the other side of the palace wall. A man shouted in a foreign language.

Johanna and the brothers reached the pier and clambered onto the quay.

They ran to the boatshed in East Harbour where they'd started and where a number of people were waiting.

Their return was greeted with exclamations of, "Thank the Triune you are back, mistress."

Johanna made her way to the back wall where the table that Master Willems used as altar still stood. She was shivering so much that she felt like her knees would give out any moment.

Her fingers were so cold that she couldn't undo the knotted sheet around her waist.

"Let me help." Greetje came to her.

Tears pricked behind Johanna's eyes. Would she need to tell Greetje that her husband was left behind in the palace?

The sheet came loose. Johanna put it on the table and unwrapped her parcel. People gasped when she revealed the crown and the staff.

"Hail the king!" a man shouted.

A path opened up between the people. Roald crossed the room. He was looking not at the items on the table but at her.

"Why are you wet?"

"I went to retrieve the crown and staff of the Carmine House so that you can be a proper king."

He still didn't take his eyes off her. "Why is your dress glowing?"

She looked down and, yes, her dress was still glowing.

"I'll explain later." What was there to explain except that his sister had turned into a malevolent ghost, and that his father had never trusted him? She picked up the crown. "This is yours."

Now he finally looked at it, reached out and ran his finger along the top of the crown.

She lifted it and set it, gently, on top of his head.

A number of people shouted, "Hail the king!"

Roald gave her a confused look. He reached up as if to check that the crown was indeed on his head, which it was. "Does that mean that this land is mine?"

"It does."

He took the crown off his head and handed it to her. "I don't want to be king. I don't know how. My father said I was stupid so I couldn't be king."

"And you believed him?"

He stared at her. "He's the king. He knows everything."

"Roald, you are the least stupid person in this entire kingdom."

He blinked. "How can my father be wro—"

"Your father was the dumb one." Squandering the family fortune on the church, fighting with the nobles who were responsible for the businesses in Saardam, going crazy after the death of his daughter, engaging a *necromancer*. All because he was unwilling to accept his son.

"Please put it back on. Your father is dead and he can't tell you what to do anymore. You are the king and I will help you."

He put the crown back, not entirely straight, and looked at her with his slightly confused expression. His eyes were clear and blue. He had trimmed his beard and his hair was brushed and clean.

Once she would have thought that outliving him was something to hope for. Now, she realised that she utterly loved him and the thought of losing him brought tears to her eyes.

She closed him in her arms where he stood, frozen, not sure what to do.

He protested. "My mother says—"

She put her finger to his lips. "Your mother is dead, too." And Johanna didn't like the callousness she had seen in Queen Cygna's actions. "It's about us now." And about the little baby growing inside her.

She held him close. As a rare sign of affection, he also put his arms around her.

People cheered. "Long live the King and Queen!"

It would have been a cheerful occasion if it weren't for the fact that Master Willems and the other men had not yet come back.

CHAPTER 18

THEY WAITED for a while, but Johanna was shivering so much in her wet dress that several people told her to go home.

"Go home. We don't want you to get sick, mistress."

"But they went out because of me."

"Which will have been useless if you die of cold. Please go home. We will wait." Greetje was trying to stay positive, but her face was pale and her eyes red. Bart and Simon had told her what they had seen and she knew what Alexandre could do.

Johanna hugged her. "I'm so sorry. I want to wait with you, but I'm so cold."

"Just go," Greetje said.

Johanna felt awful. This was all her fault. It had been her idea to get the crown and staff. Were a few trinkets worth this much?

She could only assure Greetje that Master Willems had not been carrying any religious items that would mark him a Shepherd.

"Oh, but he knows," Greetje said. "I've no doubt of that."

Her attitude made it all worse. It was likely that her husband was dead and she knew it.

Johanna went home with Roald and two other young men, carrying the crown and staff in the sheet. It was very late now, and the houses were dark and the streets deserted.

There was a light on in Father's study. That was odd, because Father normally went to bed early and would not let the light burn if he wasn't in the room. He hated being wasteful. They quickly walked to the back of the house, where the light in the kitchen was also still on.

Nellie and Koby sat at the kitchen table. When Johanna came in, both jumped from their seats.

Nellie cried, "Oh, mistress, there you are. I'm so glad that you're back. I thought—"

"What has happened?" Nellie's eyes were red from crying.

Tears welled in Nellie's eyes. "Your father."

Johanna's heart jumped. "What happened? Is he sick?" She could see him broken and battered after falling down the stairs or in bed and too ill to get up after taking some kind of sickness.

Nellie shook her head. "It's much worse than that. They came to the door and spoke with him and they took him away."

"Who?"

"I don't know! I didn't see it. I heard them, and I should have gone upstairs and stopped them."

"It's all right," Koby said. "They were strong men. I saw them and there was nothing you could have done anyway."

"Who were they?"

"Thugs. I didn't know the men in question, but they probably worked for the LaFontaine family."

Johanna's heart was thudding. "Where did they take him?"

"I don't know!" Nellie sobbed. "I don't know. I'm sorry, mistress. I don't know."

"It's not your fault, Nellie." Johanna hugged Nellie, tears in her eyes. She was so tired and so cold, and everything was falling in pieces around her. How long would it be before Alexandre found her? And then a thought: he probably knew she was back and would use Father to lure her out. By refusing to hand over the business, he had cut off the last way in which he could have been useful to them.

Roald came in from the door into the hallway. He said in a grave and serious voice, "We will free him. No one makes my women cry."

Johanna put an arm around him and he gave her a stern look.

Angry almost. It was disconcerting, coming from him. He'd never shown any of this type of concern for other people before. "I will go up to this man and I will tell this man that I am the rightful king and that he should leave."

Koby said, "But Your Majesty, I wouldn't—"

"Thank you, Roald," Johanna said.

If only it were so simple.

But something about the sincerity with which he had said it disturbed her. They had the crown and staff. They had the Carmine cloak, even if it was more brown than carmine.

They went upstairs where Johanna put on warm nightclothes and Nellie took her wet dress. "Look at the state of it. It's got burn holes and it has ripped, too. I don't know if I can fix it, Mistress Johanna."

"Don't worry about it, Nellie."

She had enough dresses to wear.

As she lay in bed, shivering under many layers of blankets, Johanna cried for Father and Master Willems and the other men. Likely, Alexandre had known who she was the moment they had come into town.

MORNING DAWNED BRIGHT AND SUNNY. The temperature had dipped below freezing overnight, and rime edged the dead leaves and bare branches of the trees in the garden.

She got out of bed before Roald did and went downstairs to the kitchen where it was warm.

Greetje sat at the kitchen table, crying into her hands.

Johanna sat opposite her, accepting tea and sweet porridge from Koby and eating silently. She felt terrible. She wanted to say that everything would be all right, that getting Master Willems and Father free, if they were still alive, was as easy as sending a letter of complaint to Alexandre.

"What is . . . likely to happen now?" she asked Koby.

Koby gave her an uneasy look. "We can only guess. There was a time that the tyrant caught a group of people having a Church service. He locked them up in the dungeons under the mayor's house, and the next day, the town crier proclaimed at the markets that the prisoners would be burnt at a public execution. We went and watched, because we didn't believe that he would do it, but he did. A lot of fighting broke out, but the tyrant was prepared for this and a lot of our remaining good young men were killed. We don't know that this is going to happen again, but . . ."

Johanna felt sick. "We have to stop it."

"That's right. It's barbaric," sounded a clear voice from the door. Roald stood there fully dressed in his outdoor clothes. "They are *my* men and I will tell that man that he cannot keep doing this to my men. I'm going to tell him that right now." He turned around.

"Roald."

He turned back to the kitchen and frowned at her.

"Have some breakfast first."

He didn't move.

"You can't do anything if you're hungry." And when he still didn't move, she pulled him into the kitchen. "Sit down." She pushed him into a chair.

Koby put a bowl of porridge in front of him. "Eat that, Your Majesty. It has lots of honey."

He nodded. "I want to help."

"Eat," Johanna said. She pushed the spoon into his hand. He was really terribly determined, and that was another thing about Roald. When he had something in his mind, he was not so easily deterred.

He started eating.

"So what are we going to do?" Greetje asked.

Johanna wished she knew. She wished she had a magician willing to help her, although there probably wasn't one who could defeat Alexandre. "I guess we'll go to the markets to hear the proclamation."

Greetje nodded, tears leaking out of her eyes.

Johanna put an arm around her shoulders. "Whatever happens, we'll look after you and the little one."

"Thank you." Greetje took a shuddering breath and wiped tears from her cheeks. "Thank you," she said again. "We'll be strong. Because nothing will ever be worth the sacrifice if we don't stand up and we don't win."

Johanna managed to convince Roald to stay at home. They were, she told him, just going to have a look to see what needed to be done. Koby said that she would light the fire in the library, but Roald showed no interest in the library today. Once he had something in his head, it was hard to get him to do something else, especially something that required him to think.

"You can help Koby with the bread," Johanna said.

And that distracted him enough to stop demanding to come. They simply couldn't risk that anyone recognised him. Men didn't usually go shopping with the women.

Johanna, Nellie and Greetje dressed in their winter clothes. Jackets, thick cloaks, hats, scarves and mittens.

They walked through the streets, pulling up their scarves against the biting wind.

There were a lot of guards at the markets. The usual line of people stood outside Alexandre's house, but there were more guards than usual, including a number of the ones who everyone called the elite guards, with bears. They were Estlander men and they reminded Johanna of Sylvan. The fact that most of them walked with bears meant that they had some magic capability themselves.

Johanna had wanted to speak to Leo Mustermans. She needed his help but didn't want to ask for it, because it would be dangerous. But there were so many guards that she didn't dare talk to him. He smiled at her when she walked past.

Johanna was between the stalls when people in the square started cheering. There was also the sound of a ringing bell. She quickly ran to a place where she could see the mayor's house.

A man had come to the top of the stairs. It was the town crier, Master Polman, who had fulfilled that role for many years. He was a thin little man with a large moustache which he twirled, as he usually did when waiting for attention.

"Listen up," the town crier said. His voice was unusually loud for a man of his size. Johanna had always thought him an arrogant little man, and that fitted his position, but the fact that he continued to work for the occupiers confirmed that his arrogance was more than a professional requirement. What had Alexandre promised him in return for his support? How easily could these ambitious men be bought? How little respect had they left after they had switched sides?

He unrolled a sheet of paper and held it up in front of him.

More and more people came from between the stalls to listen.

"Listen up, listen up!" He squinted at the paper as if unsure of what was written. "You will have heard that overnight, a group of rabble-rousers broke into the palace. They disturbed the ghosts of the people who died there. Those ghosts are now moving into the city to disturb our good citizens."

What a liar. But many people in the crowd gasped.

"Men of the guard risked their lives defending the city's property. One of the thieves was an evil magician. But do not fear. The unrest seekers have been detained. Tomorrow at noon, there will be a public punishing."

He rang the bell again and turned back into the house.

No. No, Father, Master Willems, no, no. Johanna's vision blurred. But her tears were not of sorrow. They were tears of anger. Her cheeks were burning with it. She accepted that she might get into trouble. Master Willems, too, but *Father?*

All around her, a great tumult broke out. People shouted their anger and the sound of so many voices made Johanna want to clamp her hands over her ears. But she didn't. She said to the man next to her, "If anyone wants to leave town, I have a horse for sale."

There were guards everywhere.

He frowned and then his eyes widened. "Where might this horse be?"

"It's in the warehouse next to the sea cow barn." She chose it because it was big, empty and dry. The man went around his mates and colleagues to tell them about the horse.

Johanna caught a lot of sideways glances in her direction. One or two people muttered, "Where did she get a horse?"

She just hoped that none of the guards noticed.

Johanna, Nellie and Greetje left the marketplace. Greetje was quiet, her face drawn. Nellie looked puzzled. "But mistress

Johanna, I don't understand. Leo Mustermans said he'd take the horse into East Harbour."

"Shhh. It's not about the horse. It's a secret meeting."

Nellie's mouth formed a soundless "Oh". Poor Nellie. She was always so serious and never understood hidden meanings.

The three of them arrived at the warehouse not much later. A couple of people were already waiting, amongst them Master Deim and Johan and Martine Delacoeur.

Master Deim hugged Johanna. "These are grim tidings. How are you keeping up? I understand that your father is in that group as well?"

Johanna nodded. Tears were perilously close to the surface. Father would have spent the night in a cold cell. He was old and quite frail. Maybe they hit or kicked him. And for what? Not wanting to marry Lisbeth LaFontaine?

Martine Delacoeur hugged her as well. Johanna had not expected her to be here or even to support her.

"We want Roald on the throne and we want you as a consort Queen," Martine said. "There are more of us who feel this way. King Nicholaos did some strange things that a lot of us didn't like and couldn't work with, but you are different. Roald is different. Does he even go to that church?"

That was an interesting question. Nominally, Roald went to church, but if he considered any book holy, the scriptures of the Triune were definitely not it. For now, they were united against magic and the occupation, but there was a fight against the Church of the Triune getting too much influence still to be fought.

"How are you and your husband keeping up?" Johanna asked Martine.

"Compared with you, I shouldn't complain, but Johan and my sister's husband don't get on very well. Still, we have our own room, even if it's a small one, and it's dry."

"If cold," Johan muttered, his hands in his pockets. "At times, I wonder if it's colder inside than out, in more than one way."

Martine sighed. "Yes, it's not doing the relationship between me and my sister any good."

While other people came into the warehouse asking about

"the horse", Johanna slipped into the nearby sea cow barn, where it was dark and damp, but smelled of cooking. Loesie sat huddled by a small fire. She had caught a fish which she was roasting over the flames.

"I'm not coming," she said before Johanna could ask anything.

Johanna crouched. "How did you know it was me?"

"The sound of your footsteps. The feel of your magic. It has grown stronger."

That statement made Johanna uneasy. She had felt it, too. Stronger magic meant that Alexandre could feel her, too. Stronger magic meant that he might want to confront her, and there was no way she could win such a fight.

She sought excuses. "That's because I banished the ghost like you did on the bank of the river, with a willow stick. It exploded all over me." But she knew the real reason: because the child she carried was not Roald's.

"I see that magic, but I also see other changes that are deeper. You should stay away from me. You don't want my bad magic to be entangled with yours."

"Loesie, I'm imploring you to help us." If only she knew. "There will be a public execution tomorrow. Master Willems is one of the people. My father is another."

"Cowpats. Your father is an old man. What do they want with him?"

"The company. The richest inland trader in Saardam."

She snorted. "I'll never understand people with money."

"I'm not asking you to understand anything. Just help us, Loesie. Please." Tears were very close to the surface. This was all so horrible.

Loesie said nothing.

Johanna couldn't repress a wave of anger. "I thought you were my friend."

"I can't join you because you're my friend," Loesie said. "I thought I explained why."

"You did, and I understand, but we're desperate, simple as that. We *need* you." Her voice caught.

Loesie continued to stare into the fire.

The murmur of many voices reached into the barn from the hall next door. Johanna really should be going.

"Please, Loesie. I'm not asking much and I've done my best to help you despite danger to my life. If you want to repay me, come to the market place tomorrow noon."

Loesie continued her silence, so Johanna rose, but when she was at the door to the barn, Loesie said, "Wood is stronger than fire."

"No it's not. Haven't you seen the results of the fires?"

Loesie gave her an intense look. Her eyes had misted over again. "Without wood, there cannot be a fire. Remember that."

Johanna walked the short distance to the warehouse without seeing much. She didn't know what to do. There were no other magicians she could ask, nothing else she could think of doing to counter Alexandre's fire magic. Father would be burned. Master Willems would be burned.

In the large warehouse a lot more people had turned up while Johanna had been away. Not only were Church people there, but also a group of market stallholders under the leadership of Leo Mustermans. Those groups were standing in their own parts of the hall eying each other. When she came in, they formed a path to let her through. Greetje came with her, as well as Master Deim.

After the latter had called for silence, Johanna said, "I wish I had answers, but I don't. I wish I had a power magician who had a chance of defeating Alexandre, but I don't. I only have myself and the rightful king, and the hope that we will be able to emerge from this dark time. But we will not be able to stop the deaths of our loved ones without your help, and even then it may not be possible." Her voice caught. "I'm so sorry. I wish I had better news for you, but I don't." They couldn't have stayed in Florisheim, but coming back here had been a bad decision.

"I, for one, am not going stay silent if he goes ahead with the executions," a man said.

"No, me neither." This was Leo Mustermans.

Johanna said, "Then you'll all be burned. He'll burn your houses and your families."

"For you and the king, lady, it will be worth dying, because frankly we don't have much of a life now."

Johanna had no idea who this man was, but several others agreed with him.

"We'll be there tomorrow. We'll pack the market square. We'll bring anything that can be used as a weapon. We'll fight."

A lot of men went *yeah, yeah*, and clapped each other on the shoulders.

It was terrible. It was lunacy. Johanna met Martine Delacoeur's eyes with a look of despair. Martine would understand the futility of their promises, but even she looked worn out and ready to fight one last desperate battle.

Johanna went home, feeling tired and sick. Tomorrow was going to be a bloodbath.

CHAPTER 19

JOHANNA WENT HOME feeling drained and dejected. Master Deim and Greetje came with her. None of them said anything on the way back. There was no need because they all knew the situation was hopeless.

Yet it was too late to flee Saardam again. Alexandre knew of the survival of one member of the royal family and would hunt them down wherever they went. All the people who supported the royal family were here. But they could do nothing to oust the sorcerer.

It had started snowing, small powdery flakes drifting from the sky.

At home, they found a visitor in the kitchen: Julianna Nieland, seated at the table with her hands wrapped around a steaming mug of tea.

"When did you come here?" Johanna asked.

"Ko came into town and heard about the prisoners and executions. I went to plead with my brother to stop supporting this man and to ask him to reconsider, but he told me that we're all dumb for not seeing the greatness of magic; and that we can fight, but we'll all end up trampled in the mud."

"He said that, really?"

Julianna nodded. Her eyes glittered. "I don't know what's wrong with him."

"Has he forgotten how he came to his fortune, though hard work by his father? Does he care about no one?"

"He wouldn't care about a priest or your father. He's wanted the Brouwer Company for a long time."

That was true, but Johanna had thought, mistakenly, that it was a wish he'd use polite means to get.

"I hate to think that I'd wanted him to marry you so that I'd have a sister."

"You did?"

Julianna nodded.

Now Johanna felt embarrassed. She'd considered Julianna a rival, with her fancy clothes, frilly dresses and sleek combed hair. She'd thought Julianna was arrogant and thought less of her, but it had been the other way around. She hugged Julianna. There was a lot of hugging going on when there was no hope.

And then, looking over Julianna's shoulder, she met Roald's eyes. He'd been sitting by the fire in his usual spot, and she couldn't bear trying to explain the situation of hopelessness to him. They had to fight. She had no idea how, and it would probably end in her death, but she had to try.

She took a deep breath and asked Koby, "So what is likely to happen tomorrow?"

Koby described as well as she could what had happened the last time. There would be a platform built at the markets overnight, and the prisoners would be tied to posts. There would be piles of wood at their feet.

Of course this vile man used burnings as his method of execution. He was a fire wizard. He came from a place where witches were regularly burned in the past. She guessed that was why magicians had forced their way into the Belaman Church: to force the people to accept magic and to stop the witch burnings.

Johan and Martine Delacoeur came to the door, stamping snow off their shoes.

Johanna was surprised to see them, and offered them a spot at the table and tea.

Clamping his hands around the steaming mug, Johan said, "There is going to be a bloodbath no matter what. Alexandre will have gotten some stories out of those men, such as where his enemies are. They will be chasing down the Church and other dissenters. They will be chasing down those people who left but came back, like us. There is no option but to fight, and we'll do it with the weapons we have. That's why I'm here."

He drew a slate from his pocket and wrote something on it. Roald looked on with wide eyes. Johan put the slate down. At the top, he had written *Advantage*.

The pencil hovered over the slate. "Well, what do we have to our advantage?"

Greetje and Julianna gave him strange looks, but Johanna understood what he wanted: an ex-army general would objectively analyse the situation for the best action to take.

She said, "To be honest, we don't have much at all. He's got magic, he's got people with bears . . ."

Johan drew a line across the slate and wrote *Disadvantage* and underneath that, he wrote *magic* and *bears*.

That kind of summed it up, really. There was no hope. Anyone who could help had refused to do so.

The space under *Advantage* remained empty.

Johan tapped the pencil on the edge of the slate. "Failing military strength, we need numbers."

"We have the support of most people, even if many will be too frightened to openly support us, and I can't blame them."

"Then we need to give them a reason to do so."

"Any suggestions on how to do that?" She couldn't help sounding sarcastic. She had tried doing that the last few days, all to no avail. They were out of ideas, and most importantly, out of time.

He pursed his mouth. "You have the king's regalia?"

"We do."

"Do you have the Carmine cloak?"

"Yes, but it didn't like the dip in the harbour."

"Show them to us."

Johanna went upstairs where Nellie had hung up all their clothes. The cloak looked rather shabby on its own, more brown than red, but there was a pair of trousers that she had never seen Father wear in almost the same colour. And a gold dress that used to belong to her mother, a few shades lighter than the cloak.

Johanna took all of them downstairs, as well as the sheet with the crown and the staff. Koby and Nellie were surprised to see her come in with all these things, but Johan Delacoeur nodded. "I think she's got what I mean. Put them on, both of you."

Johanna took Roald, who was puzzled, to an empty servants' bedroom next to the kitchen. She slipped out of her comfortable dress and into the dress that hadn't been worn since she was a little girl. It was a dress with laces on both sides that could be let out to accommodate a woman's condition. She pulled the knots loose and helped Roald. The trousers were a bit wide, but a belt would fix that, and the velvet cloak shimmered in the light, even if it was no longer red. She gave Roald the staff, and as she touched the wooden handle, it re-played the scenes from inside the palace: the ghost, Alexandre and his fish. For some reason, Loesie's last words came to her mind. *Without wood, there is no fire.*

"Like this?" Roald said, putting the crown on his head.

She nodded, wiped some breadcrumbs out of his beard and took his arm.

There were gasps in the kitchen when they returned.

Martine cried, "Oh, he looks so much like his father!"

Nellie said, "Mistress Johanna, you really *are* with child."

Johan Delacoeur rose from his seat and bowed to her. "Your Royal Majesties, my humble self and my wife and whatever virtues we have that may be of use to you are at your service."

Going into a magical battle with nothing other than pomp and show still sounded like lunacy, but strangely, dressing up as king and queen made Johanna feel better.

Roald was still puzzled by the whole affair. He kept asking if he was now a real king, and she said that he was and had been ever since his father died.

They went upstairs and did some really silly things in the bedroom that were most satisfactory, because if one was about to be slaughtered, one was entitled to do really silly things, even if giggling would have annoyed the servants. Things got a bit rough, and they rolled off the side of the bed.

There came a knock on the door and Nellie said, "Are you all right, mistress?"

"Yes, no need to worry," Johanna said.

They were quiet after that, climbed into bed and went to sleep.

CHAPTER 20

JOHANNA WOKE UP before sunrise the next morning. She slipped from the bed and got dressed while Roald still slept.

Koby was in the kitchen and greeted her wordlessly. She passed Johanna a steaming cup of tea and a bowl of porridge.

Nellie came into the back door when she was halfway eating it. "The podium is in the market square and people have begun to gather already."

Johanna nodded, wondering how Father had spent the night, and cringing at her immature behaviour with Roald last night.

"We must go upstairs and get you ready soon."

Johanna sighed. She couldn't have felt any less like getting dressed up, but pomp and ceremony were all they had. She followed Nellie up the stairs, remembering how she used to hate getting ready for festivities. That seemed kind of silly right now. If only getting ready for balls and ceremonies was her only problem.

They went into the dressing room and Johanna let Nellie do her thing. Roald also went down for breakfast, and other people came into the kitchen, probably Martine and Johan Delacoeur.

By the time Johanna was ready to join them, she was so nervous that she was sure she would be sick.

The gold-coloured dress didn't allow for easy sitting down, so she stood in the kitchen, wondering how long it would be before the hair pins gave her a headache.

Roald got changed rather more quickly, but he came to the kitchen with all his buttons undone. Nellie gasped, but Johanna asked, "Did anyone help you put your shirt on?"

"No." His eyes were absolutely honest like a child's.

"No one helped you with your pants?"

"No."

"That's very good." It was astonishing. Roald had never managed to dress himself properly. Maybe there was hope. Maybe he could improve and manage his own life better. If they survived today.

She did up his buttons, her hands trembling. Then they waited. Time crept slowly towards midday. A couple of boys had gone to the markets and were going to come and get them, because if Johanna and Roald turned up too early, the effect would be spoiled. They could only come after the prisoners had been brought to the podium.

Johanna felt cold and sweaty at the same time. She lifted the hoops of the dress and sat down, but had to let out the sides even more because she felt constricted. And hungry and sick at the same time. Afraid that the boy wouldn't come, and then afraid that he would come.

Finally, there were fast footsteps in the back yard and the door opened. A young voice called, "They're just about to bring them out!"

The boy was Gijsbert.

Everyone rose at the same time. Johanna picked up the crown from the table and set it on Roald's head. Nellie draped the Carmine cloak over his shoulders.

Gijsbert went out first, then Nellie and Sebastian the groundsman in his Sunday finest. Then Roald with Johanna, flanked by Martine and Johan Delacoeur. Johan wore his uniform jacket and carried a sword.

Koby and Greetje brought up the rear.

So they walked out the back yard. They weren't even halfway down the street when the first people noticed Roald.

"It's the king!" someone yelled, and people came to the doors and windows.

There was cheering and clapping and the shouts preceded the group down the street.

The king is back. The king is back and *We have a Queen.*

"Come with us to the markets," Johanna said.

"There is a burning at the markets," a woman said. "I will not be so cruel to let my children watch that." And indeed most of the people who had come out of the houses were women or children and old people.

"We're going to stop it," Martine said. "Come and join us."

A few came, and then a few more, and then a great flood of people came talking, chatting behind them. Women carried brooms, men carried shovels or picks, or the occasional pitchfork, whatever use one had in town for a pitchfork.

And so the stream of people flooded into the market square.

A great number of people already stood there, mostly the men of the families. The beggars had abandoned their line to the steps of the mayor's house, the stall holders had left their stalls.

The prisoners were being led up onto the podium in front of the mayor's house. First were the young men who had been at the palace with her. Greetje gasped next to Johanna. Master Willems was wearing a grey sack. His arms and legs were blue with the cold and bore welts from where he had been hit. One of his eyes was swollen. After him came an older woman. She walked in stiff steps, as if she'd been beaten, and blood had seeped into the back of her shift. Her body was broken but she had the most vicious look in her eyes. As she turned towards the audience, Johanna recognised her: Helena the whore who lived in the harbour and served the sailors at night and told girls about *those things* during the day.

Then came Father. Where the others had stumbled up the steps, he kept his back straight, even though Johanna could see that walking hurt him a lot. They had allowed him to keep his trousers and shoes. Maybe they hid welts on his skin. He almost tripped over the top step. A guard grabbed his arm to keep him upright and dragged him across to one of several posts that stood lined up on the platform.

People at the front cheered, but there was no joy in their cheering. A number of guards stood at the ready, facing the crowd and scanning all who were there. Checking if the people cheered as instructed.

A couple of bears lay on the edges of the platform.

By now, people at the back of the crowd were starting to notice Johanna and Roald and the rest of the newcomers.

Johanna held Roald's arm in a tight grip. She could feel the muscles under his arm tense up and relax and tense up and relax . . . She was sure that he would love to run, or start swaying.

The people opened up a path through the crowd.

There was cheering and clapping.

A cold wind tore through the square, tearing at hats and scarves. A strand of hair escaped Johanna's bun and blew across the face. She shivered. There was magic in the air.

Alexandre had come up on the stage. He now looked into the crowd. Johanna knew that he knew where she was.

"Hail the king, hail the queen!"

"We're saved!"

More and more people came to look. They pushed others aside and formed a guard of honour across the square to the podium. One of the trumpeters, in Alexandre's blue colours, rushed to the procession and played the *King's Hail*.

And so the procession crossed the markets and there they stopped, because they met a wall of Estlander guards with bears.

Alexandre jumped down the platform and wrestled himself between his men.

The trumpeter again played the short burst of notes that was the King's Hail.

Johan Delacoeur shouted, "Make way for his royal highness King Roald and his consort Johanna Brouwer!"

The whole of the audience broke out in a deafening cheer.

By now, Alexandre had come to the front of the line of guards. "What's this?" He snorted. From close up he was taller than Johanna had expected, or maybe that was because of his high-heeled boots. His eyes were green, his face quite coarse-skinned and narrow, his hair curly and brown. He wore his customary blue trousers and a cape of the same colour, held at the top with a gold clip.

He eyed Johanna up and down and then turned to Roald. His gaze rested on the crown and staff. His expression closed. He knew these were the real items and Roald was the real heir to the throne. And maybe one of his men had lied to him about Roald having drowned in the harbour and maybe he was beating himself in the head about believing it.

Baron Uti had known about Roald. Apparently his friendship with Alexandre was not as good as Alexandre suggested in the letter to the Baron that Johanna had seen while they were in Florisheim.

Johanna stepped forward. "Thank you for taking care of our town while we were away."

Several people in the crowd laughed. Alexandre glared at them.

"We will now take over as lawful descendants of Saarland's royal family." She had expected to be sick with nerves when facing him, but she felt strangely calm.

Alexandre simply stared at her. Then he said something in a low voice in Burovian to a man at his side. This man, not a guard but a fellow noble, judging from his clothing, pushed between the guards and a moment later, he came back with a dark-haired man in a dark coat with a hideously frilled white shit underneath. Octavio Nieland.

He seemed to be taken aback at the sight of the crown. Maybe he had looked for it but had been chased out of the palace by Celine's ghost.

"This is certainly a . . . surprise." His voice was as haughty as ever.

"I'm undecided if it's a surprise."

He raised one eyebrow.

"Am I surprised that you joined the invader's men?"

"You don't understand at all."

"Oh?"

"This is much bigger than the petty grievances of this ridiculous church of yours."

"It's not *my* church and I'm beginning to think that forbidding magic is not a bad thing at all. How many people have been killed through it? Oh, you don't care because they were all common people."

He went red in the face. His hand wandered to his belt where he carried a sword.

Then he looked aside, his eyes widening. Julianna had come to the front. Like Johanna and Roald and others, she had dressed in the best clothes she had. Her hair was done up in a big bun, and her eyes blazed with anger.

Octavio laughed, in an uncomfortable way. He let his hand fall away from his belt. It was a subtle gesture, but it told Johanna one thing: he might not care much about Roald, but he definitely cared for his sister.

"There is no need for conflict," she said. "We are Saarlanders. We've solved our problems without fighting for a long time." One of the reasons that Johan Delacoeur was an *ex*-army general. King Nicholaos didn't put much effort into his armed forces. "But the invaders must go. We don't need any foreigners to run our country."

"What do you know of the menace that faces us?"

"The Church of the Triune has been elevated to menace? It justifies killing and burning down half the town?"

He threw his head back and laughed. "You know nothing at all."

"Then tell us. But while you do that call off this silly spectacle."

"These people are criminals."

"My father? The only crime he has committed is to be your competitor."

Alexandre said something in Burovian that sounded sharp and impatient.

"What is he saying? Why can't he speak to us directly?"

Roald said, "He says that he has no time for talking."

Alexandre came forward and shouted Burovian words in Roald's face. Roald, true to his nature, did not flinch. He replied in Burovian and Alexandre shouted more loudly at him.

People all around cried out in protest.

Roald turned to Johanna. "He says that—"

"What does it matter what he says. What matters is this!" Octavio gestured wildly in the direction of the harbour.

People gasped and exclaimed profanities and covered their mouth with their hands. What Johanna had taken as a reaction to the argument was . . . something else.

A few people moved aside so that she could see over the water out the heads to the east, where the Saar River flowed towards the ocean.

On the water which looked like silver with the reflecting sunlight came a ship like none she had ever seen.

It was tall like an ocean faring vessel, but in place of sails, it had a tall protuberance which spewed smoke like a chimney.

Everyone around her was shouting. Some invoked prayer, others reached their hands to the heavens and chanted. Most people just stared with wide eyes. How did the ship move? How, if it was made from wood, did it not catch fire? How, if it was made from metal, as some suggested, did it float?

Magic, people suggested, and the sea breeze carried a familiar prick.

Octavio said, "Those are the eastern traders. They've been around this area for a while and they're not coming for a cup of tea. I'm hoping, since you seem determined to retake the city before they can set foot on this land, that you have brought strong magicians."

CHAPTER 21

EVERYTHING THAT had happened over the last months suddenly made sense.

This *machine* was what the Guentherite order had been trying to recreate. This was what the iron was for.

And this was why they wanted control of Saardam, why they were building the strange thing in the harbour, and similar things all along the river, and why they needed to get rid of a church that didn't allow its followers to practice magic.

While she had been talking to Octavio, several things had happened. The young men whose task it was to make use of the distraction to go to the platform had arrived there. On the platform, the prisoners were too far away from Johanna and the group to hear what had been said, and they couldn't see the water because the mayor's house was in the way. They were confused about what was happening, frowning at each other and trying to see past the guards, who also appeared to have lost interest in their charges and appeared equally confused.

Over the heads of the people between her and the podium, Johanna spotted one of the boys trying to climb the podium, boosted up by a mate. A bear jumped up, growling.

All of a sudden the guards' attention was back where it should have been. They shouted and pulled weapons.

The boy dropped himself off the platform and hid by

pressing himself against the side. But a few Saarlander guards came from the other side and tried to drag him away.

Alexandre uttered a cry of frustration. He turned back to the podium. His men made a path for him. He shouted something in which Johanna picked up the Burovian word for *kill*.

The prisoners' eyes widened.

Father was looking out over the crowd. He knew that Johanna was amongst all those people somewhere. He would have heard the King's Hail. The young man next to him was pulling on his arms, tied around the post at his back. He was shouting at the top of his voice—inaudible to Johanna over the tumult in the square—but his eyes bulged with fear.

Someone from behind fired an arrow while seated on another fellow's shoulder. It struck the bear between the eyes.

"Good shot!" someone shouted.

Johanna raised her fist. "Come on! Free the prisoners!"

Alexandre had almost reached the podium but turned around again. Seeing the crowd surge forward and one of his bears sprawled on the floor, his expression grew hard.

He raised his hand—

No. Johanna knew what would happen.

A snake made of fire sprung out of mid-air. It coiled over the heads of the onlookers and set the pile of wood at the feet of the prisoners alight with a fleeting touch.

All of a sudden everyone was screaming.

People were running away from the fire creature, other people were trying to hit the flames out with their jackets. It was a futile activity and they only succeeded in setting fire to their clothes.

A sudden wind came up. It whipped through the square and tore at hair and hats. One of the market stands was blown over. Instead of fanning the flames, the wind blew them out. Alexandre waved his hand at the pyre, but the wind blew the flames out again.

What . . .

Master Willems. He was the only one with wind magic. He stood with his face turned up at the sky, praying.

Alexandre conjured a bigger snake.

Greetje was crying at the top of her voice. "Do something. Somebody, free my husband!"

Father was looking straight at Johanna over the heads of the crowd.

Some people tried to run away, others tried to reach the prisoners. The guards didn't seem to know what to do and seemed to decide to just defend themselves.

Roald was shouting at the top of his voice, but even standing near him, Johanna couldn't make out what he said. His face shone with sweat.

Johanna remembered Loesie's words. *Wood is stronger than fire. Fire needs wood to burn.*

She meant wood *magic* was stronger than fire magic.

But was it really? Wet wood didn't burn. Live wood didn't burn. She remembered pieces of wood sprouting leaves when Duke Lothar had performed the exorcism on Loesie.

Alexandre was not a strong magician, the Baroness Viktoriya said. Johanna had wood: the handle of the king's staff. A lot of other people in the market square had wood, too. They had brooms, and the broom heads were made up of twigs. They had shovels with wooden handles. They had pitchforks and garden rakes. Master Willems controlled the wind.

Johanna took the staff from Roald's surprised hands. "Hail the king!" she called out, holding the staff over her head.

A few people in the chaos around her repeated her, and then more and even more. The chant spread over the market place like an ink stain.

Hail the king, hail the king.

Roald himself was shouting as hard as everyone else, apparently not quite clear on the fact that *he* was the king.

As they chanted, people held their brooms or shovels over their heads.

Master Willems still held his face turned up to the sky. His lips moved in prayer.

The people shouted, "Hail the king!"

Johanna held the king's staff in the air, willing it to spring into life. The fire snake dived in and out of the woodpile at the post where Master Willems stood. The wind whirled around him, putting out the flames as fast as the fire snake could light them. Gusts of wind drew sparks and strands of fire away from the creature, threatening to dissolve it.

Johanna spurred the wind on. *Come on, come on.*

The wood of the staff *moved* under her hands. Buds sprouted between her fingers. While she watched, vines grew and sprouted leaves.

A man shouted. His shovel had turned into a bush. He dropped it, but it hung in midair from fast-growing vines that extended faster than a man could walk.

All around, shovels, picks and pitchforks had also sprouted leaves. Brooms turned into living forests of glowing, snaking vines.

They reached the platform and intertwined with the wood from the woodpile. And that wood started sprouting, too. The fire snake whirled around so fast that it was hard to see where it went. Because the wood was alive, it could no longer make it burn. It only produced lots of smoke, which in turn made it harder to see.

Alexandre had climbed up on the platform and was throwing fire directly at the prisoners, but each time the wind blew the flames away.

A vine sprouted from the boards of the platform and twined around his leg. He roared with anger and cut it with his sword, but a new one grew, and another one around his other leg.

The boys were back on the platform, because the bears were busy swatting away sprouting leaves. They cut Master Willems free. He collapsed on the boards.

"Come, someone help carry him!"

Then Father. He rubbed his wrists. His face looked pale, but he was able to walk away by himself. A couple more boys assisted him down the platform. No one took any notice of Alexandre's guards, who were trying to tackle the encroaching greenery by hacking away with their swords. But Alexandre's legs were already rooted to the platform's boards, held there by thick vines. He was screaming at his men and they hacked at the wood, but it grew faster than they could cut it.

The vines crept up his torso, scrunching his jacket between wooden coils and his ribcage.

"Let me out of here, witch!"

Johanna finally lowered the staff. All the vines detached themselves and hung limp, as if the magic had just fled.

She climbed on the platform. Father watched her with wide eyes.

Alexandre's face was red splotched with white. His eyes bulged. His breathing was fast. He whispered, "You common whore."

Johanna spat in his face.

"You thought we were all killed?" she said in a low voice. "You thought you could scare the people of Saardam into supporting you? Well, you can, for a short time maybe, but if you really knew the people of this town, you'd know that they won't support tyrants."

He laughed in a breathless, wheezing fashion. "I . . . am . . . not . . . the enemy."

"You've done an excellent job so far behaving like you are."

"All . . . the . . . lowlands will fall . . . to . . . eastern magic."

"Rubbish," Father said. "They're *traders*. They come to sell things."

"We . . . can only . . . face them if we have . . . magic."

"We seem to have plenty of that ourselves."

"That . . . evil church—"

"I will hear nothing more of the church!" Johanna spat at him again. "None of your reasons justify the killing of thousands and the burning of entire cities. Not just us, but Aroden and all the villages along the river. This was never about the church. It was about power. You wanted Saardam so that *you* could negotiate with these eastern traders for this *machine* of theirs. *You* are just a power-hungry, greedy, sad excuse for a prince. You sowed fear into the hearts of all and then destroyed what people built in your name."

"I didn't . . ." His gasps came very fast now. Despite the fact that Johanna had detached the staff from the vines, the ones that held him were still tightening their grip.

"You didn't betray the very people you recruited? You didn't conjure fire dragons that destroyed the Guentherite abbot's summer residence?"

"They were . . . rebellious."

"That justified the deaths of many men?"

The vines constricted his chest so much that he couldn't speak. His face grew ever darker in colour. Spit dribbled from his mouth where his tongue had swelled so much that it stuck out between his teeth.

He lived—just—but if she couldn't stop the will of the vines to kill this man, then nothing could. She turned around because she didn't want to see this. Already, her stomach churned with revulsion.

Father was free, Master Willems had been reunited with Greetje, the other prisoners were free, and that was all that mattered. The men who had supported Alexandre had fled to the harbour and were using one of the Nieland ships to flee. She presumed Octavio was on it.

As she walked down the steps of the former platform that had become an intertwined tangle of trees, there was an awful gasp and gurgle from behind her. Turning around, she already couldn't see Alexandre anymore, but she assumed that he had become one with the trees.

The people in the square now all gathered to watch the harbour. While Alexandre's men fled, the strange eastern ship had come closer. It was a dark, square, menacing-looking thing, with smoke belching from the chimney. It was too far away to see any people on deck, but it was about to come into the harbour, and the Nieland ship was about to go out.

Both vessels halted.

A great tide of people started making their way to the harbourside, where they could see. Johanna and Roald were swept up to the front of that surge.

Had they deposed of a tyrant only to be faced with a worse opponent?

But the two ships had settled into a standoff and nothing happened. The people dispersed. Johanna asked some of her young men to keep watch and come to warn her as soon as something changed.

She and Roald walked home over the markets, where an entangled bit of bush marked Alexandre's last position. At least the growth appeared to have slowed.

At home, Father was in the kitchen, eating with trembling, sore-riddled hands. Johanna hugged him and cried on his shoulder. He was so thin. But his eyes shone with happiness.

"We're free now. You're the queen."

Never mind that she had no idea how long that would last.

Nellie came into the kitchen, and Greetje, as well as Johan and Martine Delacoeur. They had a celebration of sorts. Johan talked about fixing up the palace, but that would need removal of Celine's ghost. Johanna was too tired to even think of that.

She followed Roald to bed. There was no romping around and giggling tonight. She fell asleep as soon as her head hit the pillow.

It was still dark when someone knocked on the door.

"Mistress?" It was Nellie.

Johanna stuck her feet out of the warmth of the bed. Oh, it was so cold! She tiptoed to the door and opened it a crack. Nellie stood in the hallway with a candle.

"There is a young man in the kitchen for you."

Johanna quickly got dressed and felt her way down the stairs. The lights were on in the kitchen, and Koby was kneading dough. By the heavens, was this the time she normally got up?

At the table opposite Koby sat a young men whom Johanna recognised as one from the church.

"Has anything happened?"

"I'm afraid it has. You best come quickly."

Johanna followed him into the darkness, which wasn't quite as dark as she expected. The sky had a distinct blue tinge on the eastern horizon.

They walked in silence to the harbour. There was no longer a need to be afraid of guards or bears, but the dark realisation grew in Johanna's mind that this might be a temporary solution.

Even before they had come to the quay, Johanna already

noticed the orange glow that lit the buildings on the quay that was not morning light.

Something was on fire in the mouth of the harbour, sending smoke billowing over the water. The orange light glinted off the metal side of the eastern ship.

A couple of men stood on the quay watching the spectacle.

"What happened?" Johanna asked.

"We can't be sure, mistress. The one man who saw it is rambling about dragons, and none of it makes any sense. We sent him home. Maybe he'll be clearer tomorrow."

Dragons. In the proper use of the word, they were creatures from the far east. Not lizards, which could also be called dragons, but large winged creatures that spewed fire.

Johanna eyed the foreign ship and its menacing shape. The burning object that had to be the remains of the Nieland vessel was slowly sinking under the surface.

"Am I mistaken or are they coming this way?"

"You're not mistaken, mistress. They're coming into port."

THE DRAGON PRINCE

Book 5 of the Ghostspeaker Chronicles

PATTY JANSEN

CHAPTER 1

THE CLANG OF A GONG echoed through the hallway of the palace, a strange, foreign-sounding noise that made the hairs on the back of Johanna's neck stand up.

In slow, deliberate strides to the low beat of a drum, the visiting party from the ship of the eastern traders entered the Red Reception Room.

Upon hearing of Li Han's intended visit, Johanna had made sure that the room, unlike the rest of the palace, was in a state suitable to receive and impress a foreign visitor. For the past few days, a small army of people had been scrubbing the floor, polishing the chairs and fixing patches in the patterned wallpaper. They had gathered any furniture they could find that didn't have fire or water damage, and selected the cleanest rugs and the freshest, least damaged curtains.

But the group of people that came through the door looked so splendid that all that effort seemed akin to trying to dress up a donkey as a coach horse.

First came two mountainous soldiers in grey uniforms carrying a wooden chest on a platform with handles on both sides. From the way they walked, Johanna—seated on the ornate but otherwise quite ordinary chair that functioned as makeshift throne—judged that whatever it contained had to be heavy. They progressed about halfway into the room, set down their load, bowed in unison and retreated to both sides. Behind them came two soldiers in leather armour. They wore the same grey shift and loose trousers as the porters—Johanna judged them to all be guards. They also bowed and stepped aside.

This allowed Johanna to see the elderly couple in the middle of the group. The old man was dressed in a blue robe. He was finely built, quite short and thin in comparison with the guards. His weather-beaten skin displayed a landscape of wrinkles and sunspots, especially around the curiously shaped eyes. He had tied his greying hair in a bun at the top of his head.

Next to him stood a woman of similar age with a wizened face. Her hair was more white than grey and also tied at the top of her head. Her face was round, and she looked around the room with eyes narrowed to slits. She wore a knee-length robelike garment woven from shimmering green silk and a broad embroidered belt around her waist, with trousers of the same colour.

Women wore trousers?

The young man behind them was much taller. He wore simple black with leather armour over the top. An empty scabbard hung at his waist. Like the soldiers, he had left his weapons at the door.

Behind him were two more soldiers and then four people with an assortment of curious-looking drums. One of them carried the gong, a big metal disk suspended from a frame.

The entire party came to a halt and bowed as one. The gong made a soft noise as it swung against the side of the frame.

The old man said in a strongly accented voice, "We bow to the king and queen of Saarland and the dignified people of the King's Council."

Those wise men of the council, including Father, sat to Johanna's left. The king, of course, wasn't present, not even in spirit. He was in the garden chasing frogs. Father had even taken his chair away to save Johanna the embarrassment of having to explain his absence.

Johanna said, "I return your greeting. Rise and tell us your names and your business in our fair town." Her hands felt sweaty and the smell of polishing wax that hung around her chair made her feel ill.

The old man straightened. "My name is Li Han, brother prince of the Dragon Emperor. This is my wife Wen Mei and my son Li Fai. The Dragon Emperor, my brother, has sent us here to trade. We bring silk and spices, cloth and beads. Tobacco, cocoa, tea. Everything from all parts of the known lands and from the lands at the edge of the southern ocean. We buy cheese, wool, rugs, wood products, baskets, furniture. We trade with Phoenicians, Anglians and the tribes of the western horn. We trade all over the known world and explore the unknown world. Today I bring my son, Li Fai. He wants to make office in this city." He gestured to the younger man in black, who again bowed, his hands pressed together in front of his chest.

When he straightened, Johanna met his eyes. They carried a sharp, intelligent expression. His skin was bronzed, his lips full and dark.

She said while returning his gaze, "So you want to have an office in Saardam?"

His father replied. "Yes. Office. Warehouse. We bring goods. We sell them. River traders bring them to all the river towns. They take other things back for us to buy. Cloth, shoes, cheese. We buy them and sell elsewhere. People of Phoenicia really like cheese." He glanced at Father as he said that. Father of course had met Li Han before during his years of travelling on the river sloops. He would speak of meeting him in Lurezia where the river was deep enough for the sea traders to come a good distance inland if the wind was right.

"We have our own sea traders in Saardam," said Joris Decamp, mayor of the city and in charge of all matters dealing with the seaport. "They will not like foreigners coming in, taking their positions."

There were some nods at this in the King's Council, the group of twenty men at Johanna's left. Apart from Father and Master Deim and the shepherd of the Church of the Triune, most of them were nobles wearing their brocade and silken finery.

Someone at the back of this group said, "The Nielands could

use a kick up the backside, if you ask me. Yes, we have sea traders, but they still haven't done anything about rebuilding the ocean ships they lost. Tea is getting mightily scarce. I say let him have his office." This was Hendricus Franzen, and Johanna made a mental note of his comment.

"Old Nieland will not like that at all," repeated Joris, and that comment met with some approval.

Johanna licked her lips. What Li Han asked was no small thing. Before the fires, the Nielands had a good fleet of seafaring vessels. Many of them had been destroyed in the fire, one had never returned after a mutiny and the rest were damaged, but nevertheless, the family must be planning to repair and rebuild those ships. Li Han was a major competitor.

Johan Delacoeur cleared his throat and asked Li Han in his usual blunt manner. "Never mind the tea, spices and trinkets. They're women's things. What I'd be interested in is this: do you sell those iron ships of yours? Because there would be a long line of people wanting to buy them."

It became very quiet in the room. Everyone was keen for the answer to the question.

Li Han bowed to Johan. "We do not sell ships. We sell goods. We use ships. If we sell ships then we cannot trade anymore." He chuckled, not entirely convincingly. He had to be aware of the failed efforts of various groups in the lowlands to try to build their own iron ships, and the fact that a war had been fought over control of the port because of these ships.

Johanna asked, "If you get an office, are you going to bring more iron ships into the harbour?"

"We may. Or we may not. In the future. Not now."

Johanna glanced at Father. Did Li Han just sound coy or was he actually coy? Not wanting to reveal if this was their only ship or if they had more than one?

Father smiled at her. Well that was most unhelpful. She could use some help in deciding what to do about this delegation.

Johanna said, "One of the problems with your request is this: many people in town are suspicious of the iron ships. They are afraid and don't understand why they can move without sails."

That was an understatement. Ever since the ship had

come into the harbour, rumours had run rife about the motivations of the eastern traders, the size of their fleet hiding in a secret location waiting to pounce on Saardam and occupy the city, and also about the size of the fire dragon that—according to many—lived in the belly of the ship.

Li Han bowed again. Was he going to keep doing that every time he said something? "The people do not need to be suspicious. The idea for the iron ships came from someone from this part of the world. One of your countrymen made the first drawings for the steam machines. His name is Rinius. He is a man of great ideas."

"Rinius is a heretic!" called Shepherd Victor from his seat in the King's Council. "It is not just the Church of the Triune that considers him so. Even the Belaman Church—and they're not usually known for making wise decisions—have condemned him. He was banished to a small island off the coast of the Cape, and hanged there."

Li Han said, "Your king speaks well of Rinius."

There was a small uncomfortable silence after this.

Yes, Roald rarely shut up about Rinius and his books. It was one of the reasons that no one was keen to pressure him to come to meetings anymore. But how did Li Han know this?

A couple of men in the King's Council were keeping an eye on the shepherd; others suddenly found their knees very interesting. The outburst they feared from the shepherd did not follow, however.

Li Han continued as if oblivious to the tension, "If we have office and warehouse, we will pay the sons and fathers of this town to work for us."

"Do you think we have no work for our own men?" This was Johan Delacoeur.

The shepherd said, "Do you think our citizens will want to work for someone with magic who supports the greatest heretic of all time?"

Thomas Kloostermans, a fervent supporter of the Belaman Church said, "Yeah. I don't usually agree with him, but that man wrote a great many things that are an insult to any church, not just his—" He glanced sideways at the shepherd. "—band of lunatics."

The shepherd called out a protest at the same time as Johanna said, "Gentlemen."

They fell quiet.

That was the division in the city: those who supported the Church of the Triune and those who said it had gained far too much power.

"The eastern trader's office in our town will be an opportunity for all involved, but . . ." She met Li Han's eyes. "I'm afraid that a number of our buildings are not in a very good state. Quite a few were damaged by fire. Many were abandoned, and we may not be able to trace the owners to transfer a lease or ownership. Other buildings are damaged beyond repair."

Li Han nodded. "We can fix. You find building. We pull down and build or fix. We bring gold to pay for office."

He said something to the two mountainous guards in his own language. It sounded sharp and unpleasant.

The guards lifted the lid of the chest that still stood on the platform in front of the delegation.

Gold indeed, in the shape of coins.

There was so much of it!

Johanna still remembered the shock of walking into the king's vault when she and Roald moved into the palace and looking at the empty shelves. Somehow she had expected there to be at least some money.

Father had talked about how King Nicholaos had given a fortune to the Church of the Triune when he believed they could resurrect his daughter the crown princess Celine, and when they couldn't, to the necromancer Kylian. In panic, the king had wanted to sell his only asset—his child-like son who was utterly unsuitable for the throne—to the richest merchant's daughter to raise money. Somehow, though she'd known all that, she still hadn't realised how bad it was until she looked in the treasury.

And now the family's only hard asset—the palace—had been looted and damaged in the fires.

Johanna had already borrowed money from Father and Master Deim for the essential repairs, but she didn't want to accept too much of their generosity, because she didn't think the palace would be in any kind of position soon to pay back the loan.

Li Han's money would go a long way towards solving her problems.

If she let Li Han's son have his office.

Noticing her hesitation, the eastern trader's son took a handful of the coins and crossed the room holding them on his open palm. While he came to Johanna, she met his eyes. They were black and the shape of them was unusual but not unattractive. The rest of his face was pleasant to look at, his lips expressive, his nose broad and quite flat, not at all like the big honkers that people from the south often had. His skin had a slight yellowish tinge and was soft like that of a girl. He had no beard or moustache. His hair was black and glossy like a raven's feathers. He wore it tied at the top of his head.

He bowed and held the coins out to her. She took them. The skin on his hand was pleasantly warm and dry. His nails were neat and clean.

"It is Phoenician gold." His voice was warm, not as heavily-accented as his father's. Johanna made a show of examining the sample of gold. The coins were very heavy and carried a foreign inscription on one side and a likeness of some god on the other. Of course Johanna had seen these before. Many deals with foreigners were paid for in Phoenician gold. "Yes, I have no doubt that they're real."

She gave the coins back to him, again touching his palm. He tossed them back into the chest with a clink.

From inside his cloak, he produced a parcel wrapped in a silk cloth. "To show our appreciation, this is a personal gift to you." He handed the parcel to her. Johanna had to struggle to keep meeting his eyes. His expression was so intense and she didn't know why he looked at her like that, whether that was customary where he came from, but the intense gaze made her ears burn. She didn't want to stare back because that would be inappropriate. She heard that in some foreign lands morals were very loose.

Johanna laid the cloth on her knees and unwrapped it, glad

for the distraction. The fine fabric slid through her hands. If these people used silk to wrap things, they must be very rich indeed.

Inside the parcel she found a piece of honey-coloured wood carved into a long-tailed creature. It had a big snout with two large, open nostrils. Its mouth was open, showing a forked tongue.

"It's a dragon," he said. "This is the blue dragon. It is the symbol of our house. It's a present to you."

"Thank you. It's very pretty." Johanna traced the exquisitely carved scales on the dragon's back with her fingertips. "You speak our language well."

There was a brief flash of a smile in his eyes. "I have studied much. The office will be mine while my father travels on the ship. I have to make deals with traders in your town. I cannot expect them to know my language."

"No, that's true."

He chuckled. Had he attempted to make light-hearted conversation? "Maybe one day I can teach."

"Yes, maybe. Thank you," she said again, aware that the men of the council were looking at her.

He bowed and retreated.

By the Triune, her cheeks were burning. He had magic of some kind. There was no doubt about it.

But what about his request for an office?

She wanted to accept it.

In the past, Saardam had always been an accepting place, where people from all walks of life and parts of the known world had come together.

If someone was going to dominate the sea trade on which Saardam's wealth had relied in the past, it would be those with iron ships. It could be the eastern traders, who already had the iron ships, or the Baron, who had not succeeded in building them yet. Even without knowing Li Han well, she knew who she'd rather deal with. Father was an infallible judge of character and he had always spoken well of the eastern trader.

Yes, there was probably magic involved in the building of a successful iron ship.

Yes, many people in town would view him as a major competitor.

Yes, allowing him to settle would bring a war with the Baron a step closer simply by keeping Saardam independent.

A little voice inside her said, *Wasn't this war going to happen anyway?* Because the baron did not just want to use the port, he wanted to erase Saarland from the map. He wanted to kill the royal family and eradicate its church.

Wouldn't Li Han be a powerful ally against the Baron and his necromancer son?

"This request takes me by surprise, but I'm quite interested in your offer. I would like some time to consider possible offices that you could occupy."

There were several gasps in the King's Council. One of the men made a protesting sound, but another shushed him.

Li Han bowed. "Thank you, thank you. We come back in a few days, right?"

"Yes. Do come back." There was a seed of an idea forming in her mind but she needed a bit of time to work it out.

"Thank you, thank you." He bowed again.

The two mountainous men picked up the chest of gold and Li Han and his party shuffled backwards to the door, leaving behind a thick silence. The gong sounded again when they were in the corridor.

Johanna did not dare look at the men to her left.

AS SOON AS the eastern traders were gone from the room, several of the powerful men in the King's Council raised their voices.

"That was a rash and irresponsible decision. You cannot know what hidden motives they have for coming here," Johan Delacoeur said. His face went red, as it usually did when he was agitated. "A lot of people will be very angry."

"Those people can have their say," Johanna said. "I will listen to their arguments. I have not given him my word, only that I'm interested."

"With all due respect, Your Majesty, is that decision up to you alone? I don't think so." When Johan said *all due respect* he usually meant no respect at all.

"According to our agreement, only the king can make that decision without support from the council," another noble said.

There was some murmuring of agreement at this. Apparently a young woman who was not from a noble family was such a threat to them that they needed an entire council to keep an eye on her.

Johanna found it hard to meet Father's eyes. He and Master Deim were in the minority. *They* didn't think that she was incapable of making decisions, but the council had been one of the conditions under which the noble families had accepted the "Idiot King" on the throne.

It was a fragile agreement for a fragile position. They couldn't afford arguments.

"I cannot see why we can't rebuild our own ocean trade," a man said.

"We don't need foreigners to run business for us!" another shouted.

Another man said, "I agree. These foreigners and their gold are likely to take our best workers away from us."

"Then pay them more!" Master Deim said.

"Gentlemen!" Johanna's voice cut through their arguments. "Like it or not, we face the reality that, underneath our veneer of sophistication, Saardam is struggling to overcome the effects of the past. The invasion and occupation by Alexandre have sucked the city dry. We have no food until harvest, and not enough people are left on the farms who know how to work the fields."

"We can buy food," Johan Delacoeur said.

"Yes, but many of the poor will not be able to afford it." Not to mention that the coffers were empty.

He snorted. "They can survive off bread and water. Entire armies do it. For surprisingly long periods of time, too."

Master Deim spoke up. "The poor are those who provide the workers to rebuild the city, as well as the quay workers, the ones who unload and load our ships. Prosperity of the land is not measured in the wealth of the rich, but in how many of the poor can afford to feed their families. Because if they can, they're happy. They won't steal, they won't join rebellions. Give a poor man a job and pay him, and he will happily work for you."

"That's just what these eastern buggers are trying to do, isn't it?" That was the noble Thomas Kloostermans. "Get a foothold in the city and spread their foppish ways and foul religions. I mean—which man lets his wife wear trousers, for the sake of the holy god."

"Not many of you are old enough to remember the last time that happened," said Patricius Faber, a man easily the oldest of the council. "When preachers of this ludicrous church came into the city and subverted our merchants and workers with notions that they are somehow equal to nobles. The next thing, the king himself was taken with this rubbish, having had his senses clouded through the loss of his daughter. And no one stopped him, and we were all saying 'I told you so.' Twenty-five years on, our *women* are going to this church and are begging us to come. This church has corrupted the core of our civilisation. That's what will happen when you let foreigners in. First they give our workers jobs, then they buy things from our merchants, and then they attempt to corrupt us by appealing to the weak minds of our women."

Johanna was very much tempted to say, "Well, maybe then you should do something that those people will find worth supporting instead," but she had no energy for an argument.

Johanna shifted in her seat. She needed to get up and out of this room, because the corset made her uncomfortable. It pushed her stomach down so that her front was flat. But that expanding waist had to go somewhere. It was all squished up inside. She had to take shallow breaths because there was nowhere for her lungs to expand.

If she got up, the men would see that the dress sat wrong and that the bottom of the bodice wasn't done up at all. But, by the Triune, she was feeling unwell all of a sudden.

"If you're asking me, Your Majesty, the man's gold is bewitched," Shepherd Victor was yelling over the other voices.

A couple of the men protested.

"Look at how it makes you fight like little children. He showed you the gold and now you're all fighting over it. This man is a magician. He is using magic to befuddle our minds and cloud our senses. It was evident from the way you all looked at him. Especially Your Majesty was affected by his foul tricks of magic."

Johanna bit her lip. Arguing with him achieved nothing except cement the opinions of these men against her. Women shouldn't be leading countries. If she'd still been alive, Celine would have had to rule under a King's Council, too.

"I'm sorry, but I don't think it's in our interest that the church keep insisting on banning magic," Master Deim said. "We need magic in Saardam, even if only because everyone else uses it. It would be stupid not to teach any magic and not to attract people who know magic. When you keep banning magic, the people with magic will leave, and next time a magician like Alexandre comes, we'll be defenceless."

That was already happening. Loesie had left town two months ago. She'd said she needed to look after her grandmother's farm, but surely the increasing hostility towards magic had something to do with it.

The shepherd spread his hands. "It's not up to me to decide what is allowed or not. The *Book of Verses* says that magic is the work of the Lord of Fire and we should not get involved with it. It says in the Book of Truths: 'The man who attains his wealth through any other than the work of his hands shall be punished.'"

"That's not about magic. That's about stealing."

"Stealing and magic and other devious methods. It's all the same. Money makes good men forget their morals."

Johan Delacoeur snorted, "How easily did the church accept the king's money when he was offering?"

"The church never accepted coin," Shepherd Victor said.

"Small detail. They accepted the gifts that the king bought with money. That's the same in my language."

"The Triune teaches us to refuse the money that is given in return for favours and accept the gift given from the goodwill from a person's heart."

Master Deim said, "Oh, stop that nonsense argument. When you're poor and someone wants to give you something, you don't care if it's coin or goods or why it's given. It doesn't matter. The man pays for a service or he pays because he expects a favour."

And then other men from the King's Council joined in, debating whether accepting goods could still be considered bribery and whether the trader's generous offer of gold for the use of an office could be considered a bribe.

Some said it was and some said that if you held people to that standard, none of the powerful men passed muster, and then someone else said that maybe they needed different people in power. Within moments, they were all shouting at each other.

Johanna sat back in the chair. She really had to get out of here soon.

"Gentlemen." Johanna raised her voice. By the Triune, her head was swimming.

They fell quiet, glaring at each other.

"Bickering achieves nothing. I have no doubt all of you are well aware of the position of the city and the royal coffers. There is no money. Our citizens need money. The trader's money would solve many of our problems."

"It is tainted money!" the Shepherd Victor called out. "Tainted by magic. Bewitched. Designed to twist our minds."

"Rubbish!" Johan Delacoeur shouted back. "It's money. Gold coins. What's the magic in that?"

"Everything can have magic. Water, air, fire, wood, metals . . ."

"Gentlemen!" More forceful now. She rose.

"Tell me that metals can't have magic and I'll be quiet," the shepherd said, looking directly at Johanna. "Since Your Majesty seems to know all about magic." The expression on his face disturbed her. It was almost a madman's.

She would have said something, but her vision went blurry. She sat back hard on the chair, almost missing the seat.

Someone far off said, "Your Majesty?"

Johanna lifted her head, looking at Master Deim. His face was swimming in and out of focus.

"Are you all right? Do you need to lie down?"

Father was rushing towards her, too.

"I'm fine," Johanna said, but her heart was thudding. "Just a bit tired. It's very hot in this room."

"Let me take you to your private quarters." Master Deim offered his arm.

Johanna took it and he pulled her up. Her knees felt like they'd give out on her any moment.

"Are you all right?" His voice sounded concerned.

"Yes, I was just . . . it's too hot in this dress. We will continue with our normal meetings tomorrow," she continued to the assembled members of the King's Council, trying to school a business-like tone in her voice. To the mayor, she said, "See to it that the eastern trader gets shown possible accommodation for his business premises. I want to make sure that he doesn't go elsewhere while we decide."

Joris Decamp bowed. "I will, Your Majesty."

She let herself be guided to the hallway on Master Deim's arm. Father followed them. No one said anything until they were almost at the king's private quarters.

Then Master Deim said, "It's come to my attention that you don't appear to be as astute as you usually are. I've watched you today, and you're distracted, irritable and you keep touching your stomach. Is there something you're not telling us?"

His grey eyes were penetrating. There was no hiding it any longer. "Yes, I'm with child."

"My goodness. We must take steps to secure the kingdom."

"I've already done that." Father had insisted that she sign the scary documents about what should happen in case of her death in childbed.

"You must see a nurse regularly."

"I'm seeing Helena."

"Helena. You mean the southern whore?" He gave her a horrified look.

"She can't see customers anymore, with her face disfigured through the fire. I trust her. She has a lot of experience with women's matters."

"I bet she does." He didn't sound entirely convinced. "When can we expect a little prince or princess?"

"Helena says in late summer."

"That's not very far away." He ran a disturbed glance over her tightly-laced bodice that hid the increasingly obvious signs of her condition. "You should be resting."

"There is no time for resting."

She didn't *want* to rest, because her thoughts would drive her crazy if all she could do was sit and do embroidery and worry about what she would do if it was all too obvious that Roald was not the father of this child.

Because he was not, she grew ever more certain of that. Back in Burovia, in the farmhouse that belonged to the Guentherite Brotherhood, Kylian had bewitched and poisoned her and had in one act done what Roald had been unable to do in many.

Sometimes when she lay in bed, she could feel the child's magic flow through her lower body.

They entered the king's private sitting room, which faced the garden. Sunlight flowed in through the windows. There were a couple of books on the couch, but Roald was nowhere to be seen. He was probably in the garden catching frogs or drawing butterflies.

Johanna took the books off the couch and sat down. Father sat next to her.

"I hope you know what you're doing by suggesting that Li Han will have his office," Master Deim said.

"I don't, but I am familiar with the alternative because we've just lived through it. I figure that the eastern traders couldn't be any worse than Alexandre. For one, they're interested in money, not occupying us."

He nodded, but didn't look convinced. "I'm more worried about what the Baron will do when the eastern traders and their ship settle here."

"That's why I need to talk to you about an idea I have," Johanna said.

The men both looked at her.

Johanna began, "We have no money, but we have something everyone wants: our seaport."

"Yeah, well, that's what all this is about," Master Deim muttered.

"And the iron ships. If Li Han stays, we have those, too."

Master Deim nodded. "And the iron ships."

Johanna continued. "We can defend Saardam, but however successful we may be at protecting ourselves, Saardam will always remain a place that countries and royal families will fight over. Those who control the port decide who comes in and what they sell. At certain times, countries or families will get upset over this and they will send men like Alexandre."

Father raised an eyebrow as if curious where this was going.

"There are a great number people who want control over Saardam. They fight over magic or no magic, over this or that church, over ideals and beliefs and royal families. But at the end of the day, they would probably settle in favour of having a good relationship with those in control of the port. They will choose cooperation over a war. I'm also guessing that they will not wilfully harm—like set fire to—assets that are partially owned by their country."

Father gave her a sharp look. He seemed definitely both puzzled and intrigued now.

"I'm proposing that we form a cooperation of all those who have an interest in our port. I'm proposing that we send an official letter to all lands that have interest in Saardam. Places like Burovia, Gelre, Estland, all the areas along the rivers that are accessible through Saardam. Some will be friendly to us, some won't. We will tell them all the same thing: with their help, we will rebuild the harbour and provide services to transport goods inland and we'll have facilities where their traders can sell their goods so that their countries can prosper as well as ours."

"Yes, but we always had something like that. . . ." Father frowned.

"Then we tell them the next bit: Saardam has been destroyed and we need investment. We create investment allotments that they can buy, at a certain value each. In return for their money we give them favours, or if they can't use those favours because they never visit the city, we pay a return on their investment. We make up contracts for different levels of investment."

Father lifted his hand to his chin as he always did when he needed to think about something.

Master Deim said, "That's an interesting idea, but what does this have to do with the eastern trader?"

"Li Han? It's easy: he will be one of the biggest investors. He wants an office, so we give him an abandoned warehouse and he pays to fix it up. We get his business, and keep an eye on his iron ships. And because we don't want to be seen favouring just him, we offer the same service to others."

"I don't know that it will work," Father said.

"Trying to keep out certain groups of people certainly won't work," Johanna said. "The people who get banished, disowned or mistreated will band together and they will attack us when we seem weak, because they don't like Roald on the throne, or they don't like the church, or some other reason. That's what happened with Alexandre. King Leo and Baron Uti have an unlimited number of cousins they can send. All of them probably have magic. They're watching and waiting, making up the next excuse to invade us. Whether it's Li Han or the church or some other reason, it doesn't matter."

"Well . . ." Father said.

"I think it's a very good idea," Master Deim said. "The question is: will the stubborn King's Council allow you to carry it out? You need their support, unless Roald can make a convincing case for his support of the plan."

Johanna let her shoulders sag. The latter was never going to happen, and making the King's Council support her was an impossible task.

"I have to try." There was no alternative except continued wars and murder, including that of Roald, herself and her child.

WHEN FATHER and Master Deim were gone, Johanna asked the maid to tell Nellie to see her in the dressing room.

Johanna went down the corridor to that room. The damage from fires and subsequent flooding was extensive and had left marks almost everywhere: wallpaper was peeling, floor tiles had come up, dark stains marked the walls and all of the king's beautiful furniture had been stolen, leaving her and Roald with old things from the attic that were often also water-damaged.

There was no money to buy new furniture and no money to fix the damage. Most of the groundsmen were working for the palace in exchange for a roof over their heads and food in their bellies, but they received no pay.

The dressing room held only a row of wardrobes in which Johanna had collected all the clothes that she had salvaged from her own house and Queen Cygna's bedroom. Compared to Queen Cygna's dressing room, it was a very poorly appointed affair. Queen Cygna would have had at least a mirror, a dressing table with matching chair and a variety of items like clothes racks that seemed a luxury until you didn't have them, because you couldn't possibly leave a precious dress on the floor.

As it was, the room didn't even contain a small table for the tea and cakes that the maid had brought. The tray stood on the floor.

Nellie came in very soon after Johanna.

"You called for me?"

"Please let me out of this dress, Nellie."

Nellie went to Johanna's back, and her nimble fingers started unlacing the bodice. Johanna breathed in shallow breaths.

The dress came off. Nellie hung it over the wardrobe door with a rustle of velvet. It had belonged to Queen Cygna. It was pretty, but Johanna wouldn't be wearing it anymore.

Then the corset. Nellie started at the bottom and with each hook Nellie undid, a little shiver of relief crept up Johanna's spine. Just how tight it had been became evident when Nellie took the corset off. Johanna was overcome by a sudden wave of nausea when all her insides went back to their normal places.

"It *was* very tight. You were right, mistress. You are becoming so big. You must get the modiste to make you some special dresses."

"How about I'll do without the corset? That gives me a bit more room in the dress."

"Mistress Johanna, you can't possibly do that. What will people say?"

"No one will notice if you do the bodice up tightly. But it will be much more comfortable for me. I never used to wear corsets much when I lived with Father."

"That was different."

"Why?"

"To start off, you weren't a queen. You weren't a married woman. You were always far too much of a tomboy." Nellie counted off on her fingers.

Johanna sighed. "Yes, well, I have to go to church now and I'm not wearing the corset."

"But—"

"I'm not wearing it."

Nellie sighed. "Well, if you insist. But you should really get the modiste—"

"That's not going to help me for tonight."

"No, but if you would just stop being so stubborn, it might

help you tomorrow. You have the little one to consider. How would you like being so squished up in there that your mother can't even breathe properly, let alone eat? For what reason?"

"You don't understand, Nellie."

"I understand well enough. If you don't look after yourself, you'll regret it later. You're going to be a mother. You should take things easy. You're going to grow and grow, until you won't be able to hide it anymore. Why hide it anyway? The people are going to love it, because they're sick of bad news."

Nellie was probably right. The people of Saardam would love it. There had not been a royal birth since Celine, despite the Queen's young age—she had been seventeen when Celine was born.

The problem was not the people. It was the King's Council.

"Which dress do you want to wear to church, Mistress Johanna?"

Johanna cut through the fog of her thoughts. "The brown one, thanks, Nellie."

Nellie helped her step into the dress and pulled the heavy material over her underdress. She then started doing up the lace at the back of the bodice.

Johanna gasped. "Not so tight at the top." Her breasts were swollen and very tender.

"I know." Nellie worked her way down, pulling the lace as she went.

"It's too tight," Johanna said.

"I can't make it any looser. The lace isn't long enough."

"Then make the lace longer. Just don't make it so tight around here." Johanna pulled the bodice down over her stomach. It pushed the bump of her stomach flat. Johanna ran her hand over the front of the dress. It was very, very tight.

"Pardon me for saying this, but you're very stubborn," Nellie said. "Look at yourself in the mirror. Doesn't that look like a woman with child? How long do you think you can hide it?"

Johanna looked. Everything about her dress looked tight. Her bosom was about to burst out, the mid-section bunched up in the area between her bosom and her stomach.

Without the corset, she looked like a poorly-made sausage.

Yet she didn't want to announce her condition officially. As soon as she did, the King's Council would insist that she retire from all her duties. She did not think that Father and Master Deim alone could prevent the council making any stupid decisions. They certainly would not be able to carry out her plan for a cooperative of investors without her. They might get one or two nobles to support them, but they simply didn't have the numbers.

"Just do it up as much as you can. I'll wear a cape over the top," she said to Nellie.

"You should celebrate your condition. Otherwise you will have a child one day and people won't have known about your condition and they will wonder if the child is even yours."

"As soon as I let people know, the powerful men will want to push me aside because they will say that I can't do my duties."

"But Mistress Johanna, you are already doing your duty. You are going to give birth to the heir to the throne."

She met Nellie's eyes. There was not a shred of humour in them.

"You should be proud. You'll have seen already that it's not an easy task."

Johanna mumbled some half-hearted comment. Memories of having to hurry out of meetings with some lame excuse because she needed to vomit were not far from her mind.

But a fear grew inside her, along with the parasite child that kept taking more of her energy.

She'd taken a peek at the sparse references to childbirth in Roald's books, and had not liked what she saw. Did a midwife really ask the woman to take off all her clothes? Did the woman really lie on a bare bed with her legs spread so that everyone could see her private parts? Was there really so much blood? Apparently other women, ones who were not supposed to be the queen, invited their friends and sisters along to give support, but, having no sisters, Johanna was too ashamed to say that she had never attended a birth. Now she was afraid to ask, afraid that it would make her more scared.

That dreadful fear of shaming herself, the fear of blood and the fear of pain was gradually taking over from the fear that someone would know straight away that the child wasn't Roald's. Because they wouldn't, at least not at the beginning. All newborns were pink, hairless worms. And ugly.

Why, again, had she wanted this?

Nellie managed to lengthen the lacing and that made the dress less tight. She also took the cape out of the wardrobe. "People are still going to ask questions if you always wear it."

"I will announce it, Nellie. Don't worry about it."

Nellie draped the cloak over Johanna's shoulders. "Normally, that happens when the child has quickened."

"Yes. I'll announce it then." But she had felt the first movement two weeks ago. "Are you finished with me?"

"You are so impatient, mistress. Church isn't going anywhere. Let me look at your hair first."

Finally, after Nellie had re-pinned Johanna's hair, she left the room. Whoa. That dress still felt tight. Tomorrow, she promised herself. Tomorrow she was going to ask a modiste to make new clothes for her.

She collected two royal guards in the hallway.

"Time to go to church, Your Majesty?"

"Indeed." Their cheerful smiles made her feel tired.

The guards accompanied her across the forecourt to the coaches. Her personal driver waited there, while the stable boy brought out the two white horses. Johanna would rather have walked, but she had found that a certain level of ceremony was expected from the royal family, and as such royals did not walk through town.

It was annoying and the church was only a short distance away, and Johanna would have walked to prove that she could, and to feel that independence that she had forgotten to enjoy when she was just Johanna Brouwer.

But today she was happy to ride, because that dress was very tight and her stomach kept hardening.

The coach took off through the palace gates.

On the main market square, a temporary church had risen from the muddy building site where Alexandre had planned his monstrosity of a building for the Belaman Church.

The trenches that had been dug by prisoners for the foundations of the building had been filled up with soil. The shepherd had put up a wooden building over the top. It was only temporary while plans for a new church were made, but the new church building should be plain, the shepherd had said, and it should be built around the statue of the Triune that the king had ordered made and that the bandits had removed from the palace garden and had been dredged from the bottom of the harbour.

As Johanna alighted from the coach, churchgoers on the steps into the entrance watched and cheered. The wind whipped up and blew strands of hair into Johanna's face.

Even if she had no wind magic, the feel of it on the air was strong.

The tree that trapped Alexandre stood downwind in the market, its twisted branches reaching for the sky. Earlier this week, it had sprouted leaves, but they had grown twisted and mottled with white from the anger of the spirit trapped inside. Every time Johanna walked past, she felt a chill, a voice calling out to her to touch the tree and read its terrible history. And every time she had to keep telling herself not to give in to its call.

Johanna went up the wooden steps of the church, flanked by the guards. As she took the top step, she felt something rip in the left side of her dress.

By the Triune, what was that?

With all these people around, she couldn't feel up there to check, but it felt like part of the bodice had come loose, because cool air stroked her skin where it shouldn't. She pulled the cloak closer around her. Something had also happened to her skirt, because the hem dragged over the ground. It got in the way of her feet and she had to be careful not to step on it.

The pews were full of people: the merchants, the workers, the mothers, the common people. A murmur of voices preceded Johanna down the aisle.

"Glad to see you, Your Majesty."

"You're looking well, Your Majesty."

"Good evening, Your Majesty."

People bowed and curtsied. Johanna walked down the aisle,

clamping her left elbow to her side in case the skirt of her dress decided to come undone even more.

She arrived at the front of the church, where a row of pews was left unoccupied especially for her. Johanna sat down, flanked by the guards.

She pulled the sides of the cloak over her knees and reached up her left side under the cloak. The entire seam on that side of the dress had come apart.

This was so embarrassing. How could she make it back out of here? She could already hear Nellie berate her, *You should have a modiste make special clothes for you*. Yes, she should, but she hated standing still with people draping fabric over her and putting pins in. But there was no other option, unless she planned on going naked until the child was born.

A bell rang. People stopped talking and turned to the front of the church. The Shepherd entered from behind the altar. He wore a cream-coloured silk robe with plain red lapels. His head was bare, with his blond hair tied at the back of his head. The only piece of jewellery he wore was a gold chain with the triangle of the Triune on it. He raised his hands. He began the service with the usual words.

"Citizens of the fairest city in all the known worlds. Let us come together and celebrate the love, the fairness and the judgement of the Triune. Let us pray."

He spoke of destruction and rebuilding, of looking after the weaker people in the community. When he worked for Father, Johanna had never known that the timid accountant was such a mesmerising speaker. People listened, they hung onto every word, repeated soundlessly what he said.

His words moved from looking after each other to defending the city against threats.

"These people, they came to our town, tried to stamp out our church and our people with their filthy magic." He balled his fist. "We stood up against them. We drove them out of our town. When we stand together, we stand strong. When we stand together, the Triune will guide us. Together we will drive the magicians from the city. We pray to the Holy Father, the spirit and the ghost."

People shuffled onto their knees, hands clasped in prayer. Johanna should get on her knees, too, but she was scared that the dress would rip further, and it had to hold out for a little longer because she did want to speak to the Shepherd after the service. She didn't kneel, and found him watching her not just while she was not kneeling but throughout the rest of the service.

When the shepherd had finished preaching, people waited for Johanna to leave the church, but she told her guards that she would be staying back, so people started leaving. Johanna rose, carefully holding the ripped side of the dress by pressing her elbow to her side while keeping it hidden under the cloak with the other.

The shepherd bowed to her. He'd been preaching so vigorously that drops of sweat pearled on his forehead. "Your Majesty, I am happy to have deserved the honour that you pay me a visit."

Johanna glanced at her guards who were directing people away from where she stood. "Can we talk like old times?" Like when he was Master Willems and worked in Father's office.

He flicked his eyebrows in his oh-so-serious face. His face had aged noticeably since he had taken on the role of shepherd.

"I need your help. The whole city needs your help."

"I am forever in the service of my flock and my city and my queen." He bowed. "Tell me what you desire from your humble servant."

She thought she'd asked him to speak normally, as in old times. Then again, he had always been distant to her. With his new position, his aloofness had only increased. "I know that and thank you. I need your support for the decisions made by me and the King's Council."

He gave her a sharp look. He was part of the council after all. "I will support anything that does not go against the teachings of the Triune."

"Going against the Triune includes denying the eastern trader the building that he would be paying for? Does the Triune teach against that?"

Another sharp look. "The Triune teaches us to stand against the menace of magic—"

"There is no evidence that the eastern traders have any magic."

"That ship of theirs! Is that not evidence? Is it not enough that the people who have tried to build these machines are all dead? Isn't it obvious that some magic ingredient is needed to make it work?"

"We know how the machines work. They boil water in a vat—"

"Only to have the vat explode and kill everyone. All those people insisted that the writings of the heretic whose name I will not mention were simple instructions for building the machine. But it is more than obvious: we are missing an ingredient of magic."

"Then we find someone with this magic if that is indeed true. What Master Deim said is true: we cannot stand against evil magic unless we have magical help. The Red Baron and his necromancer son—"

"Aiyyeee! Do not say words like that in this building! Triune have mercy." He clamped his hands together and looked at the ceiling in prayer.

A bit shaken, Johanna continued, "The Red Baron and his son are waiting to pounce on us. They have control over . . . magical beings. The Belaman Church—"

"Aiyeee! Do not speak the name of that evil institution!"

Johanna continued forcefully, "The Most Holy Father has banished the Church of the Triune from his institution. He now considers us an enemy organisation. His church allows magic. They foster magic. They *teach* magic!"

He had clamped his hands over his ears.

"Listen to me. You can't make magic go away by ignoring it."

"Do not speak in here about the work of the Lord of Fire."

"Not all magic is evil. You should know that. It is about how you use it. Magic exists. People *will* use it. We must make sure it's used for our good—"

He turned his face to the ceiling and chanted, "There is nothing good in the deeds of the Lord of Fire. There is no salvation in his teachings. There is no redemption unless we renounce it. The strangers will unleash their fire dragons as soon as we show any sign of weakness. Do not speak to me of this terrible thing that brings us evil. Do not think of it."

Spit flew from his mouth. His voice grew ever shriller. He clamped his hands in front of his chest.

Whoa. Johanna backed away. What had gotten into him?

He sprinted across to the statue of the Triune, that same one they'd fished out of the harbour. It still showed gouges where it had been dragged and carried stain from the remains of algae and barnacle encrustations. He dropped to his knees on the wooden kneeling bench in front of the statue, wailing that the Triune should protect him from evil magic and that he would do three laps on the church crawling on his knees to cleanse the holy building of the evil that had been invoked today. His shrill voice echoed in the cavernous space.

CHAPTER 4

JOHANNA WAS SO taken aback by his outburst that she didn't even think of berating him for having spoken to her like that. When he was still the accountant Master Willems, he had always ruled in Father's office. He was a couple of years older than she was, so his authority seemed natural to her, never mind that she now ruled him. This whole concept of being queen unnerved her. It made her angry, too. She spent most of her life kicking against habits and "proper" behaviour, only to succumb to pressure by others when it really mattered. Even when she was younger, she might have protested, but in the end she did what Father wanted. She went and had a dress made, she went to the ball, she danced with the prince.

And now look at her.

She was a pawn of those men with their powerful friends and their money.

A *real* queen would order those nobles to do what she wanted. A *real* queen would never tolerate this silly King's Council in the first place.

A *real* queen would yell at her guards to give the shepherd ten lashes for saying what he had said to her. She shuddered at that thought.

She left the shepherd sitting on his knees and praying aloud, glad that he had never come to Duke Lothar's castle, Florisheim or the Guentherite farms where real magic and ghosts lurked in every bush. He would have been beside himself.

She made her way down the aisle of the church, where the church boys were already blowing out candles now that the service was over and most people had left.

The boys appeared quite calm under their master's outburst.

One of the boys bowed at her. "Don't worry, Your Majesty, he will calm down."

"Does he scream like that often?" Did her face show her unease so much that even a boy could see it?

"He does, Your Majesty." He nodded. He was a blond lad, very skinny. "He drives off the bad spirits that threaten all of us and lead us into temptation." He curtsied. "Your Majesty. You are second only to the Triune itself. We are your servants."

Johanna had no idea what to say to that, so she made a lame smile, stood back and watched him snuff the candles.

They were good candles, too, made from wax, not tallow, and they didn't smoke. Like everything else in town, wax was scarce and the candles had probably cost a small fortune. Obviously *someone* in the church had money. More money than the palace.

Second to the Triune or not, Johanna was glad for the darkness. When she continued down the aisle, she trod on the hem of her dress, and the fabric she was holding in place slipped from her fingers. Something said *crack* and cool air flowed over her exposed side through her thin underdress.

She managed to scramble into the coach, but by the Triune, she would have to stop somewhere to fix the damage because there was no way that she could walk like this from the forecourt up the stairs, through the foyer in the palace—where there were always lots of people—and down the corridor and past the guards who stood there. There were always lots of people about and everyone was always watching her, especially the maids.

Where could she check the damage and make a quick fix?

Father's office.

As fas as she remembered, some of her knitting work was still in a basket in the corner of the reception room. It would be very dusty and might smell of fire, but there should be a needle in the basket, even if it was a fat and blunt one, and maybe she could thread some wool through the edges of the split seam so that she could at least walk without attracting too much attention.

She notified her guard that she needed to pick something up at the office and he spoke to the driver.

The coach set off through the dark streets. The horses' hooves went clack-clack on the cobblestones. Most of this part of town had been damaged by the fires, but there were signs that the families who had some financial reserves were starting to rebuild. Ruins had been cleared, materials delivered, foundation work started. Workmen had broken down the remains of burnt walls, chipped the stones clean of mortar and stacked them neatly for reuse.

In fact there were so many piles of building material in the street that the driver had to go slow to pick a path between them.

Occasional pedestrians shouted greetings. "Good evening, Your Majesty!"

The coach with the white horses had become synonymous with the queen under Queen Cygna.

Johanna waved at the window, although it was probably too dark for people on the street to see her in the cabin.

The coach stopped at the quay, in front of the steps to Father's office. The guard opened the door.

"Do you want me to go first and light the lamp?" he asked.

"Yes, please."

He went inside and lit the oil light on the shelf in the hallway with the flame from storm light that hung from the coach's driver seat.

Johanna managed to clamber out of the coach and to the door without tripping over her loose skirt. She scrambled inside and pushed the door shut.

She took off her cloak to investigate the damage.

By the Triune, the whole side of the dress had come apart. It was an old garment, but there was no reason it should have happened other than that it had been much too tight and it had not been up to the task normally reserved for a corset. With the split seam, part of the skirt had come loose, too, and it was those folds hanging down that caused the dress to drag over the floor.

But did she have anything here that she could use to fix it? She carried the lamp into the reception room, but couldn't see the basket with her abandoned knitting things. She went into Father's office at the front, where she found it on top of the bookcase. It was indeed dusty, but there was a needle and some wool. The wool was thick and not suited to sewing, and it was hard to push the fat needle through the fabric and pull the wool through without breaking it. Johanna only managed a few coarse stitches. They were so ugly they would give Nellie nightmares, but at least they stopped the dress unravelling further. It would have to do. By now, her fingers were so cold she could barely hold the needle. It had been a long time since anyone had lit the fire in this room.

Father did not use the office very much anymore. He'd taken up a room in the palace to conduct his business. He still owned only the *Lady Sara*, and it never ventured far from port. These days, it made a lot of small trips around the local farms.

Through the cobwebbed window, she could see the coach waiting in the pale moonlight.

Behind it, Li Han's ship lay dark and menacing in front of what remained of the warehouses. A faint light burned on the deck, but otherwise there was no sign of the many crewmembers who were on board. The ship had no mast, but a fat chimney from which smoke belched when it moved.

The dark shape next to it was the *Lady Sara*—wait, what was a person doing on the deck of the *Lady Sara* in the dark? With a torch, no less?

Johanna flung the basket back onto the top of the bookcase, blew out the lamp and went outside.

The coachman and guard were waiting for her.

"Let's go home, Your Majesty. It's going to be very cold tonight."

"In a moment. Can you go and check out what a man is doing on the deck of the *Lady Sara*?" she asked the guard.

"Certainly, Your Majesty." He bowed and walked down the quay. His footsteps echoed in the stillness.

The glow of torchlight on the deck had disappeared. Johanna climbed on the coach driver's seat, but couldn't see it from there, either.

Had the person extinguished the torch when he heard people? Maybe he had gone down in the hold, whatever he was doing there. He was without a home and had nowhere else to sleep? He wanted to steal things? He wanted to set fire to the ship?

She hadn't heard Father speak of any unloading activities today. If it ever happened that the ship needed to be unloaded at night, there would be a lot more people.

Johanna waited, her heart thudding.

Her breath steamed in the glow from the light that hung on the front of the coach. One of the horses snorted.

The guard's voice rang out over the quay, followed by the sound of someone running, a thud as the guard jumped onto the wooden deck and then a big splash.

By the Triune!

Johanna climbed down from the driver's seat and made her way along the waterfront to where the *Lady Sara* lay as fast as she could without running.

"What was that?" she called to the guard on the ship's deck. At least she hoped that the man standing on the deck carrying a burning torch was the guard.

"Seems like an intruder, Your Majesty. Found this torch in the hold."

By the Triune, had this man tried to set fire to the ship? "What was he doing there?"

"No idea."

"Is there any damage?"

"If there is, it's not major. We'll have to wait until daytime to be sure." He jumped from the deck onto the quay.

By now, another person was coming down the quay from the other direction, carrying a light on a stick that swung to and fro with his footsteps.

An accented voice said, "Is there a problem?"

Li Fai.

He carried a kind of storm light, with a frame that held

finely-woven silk that glowed in the light of the flame inside. The orange glow barely lit his face with those strange and fascinating dark eyes. He bowed. "We meet again, Your Majesty."

"There was an intruder on my father's ship," Johanna said.

"Our guards said they heard a shout and a splash. That was why I came to look what is going on."

"The intruder fell or jumped in the water."

"Can he swim?"

"I have no idea. I don't know who it was."

They peered wordlessly into the inky blackness of the harbour. A breeze whipped the surface into little waves that lapped at the quayside. If there was someone swimming in the harbour or climbing out further down the quay, the sounds would be impossible to hear above the singing of the wind in the ropes and the slapping of rigging against the masts.

"I did not see or hear anything," Li Fai said. "But the ducks did. They were nervous. They are never nervous for nothing. That's why we keep them on deck. As soon as they hear something, they go quack-quack-quack—"

He did such a good imitation of duck quacks that Johanna couldn't help laughing. "You have ducks aboard the ship?"

"Ducks, pigeons, parrots and a cat."

She restrained a chuckle. It was like an animal park.

"If you don't believe me, I can show you. But not now. My parents have gone to sleep."

"Sorry. I wasn't laughing because I didn't believe you, I was laughing because of the duck noise you made."

He smiled. "I spend a lot of time on deck with the ducks. I learn their language." His eyes twinkled with mirth.

"You mean it's boring out at sea?"

"It's never boring when you have ducks."

What an odd conversation. She searched his face for signs that he was having her on, but only succeeded in attracting his dark-eyed, penetrating, intense gaze. By the Triune, what did he mean by looking at her like that? Her cheeks glowed.

"I'm serious about a visit to the ship," he said. "I understand that people are afraid of it. We are happy to show our friends. But not now. At daytime."

"I would love to, thank you." She didn't think anyone, not even Father, had been invited aboard the metal ships.

"I will send an official invitation."

"I'll look forward to it."

He bowed. "Tonight, I will ask our guards to look out for thieves and trespassers."

"Thank you."

Li Fai returned to the ship with his swinging lantern. Swish, swish, swish down the quay and swish, swish, swish up the gangplank.

Johanna waited around for a bit more while the guard walked along the quay looking for signs that anyone had climbed out of the water, but he found nothing.

The cold was starting to bite, and Johanna returned to the coach. When she got back to the palace, she would send a few guards down here to help keep an eye on the quayside and the ships.

The *Lady Sara* was a precious relic of the glory of Saardam before the fires. They'd lost the *Lady Davida* and the queue at the shipyards for new ships was long.

The precious few other ships in the harbour were the sad remains of Saardam's large trading fleet. They had lost so much and could not afford to lose any more ships.

CHAPTER 5

I T WAS ALREADY quite late, and Johanna managed to slip into the palace unnoticed by anyone except the guards. She even managed to avoid Nellie and her inevitable *I told you so* speech about her ripped dress. Likely, Nellie had already gone to bed. There was always so much work to be done, and not enough people to do it. Poor Nellie.

Johanna tiptoed into the royal bedroom.

The bedroom, where no one except she and Roald and Nellie came, was one of the poorly-appointed rooms in the private wing of the palace. It contained a large bed, a dressing table with a cracked mirror and two chairs and little else.

At least it was warm.

The fire burned low in the hearth. The heavy curtains that covered the window and a door onto the balcony resembled a set of ugly rags. Nellie had washed them when they first moved in, but some of the dark mould stains would probably never come out.

Roald lay on his stomach on the carpet in front of the dying fire and was engrossed in drawing something with his brushes on a sheet of paper. He had placed an oil lamp on the floor next to him—Johanna forgot how many times she had reminded him not to do this—and a box of brushes and paint, and a bowl with water to rinse the brushes stood to his other side. Johanna came up behind him until she could see what he was drawing: a ladybeetle.

The subject of the drawing lay on a gold-rimmed royal breakfast plate and was quite dead. Its legs stuck out at a strange angle that didn't allow it to sit belly down, but Roald's drawing showed it crawling on a leaf in exquisite detail.

"I like it," she said. "It looks like it could just walk off the page." Getting no reaction from him, she walked around him and sat down on the rug facing him.

He kept drawing.

"It's very pretty," she said again.

Roald never responded to compliments, so she continued, "The eastern traders came to visit today. They want to set up an office at the quayside."

Now he looked up. The glow from the fire made his grey eyes look golden. "I must ask Li Han to bring me some exotic creatures from his travels."

If she needed a confirmation that Roald was not stupid, this was it. Not only had he learned the eastern trader's name, he had listened to how it was pronounced. She must find out when and where the two had met.

"Roald, listen." Johanna shuffled closer to him. "You know that day when Alexandre still ruled and we led the procession to the markets where people were going to be burned at the stake, and where we raised all our wooden rakes and shovel handles and they grew into a tree that captured Alexandre and locked him in? And when the nobles who had supported him fled but their ship caught fire and they had to swim to safety?"

He gave her a blank look.

"Well, those nobles survived and some of them are still around." Although quite a few had left the city. "They're claiming that Li Han burned their ship with magic, and they're claiming that he has fire dragons and that they live inside the belly of his ship—"

"I already told them that it's a machine that works on the pressure of steam locked in a vat."

"I know you did." He had told, too, a big group of people who had been waiting in the palace forecourt back before they got the soup kitchens going. Those people were all homeless and hungry and had merely stared at him. They didn't care. They didn't believe a word he said.

"See? I did tell them." He nodded. For him, the matter of belief did not come into the question. Things were or they were not.

"Those nobles who survived don't like Li Han's presence in the city," she continued.

"But he can teach us a lot."

"Yes, he can, and that's why it's important that people like Johan Delacoeur don't get to control what goes on in the city. He was made *regent*, Roald, and I will certainly not be able to perform any duties for a while. You must come to our meetings, so that you can continue our quest to be a truly independent country. Father will help you."

He looked confused. "You can't preform your duties? What is wrong with you?"

"I'm having a child, the heir to the throne." She cringed while saying that. She couldn't bring herself to saying *your child*, while she very much doubted that the child was Roald's.

A frown. "You look healthy enough to me. Why can't you keep going to the meetings?"

"Because I'm with child. It's not appropriate." And she cringed saying that, too, because it went against everything she had stood for in her life. "The nobles will say that it's not appropriate for the queen to perform duties while she is with child. Roald, I'm not going to have any arguments against them and I'm not going to be able to hide it for much longer. You must come to the meetings. You must show them who is the king."

He stared at her. "I don't like meetings, and those men don't like me."

Johanna spread her hands in frustration. "This is not about liking you. If you're not there when I can't be present, they'll decide things that you like even less. These meetings are very important for the future of Saardam. I want to write to every country and company that uses our seaport to ask if they want to invest in rebuilding the harbour. We need the money, and if all those countries have invested, they won't attack us anymore and risk their projects."

He blinked at her. "That's a good idea. You should do that."

"But I need your help!"

"Those men won't listen to me."

"You're the king! You can tell them what to do."

He gave her a blank look.

"Roald, I need you to come to the council and tell them that you think my idea is good and that they should listen to me."

But as she already knew, it was pointless getting angry at him about not doing his duties. He just did not understand. King Nicholaos and Queen Cygna had bypassed him and appointed his younger sister as successor to the throne. Every day, Johanna was reminded of how sensible a decision that had been. Roald was present in person, but he was never really responsive to what went on around him, unless it concerned beetles or frogs, or, heaven forbid, Rinius.

She stared at the exquisite drawing he had made. He would have made an excellent monk or a student of the natural arts. He would have been good at many things, but not at being a king.

"Let's go to sleep."

"Yes." Roald gathered his paper and brushes and dumped them in the box. "I want to look at you tonight."

Johanna cringed.

He hadn't asked for a while, and she had been quiet about it. Being prodded in sensitive places was honestly something she could do without right now. It made her belly tense up. Sometimes it hurt. Yet she didn't dare say no.

Johanna undressed, first her poor old ripped overdress. She placed it on the chair with a feeling of melancholy, doubting that Nellie would be able to fix the damage. Then she pulled her underdress over her head. She watched herself in the dressing mirror as a pale form in the darkness. Her stomach was very obviously swollen, and anyone who saw her would have no doubt about her condition. She ran her hand over the firm bump and lifted her heavy breasts. They, too, felt very solid and tender.

Roald came to stand behind her, reaching for her belly from behind. His hands were always cold.

"You can feel the child move," she said. She placed his hand on her skin.

They stood like that for a while. Roald's beard tickled her shoulder.

Then he called out, "Yes!" He laughed. "I can feel it!"

He pulled her to the bed, where she took off his coat and his shirt and undershirt. He was not half as pale as she was, which didn't surprise her, given that he spent so much time in the sun in the reed beds with his sleeves and trousers rolled up. He was still very thin and his chest hairless.

She undid his belt and pulled off his trousers while he lay on his back.

They went through the usual routine. She sat on top and impaled herself on him. It was very sensitive, and to be honest, not very pleasant. He was bumping and tossing her around and she tried to keep in a position where his thrusts inside her would not hit any painful spots, never mind finding pleasure herself. That hadn't happened for a long time, and trying to explain to him what she wanted was a waste of time.

The whole thing was made less pleasant because for some reason he'd started taking much longer to reach his release.

Johanna worried about that. At the quayside, she sometimes heard the crude jokes men made about the prowess—or lack of it—of the powerful noblemen. The inability of older men to "do the job" was apparently a given.

Had that already started?

Was it something she had done or that she had allowed him to eat? Did it mean that he would never father a child?

Afterwards, when Roald had gone to sleep, Johanna lay awake, staring towards the ceiling hidden by darkness. As usual at this time of the day, the child cavorted around inside her belly. It was growing. She dreaded what the king's council would say when she turned up for a meeting when her condition was obvious.

They'd be offended. They'd tell her that they couldn't possibly have a meeting like this.

Johan Delacoeur would rule, and her idea to get the

surrounding countries to invest in the harbour would never happen.

He'd tell Li Han that he couldn't have the office.

The Baron would continue to try to get his hands on the city. Or the Belaman Church.

Li Han would leave, and Johanna would never set foot aboard the iron ship. Li Fai would leave, too, and take his ships to Anglia.

CHAPTER 6

I T WAS NOT a good morning. Johanna woke up feeling ill and things did not get better from there.

She had been told that the sickness only happened at the time that one could not yet tell that a woman was with child, but her body clearly had different ideas.

The tea she'd had for breakfast made a reappearance, and then she was hungry and ate some bread, but that didn't go down too well either.

Feeling listless and ill, she retired to the couch in the living room where Father came to keep her company.

As usual, he had needed to think about an idea before he formed an opinion on it, but his opinion had formed in favour of Johanna's plan. In fact, he'd already drafted a letter to be sent to each of the royal houses in the area, and he had come to show it to her.

He had plans, too. "King Leopold of Burovia has a lot of money and is not averse to trying new things as long as we can show clearly what his benefit will be, so I will draw up a table of returns on investment based on estimates of warehouse hire and mooring fees. I expect to be able to give a positive return after about five years. And that isn't counting any tariffs and trade levies of goods sold. We might even get this grumpypot of a Baron Uti to invest in the seaport because, without it, he'll have to import through Lurezia and he's not a friend of the Lurezian court. I very much doubt that, given the choice, he wants to fight over access to Saardam. Most wise rulers try to limit the number of wars they get involved in. Say what you want about Baron Uti, but he's not dumb."

It was worth trying to get him to invest, Johanna thought, although fighting seemed very much in Baron Uti's arsenal. If King Leopold would commit to making an investment, that would forge a bond between him and the Carmine House. In turn, Baron Uti would not attack something that his cousin King Leopold was involved in.

Father said, "The support of Estland is pretty much a given because of strong ties between the royal houses, and I don't think Lurezia would hesitate to invest either. They are not averse to trying new things, especially if they don't have to send people."

Ultimately, all of the landlocked countries in the east depended on imported goods coming in through Saardam.

Trying to make an attractive proposition to the foreign companies and countries that hoped to sell through the port was a bit trickier. Phoenicia and Anglia could easily go elsewhere, so it was all about premium customers for their produce, about quick unloading and fair quay tariffs.

Father understood what made the captains happy. He proposed preferential unloading treatment and warehouse space in return for the investment.

"For example, Anglia and Phoenicia could each own a warehouse. They would pay for rebuilding that warehouse and in return they would never have to pay storage fees."

That was a scary prospect. Storage fees had always an important source of income for the city.

The idea of foreign countries owning buildings in Saardam was both exhilarating and scary. The name Anglia struck fear in the hearts of many Saarlanders. In the past, conflicts on land had been fought with places in the east. Baron Uti usually had something to do with it. The conflicts at sea were usually fought with King William of Anglia, who had been in power for longer than

Johanna had been alive. He had a vastly superior seafaring fleet and was in the process of mapping out all the unknown lands.

If Li Fai made his office in Saardam, and if he was tied to Saardam because he owned the warehouse, the people of the city would eventually have iron ships. If Li Fai was driven out of Saardam by ignorant men "because he had dragon magic," then he might well go to Anglia and would ply his dragon magic there. If that happened, King William might well be the next ruler trying to overthrow the weak royal family of Saardam with the help of eastern magic.

Johanna and Father agreed on many things, and neither of them needed to mention the looming uncertainty hanging over this plan: without Roald's support or understanding, how were they going to get this plan past the King's Council?

While Johanna and Father sat talking, the palace guard she had sent to check the *Lady Sara* came in.

"We can't see much damage to your ship, Your Majesty," he said. "The intruder had a torch but most likely he used it for light."

"Was anything stolen?"

"Not that we can tell. Most valuable items were removed from the hold when the ship first returned." Carpenters had removed the temporary stairs and the old furniture that made up the makeshift room where Johanna and Roald had lived when the ship had lain moored at the riverbank in Florisheim. The *Lady Sara* had gone back from being a houseboat to a river sloop.

She asked, "Was the intruder perhaps a pauper, looking for a dry place to sleep?"

"We can only guess until we can question the man."

And that required knowing who he was and where he was.

Father said, "Look, if there is no damage to the ship, it's not worth worrying about. For all we know, it was a sailor looking at the sky longing for his sweetheart in some faraway town and then getting nervous when he was disturbed in a place he shouldn't have been."

Johanna's sickness subsided after some sweet cakes and tea. Father said he was going to see the mayor to talk about their plan. Apart from Master Deim, he was the person most likely to support it.

Johanna went in search of Roald.

She found Nellie instead, setting the table for the midday meal.

"Whatever did you do to your brown dress, Mistress Johanna?"

"It split while I was at church." That seemed such a long time ago and seemed such a trivial thing to worry about.

"I told you that it was too tight. It is getting really scandalous. I hope you don't mind, but I've asked the modiste to come. She will be here this afternoon. I apologise for the very short notice, but I've waited long enough. I will not have the dresses fall off you while you're in town."

Johanna sighed and let her shoulders slump. Nellie was right, of course.

"Do go and see her," Nellie said, her voice stern.

Johanna nodded.

She went to the room she used as her office, sat down and with a heavy heart wrote an announcement for the town crier.

To the citizens of Saarland: King Roald and Queen Johanna Carmine de Lacoeur van Leeuwen Brouwer announce the impending birth of the first heir to the throne, expected at the end of August. The Queen intends to keep fulfilling her duties to the people of Saardam.

There.

She debated adding *for as long as possible*, but that would be dishonest. She had no intention of giving up her position, ever.

She cringed when she rolled up the parchment and sealed the paper. There was no avoiding it.

Once the modiste came in, the news would spread like wildfire anyway. There was a King's Council meeting tomorrow. It was best that she announce the news rather than that the men hear it in some other way.

Johanna gave the roll of parchment to the guard station in the foyer and went to the dining room.

Roald had come in for the midday meal. He sat at his usual spot at the head of the table. His cheeks were red from sunburn and his jacket was probably still in the garden.

Johanna sat opposite him. "Did you see anything special in the garden today?"

"Lots of frog eggs. There are so many frogs! They're very hard to catch."

But clearly that hadn't stopped him trying. "You have duckweed in your hair."

"Oh?" He ruffled his hair, making it more dishevelled than it already was. The duckweed fell onto his plate. He blew it onto the white tablecloth while the maid came to ladle soup into the plates.

"I want to get ducks for the garden. They eat grass so the gardener won't have to cut the grass anymore."

"But they poo everywhere."

"That's good for the grass. I want to have chickens, too, and I have to grow carrots. They are good for your skin."

Johanna had intended to raise the subject of the foreign investment with him once again. He would have to sign any plan that she and Father made, and she wanted him to understand. He'd said he liked the idea. Why couldn't he just sign the document and let her do whatever needed to be done? But sadly, that was not how Roald worked. Once he got an idea into his head, he was unlikely to listen to anything else.

And frankly, his enthusiasm for the garden was infectious.

A vegetable garden would be nice, Johanna agreed. The queen's rose garden had always struck her as frivolous. Roald could grow carrots, and at harvest, she'd ask the cook to make a lot of carrot and potato soup and hand it out to the poorest citizens. He could grow cabbages, too and they could make cabbage pots and hand those out to poor people in winter.

Roald said he knew exactly how to make cabbage pots, how much vinegar and how much water to use. She suspected he had learned this at the Guentherite farm.

As usual, talking to Roald never failed to take her mind off problems.

Sitting here, with the sunlight streaming in through the window, with a view into the garden that was bright green from spring growth, it was easy to forget how precarious the Carmine House's position was.

It was such a nice day that Johanna followed Roald into the garden after the meal. He chatted endlessly about where he wanted to keep the ducks and the chickens, and where he wanted the carrot bed.

"And we can grow beans over there. No parsnips. I don't like parsnips. I'm the king. If I don't like parsnips, I can just not grow them."

Johanna eyed the empty middle of the old garden. "What shall we do with the fountain?"

When the bandits had removed the statue of the Triune that used to stand on a pedestal in the middle of the pond, they had broken the basin. The water was all gone, and the bottom was covered in dead leaves. Weeds grew in the cracks.

"We can fix it. We can keep fish, and the ducks will have somewhere to swim!"

"What about the statue?"

He frowned.

"The statue of the Triune that used to sit in the middle."

"The church can keep it."

"We can have a new one made."

"No. I don't like the faces on those heads."

The shepherd at church often asked her when the king would come to the evening service. After all, King Nicholaos used to come every day. Johanna usually made a vague reply. In truth she didn't know what Roald thought of his father's obsession with the church. She had tried to keep him away from the subject and never asked him to come. If Rinius was his hero, he would not care for the church. Rinius cared little for religion, and had paid a heavy price for expressing those views openly. Roald could get into a lot of trouble.

It was with a heavy heart that Johanna watched Nellie coming into the garden to announce that the modiste had arrived and was waiting in the Red Room. Back to playing games.

Mistress Daphne had left town or had been killed—no one was sure which. Apparently the modiste where the royal family bought their clothing, even before the fires, was Mistress Dina.

She sat in the Red Room, where the servants had put the two

makeshift thrones against the back wall, removed the chairs for the King's Council and replaced those with the couches that normally stood in this room when there was no meeting.

Mistress Dina sat on one of the couches, her basket on the floor next to her. She came from Saardam—no exotic accents this time—and she was a good bit older than Mistress Daphne had been, with her grey hair tied back from her head in a bun.

She rose when Johanna entered and dipped into a curtsy. "You Majesty. I'm your humble servant."

"Good afternoon, Mistress Dina. Do sit down." Oh, how she hated it when people simpered.

Mistress Dina sat, one hand on each knee in perfect symmetry. She looked up at Johanna like a dog waiting for her to throw a stick.

"I seem to be in need of some dresses." Johanna dropped the cape revealing the house dress that she wore underneath, a plain garment that had no laced bodice or anything that hid the rounding in her stomach.

Mistress Dina's eyes widened. "Oh. Your Majesty. Congratulations!"

"Thank you. Unfortunately, I have a problem. None of my current dresses fit me anymore."

"I understand. I will be most happy to help you. When will we have an heir to the throne?"

"At the end of August."

"That is so soon already."

"I have nothing decent to wear when I go out, so I will need something quickly."

"You're lucky. There have been many women in your situation. I might have just the thing."

Mistress Dina put her basket on the couch and started taking items out. Johanna thought back to the time that Mistress Daphne had come with her giant boxes that contained hideously frilled evening dresses. For some reason, she wanted something bold and colourful and outrageous like Mistress Daphne would propose.

But the samples that Mistress Dina put on the couch were all dark-coloured, heavy material. And then she dug up a larger bundle of material. "I have one dress here that I can adapt quickly so that you can have something to wear while I make the other ones."

She helped Johanna out of her housedress. The servants had been so thoughtful to carry the mirror from the bedroom. Johanna glanced at herself in her underdress. The bulge in her stomach was really very obvious. She put her hand on the top of its firm roundness.

"Look at you," Mistress Dina said. "When Nellie called me, I had a suspicion, but you certainly have been clever in hiding it this long." She helped Johanna into the dress she had brought. Is was dark grey and made from heavy fabric.

The sleeves came all the way down to her wrists and the bodice buttoned up right up to her chin. Instead of at the waist, the skirt went all the way up to just under her breasts.

She looked at herself in the mirror. The fabric was so heavy and thick that the folds hid the curve in her stomach. Johanna pulled the fabric around her so that it drew taut around her front.

"Yes, the dress hides it very discretely."

Yet it was very obviously a type of dress that would only be worn by a woman with child. Johanna wasn't sure that now she announced it officially, she wanted to hide it discretely. She'd want Mistress Daphne to design something outrageous in bright pink with a huge frilly bow, or something ridiculous.

"It's going to be summer. I'll be so hot in this dress," Johanna protested.

"Well, you can't wear any of those Lurezian flimsy gowns. Imagine, in some of those, people can see right in between here." She held her hand over her bosom. "You are already quite heavy in the bosom. You do not want men staring at the rounding of your bust or your stomach. You want a dress that covers all the indecent bits. It's not meant to be flattering. Mind you, you will have no waist so being flattering is nigh impossible."

No, indeed. Johanna stared at herself in the mirror, dismayed at the dreadful dress. Was *this* what she was going to have to wear for the next few months?

Mistress Dina made her stand with her arms wide while she measured and scribbled on her slate. Then, with all the measurements taken, she told Johanna to keep the dress on.

"It's a bit wide in the shoulders. I will fix it later, but it's almost church time and you can't possibly turn up to church in your house dress."

Johanna looked wistfully at the dress draped over the back of the couch and again at herself in the mirror. The dress was a horrible, shapeless thing. She looked as if she were going to a funeral. Even her dark red cape was going to be outrageously colourful compared to this thing.

She looked like . . .

Like the old women who sat in the back of the church.

And then Johanna realised that this was a setup. Mistress Dina was sent by the shepherd or someone like that. Get her to dress properly in church-approved clothes.

Because no one in the church thought that her clothes were dour enough.

Hot anger made her cheeks flush.

The church was trying to make her and Roald theirs, as they had done with King Nicholaos.

HAD SHE BEEN plain Johanna Brouwer, she would probably have stopped going to church at that point. She had only started going to church a few years before the fires, because so many people spoke about it, and because the services were very well attended and the wooden pews told her many stories about the people who sat in them.

But she had left Johanna Brouwer behind ages ago, and more than ever, she realised that her survival, indeed the survival of Saarland as independent country, relied on a careful balance between the Church of the Triune and the Belaman Church, between magic and those who abhorred it, between true Saarlanders and those from elsewhere.

Had she been plain Johanna Brouwer, she might have barged into the service late wearing her clogs, stormed to the altar and yelled at the shepherd at the top of her voice for trying to make her do what he wanted. She'd have dressed in the most colourful dress, too.

But she'd been young and naïve and if it weren't for Father she would probably have ended up at the bottom of the Saar River.

So she wore the dour dress, but even Father noticed it. He frowned. "Is that your new dress? It's not like you at all."

Johanna mumbled something about being proper.

"Dear child, when have you ever worried about something being proper?" Master Deim was just coming in. He eyed Johanna's dress. "Yes, that's very . . . unlike you."

Johanna made a lame excuse. "Mistress Dina came with Nellie's recommendation. She's been modiste for the royal family for years."

"Hmm. Very motherly." That dress had to be bad if even Father noticed it.

Not so long ago, she had worn clogs to church. How quickly things changed.

Father nodded his approval. "Well, at least no one at the King's Council will be speculating anymore."

"Did they speculate?" Not that it should surprise her.

"There was some rather crude talk, which I put an end to. Tomorrow's meeting will be interesting if you are going to be stubborn about being on the council."

Interesting was not the word Johanna would use. One thing she appreciated about Father. No matter how much he, as a man, would disagree with her desire to continue working, he had never said anything about it.

Fortunately, the day had turned quite cold, and Johanna could wear her cape over the top without dying of heat stroke. She was glad of the comfort the coach offered her on the way to church.

A group of citizens waited on the steps and under porch, sheltering against the steady drizzle that had started to fall. As soon as the driver opened the coach door, a cheer went up.

A man shouted over the top of all the voices, "Three cheers for the queen and the royal heir!"

People shouted, "Hurray, hurray, hurray!" And then they clapped and shouted "Congratulations!"

In her new and very dour "proper" dress, Johanna felt like a dressed-up doll. No, she was a puppet like those in the puppet theatre. Someone else did the talking. She just did whatever people expected. Her body was reduced to being a vessel to carry the royal heir.

It's your own fault, a little voice inside her said. *No one ever said that it would be easy.* As sole heiress of the Brouwer Company, her life was always a commodity anyway. To be married off.

Sleep with this man and beget him an heir. That was her function.

A very, very small corner in her mind found it funny that the child that would be born in August carried no Carmine blood and would probably have a good deal of magic.

Inside the church it smelled of wet fabric and musty clothes. Most people would have walked here through the rain. Most people who came to church were the merchants and workers. Very few nobles would ever have set foot inside this building or even its predecessor, or, for that matter, any of the other Church of the Triune buildings in town.

Johanna sat down at the usual pew at the very front of the church. She could still feel people's gazes and hear people talking about her and the impending birth. Most of the talk was good, happy. Nellie had been right.

Then someone behind her said in a clear voice, "What is *he* doing here?"

And someone else gasped.

Johanna glanced at the guard next to her. He had half-risen from the pew and looked out towards the back of the church.

"Who are they talking about?" she asked him in a low voice.

"Have a look yourself. You wouldn't believe me if I told you."

She looked over her shoulder.

At the very back of the church there was an area for latecomers. There were always people who came after the service had started and couldn't get a seat, and a few people always preferred to stand. They were usually the same people: a farmer who lived just outside the town and who complained that sitting hurt his backside, a quay hand who was so tall that his legs didn't fit comfortably between the rows of pews.

Today, someone else had joined them: a man in a thick fur coat with black hair tied back in a bun. Li Fai.

Whether it was coincidence or a work of magic, he found Johanna's eyes over the heads of all those people.

She felt like screaming at him, *Leave! This is not a place that's friendly to you!* She wondered what had possessed him to come here. If he was naively curious about what people did at church, this curiosity would kill him one day. If he had a plan . . . what plan could possibly involve a church that preached against his very existence?

If she were plain Johanna Brouwer, she would have gone to him right now and asked him if he knew what he was doing. But if she were plain Johanna Brouwer, she would probably hardly know who he was. Or she would, like most people, be afraid that he was an evil magician.

Even if she entertained that thought to get up and warn him anyway, it was too late for it now, because the congregation hushed and the shepherd came to the dais. He wore his usual cream-coloured robe and a red scarf that hung down both sides of his neck. The sign of the Triune—two triangles with the sides intertwined—was embroidered in gold thread on both ends of the scarf and the tassels dangled as he walked.

He met Johanna's eyes and bowed. Then he opened the big, leatherbound *Book of Verses* that lay on the dais and started the service. Today, he spoke about the good of the holy god and how that good lived on in each person.

He seemed . . . distracted, for want of a better word. He was constantly leafing through the book looking for specific cita-tions. Twice he forgot where he was. Johanna noticed that he looked thin, and his hands trembled. Several times, he glanced at the back of the church where Li Fai stood. Johanna was afraid that he was going to make comments about "heathen invaders", but he did not.

After the service, he came down the steps and bowed to Johanna. "You have formally announced the impending birth. My congratulations."

"How is Greetje?" His wife had to be very close to giving birth.

"Very well."

"She must be getting very tired. I have hardly seen her in the past month."

"She has been busy." He glanced aside. "All of her work has been in the house. It's not a good idea for a woman in her condi-tion to go about in the streets."

Johanna wanted to argue why not, and that women on farms didn't seem to have those restrictions, but other women had already assured her that she'd be too tired to do anything that wasn't essential, and her first consideration should be for the child. Never having had a child, Johanna couldn't dispute their statements. What did she know about it anyway?

She wanted to talk to Li Fai, so she made some sort of an excuse and went down the aisle towards the back of the church. But there were so many people wanting to congratulate her that by the time she came to the area behind the pews, Li Fai was nowhere to be seen.

The church buzzed with rumour about him, but so many women crowded around to offer Johanna help and advice that she couldn't hear what was being said. The women offered to make clothes and bedding for the little one. They offered to help look after the child, wet-nursing even.

It made Johanna feel uneasy. This was actually getting serious. It was happening. This annoying thing that grew inside her would always be part of her life. There was no going back.

That was a scary thought.

She looked over her shoulder, but the shepherd was gone, too. That was strange. He normally never let an opportunity pass to talk to the congregation.

Johanna put the facts together.

Li Fai coming to church, now gone. The shepherd nervous, now also gone.

"Let's go," she said to her guard, who today was Anton, a soft-spoken orange-haired giant. With his imposing figure, he had no trouble clearing the aisle and preceded her to the doors.

"Wait," Johanna said when she was in the coach and he was about to shut the door. "I'd like you to walk around the church, especially the back of the building where few people go except the shepherd."

"Anything in particular you want me to look for, Your Majesty?"

"Anything unusual, but in particular people having arguments."

He nodded without question and vanished into the night.

Johanna waited in the coach while the last of the congregation filed out of the church. It was very dark in the porch of the church, and a few pitiful street lamps reflected in the wet wooden steps.

Up on the driver's seat, the coach driver sneezed so loudly that it echoed over the market square. His movement made the coach wobble a little. One of the horses snorted, probably having been suddenly awoken from its nap.

Johanna giggled silently. She had no idea why she found it funny when people sneezed.

But now there was a sound of a key being turned in a lock. A moment later a figure in a rain cloak walked across the porch and down the steps. This person was too small to either be the shepherd. It had to be one of the altar boys.

Johanna opened the door to the coach. "Excuse me."

The boy—because it was indeed an altar boy—gasped audibly. "Oh. Your Majesty. I didn't realise you were still here."

Johanna managed to stop herself from saying *The coach would have been a pretty good indication*. "I was wondering if there is something going on with the shepherd. Normally he closes the church, doesn't he?"

"Yes, he does. He asked me to close tonight."

"Did he say why?"

"He didn't, Your Majesty."

"Is it because of his wife?"

"I honestly couldn't tell, Your Majesty. Could be."

That was typical of Master Willems: he rarely spoke about his family or anything that could be considered personal information.

While they stood there, Anton came around the corner of the church building. He shook his head. "Nothing. All quiet."

Johanna sighed. Maybe she was seeing things. "Let's go home then."

"As you wish."

Johanna went back into the cabin, and Anton climbed on the bench next to the driver. The coach set off.

The rain had gotten heavier in the past few minutes. Drops streaked over the little window and restricted Johanna's view of the deserted streets. The coach went the long way. In the past few days, the town council had started repaving the main street from the markets to the palace, and with the rain it would be muddy. So they went along the stately houses along the main canal and turned left into the street that ran from the markets to the harbour.

They were almost at the markets when Johanna became aware of voices: men shouting. The coach slowed down and then stopped.

Anton said, "All in order?"

A man replied. Johanna couldn't hear what he said. She opened the door to the coach far enough that she could stand on the top step and look into the street. Cold rain hit her face.

Five men stood in a circle. Four wore dark clothing and hoods that covered their heads. One of those carried a torch.

The fifth man, with his back against the steps to the front door of a stately house, was Li Fai.

He met Johanna's eyes over the rump of one of the horses. An expression of relief came to his eyes.

Johanna couldn't see who the other men were, but one wore a long coat of thick felt or some such. It was a fine-looking garment that a pauper could never afford. The other men weren't paupers either.

"Do ride with us." She put on her most innocent voice. "The weather is positively awful. We can go past your ship. I wanted to ask some questions, if you don't mind being questioned at this time of day."

He bowed. "I'm at your service." In long strides, he walked past the four men to the coach. As he passed, one of them turned his head, allowing a brief flash of torchlight to strike his face.

It was Octavio Nieland.

CHAPTER 8

LI FAI CLIMBED into the cabin and sat down on the bench opposite Johanna. Anton shut the door behind him, enveloping Johanna in the smell of wet clothing and the faint tag of a foreign perfume.

The coach jolted into motion.

"Thank you," Li Fai said, pressing his hands together before his chest and bowing.

There was a short silence, thick and awkward.

"Were they bothering you?"

"They were asking things I don't know."

"Do you know any of these men? Have you met them before?"

"They have businesses in the harbour, don't they? One is from the Nieland family?"

Johanna nodded. "What did they want to know? They didn't hurt you, did they?" It was far too dark in the coach to see if he had any injuries to his face.

"No." He let a short silence lapse, in which Johanna filled in, *Not yet*, and then continued. "A few months before we came here, we put in at Seneza. We come there often."

Johanna had heard sailors talk about Seneza. She didn't think Father had ever been there. Lurezia was about the furthest south one could travel on the inland rivers. Seneza lay at a rocky point where the Golden Sea joined the southern Lamorian Ocean. From accounts, she had heard it was a sunny and dry place, with a jumble of ochre-painted houses and many ancient temples and churches. It had been the home of the Belaman Church for hundreds of years, and it was because of its location that the church had so easily spread across the known lands.

Seneza was also an important port city, which was why Li Han would have been there, going in and out of the Golden Sea to Phoenicia and many of the rich lands in that area.

"While we were in Seneza, something important was happening there, except we were unfamiliar with it at the time. Apparently there was an inquisition in the Belaman Church."

Johanna nodded. The one where the Most Holy Father Severino had declared the Church of the Triune banned from the Belaman Church.

"On the evening before our departure, a man came to us. He asked if we were going to Saardam, and we said we were. Then he asked us if we could take a crate and deliver it to the shepherd of the Church of the Triune. We said we could. He paid the fee. We did as asked."

"Was that why you were in the church tonight?"

"No. We delivered the crate when we first moored at the quay weeks ago. But people have been asking about it since. I was . . . simply curious about the church and trying to understand why so many people are looking for this thing. I was going to ask the shepherd what was in the crate."

"You didn't look at it while it was on your ship?"

"We trust our customers and do not open their cargo." He sounded indignant.

"I'm sorry. I just thought you might have had to inspect the contents or something. Did you end up asking the shepherd what was inside?"

"He left the church before I could go to him. It was very busy."

Indeed, it had been, but also, having seen Li Fai, the shepherd had left the church quickly. "And these men who were just talking to you, they asked about this thing as well?"

"They did."

This was getting ever stranger. "What did they want to know?"

"They asked me where it is, not believing me when I said we delivered it to the shepherd. They say the shepherd tells them he doesn't have it. So if he doesn't have it, what did he do with it? Why should that be our business? We delivered it. Our business is finished." He spread his hands. "But still they come. They believe the shepherd, and not our words. We don't have anything to do with it. We don't have it anymore."

"Who gave it to you, in Seneza?"

"It was a man from the church. He paid us on the spot and didn't want his name recorded. That is not unusual. Some people are very suspicious. He was quite old and was wearing . . ." He made a movement down his front indicating a long garment. "He was a monk."

"A habit?"

"Yes."

Very strange indeed. "Have any of these people told you why they want it?"

"They seem to think it is worth more than the gold we brought."

The coach was turning onto the quay. The wheels rattled over the cobblestones.

She spoke in a low voice. "Did the crate contain something of . . . magic?"

"Magic?" He frowned.

"Yes, like . . ." Her heart was thudding hard against her ribs. "Like if I touch a piece of wood, the wood can tell me what it has seen in the few days before. Some people can see things on the wind, or in water." She didn't know why she was saying this. He was still frowning and clearly had no idea what she was talking about.

From the brief encounter in the palace, she *thought* he had magic, but maybe he didn't. Maybe there was no magic in his homeland.

Still, she continued, speaking even more quietly now. "Some people can make trees grow very quickly. So quickly that they can trap their enemies inside."

His eyes widened. "The tree in the market square. The one with the ugly speckled leaves." His voice was no more than a whisper. "It cries."

Johanna nodded, and she knew for certain. Only people with magic could hear the cry of Alexandre's angry soul. "This is what I mean. Some people can make trees do their will. Other people can shape fire into creatures."

"You call that magic?"

"Yes. What do you call it?"

"Art." He drew something from his pocket and held it in the palm of his hand: a finely made octagonal wooden box. A faint orange glow emanated from a dragon pattern of inlaid wood and mother-of-pearl on the lid.

Johanna held her breath.

"Touch it," he said.

She reached out and brushed the very tips of her fingers over the wood. She saw the inside of a ship's cabin. A couple of lamps hung from the ceiling. Li Han sat by the window. On his lap he held a bundle of cloth that looked like a jacket or robe and he was pulling a needle with bright red thread through the fabric. On the back of the jacket he had embroidered the top half of a dragon in exquisite detail.

Li Fai's mother Wen Mei sat at a desk surrounded by jars of paint and brushes. She was painting on silk cloth held in a wooden frame. Johanna recognised the flowers she was drawing: a daisy, a dandelion, buttercups, cornflowers, poppies. Behind her on a low shelf against the wall stood a number of finished drawings, of ducks, rabbits, deer, cows, and one with a couple of green frogs.

"Do you see what the wood says?" Li Fai asked.

"Yes. I see your parents. Your mother is drawing plants and creatures from our land. Your father is doing embroidery."

He nodded. "The box contains my art." The glow of the dragon pattern on the lid had intensified.

He opened the lid and some brightly glowing thing came out.

Johanna gasped and withdrew her hand.

The thing cavorted through the air between them, trailing sparks in its wake. Eventually it settled in the palm of Li Fai's hand. It was . . . a miniature dragon. It crouched like a dog waiting for its master to throw a stick, swishing its tail. Its eyes were buggy like a frog's, and roved from Li Fai to her and back.

Li Fai said something and it jumped into the air before running over his arm, across his shoulder, behind his head, over the other shoulder and down his other arm. Then it jumped onto Johanna's knee. She gave a squeak and shrank back. It ran over the seat before jumping onto the ledge under the window in the coach door and jumped from there onto her shoulder, and used that as a springboard to jump to Li Fai's hand, where it sat back on its haunches, waiting for the next command.

"What is it?" Johanna asked. She ran her hand over her knee, checking the dress for fire damage, but found none.

"This is my art. This is my dragon. It does what I say." He again gave it a command, and it jumped from his hand to Johanna's knee and crouched there, looking at her like a little puppy.

"It's cute."

"You can touch it."

She carefully reached out and touched the creature's back. It was smooth and firm. "It's warm." The flames that trailed off the flanks and the comb-like plates over the creature's spine weren't hot, as she expected.

"That's because it's a dragon." That clearly explained everything.

"I'm not familiar with dragons."

It yawned widely, and then dropped onto its belly, resting its head onto its forepaws.

"It likes you."

Johanna chuckled. "Where did you get this creature?"

"You don't 'get' dragons. When a child with the art is born, the child's grandfather goes to the dragon temple and receives a box. The child is then schooled to fill it with whatever art he or she excels at."

"So . . . if I grew up in your lands, my box would have. . . ?"

"A small tree."

Johanna tried to imagine what that would look like. She imagined opening the box and a little tree would gently unfold from inside. The branches would be supple and thin, waving as if moved by an unseen breeze. That breeze, of course, would contain stories other people could read. The tree drank the water that told yet others their stories. In that moment, she understood the power of wood magic and knew that she had never understood it before.

Her voice was soft when she said, "Could you show me how to make a tree grow in a box?"

He shook his head, his expression sad. "I don't know if I can. I can try, but it is something for a child to learn. I haven't taught children."

"Do you have any children?"

"I have not yet been married."

Which wasn't the same thing at all, but it seemed rude to point out the difference.

She was vaguely aware that the coach had stopped. Li Fai snapped his fingers. The dragon jumped up into the wooden box, leaving a warm spot on Johanna's knee. Li Fai shut the lid. The mosaic dragon on the lid glowed for a second or two before fading.

There were footsteps outside, followed by Anton opening the door. "We're at the gentleman's ship, Your Majesty."

A blast of cold air came into the cabin.

Li Fai put the box into his pocket. He bowed to Johanna, meeting her eyes. "It was an honour to be given a ride with you."

"It was my pleasure."

He rose and hesitated at the top of the steps. He said in a low voice, "The crate we carried for the shepherd was art. Even when I wasn't in the hold, I could feel the chill of it. My father was upset with me when I said we should throw it overboard. He agreed to take it and he got the monk's money. My father does not have art. He doesn't understand. I said I wouldn't have taken it, because the art is not a good kind. There was much death in the crate. If it is lost, do not look for it. It is a bad thing."

He bowed again and then he was gone, leaving behind a cold silence that didn't dissipate even after Anton had shut the door.

CHAPTER 9

JOHANNA STARED OUT the little window while the coach made its way back to the palace. She felt dumb and ignorant. There were places out there where magic was taught routinely to children. Why did she have to be born in a place where it was swept under the carpet, denied and even forbidden?

She imagined Father going up to a building called a "dragon temple" and coming back with a box for her to contain and focus her magic. Her life would have been . . . so much happier. Instead, she'd been angry, she'd bumbled through dealing with magic and trying to hide it. She'd thought that by going to a church that forbade magic she could change people's opinions of her. Obviously Master Willems still thought that.

What a fool she'd been.

On the driver's seat, Anton and the driver were telling jokes. Their laughter echoed in the empty streets that glistened with the rainwater.

The coach dropped Johanna off at the bottom of the palace steps. A guard with flickering storm light met her there and accompanied her to the entrance.

Johanna pulled the sides of her cloak together. It always was cold and blustery here. The sea wind whipped up across the wide expanse of the Saar delta on the other side of the palace.

She just came into the foyer when another guard entered from the hallway. His face showed an expression of relief as if he'd been waiting for her. He bowed. "My excuses for the late hour, but you have a visitor, Your Majesty."

Her heart jumped. "Who is this visitor?" Her first thought was *Li Han*, wanting a reply about the office, and she was not in a position to give him that reply yet. There was the King's Council still to be convinced of her plan. Yes, she could override the council and give him permission to find an office along the quayside, but doing so would make her life pretty hard, because many of the men in the King's Council would never cooperate with her again.

"She didn't say her name. I asked her to wait in the Red Room."

"I'll go and see her now."

Her. Not Li Han, obviously. Johanna's next thought, while walking down the hallway, was *Loesie*.

It even made sense. Loesie could feel magic and if this thing that Li Han had taken to the shepherd was something of great magic, Loesie would know about it.

Johanna reached the Red Room. Because there were no meetings tomorrow, no one had bothered to light the fire in the hearth and it was unpleasantly cold in the room. The air smelled of moisture with a faint whiff of mould.

Someone had lit a few oil lights, but they did little to dispel the cloying darkness that hung in this room at the best of times.

On the couch in the middle of the room sat a small person hiding under a hooded cloak of green velvet. This was definitely not Loesie, because she wore only black.

As Johanna entered and the guard shut the door behind her, a pair of pale, slender hands came out from under the cloak and pushed back the hood.

Greetje, wife of Master Willems, now Shepherd Victor.

But what a sight she was. Her hair hung loose down both sides of her face, her left eye was swollen and a nasty bruise coloured her cheekbone.

Johanna gasped and raised her hand to her mouth. "What happened to you?"

Greetje's chin trembled. Her eyes glittered with tears. Her voice was hoarse, no more than a whisper. "He's gone mad."

"Who?"

"My husband." The tears rolled over her cheeks.

"He did this to you?" Timid, shy Master Willems?

Greetje nodded, choking out a sob. She gingerly wiped her face, wincing as she touched the bruised cheekbone.

"But how is that possible? He is the shepherd." But that of course didn't guarantee his behaviour.

Johanna saw the shepherd as he had made his way out of the church earlier that night. He hadn't even stayed behind after the service to answer questions and talk, as he usually did.

She saw him as she had left him in the church last night: kneeling, praying and chanting, just because she had said the word "necromancer" and hinted that he might want to use his wind magic for the good of Saarland. Because they could do with as many magicians as they could muster. Earlier yesterday, he had argued vehemently against accepting Li Han's money based on a fear of any magic Li Han might have.

She felt cold inside.

"How long has this been going on?"

"He's never hit me before, but he's been acting so strangely in the last few weeks. It's getting worse."

"Any idea why?"

Greetje shook her head.

"It wouldn't happen to have anything to do with something that he received from the eastern trader?"

She continued shaking her head, although she didn't meet Johanna's eyes. A tear tracked across her cheek. She sniffed. "He's just gone mad."

"Can you tell me what happened? You said he'd been acting strangely, but what does he do that is strange? What does he talk about at the dinner table?"

Greetje laughed, not in an amused way. "He rarely still comes to dinner. When he comes home, he goes upstairs. A room up there used to be a spare bedroom. We were planning to put our little one in there when he or she doesn't need nightly feeds anymore, but he's taken over the room with scary things."

"Like what?"

"The room has dark wallpaper. It used to be his grandfather's smoking room and it still smells of smoke. It has heavy curtains which are always closed. He's put an altar against the wall and filled it up with . . . awful things, like animal skulls and sheep's horns and chicken feet and teeth of things that live in the sea I can't even begin to imagine." She shivered. "There are crudely-made stone statues and puppets made out of straw."

Johanna thought of the primitive altar she had seen when staying in that really poor village on the edge of the shifting sands. She suspected these things were all religious relics.

"When he comes home, he doesn't talk to anyone. He sits on his knees and prays. Often, he cries. He stays in that room for hours on end. His father will ask him to come out, but he never replies. Even if he does come out, he's not really there. He stares into the distance and then he will just snap at someone for no obvious reason at all." Greetje sniffed. "I don't understand. He used to be so nice and gentle. Now, he spends much longer at church and he screams at me when he comes home. He screams at the servants. He doesn't eat. He scares everyone. He sits on his knees in that room all night, praying. Sometimes he cries."

"I really need you to answer this: did he receive anything in a crate recently? Something that was taken to him by the eastern traders and that came from a monk in Seneza?"

Greetje looked at her with wide eyes and shook her head. "Not that I know, but he doesn't tell me anything anymore."

"Then tell me why he hit you."

"I just couldn't bear to listen to his crying and pleading anymore and went into that horrible room. I asked him to please tell us what bothers him so much, so that we can help him, and then he got up and came at me at me." Her mouth trembled. "He took me by the shoulders and pushed me into the wall. He yelled at me that we were all going to die, that the Triune would pass judgment and that we would all end up facing the Lord of Fire because we weren't worthy. I asked him why ever he thought we weren't worthy, because I said he was doing so many good things, and then he started screaming. I was really scared because I'd never seen him like that. His eyes were all red and there was spit flying out of his mouth. I didn't even hear any of what he was saying. He looked like a madman. He screamed at me to get out and hit me in the face. Thankfully the groundsman came in. He pulled him away from me, but you should have seen the look in his eyes. As if he could kill me."

She sobbed into her hands, her shoulders shaking with cries. Johanna put her arm on Greetje's shoulders. Goodness, her shoulders were so thin that she could feel the bones through the coat. "I'm sorry for bothering you, but I have nowhere to go. I have no family left."

Master Willems, too, had no family that she could call on for support.

"Of course you can't go back there," Johanna said. "I simply will not have it."

"Please don't call the guards or anyone. He's not himself. I don't know. Something has taken possession of him. Please, he's not a bad man."

"Maybe not, but all the same, you can't go back there in your condition until he calms down. You have the little one to think about."

Greetje looked down and sniffed. "But he will be so angry with me."

"We'll worry about that later. First, we'll give you a safe place to sleep. How long before the little one is born?"

"It could be any day now. I'm so tired."

Johanna called for Nellie and they installed Greetje in the guest room. The maid brought a nightgown which Greetje put on over her round belly. She looked terribly out of proportion, with her arms and legs very thin and her belly hideously swollen. Her navel had even turned inside out and sat like a little bump on a tightly-stretched water bag.

She was exhausted and had evidently been very cold. She was asleep in moments, her cheeks glowing healthy red.

Johanna and Nellie tiptoed out of the room.

"Well, that is a really terrible thing to have happened to her right now," Nellie said. "What are you going to do about the shepherd, Mistress Johanna?"

Johanna sighed. "I don't know. It worries me. The church has so much power over the people. Greetje is right: his words have become so much angrier recently. There is clearly something going on. This is not how it used to be under Shepherd Romulus."

"No, but Shepherd Romulus had it easy. He never knew about the decision by the Belaman Church to expel the Church of the Triune. He never saw his life's work burned to ashes. The church was new and no one challenged him."

Johanna felt cold. She was going to say, *Don't you start making excuses for him, too, Nellie*, but she wasn't even sure that Nellie would understand. She had come from a church family after all. Was there anyone except the nobles and Father who did not crawl at the shepherd's feet?

Sometimes Johanna thought that ousting Alexandre had been the easiest of their problems.

She said, "Greetje will stay here for a while until we sort out what's going on. Ask the modiste to come and bring us some gowns for a newborn." She held up a finger. "Not Mistress Dina, please."

Nellie gave her a wide-eyed look. "Whatever is wrong with Mistress Dina?"

"Find someone a bit younger who can dress both the child and myself in more cheerful clothing."

"Whatever is wrong with your new dress, Mistress Johanna?"

Johanna spread her arms. "Do I look like a picture of happiness?"

Nellie looked her up and down and frowned. "You look decent to me. Very appropriate."

"I don't want to look decent. I want to look happy. If I have to wear this horrible hot dress, I want you to get me a big silk ribbon to tie around my belly."

Nellie gasped.

"I don't want to look like I'm at a funeral. Find someone, please, who can make me a dress that's comfortable and a bit more cheerful."

Nellie's expression was still bewildered. "I'll do my best. You do know that Mistress Daphne is no longer in town?"

"I do." It was the last thing Johanna had ever expected to be sorry about.

THE RAIN CLEARED overnight for a sunny morning. At breakfast, Roald announced that he was going to start on the vegetable garden. The day was clear, the sky hazy blue and the lawn full of daisies and buttercups. Johanna wished that she could go outside with him, but there was so much still to be done.

The maid confirmed that Greetje was awake and had been brought her breakfast.

Johanna went to see her. In the hallway, she asked a guard. "Has the shepherd been here to visit his wife yet?"

"No, Your Majesty, he hasn't."

That was a bit worrying. Johanna hoped that he was all right. Maybe, if there was time, she should go and see him and ask him about this mysterious crate.

Greetje lay back in the pillows in the bed in the guest room. Sunlight streamed in through the window. A tray with an empty plate and a teapot stood on the table next to the bed. The blanket was pulled up over her belly.

In the daylight the bruises in her face stood out like huge purple blotches. The eye above the bruise had gone red and bloodshot.

She brought her hand to her face when she noticed Johanna

looking at it. "It doesn't hurt so much anymore, but it probably looks terrible."

Johanna nodded. "It's very colourful. How are you feeling, other than that?"

"Tired, but that is probably a permanent thing until I have this child." Her eyes glittered with tears again. "You know, I'd imagined that we'd be a happy family. In the beginning, he told me that he really wanted to be a father, but he lost interest. I don't know what's wrong with him."

"Do you want me to try to talk to him?"

Did Johanna imagine it or did Greetje actually wince at the thought? "I can't imagine that it would do much good."

"But you can't continue like this."

Greetje shrugged.

Well, if the worst came to the worst, she could always let Greetje stay in return for work in the kitchen or laundry. However, the palace was fast filling up with people who were there because she felt sorry for them rather than that they were good at their jobs.

It was not to be helped.

Johanna sent a guard to tell Helena to see Greetje, and went to her office to tackle the urgent correspondence. That pile contained some issues that she should deal with, before the inevitable and probably soon time that the men would no longer let her attend the meetings.

One of those issues was that letter from Joris Decamp, Saardam's mayor, that detailed the pitiful state of the city's stores of grain and potatoes. It was another few months until harvest, and while it was summer, the farming villages had been hit by the fire demons even harder than the city. Crops had gone unplanted because there was simply no one left to do the planting and work the fields. Unless they could get some crops in the ground, the summer would be bad, but the next winter would be devastating.

Another worry was the slow pace of repairs to the city that left many without decent roofs over their heads and forced citizens to walk long distances because canal bridges had been burned.

A few weeks ago, Johanna had asked the city's carpenters,

bricklayers and stonemasons how much it would cost to rebuild two key bridges over the main canal.

She had received a stack of quotes, but every single one of them was hideous, as if the city's carpenters had decided en masse that since she was a woman, she couldn't possibly have any idea of how much a new bridge would cost to build. As if she had any of that kind of money to spend.

At least, Li Han's gold would go a long way towards solving those problems in the short term. In the long term, she would just have to convince them to let her write to foreign royal families and merchants to convince them to invest in Saardam's port.

She had the letters all ready. The only thing needed was the approval of a bunch of self-centred men.

After she had sat there staring at her desk and not doing anything, there was a knock on the door and a courtier came in with the news that the King's Council was gathering in the Red Room.

This was it.

Johanna rose from the desk, feeling nervous and sweaty. She checked her reflection in the window: it showed a very proper, very prim young woman with a slight telltale rounding of the stomach. When she pulled the dress flat over her stomach, the bump became more pronounced, and sucking in a breath no longer made it disappear.

Clearly, there was no avoiding the issue.

She picked up her letters and her plan that detailed investment amounts and lists of proposed benefits and went down the corridor to the Red Room.

The men had been talking, but fell quiet when she came in. Johanna crossed the room under their penetrating gazes. She felt like a stock animal for sale.

In total silence, she sat down on the makeshift throne, her pile of papers on her lap. "Well, then, let's begin."

This was followed by an intense silence.

Then Thomas Kloostermans spoke up. "We are of the opinion that you should not be working in your condition." He was a pompous fellow, dressed in an ostentatious white shirt with an abundance of lace on the collar.

"That is a matter for me to decide, isn't it?" She gave him a stern look, but by the Triune, her heart was thudding against her ribs.

"Well . . . Your Majesty. I don't think so. Anything you do will harm the future heir to the throne. The royal family is already in much danger. We cannot risk losing another heir."

"And that apart from the fact that it's simply not appropriate," Patrice Faber said.

"Yes, scandalous," another added.

This statement brought a lot of agreement from the men. Father and Master Deim both watched, their faces blank. The shepherd wasn't there, not that he would have supported her, but that was another thing to worry about.

Johanna picked up the top sheet of her plan. "Gentlemen, why don't we start the meeting. I have many other things to do. I have a proposal that will bring prosperity and lasting peace to Saardam. If you're all quiet, I can read it out—"

Old Patrice Faber said, "What would these foreign visitors think of us, letting a woman work like that. No wonder her decisions have been irrational lately."

Irrational? "Excuse me, I am your queen—" *and you should shut up.*

"Darling, you are the consort. In absence of the king, the King's Council has been instated to make sure that the country stays on the right path until such time that the King's heir—" and he looked pointedly at her stomach "—is old enough to reign in his own name."

"What if it's a girl? What if—" Johanna had to stop herself. She'd almost said it *what if this child is not even Roald's.*

"Dear girl, you will not stop at one child. Where there is one, more will always follow. Your task is to bring a healthy heir into this world."

"My task is to look after the king's affairs because he cannot look after his own."

"That's what *we* are for."

"Roald doesn't want you."

"Then he should turn up to meetings and tell us so. You have been all too quick in speaking on his behalf."

Johanna spread her hands, and let them fall. Every single one of the men, except Father and Master Deim, regarded her with hostility. She met Father's eyes. The expression of defeat on his face hit her hard. He glanced at the door as if he wanted to say, "Just go. It's not to be helped."

Johanna looked around the wall of hostile faces. She found it hard to breathe. She wanted to scream at them that she would bring Roald in and he would tell them that she could keep working just fine. But Roald had never performed on command, and there was no reason why he should do so now.

Thomas Kloostermans gestured at the door.

Unable to find anything to say to counter the demand, Johanna got up.

"Would you like some help?" Master Deim said.

Johanna nodded. She was trembling so much that she feared her legs would give way before she made it to the door.

Master Deim took her arm. Before leaving the room, he said in his gentle voice, "I will represent the Queen's viewpoint. In most cases, it also happens to be my own."

Johanna barely knew how she made her way out of the room.

"It's not fair!" she burst out when they were in the corridor. Hot angry tears pricked in her eyes. In the trek through the forest with the bandits, she had learned some interesting words. She felt very tempted to use them.

"I know, child. But you do have to agree that the heir to the throne should be your first concern. Don't worry about the council. Your father and I will represent you and your plans."

"But you don't have the numbers!"

"Neither do we have the numbers when you're there."

"But . . ."

He shook his head. "I know these types of men. They always say no to everything at first. But if they give me the chance to explain, I'm sure they will see the wisdom, or at least enough of them will for the plan to pass."

"But I want to do it!" It was *her* idea.

"I understand. For now, be calm and quiet. You'll get your chance." He smiled and went back into the room.

Johanna went back to the living quarters, still clutching her papers. She was seething inside. She should have screamed at them. She should have told them that she wasn't going anywhere.

And then what?

These powerful men could easily make her life impossible.

And it was not as if she hadn't known that this was coming. Fighting it was useless because, though she might be the queen, these men had much more power than she did. She guessed she'd have to resign herself to a lifetime of battles for the city. Master Deim and Father alone could never sway the council to go ahead with her plan.

While she stood there, a guard came towards her in the corridor, followed by a middle-aged woman who was taller than him.

Helena of Karathos must have been a striking beauty in her youth. She had long legs, long arms and slender fingers. She was probably in her late forties now. Johanna had never seen her in her prime, but apparently before the fires, there were still days when sailors were said to have big fights over her.

Not so much anymore. Her eyes were still dark, her eyebrows heavy and her hair—or whatever was left of it—raven black. These days, it was not so glossy anymore, occupied as she must be with tending the weeping burn wounds on the right side of her face.

"It's getting better," she said previously when Johanna had asked about it. "I keep it clean and more of the wound scabs over."

Her injuries would leave her with permanent ugly scars and must hurt, Johanna guessed, but Helena hadn't come here to talk about that.

"She's not far off," she said in her dark voice with thick accent. "Maybe tonight, maybe tomorrow, maybe next week. Not much longer than that. The child is big and she is very uncomfortable. It's the first one for her, yes?"

Johanna nodded, feeling uncomfortable.

"Call me when her pains start. I will come."

Johanna offered Helena some tea, but she said she needed to go to another woman with pains, so she left quickly.

Johanna strode into her office. She was tempted to slam the door, but that would seem childish.

Women were only good for producing heirs. It had always been that way and it was pointless to fight it.

With tears in her eyes, Johanna pushed the pile of draft letters aside. They would never be sent. There would not be investment in Saardam. There would be wars. Li Fai would not have his office. She would never see the little dragon again, never learn about her magic. Everything she had done was pointless. Her life was pointless.

She went to the window, leaning her forehead against the cool glass.

The royal office looked out over the former rose garden, and while there were signs that Roald had been working on a garden bed, he, and the guard who would accompany him, were nowhere to be seen.

From her position, Johanna could see the ravaged glass doors of the garden room. Throughout autumn and winter, the room had lain open to the elements. Dust and leaves had blown in, staining the floor and walls, causing mould to grow on the curtains. Animals had roosted in there, and bandits had camped there. The room would need a great deal of work before it was beautiful again.

Johanna left the room and went into the garden.

The air was warm and smelled of grass and flowers. Queen Cygna's rose beds were badly overgrown with weeds. There were dandelions and poppies, cornflowers and daisies, wild carrots and a variety of garden plants that had run riot, like foxgloves and lupins.

When Alexandre's henchmen took away the statue of the Triune that used to stand on a pedestal in the middle of the pond, they had knocked down the wall that used to be on the river side of the garden. Some of the rubble still lay in the garden beds. Last autumn's floods had invaded the garden beds on that side and washed away the soil that, Johanna had been told, the queen had brought in because the clay of the riverbank was too gluggy to grow roses. Now the garden bled into the reed beds and was more ideal for Roald than the old garden had ever been.

Johanna went to the old gazebo. The vandals had set fire to the roof, but the stone pillars that supported the roof still stood and the vandals had not been able to move the stone seats.

She sat down on a bench with a seat warmed by the sun.

The presence of the king was only indicated by the two palace guards who stood in front of the reed beds, while a group of courtiers hovered around a table that evidently contained Roald's morning tea in which he took little interest, as usual. Johanna had told them repeatedly not to bother, but they insisted that the king "had to eat well" and was "much too thin". Yes to both accounts, but trying to get Roald to do it was an effort that was best spent at the dinner table.

Johanna went to the table and took a cake from the plate held out to her by the courtier.

She was just about to join Father whom she spotted on another bench when there was a shout from the reeds, the tone of the voice distressed.

The guards looked at each other and frowned. Johanna looked at Father. The courtiers gasped.

"Was that His Majesty?"

The guards had already taken off into the reed bed.

Johanna called out, "Roald. What's going on?"

He would not answer that of course. He never did.

Johanna ploughed into the reeds after the guards. There was a narrow path where Roald usually walked. The ground was pretty soggy and she had to step carefully from one patch of flattened reeds to the next so her shoes didn't sink into the mud. Her dress snagged on sticks that had washed up during the flood.

"Roald!" she called.

Something went, "Eeeeh! Eeeeeh!" in the reeds.

That sounded like his voice.

"Roald!"

A courtier caught up with her. The man ran past her through the reed bed with a splosh-splosh-splosh and disappeared into the greenery in the direction of the river.

There was another shout, this time from one of the guards at the front.

Johanna hesitated. The ground got *very* wet here. More mud and puddle than dry land, really.

She kicked off her shoes off and continued clumsily. The reeds were hard to walk on with her soft feet. The water was cold and the mud squished—eeew—between her toes.

The hem of her dress got wet. She could see glimpses of the courtier's back between the reeds. He was heaving something heavy.

By the Triune, Roald was all right, was he?

But his voice was still going, "Eeeeh! Eeeeeh!"

He did that when he was distressed. He would be swaying, his eyes wide. She had to get to him quickly, to comfort him.

The courtier blocked her path. "No, Your Majesty. You shouldn't see this in your condition."

"The king needs my help." She was already getting tired of the *in your condition* that her close maids, courtiers and guards used as excuse to make her sit still and do nothing. That would only get worse.

"I will bring the king to you. Wait here."

The man turned around. She could see Roald's legs in between the reeds behind him. He was sitting in the water and looked indeed to be swaying and crying. The courtier tried to pull him up, but he squealed even more.

No, he wasn't going to come if the man was going to force him like that. He'd only scream and roll on the ground, and then he'd be all wet and muddy and everyone in the palace would talk about it for days.

Never mind waiting here, and whatever she shouldn't be seeing *in her condition*. In the past year she had seen so many awful things, there wasn't much that could still upset her. She followed the little path through ankle-deep water, holding up her dress. Her bare feet grew numb with the cold.

At the end of the path, where the reed bed made way for shallow water, one of the guards stood looking at a large and pale thing that lay in the water that was just deep enough to cover it. It took Johanna a few seconds to realise what she was seeing Pale grey cloth waved gently in the lapping water. An open hand reached for the sky.

Johanna raised her hand to her mouth.

A body, the form distorted by ripples in the water. A man, someone well-clad. As far as she could tell age on dead bodies, he looked quite young, had blond hair that floated about his face. His eyes were half open. His nose and chin were the only things that broke the surface, but water lapped in and out of his mouth.

She knew him. It was Auguste LaFontaine, the young nobleman who, just a few months ago, had been his family's message boy when they were trying to get Father to marry into their family.

Johanna stared, feeling sick. Roald was still squealing, but his voice sounded far off.

How did he end up here? She could see no sign of violence on him.

He'd drowned.

She was taken back to two nights ago, when she had clearly heard the splash of the man who had fallen or jumped into the water from the *Lady Sara*'s deck. She and Li Fai had looked, but hadn't been able to see anyone. The harbour was upstream from here.

Auguste LaFontaine had been snooping around on Father's ship?

A bunch of court guards splashed up behind her.

"Let us deal with that, Your Majesty," said the guard captain. He gently pulled her back to the reed bed.

Roald was still squealing, swaying, clamping his hands over his face.

Johanna crouched next to him. "Listen to me." She took his wrists and forced him to sit still.

He still resisted her, trying to keep swaying against her grip.

"Sit still! Maybe you like getting wet, but I don't"

He relaxed a bit. She was able to pull his hands away from his face. His eyes were still wide. Sweat glistened on his forehead.

He squealed, "There is a ghost in the water!"

"It's not a ghost, but someone has died."

"He's all white. Did you see that? He's all white. He's been touched by magic!"

"It's just the colour that skin goes when someone is dead and the body lies in the water."

"The frogs! What did he do to the frogs?"

"It doesn't bother the frogs."

"But the frogs will be scared!"

"Come, Roald. Get up. You'll catch a cold."

She heaved herself up and pulled him up with her. A guard rushed to help. A couple of others splashed into the water and gathered around the body, staring, speculating what he'd been doing there.

Johanna and Roald made their way back to the garden, where courtiers came to help them. It seemed that the commotion had caused the meeting of the King's Council to be halted. The men had also come into the garden. They stood on the grass, looking out of place in their finery and out of their element in the sunshine.

Father rushed up to her. "Dear daughter of mine, what is going on? Are you all right?"

Johanna told him.

His eyes widened. "Auguste LaFontaine?"

"I'm wondering if it was him we disturbed at the *Lady Sara* two nights ago."

Johanna should go inside with Roald. He was wet and shivering. When he had an attack like that, he was usually very tired, but the guards were now carrying the body out of the reeds into the garden. They put Auguste down on the grass. His body had gone rigid. His arm stood out at an angle as if he was pointing at something.

The chief guard who stood next to Johanna judged that he'd been in the water for no more than two days.

"He doesn't float yet," he said in a tone that suggested he had experience in this matter.

Johanna wasn't sure if she wanted to know this much detail. She felt ill.

One of the guards gestured to his superior.

"Excuse me, Your Majesties." The chief guard went to join his men who bent or crouched over the body.

Father went and had a look as well, and then he gestured for Johanna to come, too.

Dragging him through the reeds had twisted Auguste's shirt and exposed the soft underside of his lower arm, where the skin was marked with an ink stain about the length of her thumb, in the shape of a dragon.

The same symbol as the carving that Li Fai had given her.

JOHANNA QUICKLY TOOK Roald into the bedroom, and then she went to look for Nellie. She had to tell the whole story over again, also about seeing the man on the *Lady Sara* a few nights ago.

Nellie's mouth fell open. "But why would he be sneaking around on your father's ship, Mistress Johanna?"

"Wouldn't it be good if we knew that?"

There were many possible reasons why Auguste might have been walking over the deck, maybe spying on Li Han's iron ship next to the *Lady Sara*. Maybe to do damage to Father's business.

A chill went over her.

The door opened and a courtier came in. "Your Majesty, your father wants to see you in the Red Room."

"I'm coming." Johanna looked at Nellie. "Are you going to be all right with Roald?"

"I just give him the usual treatment?"

"Yes. Give him warm milk with honey and books about frogs. Lots of frogs."

Nellie assured that she would look after Roald, who was already going through the shelves for a book to read, and Johanna went to the Red Room, where Father sat on the couch close to the hearth.

"I've asked Li Han to come," he said. His expression was grave. "Some members of the King's Council will be here, too."

Johanna's heart skipped a beat. "Do you really think Li Han has something to do with this?"

"I don't know. I don't think so. At least, I hope not." But he was worried, clearly. "Some people suggested to me that Li Han may try to get rid of all his competition who are trying to build the iron ships and that he's here and wants an office for that reason: that he is looking for ways to kill his competitors or ruin their businesses. I don't think that is true at all, but now that this has happened, I don't know how I'll be able to defend my position."

A deep hole of despair opened up in Johanna's mind. "If we had a water magician, we'd know what happened." Or at least they would know whether Auguste had been pushed or jumped and simply met with misfortune while sneaking around in a place where he wasn't supposed to be.

"If I'm correct, I heard you mention a water magician." Master Deim had come into the room. "I am not sure how that would help. A water magician can tell how he ended up in the water, but it might just have been too dark to see who was chasing the fellow or why he jumped."

Johanna gave him a sharp look. That was as close an admission she'd heard from him that *he*, in fact, was a water magician. "Chasing?"

"He jumped off the *Lady Sara*'s deck. He tried to swim, but the current was too strong and he got swept out of the harbour. Shouldn't have attempted to flee that way while the tide was going out."

"There was nowhere else for him to go, because we were on the quay."

"It was still stupid. The water is too cold. I don't think he was a good swimmer."

"What about the mark on his skin?"

Master Deim shook his head. "I have no idea. He must already have had it when he got into the water, but not too long before that. It's drawing ink. It would come off within a few days."

"So, what? We disturbed him at the *Lady Sara* where he was doing something mysterious, he tried to swim, but drowned? That doesn't account for the mark on his arm."

While they were speaking Johan Delacoeur had come in, followed by Thomas Kloostermans and Joris Decamp.

"The matter seems clear to me," Thomas said. "This eastern stranger captured him, gave him this mark, and then he jumped when escaping."

"It's a warning," Johan Delacoeur said, nodding.

Johanna protested. "That doesn't make sense. If that were the case, Auguste would have run to us and not from us. Also why would Li Han capture this man? Why would he draw in ink on his skin?"

"Evil magical foreign ways," Thomas said, his voice dark. "Who knows why these people do things? It's only a matter of time before the dragon comes out of that ship and roams the city. And you will all be sorry when all I can say is, 'I told you so.'"

"Oh, stop it with your stupid superstition!" Master Deim called out. "We're trying to solve a crime here. The witch hunts have long gone."

"Tell me with an honest face that you truly believe that these people have no evil magic."

"No *evil* magic," Master Deim said, his voice soft. "I believe that."

"You are wrong! *All* magic of this type is evil." Thomas Kloosterman's eyes looked like they were about to pop out of his head.

A chill went over Johanna's back. It was unlikely that Li Fai's little dragon was as harmless as it had looked. She said, "That is all very well, but why would Li Han purposely put this mark on Auguste's arm and then kill him to advertise what he's done? Why would he even want this young man dead?"

"I have no idea, but we can ask him right now." Thomas gestured to the door where a courtier had come in.

The man confirmed, "The eastern trader is here."

"Do let him in," Master Deim said.

The courtier disappeared again, and a man came into the

room, flanked by two massive guards who each wore armour and looked dangerous despite having left their weapons at the door. The much slenderer man in between them was not Li Han, but his son.

The guards accompanied him to the middle of the room, where they stopped and let their master walk to the throne alone. Li Fai bowed before Johanna. "Your Majesty, it is always an honour to see you."

Johanna cringed at seeing the smile in his eyes.

Today Li Fai was wearing a white shirt with a brocade jacket over the top. His hair was tied in a sleek bun at the back of his head.

He remained standing in a bowed position.

"Do get up," she said, glancing at the nobles.

He did, meeting her eyes. He was so serious. Doing his job. Representing his father's company.

"I'm afraid I don't have a pleasant reason for calling you here." She cringed.

"Oh?"

"I will show you. Come."

She led him into the corridor.

He walked next to her, his footsteps silent like a cat's.

They went into the bare, damaged ballroom. Alexandre had made a start at cleaning up this room, but hadn't progressed any further than to clean up and repair the doors to the garden room. That particular room was still in its ruined state. The guards had placed the body on the stone floor.

They gathered in a circle around it—Father, Master Deim, the three men from the King's Council and a couple of guards, including Li Fai's.

Li Fai's face did not show any emotion at the sight of the drowned man. He looked puzzled until she pointed out the ink mark on his arm. Then his eyes widened briefly.

"This is the mark of your family. Do you know anything about how this came to be on the man's arm?"

"You think I did this? Why would I put this stamp on a man's body?"

"I'm presuming it was put on before he entered the water

from our ship two nights ago. Right now, I'm not drawing any conclusions about who put it on or why."

Thomas Kloostermans snorted.

Li Fai's gaze shifted from her to Father, to the three nobles and back. "The brand is for marking our merchandise. It's not for people."

"You draw this sign on your products?"

"Yes. It's a stamp. We use it to put on bags and crates."

"You're certain that you or your crew did not put it on this man?"

"No. It's for things, not people. It's a stamp, not a brand. You put it in ink and stamp it on bags. We don't trade in slaves."

"Do you keep the stamp in a place where someone could steal it and use it?"

He frowned. "It is usually in a cabin on the deck of our ship."

"Would you miss it if someone took it for half a day or a day and put it back later?"

"Depends on if we need it. Some days the cargo manager doesn't use it."

"Did he use the stamp yesterday?"

"No. He only uses it if stock is loaded or unloaded. He keeps it in a box with a pot of ink and an ink pad."

"Could someone have stolen it?"

He gave her an affronted look. "That's why we have the ducks."

Yes, he had told her about them. "However, it looks like someone has used this stamp."

"I don't know how. The ducks always make a noise when anything moves on the deck. There are always people on the wharf. I don't know how anyone could have taken the stamp." His voice had lost the even tone, and his accent became more pronounced. "We have nothing to do with this man. I don't know why he jumped. I came to the quay to check. We have not spoken to him. I have never seen him before. I don't know who he is."

Johanna cringed inside.

Li Fai gaze's darted from one person to the other. His eyes were pleading when they met Johanna's.

Johanna said, "If you haven't done this, who would have?"

"I don't know." He glanced at the nobles again, and back to Johanna.

"Have people made threats to you or your family recently?"

"Yes. But that is normal. It happens wherever we go. People don't like us or our ship, and they make threats."

"Who are these people in Saardam?"

"I don't know them. They don't show themselves. They write letters. Sometimes there is a fake name on them, most of the time not. They tell my father to leave. They tell him that he will be killed. It's the same everywhere. We get used to it."

That was a rather terrible way to live.

"But talk and trying to scare us is easy. Writing letters like a coward is easy. Doing the things they threaten is not. My grandfather always says that. Words are easy but deeds are not. Sometimes people try to steal things from us, or yell bad words at our crew, but we get used to that. This . . ." He nodded at the dead man—

"Can you swear to us that you have nothing to do with the mark on this man's arm?"

"Yes, I swear. I have not seen this man. I have not touched this man. I have nothing to do with him."

Johanna believed him.

The three men from the King's Council watched with unemotional faces. Johanna didn't think that they believed him.

It was rather macabre holding council with a dead body between them, and the waft of wet clothes mixed with the beginnings of decay did nothing to calm Johanna's queasy stomach, so she led the group into the foyer, where the rest of Li Fai's entourage waited.

"Well," Johanna said to him. "I am still interested in your plan for an office, but we first need to establish to the satisfaction of the King's Council that neither you nor anyone in your crew have any responsibility for the death of this man."

He nodded. The expression in his eyes of confusion, bewilderment and hurt disturbed Johanna deeply. He spoke the truth, she was sure of that. Not only that, she wanted him to teach her magic.

He bowed and left with his entourage. Johanna looked at his back until he had gone through the palace gates.

"How do we know that he's speaking the truth?" Johan Delacoeur said. "If it's true what he is saying about the ducks, then the only people who could have had access to the deck at times when no one else was there were the members of his crew."

"Auguste LaFontaine is a son of a respected family," Thomas Kloostermans said. "I'm sure the family will be highly affronted if he stands accused of larceny. It's most inappropriate."

"I told you my version of the story," Johanna said. And she very much wanted to challenge the respectability of the LaFontaine family. Or, for that matter, that of some other "well-respected" families.

Thomas waggled his eyebrows. "If the man you saw jump in the water was indeed Auguste."

"It was," Master Deim said, his voice firm. Thank the Triune for Master Deim.

"How do you know?" Thomas shifted his gaze, lifting his chin.

"I know. I saw him." Master Deim kept a straight face. He crossed his arms over his chest and gave Thomas a cold stare. *Magic* was the answer, and Thomas would know it. That was the crux of the matter. As a staunch supporter of the Belaman Church, Thomas Kloostermans would support only the type of magic sanctioned by the church, and opinions over exactly what sort of magic that was varied wildly.

He snorted. "To me, it is clear. That gold brought by the slitty-eyed stranger has bewitched you, and your words are muddled by it. This man and his family are trying to scare us with magic. This is what Alexandre was trying to protect us from. He was doing it poorly and angered a lot of people—"

Johanna burst out. " 'Angered' does not quite cover the fact that he killed many people and burned their houses!"

Thomas lowered his voice. "I didn't say he was skilful or good. I said he was trying to protect the land from the influence of foul dragon magic, and match the menace of the iron ships with iron ships of our own. This murder of a son of one of our respected noble families proves that the threat is real, and that these people are not here to our benefit." He sounded like he was speaking through clenched teeth and made a point of looking at her stomach.

Johanna responded equally terse. "They are here for business. We have to do business with them, or they will do business with Anglia." Why was that so hard for these men to understand?

"If he can prove that he's got nothing to do with this death," Master Deim said. "But I don't think that will be too hard."

Thomas Kloostermans glared at him. "So you believe."

"I *know* that. But rest assured, the palace guards will investigate and they will find out what happened."

It seemed that there was no more to be said.

Thomas Kloostermans huffed something about being busy and excused himself. Johanna watched him go down the steps into the forecourt.

Johan Delacoeur nodded to her. "My congratulations on the impending birth. I don't think anyone has said this to you today."

"Well, thank you." The next thing he would start talking about how she should rest and do only womanly things like embroidery, so she changed the subject. "I don't think anyone has been in the mood for congratulations. It's a dark day."

"If you ask me, Your Majesty, I'd say that Auguste was asking for trouble. If he was snooping around the eastern trader's ship and one of those mountainous deck hands pushed him over the side, it could only have been his own fault."

"But they didn't, and he fell off the deck of the *Lady Sara*. Li Fai came to check because he heard a noise. That was the only time he became involved."

"If you say so."

"I was there."

"We'll see." Clearly he didn't believe her. Was there anything more frustrating than dealing with these men who thought she made things up?

He dipped his head to her and also left.

The next person in line, Joris Decamp, came up to her. "I'm sorry to bother you, Your Majesty, but the LaFontaine family is asking me a lot of questions, mainly about getting access to the body so they can hold a funeral."

"They can come to pick him up." Everyone who needed to have seen the dragon mark had seen it.

"They also told me that they launched their own investigation. They're not happy with what they called our lax approach."

"They're not happy that we haven't gone and arrested Li Han and put him in jail?"

He gave her a penetrating look. "Many people question your trust in the eastern trader. They don't understand why you believe his words and disregard the words of the town's citizens."

By "people" of course he meant nobles. Those came with the agenda of defending the city against the eastern menace and the evil church.

Normally, Joris Decamp tended to support her, but this made it clear how fragile her position was. They tolerated her because of Roald, because there was no one else to take the throne. As a woman, they were only willing to treat her seriously as long as she said womanly, obedient things.

The worst thing was that she was utterly dependent on them, and they now had control of everything and would destroy all her plans.

CHAPTER 12

JOHANNA MADE SOME sort of excuse and went to her office.

These men were going to destroy everything for the sake of their opinions. Just because they didn't like the church, and didn't like Li Han, and they were afraid that Li Han would put some of them out of business that they could have spent the past few months rebuilding, but hadn't.

Just because . . .

Because they were nobles and it was their sole purpose in life to stop her ideas. Because she was a woman. Because she was not a noble. Because she had saved the crown prince's life while they hoped he'd die, because she married him while their daughters thumbed their noses at him.

Because the *common citizens* of Saardam would benefit from her plan.

And though she didn't know how, she wasn't going to let them destroy her work.

She pulled a piece of parchment out of the drawer and spread it on the desk. Then she opened the pot of ink and selected a pen from the tray. Clearly, Roald had been rummaging in her writing things again, because there was charcoal in the tray. She'd already told him several times to keep it separate because it made everything black.

She wiped her hands on the dress—it was almost black anyway, dipped the pen in the ink and wrote:

To Li Fai. She hoped she spelled that correctly.

The events of today disturb me greatly, but I want you to know that I do not hold you or any of your crew in any way responsible for the death of this poor man. Some members of the King's Council may not believe you, but there is no doubt in my mind that you are speaking the truth.

She signed off with simply "Johanna" because anything else felt preposterous.

And then she added:

P.S. I very much enjoyed your openness in discussing magic. It is a difficult subject in this town because most people are afraid of it. I hope we can continue our discussion soon.

She let the letter dry for a moment and then rolled it up and sealed it before she could change her mind. She would not allow these nobles and church people to chase Li Han to Anglia, because he was innocent.

She went to the guard station and asked the young man there to see that it was delivered.

Next, Johanna went into the garden.

Most of Queen Cygna's rose bushes in the higher part of the garden had survived a year of neglect. Not having been pruned, they had become gangly, but the more hardy varieties were sprouting flowers. Johanna found a pair of pruning shears in the tool shed and set about cutting flowers that had just opened. A courtier came to ask what she was doing, and she informed him that she was cutting flowers for the poor man's funeral, and that reply seemed to satisfy him.

It was a bit strange being in the garden while Roald was inside. The flower baskets that she retrieved from the garden shed showed her images of Roald pottering about with jars and buckets. In one vision, a green frog climbed over the edge of a pot and jumped to the ground. Roald ran after it over the lawn. It made her laugh.

She divided the roses between the two baskets and took them inside.

Then she called for Nellie, who came to see her in the office, frowning at the roses.

"I want you to do something for me." Johanna took one basket. "For this basket, I want you to find some jam or compote from the cellar, or some spices or tobacco from Father's store. I want you to take it to the Nieland family with my apologies for forgetting Octavio's birthday."

"But that was two months ago."

"Yes. I've forgotten it."

Nellie frowned at her. Johanna could almost see her thoughts trying to work out whether she was serious or not.

She picked up the other basket. "To this one, you will add a little singlet and a blanket or some such and take it to Josefina LaFontaine, who I understand has given birth to a girl." She picked up a notebook from the desk. "Give her this, too. Tell her that I want Josefina to teach the girl how to read. And give the flowers for her cousin's funeral."

Nellie nodded, but she still look confused.

"When you visit these families, you will leave the entire basket there, and a couple of days later, we'll send someone around to collect the empty basket."

Nellie gasped and raised her hand to her mouth. Now she understood. "But Mistress Johanna, you can't go snooping on people like that. Why would you do this? You said you'd finished with this . . . magic."

"There are things I need to know."

"Why not leave the investigation to the guards?"

"There are things no one will tell the guards—especially the women, because I bet the guards will be hesitant to question the noble ladies."

"But you can't just . . . eavesdrop on those families—"

"Yes, we can. A man has died. Another man has hurt his wife. Yet another man has threatened someone in the street about something they are looking for. I have suspicions that these things could be related."

"You are speaking in riddles, Mistress Johanna."

"Has the shepherd been here?"

Nellie blinked at the sudden change of subject. "No, he hasn't. It's very strange—"

"Then we will send him a basket, too."

"Mistress Johanna! You don't spy on the shepherd!"

"Just do it, Nellie. Unless Greetje is ready to go back home, but I don't think she should until we know what's going on."

"No, she won't. Not yet. She's not been feeling well. I think her pains will start very soon."

"Then go to him and tell him that. Deliver a basket with some singlets and a blanket."

Nellie nodded, looking unhappy. "I really thought you were finished with this wood magic. I mean, that horrible thing that happened to the poor man having his life squeezed out of him by a tree would have been enough to put everyone off. Of course he is an evil man, but did he deserve to die like that?"

"Nellie, you never cease to surprise me with your capacity to judge people kindly."

"It's what the Triune teaches us to do. I'm a forgiving person, because holding grudges just makes you horrible and grumpy."

"But, you're talking about Alexandre. . . ."

"A horrible man, by all accounts, but like all people, deserved to be treated with dignity, because when you start treating people poorly, that is the end of the world."

"Then, Nellie, if you feel like that about what I asked you to do, I can ask someone else to go."

Nellie's eyes widened in shock. "No, Mistress Johanna. I would never allow that!"

"But you just said . . ."

"What you tell me to do is what I do. You are much wiser than I am and I trust that you ask me for a good reason. To be perfectly honest, Mistress Johanna, and don't tell anyone I said this, those horrible arrogant families could do with being taught a lesson."

Johanna laughed, and then turned serious again. "As long as no one dies."

"Yes." Nellie nodded.

Johanna sighed. "I'm sorry to ask you to do this, but you know most times I feel that you're the only friend I have. If . . ."

She shuddered. "When the time comes that the pains start and the child is about to arrive, you are the only person I want with me, besides Helena."

Nellie looked at her with wide eyes. "Oh!" And then her eyes glittered. "Oh, Mistress Johanna!" She wiped her eyes with the end of her sleeve. "Look at that. You're making me cry."

"It's true," Johanna said.

"Oh, mistress Johanna!" Nellie wiped at her eyes again.

Johanna's eyes pricked, too. Words about how scared she was of the pains were on her tongue. Or about how she was almost certain that Roald was not the father of this child. Kylian had made a pass at Nellie. She would understand how overwhelming his magic was.

Johanna also asked Nellie to collect any wood that she could find from the warehouses and quayside near the *Lady Sara* and Li Han's ship. She drew a map of the part of the quay and indicated spots where there might be wooden items that could tell her a story.

"You have to write down precisely where you collected them," she told Nellie.

Some of the places would require a man to visit without raising eyebrows, like the inside of the warehouses. Nellie said that any of the groundsmen would be happy to go if she asked.

"I don't want people to get into trouble," Johanna said.

"People are happy to take risks. They adore you, mistress Johanna."

Nellie took her task seriously. She wanted to know if the type of wood mattered. Johanna explained that willow wood was the best, but any other wood would do. She said the best things were items that weren't used too often. Things like tables and benches typically only told stories one day old, because they were used so much, and newer memories took the place of older ones.

By the time the maid came in, wondering why Johanna hadn't called for the coach, she realised that not only had she forgotten to get dressed, she was going to be late to church.

NELLIE GASPED WHEN she realised that. "Oh, mistress Johanna, how terrible! Quickly, I'll help you get ready."

"No, Nellie."

Nellie stared at her, eyes wide. "What do you mean, no?"

"I've been thinking about this. We have Greetje here and the shepherd hasn't even been to visit his wife. Is that an example of a caring man or one who is sorry about what he has done? Even before this happened, I've been very concerned about the way the shepherd has been preaching in church. It's like he's gone mad, like he's trying to get people to sign up to go to war. You can't make magic go away by ignoring it. He should know that better than anyone. Something has happened that has made him act like this and I don't think we should give him any more power than he already has until he calms down and we find out what it is."

"He's afraid of magic."

"He's a wind magician. Everyone knows that. I don't understand what is going on with him. You know, I have looked in the *Book of Verses* but can't see where it says that magic is forbidden."

"But even Shepherd Romulus used to say this."

"Yes, but I don't think the couple of verses that he always quotes mean what he thinks they mean. The most important quote is two lines from *The Book of Revelation* that say, '*And those whose magic turns to evil, let them burn in doom.*' The church of the Triune interprets this as meaning 'no magic', but the Belaman Church uses the same version of *The Book of Revelations* and they interpret it differently. The church has always fought their own battles about magic. The Belaman Church uses the word magic to mean belief, for the holy teachings. Shepherd Romulus would have been talking about that type of magic."

"I don't know, Mistress Johanna. It all seems very confusing to me. None of these supposedly important men ever seem to say what they actually mean. If they talk about a woman's 'situation' they mean she's with child. If they talk about 'magic' they really mean the belief of the Belaman Church?"

"Our shepherd doesn't. He definitely means real magic."

"But Shepherd Romulus didn't?"

"I don't think so. After all, true magic is not common in Saardam. He received his teaching from the great seminary in Lurezia."

Nellie sighed and shook her head. "It's all so complicated. But for what it's worth, I think that the church would be a bad enemy to have."

"It is, but instead of going to the nightly service—because how much gossip would I start by coming in late—"

"Less than by not going at all?"

"I don't know about that. But anyway, I don't want to disturb the service and call attention to myself, so I'm going to light a candle for Auguste LaFontaine in the Belaman Church—"

Nellie gasped.

"Mother used to go the Belaman Church. I could call myself a member even if I haven't been baptised. I think you taught me something today about treating someone with dignity, even if it's someone you don't like and who hasn't treated you with dignity. Next time Auguste's family come into the church for the funeral, they will see a candle with a card that has a royal seal and they'll know that I sympathise with their loss. And also, Nellie, just because the old bearded men of the Belaman Church don't like the Church of the Triune and declare that it's no longer part of their church, that doesn't mean we have to agree with that. As far as I know, they teach the same things and fight against the same evil magic, even if they use different names for it. Anyway, after I've lit the candle, I'll go and pray in shepherd Carolus' church. They don't have evening services, so I can enter there without disturbing anything."

So it was done.

The home of the Belaman Church, the small but ornate building around the corner from the marketplace, had "miraculously" survived the fires. The Holy Father Fabricius was Burovian. He spoke with a thick accent that noble children often mocked—and got clipped on the ear for doing so.

Johanna used to go to this church to pick up her mother. In those days, the streets seemed so much more colourful.

Her early memories were of walking down the street on Father's hand and seeing people stream out of the little building of the Belaman Church. There had been a wedding and all the guests were dressed in vibrant colours. Some of the women wore costumes that included headbands with hundreds of dangling coins. They were colourful people, mostly dark-haired and olive-skinned. Several men were playing lutes while the happy couple, both in cream-coloured silk, stood on the church steps.

Whatever happened to that Saardam?

Those people must have left, too, gone to Lurezia or any of the big towns.

Johanna alighted from the coach in front of the building. It looked smaller than she remembered, and had recently been cleaned.

She went up the steps and pushed the door. It creaked.

Johanna peeked in. The noise brought no reaction from inside. Candles flapped in sconces attached to the pillars that supported the roof.

Johanna took a candle from the box on a table in the foyer and dropped a Phoenician gold coin in the donations box.

She then walked down the aisle. There was such a difference between this church and the wooden building of the Church of the Triune. The walls behind the altar and along the sides were covered in brightly painted murals depicting scenes from the *Book of Verses*. There was a lot of gold and blue paint, and neither of those colours was cheap. Almost every side panel of the outer wall told its own story. Sometimes there would be a statue or a little altar dedicated to this or that saint. The floor displayed elaborate mosaics.

She couldn't help but think of the splendid building in Florisheim where she had prayed to the saint Magdalena whom the people in Florisheim worshipped as saint of mothers and children. And the saint had granted Johanna her prayers. Even if Roald's seed didn't work, the saint had granted Johanna a child.

She placed the candle on the tiered shelves where other candles burned and leaked wax all over the wood. She inserted her card in the groove in the wood that ran along the front edge of the shelf. *In the memory of Auguste LaFontaine, in sympathy with those who mourn his loss. Queen Johanna Carmine de Lacoeur van Leeuwen Brouwer.*

She knelt on the bench and said a few words of prayer.

Only when she rose again did she become aware of the dark-robed figure kneeling at a bench in front of the giant mural of the Lord Saviour. The mural depicted Him as a bearded man. His friendly face had always fascinated her as a child.

The man who sat on his knees was the Holy Father Fabricius.

How long had he been sitting there?

He didn't look up, but sat with his head down, his hands folded in prayer. Johanna sat on the frontmost pew and waited until he raised his head.

"It is a good thing to see you here, Your Highness."

"I came to light a candle for the poor young man who drowned in the harbour."

He nodded. "It's so sad."

"Tell the family that I sympathise with them." She rose and stepped into the aisle.

He dipped his head. "It is terrible. Magic stirs in the belly of this town. Every time something bad happens, I tell the citizens: there will be death and destruction until you vanquish this foul magic."

His eyes were intense.

Johanna nodded a lame agreement and retreated down the aisle, remembering suddenly why she had started attending the

Church of the Triune's services. The Holy Father Fabricius always said things like this, as if it were his task to make everyone afraid.

The coach that waited in front of the church then took her to the much smaller church building two streets away that was the home of Shepherd Carolus.

He was a much more cheerful fellow and came to Johanna with open arms when she entered. Since coming back to Saardam with him, he had tamed his straw-like hair, but he was as tall and gangly as ever.

"Welcome, welcome. I feared we'd never see you again in this humble building. Come and share a prayer to the Holy Father."

They did. Because all things in the church came in threes, Johanna dedicated her prayer first to Auguste LaFontaine, then to Roald in the hope that he wouldn't remain scarred by finding the body and then to Li Fai *because he is innocent and doesn't deserve all this trouble*.

"What brings you here today?" Shepherd Carolus asked when they finished.

"I want to ask you something."

"Ask away."

"Tell me if it's an inappropriate thing to ask or if you don't want to talk about it. I'm asking this as a citizen with concern for the safety of our city."

The laughter faded from his face.

"Apparently, when he came to Saardam, Li Han brought in the hold of his ship a crate that had been given to him by a monk in Seneza to be delivered to Shepherd Victor. It seems that many people are keen to get their hands on whatever is inside. Word goes that the shepherd doesn't have it, but no one knows where it is."

"Oh, he has it all right."

"What is inside?"

Shepherd Carolus sighed and shook his head. The serious look on his face didn't suit him terribly well. "Rumours abound about this thing. Word goes that when the Most Holy Father Severino of the Belaman Church made the decision to cast the Church of the Triune out, he also no longer wished to hold onto the relics that the Church of the Triune had trusted him with."

"Did he have any of our relics?" This was the first she heard of it.

"There is some discussion over that. The Church as we know it and we practice here . . ." He gestured around the empty pews. ". . . is quite a new thing, but apparently the forebears of the Church of the Triune arose in poor farming communities in the area where Saarland, Estland, Burovia and Gelre join. Those poor people are very much into relics because they have so little and treasure each possession."

Johanna nodded. She had seen the heartbreaking poverty of those people and the incredibly poor land they farmed, and where the father was happy to receive coin from bandits seeking pleasure with his daughter.

"It is said, but I don't know how true any of this is, that the early shepherds came from that area and brought their relics, which were later transferred to the Belaman Church for safe-keeping."

Johanna frowned. "But they're objects, things made out of wood or stone. Or bones. How can they be more valuable than gold?"

But as she said that, she already knew the answer: they were objects to which *magic* was ascribed.

Shepherd Carolus continued, "Other people say that the relics didn't belong to the church but to some ancient pagan settlement which died out. They say that the relics impart witchcraft on those who have them. And other people again say that this crate is something sent by the Red Baron under the guise of being a religious relic in order to bring about our destruction."

"Now *that* is something I can believe."

"Whatever it is, Shepherd Victor has the crate."

"At the church?"

"I don't know. I've asked him if he wants help in dealing with it, but he keeps changing the subject. If it were something simple, he would have dealt with it. I don't think it's simple, which goes against the most obvious answer: that the contents are sent by the Baron purely with ill intent. In that case, the shepherd could just toss the crate in the fire and be done with it. I think there *are* relics of some description involved."

"What sort of things would relics be?"

"It could be anything. Many of the old relics are not pleasant things. I've seen relics that are necklaces made of human teeth. Some relics are the bones or scales of strange animals. There is usually a horrible story related to the relic, and many are objects of dark magic and shouldn't be disturbed for that reason, especially not in here in Saardam, where some like to think we have no magic."

"Could one turn a magic relic harmless?"

"I guess you could. I guess that might be what he's trying to do."

"Or destroy it?"

"Hmmm. A magic relic would unleash terrible powers if you tried to destroy it. You'd have to be very careful that you didn't end up with a worse situation than when you started. But again, I don't know much about it, much less about what's inside that box that he's got. But one thing I want to say. He loves that girl and would never harm her. If this thing made him do that, then it's something terrible indeed."

After some small talk with the shepherd—and it was good to see him again—Johanna went back to the palace.

She needed something to eat before going to see Greetje, but as she sat in the kitchen, Nellie came in, carrying a pile of bedsheets, her face red.

"Oh mistress, there you are. I've called Helena. Greetje is complaining about cramps."

CHAPTER 14

JOHANNA ARRIVED AT Greetje's room at the same time that Helena came out. She shook her head in response to Johanna's unasked question. "Not yet, but she is very close. I'll come back tomorrow morning."

"Can I go in?"

"Yes, of course."

Johanna went into the room. Greetje sat in the bed, nibbling at a slice of bread that stood on a plate on the cover. Her stomach was so round and big that she had to lean back.

She looked at Johanna when she came in, but said nothing. Johanna sat down on the chair next to the bed. "How are you feeling?"

"I'm sick of this. I can't sleep, I can't walk, I can't sit, I can't breathe. Everything hurts. It's not fun at all."

Johanna could see that. "It won't last much longer."

"No." Greetje stared into the distance.

A moment of uneasy silence passed.

Then Johanna said, "I need to talk to you about something."

"Oh?" She turned to Johanna. There was a slightly alarmed look in those grey eyes.

"I asked you yesterday about a crate that your husband received. You said that you didn't know anything about it."

"I don't." The answer came a bit quick for her liking.

"Has he mentioned anything to you about it?"

"No. Not that I know."

"You're sure?"

"Yes, why do you keep asking?"

"Because it's important, because I think your husband might be in trouble."

"He's not hiding anything from anyone, if that's what you think."

Obviously, he was, and Johanna was unsure why Greetje was becoming so defensive on behalf of her husband who had mistreated her. "But at the same time you have to agree that he's not himself and that there has to be a reason. I spoke to Shepherd Carolus."

Greetje gave her a sharp look.

"He says that rumours are that following the verdict by the Most Holy Father Severino of the Belaman Church that the Church of the Triune can no longer be part of that organisation, he arranged to ship back to Shepherd Victor the relics of the church which had been held in safekeeping by the Belaman Church—"

"That's a lie."

"I didn't say it was the truth. It is what people are talking about on the streets. Failing better information, they consider it the truth."

"It's still a lie. The whole thing is a lie."

"For something that you say your husband doesn't have, you seem to know a good deal about it."

"He talked about it."

"Then what did he say?"

"Why is this so important? It's just a thing."

"There are many objects that are not *just a thing*. Is the king's crown *just a thing*? Is his Carmine Cloak *just a thing*? Or is a flag *just a thing*? And the statue of the Triune that Alexandre's men went to the effort to drag to the harbour and drop there, if that were *just a thing* do you think the church would have made such an effort to raise it and clean it?"

Greetje looked down at the bedspread. There was one piece

of bread left on the plate that stood next to her, and she picked crumbs off the crust.

Johanna continued. "Things can be symbols, but worse, things can contain magic. I am beginning to suspect we're dealing with such a magical thing. If your husband is in any way as stubborn as he used to be when he worked for Father, he would not admit this. Because magic doesn't exist, according to the church—"

"I don't know what you're getting at. You're making underhanded comments about my husband. He's a good man."

"He may need help, Greetje, and he may be too stubborn to admit it. And something doesn't add up in all your tales. I don't think you're telling the entire truth of what happened."

"I am!" Her eyes were wide.

"Or you're leaving some key bits of information out. I don't know why and I don't need to know exactly what went on in your family, but tomorrow, I will be sending guards to your husband to ask him about it, because in the time you've been here, he has not once come to the palace to check on you. If you think like me, that's not normal, and if you think that he is going to tell the guards something that you haven't told me, that's not going to look good, is it?"

Greetje looked up at her. Tears welled in her eyes. "I don't know why everyone is so mean to me. I should have stayed at home."

Maybe you should. "You're tired, and maybe it's the wrong time to be worried about it. I'm going to write some letters. If you want me, I'll be in my office." Johanna rose.

"No. Don't go. I'm scared."

"The birth pains are a natural thing. Your body will know what to do." Helena always said this, anyway. Johanna felt terrible, because she was scared, too.

"No. It's not that."

"Then what?"

Greetje hesitated. Met Johanna's eyes. Looked down again. Then she said, her voice barely audible, "I looked."

Johanna went back to the chair next to the bed and sat down

again. The child inside her was giving her a most unbecoming set of kicks.

Greetje continued, "That crate you were talking about? It's in his room upstairs, with all the skulls and the teeth and the other terrible things that he collected."

"Why did you say he didn't have it?"

"Because . . ." Greetje's lip trembled. "Because it is an evil thing. Because . . . he made me promise not to touch it or look at it . . . because . . ." She covered her face with her hands.

"What, Greetje?" Johanna's heart was thudding. "Because what?"

"Because . . . I couldn't help myself and I was stupid, and I looked anyway when I thought he wasn't watching . . ."

She burst out into tears, sobbing so hard that her words came out as incomprehensible wails. Johanna moved from the chair to the bed. Greetje fell into her arms, crying into her shoulder in long, gasping wails. Johanna patted her back.

"Why did you do it?" she asked when the worst seemed to have passed.

"Because I'm a stupid woman! He even told me that. But honestly, this thing was calling out to me from the moment he brought it into the house."

Johanna shuddered, thinking of the twisted tree that held Alexandre prisoner that called out to her when she came to the market place. "So, what happened that you haven't already told me?"

"I've not told you any lies!"

"No, but you held back information."

Greetje's mouth twitched. After a short silence, she started in a low voice. "So he brought this thing home and as soon as he took it inside the door, I could feel its evil. I asked the old maid who has been with his family for years, but she said I was making it up. She always thinks I'm crazy. Then I asked my husband, and he said that it was something he needed to deal with, and that I shouldn't go into the room upstairs until he said it was safe. I was not to open the crate or look at it or have anything to do with it. That's when he started spending so much time there praying, and sometimes crying. And I really could not stand it anymore so I told him to take the thing out of the house, and he said he would but he didn't. I asked the maid to tell him the same thing, because he listens better to her than to me, and he got angry with me for pulling his trusted maid into it. And then I thought enough is enough, so one day when he was at church, I went into the room."

Her chin trembled. She took a big, shuddering breath.

"The crate stood on the table in the middle of the room. The lid was off, but I couldn't see into it from the door. And, I don't know how to say this, but it was calling out to me."

"I understand that feeling," Johanna said.

"He had pleaded with me not to go into the room, but I so desperately wanted that crate out of our house. I was going to pick it up, walk outside and dump it in the canal." She stared at her hands. "But I had to get close to it first. As I came closer to the table, I told myself I was not going to look inside. I was going to put the lid on. The lid was on the floor, leaning against the table leg. I crouched so that the bottom of the box was out of my view. The inside of the box was lined with red velvet, I could see that, and I was wondering what sort of thing justified this luxury. But I didn't look. I crouched to pick up the lid. It, too, had red velvet on the inside. I turned it over so that the velvet faced the bottom, and I held it in front of my face so I couldn't see into the crate. Apart from the red velvet lining, there was also something like a gold staff with a ruby on top. I could see that. I thought that wasn't such a bad thing to look at, but I promised him that I wouldn't, so I kept the lid in front of my face. And then I bumped into the table because you know I couldn't see where I was going. The golden staff thing fell over and the ruby hit something that made a dull hollow sound." She shivered visibly.

"And you looked."

"I looked. A black thing, a bit bigger than a man's fist, lay on the velvet. It was a bit bumpy and round on top and it was this round part that the staff had hit. At first I couldn't make out what I was looking at. It was dark in that room, and black is not the usual colour you'd expect . . ." Tears welled up in her eyes.

"Not the colour you'd expect what to be?"

"It was terrible. As soon as I looked at it and I realised what it was, I saw these . . . these . . . horrible visions. This girl screaming and screaming like an animal. A man with a knife, cutting her. There was blood dripping from his hands, on his clothes, even in his face." Greetje covered her face with her hands. Her shoulders shook. "I couldn't stop the visions. I couldn't stop her screaming, I couldn't stop him slashing at her. I could feel her pain."

She took a few fast breaths.

"And then I was yanked away. My husband was yelling at me at the top of his voice, saying all these horrible things. Holding me with my back against the wall. I screamed that I *had* to go back into that room. I was trying to get out of his grip, scratching his arms. This was when he hit me. I've never seen him so angry . . ." She cried in big racking sobs. Her shoulders shook. Her whole body shook.

"What was the black thing in the crate?" Johanna asked when Greetje had calmed down a bit.

"It was . . . it was . . . a skull of a newborn child." She started crying again. "It could have been our child! Murdered. With rubies stuck in the eye sockets."

Johanna held Greetje, waiting until she calmed down again.

"At the time when the Church of the Triune came to Saardam, there was a Belaman Church monastery in town."

Johanna had heard about that.

"Apparently, the abbot took a liking to deflowering young girls and would keep seeing these girls as a part of their repentance for whatever minor disobedience they had come to confess. Whenever the girl became with child, the monks would hunt her down and kill the girl. They would sometimes cut out the child to make sure it died. Apparently one girl managed to escape the monks until the day her child was born. The babe drew one breath before her head was chopped off and the mother cut to pieces. That is the skull of the child in the crate."

"And it's a church relic?" That was horrible. Disgusting.

"After this happened, a lot of people took to the streets and burned down the monastery and chased the monks out of town. The Church of the Triune gained a good deal of influence because of this. And because the newborn girl had drawn a breath, she became a ghost. Murdered people often become ghosts. No one murders young children. They're the most horrible powerful ghosts. Demanding, crying, powerless in anger. The church kept this skull to protect the citizens. My husband has been seeking ways to destroy it. I was so stupid to undo all his work. I should have listened to him. I'm not worthy of him."

"Come on, now. It's not easy to withstand a thing of evil magic. Even the best magicians have trouble with that." Johanna put a hand on Greetje's knee. "He will have to accept help. We'll talk to him tomorrow."

Greetje nodded, although she still looked scared.

Johanna rose. "You look exhausted. Go to sleep now. We'll talk to your husband in the morning."

Greetje leaned back in the pillows. She looked so pale and tired that she would probably be asleep very soon. Johanna also had a feeling that her pains would start before morning.

CHAPTER 15

JOHANNA WAS RIGHT about Greetje. Nellie woke her up when it was barely light, sneaking into the linen cupboard in the room.

"What?" she whispered.

Roald was still asleep. Nellie put her index finger against her lips, so Johanna rolled out of bed and followed her into the hallway.

"The pains have started," Nellie said. "Helena should be here soon."

Johanna went into the dressing room and got changed into her housedress. Her hands were sweaty with nerves while doing up the buttons over her own swollen stomach. Guess she was about to find out what was going to happen to her in late summer. The child mocked her by doing somersaults inside her.

Greetje sat on the rug in the middle of the room on her hands and knees. She didn't look up when the door opened, but let her head hang forward. She still wore the nightdress that Johanna had lent her. The fabric was thin, and the light that came into the window showed Greetje's body under the dress. Her belly was round as a water bag ready to burst. She moaned softly and rocked from side to side.

Nellie had dragged a little table into the room where she had lined up neatly folded towels and swaddling cloths, clean sheets, a jug of water, soap, and a little white gown.

The fire blazed in the hearth, even though it wasn't particularly cold.

Helena came in, lugging the bare wooden birthing chair that Johanna had sometimes spotted her carting through town. She plonked it on the rug next to Greetje, who eyed it suspiciously. Bare and made of dark wood, and with no seat except a narrow ledge, it looked like a piece of torture apparatus.

"Sit there," Helena said, after she put down her other things in the corner of the room. Johanna thought she spotted knitting needles and wool.

Greetje heaved herself up, wincing. "Do you want anything off?"

"Just the underthings. Leave the gown on."

Greetje sat on the chair, moving gingerly. The only way to sit on it was with her legs spread and it was not very elegant. Helena knelt on the ground, feeling under Greetje's gown.

Greetje gasped. She let her head hang forward, breathing deeply. She let out a soft moan.

Helena sat back and waited for the pain to pass.

Johanna involuntarily placed her hand on her own swollen stomach. It had tightened into a hard ball.

Greetje met her eyes. "I'm sorry. It really hurts."

"No need to apologise," Johanna said. She sat down in the single chair in the room. Her stomach had relaxed, but now she badly needed to use the outroom.

Helena asked a bit about when Greetje's pains had started and how often they came.

Greetje had to stop talking a few times, but it seemed a quiet affair, not the frantic screaming that Johanna had heard other women talk about. If it was like this, she could handle it.

Helena climbed to her feet. "It's early days. This will take a good while. I don't know that it's necessary for you to sit in the room. Maybe ask a maid to check in with me every now and then. Have breakfast, do your normal things. I will call when there is progress."

Johanna nodded.

"Do you want me to bring some tea?" Nellie asked.

Helena said that she did, so Nellie left with Johanna. The cool breeze through the corridor made her shiver.

"Phew, it was really hot in that room," Johanna said.

"It's to keep out the bad air," Nellie said. "We don't want the little one to catch a cold."

"Do you think you can still go out and get me those pieces of wood that we were talking about yesterday? The longer we leave it, the more irrelevant images the wood will store."

"I'll do that right after I've brought the tea."

"Thank you, Nellie."

"You go and have breakfast."

Johanna didn't feel like it was fair for her to eat while Greetje suffered, but on the other hand if she didn't eat anything herself she would faint.

She found Father and Roald at the breakfast table talking about frogs. Or at least Roald was talking because Johanna had no doubt that Father had heard Roald's story many times before.

She sat at the table and ate a few pieces of bread and jam while listening to Roald. He *still* wasn't eating, so when there was a little pause in his story, she deposited half her bread on his plate.

"Eat it."

He stared at her as if the fact that you were supposed to eat at the table was a new notion. "What about you? You have to eat."

"I will eat later." The few bites she'd taken of the bread sat uncomfortably in her stomach. Eating more was not going to help.

"I heard rumours that you didn't go to church last night," Father said.

"No, I was busy, forgot the time and was too late. I went to light a candle for Auguste LaFontaine."

Father raised his eyebrows. "Different church?"

"It was the right thing to do. I'm not sure that I agree with how much influence the Church of the Triune wants to have over the royal family. I think we may need to step back a little."

"That took you long enough to realise," Father said.

Typical for Father, he kept changing his mind about why he disliked the church. It seemed he was determined to dislike them no matter what they did.

"The church did many good things for common people at a time that they needed it." She thought of Greetje's horrid story about murdered girls. "They're still doing good things. They give people food."

Father said, "They buy souls with every food package they hand out. They shouldn't be feeding the people, the royal family should."

"What with?" She spread her hands.

She was starting to feel really ill and excused herself from the table just in time. By the Triune, women had told her that this sickness was meant to let up once your stomach started growing. Her body clearly had different ideas.

After a quick rest, Johanna then had to go to the kitchen, where the cook gave her some cake and soup. Halfway through eating that, Nellie came in again.

The cook asked her, "Do you still want to boil the water? It's been boiling for a long time now."

"Put it aside. She's going to be a fair while."

"How long?" Johanna asked, feeling chilled.

"Helena says it's very slow. No need to hurry to the guest room. I'm about to go out to run your errands, Mistress Johanna."

Johanna sat at her desk but succeeded at nothing more than staring at the letters she had been writing before the King's Council so clearly dismissed her. She thought of going to see the shepherd, but he could do nothing until the child had made its appearance. She went to have a look in the guest room. Greetje lay on her side in the bed, moaning, while Helena sat knitting. Nothing much happening there.

Johanna wandered to the guard station to ask how they were going with the investigation. Anton was on duty there and didn't seem to have much to do.

He told her that Auguste LaFontaine's body had been delivered to the family. The guards had spoken to the young man's family and friends.

"There is something going on with those people that he's friends with," he said. "We'll have to ask further when they're more amenable to speaking to us, after the funeral."

"Do you think they know more than they're telling you?"

"Certainly, but they're pretty protective of each other now. Their versions of events line up far too perfectly. We can loosen them up later. They have weaknesses we can explore. They're a bunch of raucous young men with none too good a reputation, if you get what I mean."

Johanna had to think of Nellie and her "these men don't say what they mean" speech. She guessed that "none too good a reputation" meant that the young men frequented whorehouses.

"Is Octavio Nieland one of those friends?" she asked.

"Octavio wouldn't call himself a friend of a bunch of young louts like that. They're more like his lackeys."

He didn't have much other news, so Johanna went to her office. The pile of draft letters mocked her from the corner of the desk.

It said to her *Look at you, little queen. You had notions that you could escape the fate of so many women before you. You thought the men would listen to your ideas. You thought that they would give you power. But whatever you do, you'll always still be a woman and they will never, ever take you seriously.*

She picked up the pile and leafed through the names.

Everything she did was pointless. Baron Uti, King Leo and King William wouldn't even know who she was. They'd say "The consort of WHO?" And they'd laugh and laugh.

She might as well throw the whole lot in the fire. Let the men do whatever they wanted. Learn to knit and sew and make pretty newborn outfits. Hold tea parties for the noble women. Admire their dressed-up brats. And grow roses.

After all, that was all Queen Cygna had done. No doubt she'd been a fighting spirit once, too, in her youth in the northern country where she had grown up. Maybe she'd dreamt of having her own fishing boats. One day, her father would have told her she was to marry a prince in another country. She would have cried, but she would have done as her father ordered, because that was what good girls did. After all, he was a prince.

Tears came to Johanna's eyes when she thought about it like this. In all the talk about the tragic circumstances of the royal family, Queen Cygna was rarely mentioned.

Nellie came to her room later in the morning. To Johanna's question about Greetje, she said that there was not much progress.

She carried a basket from which she dug a couple of items made from wood: a wooden spoon from the kitchen in the armoury and a twig from a broom in one of the quayside ware-houses that belonged to one of the noble families of interest.

"It's quite hard to find things made out of wood that are small enough for me to carry," she said. "I don't know if these are any good. There are also a lot of people around, and I have to be careful."

Johanna had to smile when she imagined Nellie snooping around and *stealing* a wooden spoon from the armoury kitchen.

The spoon showed her a good view of the cook going off at a kitchen hand while soldiers lined up with their plates. The language was . . . interesting.

The broom twig was the most informative, except the broom had been in the broom cupboard and the images included a glorious view of the inside of the cupboard, while two male voices spoke in the main room. They spoke about nothing inter-esting—warehouse space—but the way in which they referred to her as "the little queen", as if she were a child, disturbed her.

"I'm sorry if they're not very good," Nellie said.

"It's all right. I didn't expect any of these pieces of wood to tell us precisely what we want to know. That would have been crazy coincidence. We'll probably have to go a few times while he guards are doing the formal questioning."

Nellie looked in her basket. "I swear there was something else. There were some wood chips from the saw mill." She rummaged in the basket and found the wood chip: a chunk of willow wood that looked to have been separated from the block with an axe.

In fact, the blow of the axe was exactly what Johanna saw when she put the splinter on her hand.

She winced.

Nellie said, "Oh, mistress Johanna, are you all right?"

Johanna saw a group of young men fighting on the sawdust-covered floor in the sawmill. No, they were play-fighting, laughing and being silly. They were probably drunk.

One young man had taken off his shoes and he carried another over his shoulder through the warehouse. That young man was yelling at him and pummelling his friend's back with his fists.

The one carrying his mate was Auguste LaFontaine. He flung the other man off his shoulder into the sawdust. His friends pounced on him with a slate sponge, covering his face in chalk. There was much laughter and silliness.

By the Triune, how drunk were these men? It was embarrassing to watch.

"Mistress Johanna?" Nellie asked.

"Yes, this is a good one." Johanna put the wood chip on the table. "Get me more from there and perhaps the quay outside."

Nellie nodded and left the room. She looked happy, and Johanna couldn't bear to tell her how pointless it all was.

CHAPTER 16

JOHANNA SPENT MOST of the afternoon on the couch in the living room. She felt tired and ill, and her feeble efforts to do some embroidery didn't come to much. Even Nellie was surprised about it when she came in to bring tea.

She nodded at the work on Johanna's lap. "That's an unusual sight, if you don't mind me saying so, Mistress Johanna."

"I thought, since it's my child, I better start taking an interest in the things that an expectant mother is supposed to do."

"Oh, but myself and the other girls can do all that. Just you keep busy with important things."

Johanna sighed. "They don't want me, Nellie. They're not going to listen to me. Roald is not going to turn up to meetings and help me. I'm tired of fighting these stupid, pompous noblemen."

"Just have a good rest. Your body is working very hard. No wonder you feel listless."

But Johanna felt it was more than that. She just thought that by giving up her freedom and marrying the prince no one wanted to marry, she expected at least *some* people to be grateful for saving the royal family. But in truth no one cared, at least no one who had any power in Saardam.

So instead she found herself in this gilded cage without real supporters beyond Father and Master Deim, and without friends.

Later in the afternoon, a courtier came into the room. "I'm sorry to disturb you, Your Majesty, but this arrived for you." He carried a roll of parchment held by a white ribbon.

A silk ribbon, tied in a neat bow. The stamp in the sealing wax depicted a tiny dragon.

Johanna sat up and took it from him, her heart thudding. She broke the seal, pulled the ribbon and unrolled the parchment.

At the top was another dragon, this one hand-drawn in exquisite detail, by Li Fai's mother, Johanna guessed.

Underneath, it said,

To Johanna, esteemed Queen of Saarland.

She had to laugh at that.

The letter continued,

I appreciated your previous correspondence. The palace guards have been to our ship, and I am confident that they have seen the truth that we had no involvement in the poor man's death.

I have also noted your interest in the arts. I have asked my mother what can be done for a person who has grown up without a box. She has shown me some things I would like to try. If you're amenable, we could arrange a meeting in a mutually agreed place.

It was signed Li Fai.

Johanna held the letter to her chest, breathing its unfamiliar perfume. The eastern people didn't seem to have any customs that resulted in women being disregarded. They even wore trousers. Maybe she should hide on board the ship when it, inevitably, left Saardam for Anglia.

It was a silly thought. Of course she would never leave Father, but just the thought that no one on Li Han's ship raised any objections about Li Han's wife travelling with them made her own situation sting even more.

She cast her feeble attempt at sewing aside and went to the office.

In reply to Li Fai's letter, she wrote,

I would very much like to have a meeting. Magic is not taught to children in Saardam, since only few have it. In my limited travels, I have searched for people who could teach, and have never found anyone willing to do so. It is perhaps unwise for you to come to the palace in the current climate, and inappropriate for me to visit your ship, but we could meet at my father's office at the quay. Let me know if tomorrow two hours after midday would suit you.

Surely Greetje would have had the child by then.

She rolled up the letter, sealed it and went to the guard station to have it delivered.

Next, it was time for the evening meal. Nellie didn't show herself and neither did Helena, so Johanna ate quickly and went to the guest room to check on the progress there.

Greetje lay with her eyes closed on the bed. Her shoulders went up and down with deep breaths. She looked asleep, but probably wasn't. Helena was asleep in the chair, leaning back with her mouth open. Johanna didn't want to disturb either of them, so she left the room quietly. She'd best go to bed early. Most likely, she'd probably be called in the middle of the night.

But when Johanna woke up with a shock, it was to light streaming in through a crack in the curtains. She jumped out of bed, flung on a dress and went to the guest room.

Even before she entered, it was obvious that the birth had not yet happened. Johanna had quietly hoped so, but she could hear Greetje's distressed cries in the hallway.

By the Triune, this was the part that women spoke about. Her voice barely even sounded human anymore.

Suddenly scared, she hesitated with her hand on the door handle. Her stomach was tight like a rock. Her breasts tingled so much that it almost hurt. But she knew: this one thing was inevitable and she would have to go through it herself. She should face it.

The guest room was dark and hot. The curtains were drawn, the windows closed so that no evil spirits could come into the room.

It took Johanna's eyes a while to get used to the darkness despite the candles on the table and the mantelpiece.

Greetje sat on the birthing chair, stark naked and panting noisily. As Johanna shut the door behind her, she started crying again, an inhuman kind of *uuhh—uuhhh—uuhhhh* that made

Johanna want to clamp her hands over her ears. It lasted a good while, then Greetje leaned back, her swollen breasts heaving with her deep breaths.

Johanna sat down next to Nellie on the corner of the bed.

Helena wiped Greetje's face, which shone with sweat. Her hair hung in sweat-soaked strands along the sides of her face.

In the moment of relative silence, Johanna whispered to Nellie if she wanted her to do anything, but Nellie said, "When the little one is out yes, but not right now. I've got the water on the stove. To be honest, it's been there all night. Helena says that it will be a while yet."

Did that mean she was going to scream worse?

So Johanna sat on a chair in the corner, while Greetje started crying again, and Johanna's stomach tightened and her breasts tingled.

It was as if the child inside her reacted to another mother's agony. As if it wanted to play, too. Johanna put her hand on her stomach. It even felt hard. She broke out in sweat.

A maid came to bring tea, but Johanna let hers sit on the table next to her, afraid that anything she drank would come straight back out.

Helena took a quiet moment to gulp some tea and eat a piece of cake.

"Is she still all right?" Johanna asked. She *had* to distract herself from her panic. Her child was not ready to be born yet.

"First one is always very hard," Helena said.

Well, thanks for that. Johanna felt even sicker. The child inside protested with a volley of kicks in he stomach.

Greetje started crying again, so Helena abandoned her tea.

If Johanna had thought that the agony couldn't get worse, she'd been wrong. The pains came quickly, one after another. Greetje screamed so much that she grew hoarse. Helena made her drink water, but she threw up almost immediately, all over herself. She hadn't eaten for more than a day, and most of it was stringy yellowish slime. When Helena tried to wipe it off, she screamed obscenities such as Johanna had never heard a woman use, certainly not one who was married to a man of the church. She managed to get herself out of the chair and stood in the room stark naked, bruised, her hideously swollen stomach out of proportion with the rest of her body, crisscrossed by bright red stretch marks. She yelled that she wanted it to end and she didn't want to die. The tears were running down her cheeks.

Helena ordered her, "Then stop crying and start pushing. You're ready."

"I can't."

"You have to."

"I can't! It hurts."

Helena grabbed both her shoulders and pushed her down on the chair.

Greetje protested. "Ow, you're squeezing me."

"Then listen." Helena's voice was intense. "You're going to push like you've got to shit, and it's a really, really hard and big one, and you can't get it out. It's stuck down there, but you've been sitting on it for a few days and it hurts so much that it can't wait any longer. It's going to take a long time and it will hurt, but you push, and push until you're red in the face and your eyes go red. You push because if you don't shit, you die."

"Ew. How crude."

"That's what birth is like. It's crude. It's hard. It's messy. It's painful. If you don't do it, you die. So you push your guts out! Come on. Close your eyes and when the pain comes, push, push, push!"

Greetje closed her eyes, and when the pain came, she pushed, first carefully.

Helena kept shouting, "Harder! Like you have to shit. And you have to get that shit out of there."

Greetje went red in the face.

And again and again. She held her breath while pushing, going red in the face, and then let it out with an explosive sigh.

Again, and again and again.

Not making much progress.

Johanna now grew aware of how hungry she was. She eyed the remains of the cake, but decided against it and drank some cold tea. And coughed it back up.

Nellie gave her a concerned look. "Are you all right, Mistress Johanna?"

"I think so." She *hoped* so. The child was kicking her in the ribs. It almost hurt.

It was so, so agonising to watch, and it took so long, and Greetje's strength wilted to the point where she could not push anymore. She didn't even cry anymore, but drifted off between pains.

Helena cast Johanna a worried look. "She's ready but the child is big and sitting high and she's exhausted. I think her body is giving her a rest before giving it one more try."

There was a really morbid undertone in her voice. *One more try* was going to be the last try.

All of a sudden, it was too hot, too stuffy, too scary in the room. Johanna *had* to get out of there. She slipped out into the corridor.

The light outside hurt her eyes. It was now afternoon and golden sunlight slanted in through the windows.

She briefly went to the kitchen to get something to eat. The cooks were already preparing the evening meal, and the kitchen smelled of hearty soup. She forced herself drink some tea and walked around aimlessly, feeling sick and sweaty and afraid. If she didn't eat so much, then would her child be smaller?

When she came back into the room, Greetje's pains had started again. She trembled all over and was crying. "I can't do it, I can't, I can't. It's my punishment from the Triune, for being dishonest to my husband."

"That's rubbish!" Johanna was surprised at how angry she got. "I'm going to tell your husband that he's going to stop preaching that rubbish about not being good enough and taking up arms against the enemy as redemption."

Helena instructed Johanna and Nellie to each hold up Greetje between them. "I hope a change in position will make the child fall into place. It's still sitting too high. She needs all the help she can get."

Johanna and Nellie heaved Greetje off the chair. She was very slight and not heavy, even with the added weight of the child. Her arm on Johanna's shoulder was clammy and her muscles trembled. Helena instructed Johanna and Nellie to keep a good hold on her while she placed one of Greetje's feet on the back of the birthing chair and the other the arm rest of the other chair so that her knees were bent, her legs spread wide and Johanna and Nellie held her entire weight. When a pain came, Johanna could feel all of Greetje's body tense up. She'd push, she'd let out a loud *uhhhh, uhhhhh, uhhhh* like a mortally injured animal.

The pains rolled on relentlessly. There was almost no rest between them. Johanna felt deeply ill.

She was afraid and with each pain she became more terrified. She had to hold on tightly to Greetje's arm because she was drenched with sweat.

She pushed, screamed, panted, howled, swore, pleaded.

This had now lasted for the best part of the day and Johanna could feel Greetje's strength ebbing. It was not going to happen.

Johanna was doing none of the hard work, but even she was starting to feel tired with the effort of holding onto Greetje's sweat-drenched shoulder.

Helena showed no sign of giving up. In fact she was starting to encourage Greetje again. She shouted at her when she let her head hang for too long. And Greetje pushed and swore and howled.

Helena dropped to her knees. Both she and Greetje were screaming. Helena at Greetje, Greetje out of pain. Nellie started yelling, too, "Come on, come on!"

Johanna hoped that this was over soon, because she was going to throw up.

Finally, finally, something happened. A little head emerged, covered in wet hair. Helena helped ease out the child from between Greetje's legs. From her position, Johanna couldn't see it very well, but the face was all scrunched up. The body was pale and waxy and looked like something dead that had been in the water for too long. When the child was free, a gush of blood and mess came out.

There was a moment of intense silence. Helena's hands holding the child were covered in blood. Was it too late? Had it taken too long? Johanna couldn't help but think of the child's skull in the box. Her vision wavered.

Then the little mouth opened and uttered a weak cry.

"Oh, by the Triune," Nellie called out in relief.

Johanna and Nellie lowered Greetje onto a towel on the bed. She was shivering and crying. "It was so terrible. I'll never, never do that again."

Her legs were covered in bruises and slick with blood. Her belly was floppy, the skin wrinkled. Her chest was covered in red blotches and her eyes were shot through with blood.

"Calm down, it's over," Nellie said. She dipped a washcloth into the boiled water which had long since gone cold, and started washing the muck off Greetje's lower body. Then she dressed Greetje in a clean nightshirt and tucked her in bed. By this time, Greetje's eyelids were drooping.

Johanna shivered. Her dress had gotten wet with birth fluids and felt disgusting and cold around her ankles.

Helena had wrapped the child in a cloth which made it stop crying. "Hey, hey, it's over. Look. It's a little boy."

She put the child into Greetje's arms, but Greetje was barely conscious and didn't even have the strength to hold it. Or to smile. Her eyes were half open, unfocused. Her face was more grey than pink. Her hair still wet and stringy from sweat. Her cheek was still blue from the bruising. The birth had lasted more than a full day and Greetje was utterly spent. She didn't want a boy. She didn't want anything at all.

It was not a happy occasion.

There was much cleaning up to do in the room, and Johanna helped Helena and Nellie. Nellie took the child to the next room, giving the boy a tender look. He was quiet. His face was red and swollen, his head bumpy and eyes gummed shut. He was ugly, to be honest, nothing like the cute little ones that Johanna had seen whenever she visited friends. He had suffered as much in the process as his mother had.

There was no cot, so Nellie had made a bed in one of Loesie's baskets. "I think I might ask a wet nurse to come for today," Nellie said. She stroked the boy's head.

For the thousandth time that day, Johanna wondered why she had ever wanted to have a child.

"That was not particularly pretty," Helena said, coming into the door.

"Is she asleep?" Johanna asked.

"Yes. She'll need bed rest for ten days. I'll come back this evening to make sure he's feeding properly. After all this, I'm exhausted, too."

"This is not how it normally goes?" Johanna felt somewhat relieved.

"I was about to think that we were losing her when she finally managed to push the child out. She is small. The child was big. It happens. I'd be dishonest if I said it will be easier for you. It may. It may not."

Johanna felt ill.

She knew that each time a woman became with child, she was tempting fate. It was not for nothing that Master Deim had made her sign documents that made Johan Delacoeur the regent in case something happened to her. The risk was so great. Her own mother had died while with child.

She decided: she would have this one child as heir for Roald —she didn't care whether or not the child was his—and then she'd find herbs that women in Florisheim were said to use to stop having children. Maybe, too, Roald would lose interest. That would be great. No more horse riding while having something big stuck up her private parts.

At any rate, she'd seen enough of this childbirth business to last her a lifetime.

IN JOHANNA'S DREAMS, she lay on her back with her legs in the air. Nellie was screaming, but Johanna was puzzled why. Helena sat on the couch knitting a huge sock, saying that she wouldn't do anything if there wasn't any tea. Roald was in the room, too, and he was saying that he couldn't possibly look at her with all these people in the room.

Johanna knew she was supposed to feel a lot of pain, but she didn't. Still, she knew she was expected to scream, so she did. She woke up with a shock, her heart thudding and her stomach tight. Her mouth felt dry. She hadn't *really* screamed, had she?

Sunlight flooded the room and Roald was gone from the bed.

Johanna rolled out of the bed and opened the door to the hallway.

Nellie just happened to be walking past. "Oh, there you are."

"You didn't come to wake me."

"I did, but you were fast asleep so I thought I'd let you rest."

Johanna didn't feel rested. In fact, she felt more tired than she had going to bed. "How is Greetje?"

"Still sore and tired, but the boy is feeding well."

"Has anyone told the shepherd about the birth?"

"A guard went out this morning."

"Where is Roald?"

"In the garden."

Everything was under control. Not even a dead body could keep Roald out of the garden for long.

Johanna went into the dressing room, followed by Nellie.

Nellie told her about how she had the baskets ready to go out to the LaFontaine and Nieland families.

She put a basket on the dressing table. From inside, she took a little woollen blanket, a tiny singlet with the letters ML embroidered on it, and three napkins.

"What is ML?"

"Josefina LaFontaine's little one is called Marie. I'm sorry for taking these things from your cupboard, but I can make some new ones before the child comes."

Johanna nodded. She was in awe of all the things Nellie did. "Do you ever sleep, Nellie?"

"Not as much as you do at the moment. But you need it, so don't worry about me, Mistress Johanna."

Nellie didn't even understand why Johanna was asking. "I also got the wood you asked for," she continued while doing Johanna's hair. "I've put it in your study on the desk. To be perfectly honest: I didn't get it, but I asked one of the groundsmen because he wouldn't look so much out of place in those warehouses."

"There's no need for you to get into trouble about this, Nellie."

"What trouble? He was glad to help. People support you more than you give them credit for."

Did they support her as mother of the heir to the throne or as someone who could help fix this broken town? That was the big question.

"Don't look at me like that, Mistress Johanna."

"Like what?"

"You don't believe what I said. I can see that in your eyes."

"It's not so much that, Nellie, it's that I think they want me to be a quiet little queen who wears pretty dresses and holds tea parties."

"I don't think they want that at all."

"But you want it."

"Mistress Johanna, whatever makes you think that?"

Nellie's eyes were wide.

Because every time I want to do something that's different, wear a different dress or create a fuss, challenge the church or whatever, you tell me not to.

But she let it rest. Nellie *did* support her a lot.

Johanna went to the kitchen for breakfast. The cook brought her porridge with cream and jam, and for the first time in days, she felt well enough to eat all of it.

She then went to her office where Nellie had left two little boxes. As instructed, Nellie had put a little note with each. One box contained wood chips from the sawmill, the other another twig from a broom from the warehouse where Li Han's ship lay moored.

The wood chips showed her the same young men, including Auguste, hanging around while one of their mates was working at a bench chipping away at a block of wood.

He put his hammer and chisel down. "Finished."

He showed his mates what he had been making, but Johanna couldn't see that from the position on the floor where the wood chips had been.

The other young men appeared impressed. "You roll the paint on like this." He dipped the wood block into a paint-soaked cloth and stamped the block onto someone's arm.

Auguste yelled, "Hey!"

He held out his arm. The stamp had left a black shape of a dragon. "Hey man, what are you doing?" He rubbed at the spot but the ink didn't come off. "Look at it. I'm supposed to go out to dinner tonight."

"Do you think it's good enough?" one of his mates asked.

Another said, "If it stays on his arm, it has to be. He's the most slippery bastard in the entire kingdom."

His mates laughed, but one remained serious. "I don't know. It's definitely similar, but this one lacks in workmanship, so that when all the bags stand next to each other, he will be able to tell the difference right away."

"Are you criticising my whittling skills now?"

"I say it's good enough. We only want the stuff to pass the harbour master's inspection. It will be good enough for that."

His mates all agreed.

Johanna withdrew her hand from the wood chip. Well, *that* was interesting. She rose from the chair and went to the guard station. The guards were unfamiliar with her wood magic, so she had to talk in general terms. She made up that Nellie had heard rumours when running an errand to get something from Father's office. She also couldn't give the names of the louts, but *Auguste's group of friends* would probably yield those names when they asked around.

The guard frowned at her. "Some kind of illegal importing racket?"

"That's the rumour. And they've falsified Li Han's stamp to make it look like whatever they're bringing in is coming in under his name."

"That's disturbing. Any idea what sort of goods they might try to smuggle?"

Johanna shook her head. "I don't even know how much of this rumour is true."

"But we will surely check it out." His expression cleared. "Oh. By the way, someone brought this for you." He grabbed something off the shelf in the guard station and held it out to her.

As soon as Johanna saw the rolled up parchment with the white ribbon, she knew what it was about: she had completely forgotten about yesterday's meeting with Li Fai.

Oh by the Triune.

She took the message into her office where she broke the seal and pulled the ribbon with trembling hands. She unrolled the parchment.

It said,

I hope this finds you well. I have been informed of your condition and assume that this was the reason that I didn't see you at your father's office. I remain interested in meeting you. If you are well enough, please let me know a new time.

Johanna cringed all the way through reading this. How could she have forgotten about this? This was important. How *dumb* could she get?

What to do now?

Johanna pulled out a piece of parchment and her pen, and wrote,

Please accept my apologies. I will explain when I see you two hours after midday today at the same place.

She rolled up and sealed the parchment and went to the guard station to have it delivered.

CHAPTER 18

AFTER THE MIDDAY meal, Johanna told Nellie that she wanted to go out.

Nellie had just taken delivery of the first of the dresses that Mistress Dina had made for Johanna. This particular one was dark blue. Being made of velvet, it was also warmer, which was a problem, because the day was sunny and bright, more summer than spring.

Father stood at the door to his quarters when she left. "That dress looks even more 'proper' than the grey one."

"Does it?"

The sleeves were equally long, the neckline equally high and the top equally shape-less.

"I take it you're going out?" Father said.

"Yes."

He nodded.

"You're not even asking where I'm going?"

"I trust it's some place where you can do important things for the country. You're big enough to look after yourself now. I trust you won't get into trouble."

This made Johanna hesitate. Why *was* she in such a hurry to see Li Fai?

Yes, she didn't want to give his father reason to pull up anchor and go to Anglia.

Yes, she had never met anyone who'd been willing to teach her anything about magic.

Why did Father's question made her feel guilty, as if she was doing something untoward?

Father spread his hands. "But mostly, I've learned that whenever you're going somewhere or doing something, when you have it in your head that you want this, I can yell at the Moon for all I like, but you don't listen. And you know, it used to scare me, but I've also learned that whatever you do, you might not do in a way that I would have done it, but it turns out all right just the same."

Johanna laughed. "Well, that's a profound bit of wisdom on such a nice sunny day." Yet, the conversation chilled her.

She was far too keen to see Li Fai, and if she wasn't careful, it would lead to rumours. That wouldn't be so bad if only the rumours were true.

She continued into the foyer and down the steps, where the driver waited seated atop the coach holding the reins to the two white horses.

Johanna climbed in, assisted by a guard, and the coach set off.

Inside the luxuriously-appointed cabin, Johanna stared at the empty bench opposite her. Li Fai had sat there when he explained about his magic box. The little dragon had gambolled over her knees while she sat in the same spot as she sat in now. She could still see Li Fai sitting opposite her, with his very serious face.

No one else had ever talked to her about teaching magic. She had spent so much time in Florisheim looking for someone. The books in the monastery, her visit to Magda, none of them had ever told her what to *do* with magic.

As soon as she saw Li Fai's dragon box, she had wanted a box with a tree.

That was the crux of the matter. Nothing else.

Of course Johanna arrived at Father's office early. The coach dropped her off at the steps. She pulled her cloak about her shoulders while climbing to the front door.

It didn't look like anyone had been here since her fumbling

with the ripped dress. Father did most of his work from the palace these days.

The first door on the left led to the official reception room. It contained two couches and a chair, a low table and, around the walls, bookcases with glass doors. The room looked tidy, but so much dust had collected on the seats of the couches and the table that she it would be embarrassed to use it. Father never used the reception room much, even when he still came here every day. It was too formal, he would say. The room had a window that looked out over the street, which made it unsuitable for holding this meeting. If Li Fai was going to do magic, she didn't want to take the chance that people might see it.

Father's office was at the back of the building and more suitable. She opened the door to air the room, but realised that if she wanted a fire in here, she should have come earlier.

It was not to be helped. She went back to the reception room. The coach had gone. As per her instructions, it would wait around the corner.

She eyed the people on the quay. Couldn't see Li Fai.

If, a year ago, someone had told Johanna how she would be looking at the quayside activities, she would have laughed. As queen? With child? The *Lady Davida* burned? An iron ship in the harbour?

Had there ever been a time, back then, when mooring spots at the quay were unoccupied? When you could see substantial stretches of water in between the ships?

The wreck of the *Lady Davida* was somewhere on the bottom of the harbour, Adrian's watery grave. Father was still talking about building a new ship, but everyone wanted new ships. The shipyard had trouble getting wood, because people had a greater need for houses. It would be a while before the harbour filled up again.

Now she spotted Li Fai. He was coming down the quay in the company of one of his mountainous guards. Workers unloading ships and fixing fishing nets barely glanced at him. So much for a hostile reception. He even greeted one or two of the workers.

He came up the steps to the front door. The knocker fell on the wood.

Johanna went to the hallway to open the door. Li Fai bowed.

"Do come in." She wasn't sure what to say to the guard, but he seemed to assume that he'd wait outside.

Johanna closed the door, shutting off the sounds from the street. "I'm sorry about yesterday."

"You are well?"

"I was not the problem. Someone . . . close to me was . . . unwell." It seemed inappropriate to go into too much detail. Johanna could still hear Greetje's screams and they still made her shudder. "Let's go to a more comfortable room."

She preceded him to the office. Coming here with a visitor would of course mean that she should sit in Father's chair. The tall, heavy chair with the leather-covered seat almost swallowed her. But the velvet of the dress had as much grip on the shiny leather as shoes on ice.

She straightened her back. "Well, uhm . . ." This was awkward. All of a sudden, she realised the wide variety of political rumours that might start if people knew she was here with him. Planning behind the King's Council's back, consorting with the enemy, using evil magic.

He dug in his pocket and placed two boxes on the table. One was the octagonal dragon box she had seen before. The other was plain. The wooden polished surface gave no indication of its contents.

He didn't need to say that the box was hers. The wood sang out to her.

"Can I touch it?" She held up her hand.

He covered the lid of the box with his hand until she withdrew. "We give a box like this to a child to store their art. The box itself can be either just a pretty thing or very significant. If it can be made from the same material that the gives the child their art, then it makes the art more powerful. The art of wood is much-coveted around the known lands. It might not be spectacular and might take a long time to master properly, but its power is infinite."

Johanna looked at the other box with the little dragon on the lid. She felt like protesting. *But . . . Dragons!* Yet every single person who knew more about magic than she did always told her the same thing. *Wood is stronger than fire. Without wood, there cannot be a fire.* Even Loesie had said this.

"I don't have the art of wood and I don't know how this box would work for you. It is not exactly the type of box we would use for children, but we have no children on board and have no reason to take those boxes. This is a simple box of the same wood. My father had it in his cabin."

"This isn't just normal wood, is it?" None of the type she was familiar with anyway. Most of the lid was straw-coloured, mottled through with flecks of brown and red. Yet the surface was polished smooth as glass. The wood's fibres shone like silk when the light fell on it at a certain angle. In the surface of the lid, the direction of the wood's grain changed in two places, giving the impression that the lid was twisted while it was perfectly flat. It was a curious thing.

Li Fai continued. "Wood artists tell me that different types of wood have different strengths."

Johanna nodded. Willow wood was best of the wood types she knew.

But she also knew without touching the box that it was made from a type of wood much stronger than that.

"This wood is from a pine tree that grows on top of the world in mountains so high that the slopes are a wasteland of broken rocks and snow. The trunks are usually split and stunted, and instead of growing straight like normal trees, they twist over the ground, sometimes trying to rise, like a creature rolling on the ground in a terrible sickness. The trees fight the icy winds that come to its home from all over the world. They drink the rain and snow that fall from the clouds that float over all the lands. The trees are ancient because they grow very slowly."

"That sounds like a very wise type of tree."

He nodded. "People with the art of wood do not touch it lightly. This wood has a very long memory."

She understood, and shuddered at the thought of the stories such an old and wise tree would have to tell.

"But you must touch it, if the box is to become yours."

She reached out again, but he grabbed her wrist. "No, not

yet." His expression was serious, and made her feel like she had almost done something extremely dumb.

Johanna withdrew her hand, still feeling the warmth of his touch on her wrist.

He rose from his chair.

In the corner of the office was a table where Father tended to put things that came from the warehouse. It contained a messy stack of bags and lengths of rope to tie them. He pulled out a couple of the ropes.

"I'm sorry I have to do this, but it's for your own protection."

He crouched next to her and tied a rope around her leg and the leg of the chair. He tied a knot in the rope.

"Hey, what does this mean?"

"Again, my apologies. People can have very strong reactions to the wood. There are stories of people having jumped up and injured themselves. With young children, a parent usually holds the child on their lap, but if I did that, you would not find that appropriate." He glanced at her while tying up her other leg.

She was trying to decide if he'd meant it as a joke. His face remained completely serious.

Then he knotted two lengths of rope together. He looped this around the backrest and to the front.

"Not too tight. I'm with child."

"I know."

His fingers were soft-skinned and gentle. The rope was rough. The words were on her tongue, *Look, I'd prefer if you held me.*

Appropriate it was not, but some part of her didn't care about what some stuffy noblemen considered appropriate. She wanted to feel the dragon magic and see the little dragon again.

He rose. "I'm leaving your arms free. You can wave them around, but I'll stand far enough back so that you can't reach me."

Johanna felt chilled. "This is not going to harm the child, is it?"

He inserted his fingers between the rope and her dress. "It's not too tight." The back of his hand brushed her dress.

Johanna took in a sharp breath. She was going to say, "Hey!"

but a stream of magic went through her that made her entire body tingle. Whatever magic that was, she didn't see any images, but she could feel them.

The call of the wooden box on the table.

The sighing of the wind around the building.

The slapping of the water against the quay.

The straining of the little dragon inside the other box, butting its head against the lid to get out.

The keening of Alexandre's spirit trapped inside the tree.

The cramped struggle of the child inside her.

All those things combined into a big throbbing vein of magic that coursed through her body.

Li Fai's dark eyes met hers. "The child has the art and it's at least as strong as yours."

That's because the child is Kylian's. Sweat broke out on her back.

He withdrew his hand.

Then he turned to the desk and picked up the plain wooden box. Johanna held her hands up, her heart thudding.

He held the box a hand's width above her palms. "Understand that the great power of this wood is not that it shows the past. It is that it shows possible futures."

He lowered the box in her hands.

Johanna's vision went dark.

GHOSTLIKE **FIGURES** emerged from the darkness, hazy at first. Johanna had to blink her eyes a few times before she could see properly.

She was in the church, in a pew about halfway down the back, a place she might once have occupied when she was simply Johanna Brouwer.

It must be night, because the little windows near the ceiling were dark. The only light came from the candles that burned in sconces along the walls and on the pillars that supported the roof.

She was standing and all the people around her were standing, too. Johanna didn't recognise any of them.

At the sound of a bell, a procession of people started making its way down the aisle to the front of the church. They wore long dark robes that covered their heads and hid their faces.

No one in the regular church services wore those robes. Not even at funerals. And what were they all doing here? The service usually only involved the shepherd and a few altar boys.

The person at the front could be the shepherd. Maybe, maybe not. He was tall enough to be a man, but walked with a limp, like an old man. As he passed Johanna's position, he turned to her, but she still couldn't make out a face inside the shadow of the cowl, only the faint glint of an eye.

A draft of wind tore through the church, ruffling bonnets and hair.

It chilled her to the core of her body, but no one around her reacted.

"Hey!" she said to the woman next to her. She just sat passively staring into nothingness. Her face was pale and her eyes didn't move. For a moment, Johanna thought that she was surrounded by dead people, but then the woman blinked.

"Hey!" she said again, but the woman didn't react.

The procession slowly made its way to the front of the church. The first man climbed the steps. From within his robes, he withdrew a bundle of red cloth and laid it on the altar.

The cloth crumpled to the table, except for one lump about the size of a man's fist.

All the members of the procession now stood in a half-circle behind the altar, except the man who had carried the parcel, who leaned on the altar as if his back pained him. His hands were pale, the fingers thin. Some of his fingertips looked strangely dark.

He lifted his hands and pushed back the hood. The man's head was bald, his eyes deep within their sockets. His nose was thin, his lips dark and his cheeks sunken and scabbed.

But even if he resembled a walking skeleton, Johanna recognised the shepherd, Master Willems.

With trembling hands, he pulled back the red cloth. A gust of wind almost tore the cloth from his hands. It buffeted the windows, rattled the doors. A tiny door to the side of the altar that led to the bell tower creaked open and then slammed shut.

The blackened skull underneath looked even eviler than when Greetje had described it. The two rubies in the eyeholes glowed with ghostly red light.

"Behold the evil that attempts to invade our city!" The shepherd's voice was shrill. "It has taken many of us already. It has taken three altar boys, it has taken my housekeeper, my wife and son. I have tried in vain to protect you from it, but I cannot do this alone. We must sit on our knees and pray. Oh holy god, I place this terrible thing before you so that you can smite it before the eyes of the people, before it destroys all that is dear to you."

At the front of the church, a woman started crying. Johanna leaned sideways so that she could see who this was. To her great discomfort, she recognised herself.

Alone, no longer with child.

A cold feeling took hold of her. What terrible thing would happen that made her wail like this? What would happen that made the people of Saardam sit quietly and watch their queen cry without a single sign of emotion? That would allow her to walk up to the altar in the middle of a service to face the skeleton-like men in their long robes? To accept a hammer from one of them?

She turned to the altar.

That child's skull? That was the child she carried. Conceived in that place of dark magic. Resurrected. Imbued with Celine's ghost. The *necromancer*'s child.

Johanna in the pew watched herself stand over the altar, hefting the hammer above her head. The glow from the skull's ruby eyes turned her face red.

The shepherd faced the congregation, raising his arms. His sleeves fell back, revealing just how skeletal he had become. His forearms were thin as sticks, his elbows swollen. A red rash covered his skin, with ugly sores and scabs.

"Believers of Saardam, today we bring to you the destruction of the evil that has plagued us for months. We have brought into our midst a former member of the church who went on to betray us, but who is the only person who can destroy this thing of evil: the mother of the necromancer's daughter. Go now, smash this evil and let us live in peace without magic."

Johanna at the altar brought the hammer down.

The black skull shattered. Fragments flew off the dais, some landing on the steps. One of the rubies bounced to the shepherd's feet.

A deep male voice laughed.

And laughed.

For a few terrible seconds the congregation was as quiet as death. Everyone stared at the fragments of the shattered skull.

Johanna was just beginning to think that it was over, when the fragments started to crumble, and crumble, and turn into fine black dust that *oozed* over the red velvet like slime. The trails joined to form blobs and bigger blobs.

The shepherd gave a strangled noise. The ruby that had landed at his feet had melted into a red jelly. The glob crept towards him like a headless slug.

A woman at the back of the church screamed, "There, there!"

She was pointing out the open church door.

A white ghost drifted in, followed by another and another. People screamed, trying to push away from the aisle, even if the ghosts paid no attention to them. They made for the shattered relic. Johanna near the altar could feel the icy air as they passed, and melted into the ever-growing blob of slime.

More ghosts came in a frantic rush. The shepherd's cup and staff, standing on a shelf behind the altar, were yanked from their places and absorbed.

And then a man close to Johanna in the pew bellowed an incoherent shout. As he opened his mouth, a cloud of mist flew out, over the heads of the congregation, and joined the blob. The man fell face down on the bench.

A woman—his wife probably—rolled him over. His eyes were wide open. The irises had gone white.

She started screaming.

Similar screams also went up elsewhere as more and more trails of mist were sucked into the growing blob. People tried to run, were struck by the invisible magic and fell where they stood. Others tried to climb over the growing piles of bodies, only to be struck themselves.

The blob grew and grew, extending tentacles outwards, picking up bodies in its hunger for living souls.

It grew into a structure that resembled the ugly algae-covered growths that sometimes washed up on the shore. A red glow throbbed within, like a giant heart. With each beat, the structure grew and grew. Its tentacles now reached for the roof of the church, frantic, probing. It pushed at the windows up there, dislodging panes of glass. It reached onto the roof. Its heart throbbed so hard that the air vibrated with it. *Whoop, whoop, whoop.*

It was still sucking souls, mostly coming in through the door of the church or the broken windows. Each soul made the thing grow, made the heartthrob louder.

And then with one last *WHOOP*, it exploded.

Johanna ducked between the pews. Dust and debris flew over her head.

When she looked up again, the roof of the church was gone. The shepherd and the hooded men who had come with him lay like desiccated skeletons on the floor.

Now most of the noise came from outside.

Johanna made her way to the door of the church as quickly as she could, stepping over debris and arms and legs of dead people. Clouds of smoke blew through the church, and from somewhere behind the altar came sounds of wood popping in flames.

She stopped at the top of the steps.

All of Saardam was on fire. The houses along the market-place, the palace, the remaining warehouses along the quay, even the few ships that had survived the previous fire, even Father's sea cow barn.

She ran through the streets strewn with bodies to the harbour.

The flames reflected in the still water of the harbour, in the place where Li Han's iron ship now lay. A chain of men was passing up buckets of water to the quay while others ran to and fro from the quayside to a burning building, tossing their futile efforts into the roaring flames.

The king's armoury!

Johanna wanted to scream at them, "Get out of there!" but she had no voice.

As she watched, the roof of the building burst open and a fireball bloomed from the inside. Debris flew outwards.

The men abandoned their buckets and ran.

Too late. The expanding explosion engulfed them.

One jumped off the quayside, but the flames licked his back in midair. He fell into the water, a burning figure, and did not come back up.

From the fire emerged a vaguely human shape that, as it walked over the quay, resolved into a man. His clothes were on fire, his hair was on fire, but he kept walking as if that didn't bother him.

She recognised his face: Alexandre had broken free of the tree that had trapped him. Someone else emerged from the fire behind him. Kylian, his orange hair trailing flames.

He laughed, and pointed at Johanna.

A sharp pain tore through her body. Johanna clutched her stomach, to find that she was yet in another possible future and the child was still inside her.

"What are you doing?" she gasped.

He laughed. His hand leaked fire, which he casually flicked at Johanna. It danced over her stomach. Another lancing pain tore through her.

"I am with child!" she gasped as soon as she could speak again.

"As if I didn't know that."

"Then be careful."

He laughed.

"It's your child."

"I know that. It's time for the child to face the world."

Johanna gasped with the pain. She stumbled back until she hit the wall of a house. Stood there gasping. She could feel the child's head pressing between her legs. It burned like fire. Something wet ran down her legs and when she shifted, she left bloodied footprints. The child was going to kill her.

She screamed and screamed.

"Hey, hey!"

Johanna bent over, gasping, clutching her stomach.

"Calm down, calm down," a man's voice said.

Li Fai's face swam into focus. He was looking at her with an expression of concern.

She was still on the chair in Father's office. Pale sunlight slanted into the window. A pigeon crooned on the roof.

"Oh!" Johanna gasped, and burst into tears. "That was the most horrible thing I've ever seen." She cried with relief. She was safe. There was no fire. The shepherd was not a walking skeleton. The relic was whole. Her child was unborn. Greetje and her son were alive.

Everything was all right. For now.

Then she looked up at Li Fai. "You're saying that this wood shows the future?"

"Possible futures."

"But that's horrible."

"Then you must take steps to prevent those futures. Are you all right?"

"Yes, I'm all right. I think." She was still catching her breath. A ghost of the pain lingered in her stomach.

Prevent those futures, he said. That was easier said than done. Many girls before her had tried to rid their bodies of children that had taken root. Many had died in the process. But if she would die giving birth anyway, then surely it was better if the necromancer's child died with her?

She felt sick. Sweaty, trembling.

Li Fai knelt at her feet to untie her legs. Wherever he touched her, his magic sang in her veins.

She set down the wooden box that she still held in her hands. She said, "Li Fai."

He looked up, his perfect eyes meeting hers.

"I need your help."

"I'm always happy to teach."

"No, please. I need your help. Your dragon. Your magic. We need it badly."

The ropes that had held her feet were now undone, and he moved behind the chair to undo the knot that held the rope around her body.

She swallowed hard. "The child . . . I don't think it is the king's. The crate you brought for the shepherd contains a newborn's skull. It's a horrible church relic. The shepherd just said. . . ." She had to stop to compose herself. "He said that I was the mother of the murdered child resurrected. The father . . ." She sobbed. "The father of the child is an evil magician. A necromancer. He plays terrible games with people. This child is a resurrection of the murdered child whose skull is in the box."

"How does the shepherd know that?"

"I don't know. He's the shepherd. He knows things like this." Johanna hid her face in her hands. "He is also a magician." What else could she have done to prevent this? She'd been doomed from the moment she danced with Kylian. The moment she first laid eyes on him. The moment he kissed her.

If only she hadn't listened to Father and hadn't gone to the ball. If only Roald was able to father a child. If only she hadn't been so keen to come to the Guentherite farm where she had witnessed Kylian's necromancy, and where he had bewitched her.

But what would she be, except dead many times over, if she hadn't done any of those things?

She met Li Fai's eyes. "Please. Do you have anything, magical or no, to get rid of this child? It's evil."

Li Fai pulled her up.

Johanna rose so quickly that blackness encroached on her vision. Whoa.

"Careful!"

A pair of hands steadied her. Li Fai had to use all his weight to stop her falling. When she had regained her balance, he said, "Evil is rarely born. It is made, through lives lived in deprivation and lack of opportunities or learning. If I may?" His hand hovered over her stomach.

She nodded.

He laid his full hand on the swelling. His eyes widened briefly. Johanna's heart jumped.

He said, "The child's art is strong. If you teach her well, she will be a good queen."

But Johanna hadn't missed that first reaction, that brief expression of horror that confirmed her deepest fears.

"I can't have this child!" Tears leaked out of her eyes over her cheeks. "I have to get rid of it."

"We have herbs that stop a woman from becoming with child. We have magic that expels a child that has just started growing. We have nothing that can stop a child growing once the woman's belly has started swelling."

Johanna cried, in big sobs. "I don't know how to teach magic. No one teaches magic in Saardam. No one has magic. Please, help me."

He gave her a stern look.

"About three years ago, when my family was in Lurezia, we met an astute businessman who had a very successful river trading business. My father liked this man a lot. He bought an awful lot of my father's goods, far more than any river trader did. When my father asked this man why he did so well, he said that he had a clever, hard-working daughter who did a lot of his dealing with buyers, making sure that accounts were paid on time, and who would have ideas that made a big difference to the business. For three years, I looked forward to meeting her."

Johanna fell quiet.

A deep shame crept up in her.

What had happened to that Johanna Brouwer? Why had she let the King's Council push her aside? Why hadn't she sent those letters about the investment in the port of Saardam yet? Why had she been afraid of a bunch of pompous, huffing and puffing nobles?

Because they don't listen to me.

A voice, sounding like Master Deim, responded in her thoughts. *Then you must make them listen, child.*

Johanna wiped her eyes with the back of her hand.

Li Fai was still looking at her.

"I'm sorry, I . . . let myself get carried away. I swear you can still meet that merchant's daughter."

Ho nodded. "I will look forward to that."

She knew what she must do. She had been wrong to let the King's Council have their way. Wrong to try and remain polite.

She grabbed her cloak off the backrest of her chair.

"You're leaving?" Li Fai asked. "You haven't even opened the box."

True. She held out her hands as he gave it to her.

She braced herself for another onslaught of images when she touched the wood, but this time the vision was gentler .

The box took her to a sun-filled meadow with flowering buttercups. The sky was blue, but the larks were no longer singing. The trees were still green, but autumn was in the air. Johanna lay on the riverbank, watching the water flow past the waving reeds, while willow fluff drifted on the air. Her feet hurt from carrying her and her hugely swollen stomach from the jetty that she could see in between the willow trees. Saardam lay on the other side of the inlet. The church tower poked out of the jumble of houses.

Li Fai sat next to her. He had ditched his armour and his black clothing and wore a simple white tunic and blue trousers, such as Saardam's merchants would wear. His hair was loosely tied in a ponytail. He held a parchment on his lap that contained a map. New canals, streets, an entirely new part of the city which would be built right here, after they built a bridge over the creek.

But right now, he rolled it up, bent over her and gently kissed her lips.

Johanna yanked out of the vision, heart thudding.

And Li Fai in Father's office was looking at her with the same intensity.

He smiled, oh so innocent. "You were in such a hurry to get out. Open the box."

Johanna did. A puff of dust blew out. It whirled and shaped itself into strands and thicker strands. It formed a miniature trunk with real bark, and little branches and tiny green leaves.

She laughed. "It's a willow tree."

"It is your art. Carry it with you always. You can call on it when you're in need. Do know that this is only the start."

"Will you teach me more?"

"Where I can."

His gaze was so intense that it made Johanna's ears glow. *Possible futures* were really no more than that, were they? Images borne of wishes and fears. They did not necessarily become true, did they?

Johanna slipped her cloak over her shoulders. "Those horrible things I saw in the wood will not happen. I'm going to stop them from happening. I will write letters to all the royal families and other people interested in the port so that we can stop future wars. I will go to the shepherd and demand that he accept help in destroying the church relic. When my daughter is born, I will teach her not to become like her father."

He nodded at her. One corner of his mouth moved up a fraction.

CHAPTER 20

JOHANNA HAD STAYED away much longer than she had expected. It was now time for supper before getting ready for church. And she was going to church tonight. She was going to confront the shepherd, and was not going to back down.

In fact, she wasn't going to take no for an answer ever again. She had asked Li Fai to come to the church as well. If what they were facing was as bad as her visions had indicated, then she would need him badly.

In the dining room at the palace, she found Father and Roald at the dinner table. Father had the stack of letters and the draft plan on the table. For a change, Roald seemed to be listening.

Johanna sat quietly on the far end of the table, and ate while watching Father explain the plans that they had prepared and that had so skilfully been thwarted by the King's Council.

He explained about the investment allotments which anyone could buy for warehouses and other necessary structures to be rebuilt. He explained about the warehouses and offices.

It was *her* idea and her plan, but Father was doing very well at keeping Roald's attention, so she simply listened.

Johanna could see it now. If they were successful, there would be a need to build a bridge across the creek and build warehouses on the land on the other side, where she and Li Fai . . .

Her ears glowed. Just *thinking* about this was inappropriate. She should stop this while she still could. Her current situation was bad enough.

But those eyes . . .

And his singing magic.

And the little cavorting dragon.

And all the things he knew that she had never been taught before.

Including how to completely, utterly, hopelessly fall in love.

That realisation shook her. It was silly. It was stupid, impossible.

But many royals had mistresses and secret lovers said a little voice inside her. It was not that she didn't love Roald. She did, like a brother. And it was not as if he'd shown much interest in her in that way recently.

She stared out the window, her chin leaning on her elbow, while Father exhausted Roald's willingness to listen to the plans.

After dinner she asked for Nellie to see her in the dressing room. She came in carrying a stack of clean nappies which she put on a shelf. "That boy sure knows how to dirty his bottoms. He has a good set of lungs on him, too."

"Has she named him yet?"

Nellie shook her head. "She's still wondering why her husband hasn't been to see her."

"Maybe because he has other things to worry about?"

Nellie gave her a sharp look. "I haven't heard that tone in your voice for a long time, mistress Johanna."

"Welcome it back."

"Did anything happen?"

Yes. I fell in love. "No. I'm sick of waiting for those stupid men to solve my problems. I'm done with being polite. I don't think I'd ever be much good at embroidery and knitting."

"No, mistress Johanna."

"Is that a statement of criticism?"

"It's the truth. Also, if you ask me, mistress Johanna, things get awfully boring around here if you try to be polite."

Was that honestly a smile in Nellie's eyes? "Anyway, Nellie, could you do my hair?"

"Are you going to church tonight, mistress Johanna?"

"I sure am."

So it was done. Not much later, Johanna made her way down the palace steps to the waiting coach.

It was only a short ride to the church, but it was busy in the market place and the driver had to ring his bell several times.

Johanna alighted from the coach at the bottom of the church steps. Many people were going up the church steps and filing into the doors.

Johanna walked down the aisle and sat down in her pew at the front. She looked over her shoulder. Li Fai had also arrived. He even stood talking with the old farmer who complained that sitting hurt his backside.

It looked like the service tonight would be well attended. She spotted some women with little gifts. Likely the news about the shepherd's son had gotten out.

Behind the altar, two boys were lighting candles. One of them carried the big *Book of Verses* to the altar and opened it at the right page. It was that same altar where, in her vision, Johanna had shattered the skull.

She shivered.

The boys were ready with their preparations and took up position at the back.

They waited.

And waited.

Where was the shepherd?

"He should have been here by now," Johanna said to Anton.

"I don't know, Your Majesty."

People at the back were also getting restless. Some half-rose and glanced at the door—which remained open and empty. The altar boys had trouble standing still. One of them was nervously shifting his weight from one foot to the other and back again.

Johanna rose and gestured for the boy to come down the steps. "Do you know where the shepherd is?"

"No, Your Majesty."

"Did he say he was coming?"

"He didn't say that he *wasn't* coming, Your Majesty."

"Will you run to his house and see if he has fallen asleep?"

"Yes, sure, Your Majesty." He ran out, his tunic with tassels flapping.

There was a sound at the door, and voices. A moment later, the boy came back in the company of Shepherd Carolus, who strode down the aisle towards Johanna. His face was red and his straw-like hair even more dishevelled than normal.

"Oh, You Majesty, you must come. Something is going on with the shepherd."

Johanna rose, her heart thudding. This was it.

She and Anton followed the Shepherd Carolus down the aisle. Johanna gestured for Li Fai to come with her. He came, giving her a tiny comforting smile that warmed her.

She returned a polite nod, hoping it wasn't too formal, or too informal, or that it would start rumours. He was only a business contact, right? Only a friend.

He followed her into the coach where they sat on benches facing each other without saying anything.

When the coach stopped, Li Fai reached for her hand. His skin was warm and dry, in sharp contrast with her hands, which were cold and sweaty.

He said, "Hey. You will be fine."

Johanna nodded, trying to believe it.

"You saw the possible futures in the wood."

She nodded again. Out of the three possible futures she had seen, there was only one she wanted.

She began, "Li Fai . . ."

But now Anton came to the coach door and opened it.

The Willems family lived in a moderate house in a relatively narrow street that connected two main canal streets. This far from the palace, the fires had spared or only slightly damaged most of the houses. Because this area had a high concentration of church families, many of them had fled after the occupation; and while a good number had returned, the fate of many others remained unknown. Both Master Willems' parents had been killed by Alexandre's barbarians, and he and his young wife had lived in the house ever since.

It was not a lavish or large place. Dark curtains obscured the windows on the ground floor. On the upper floor, some glass panes were broken or missing, replaced by small pieces of wood. Someone had scrubbed the steps even if they hadn't been able to remove burn marks from the walls and servants' door.

Johanna went up the steps to the main entrance. She dropped the knocker on the door and waited while Li Fai remained at the bottom of the steps.

And waited.

And knocked again.

The sound of voices drifted from somewhere. When she held her ear to the door, it seemed the sound came from inside the house.

She went down the steps to the servants' entrance.

Voices came from inside that door, too, and when she knocked—no knocker here—someone opened the door quickly. A young maid, whose eyes widened when she saw Johanna. She dropped into a curtsy.

"Oh, Your Majesty. You should have knocked upstairs."

"I did. No one opened the door."

"Oh." She put her hand over her mouth. "I'm sorry. Come in."

She followed the maid into a dim hallway with a very low ceiling, and through a side door into the kitchen. It was not as big or well-appointed as the kitchen in Johanna's house, and the ceiling was really low, making the room pokey and dark. A couple of pans stood on the stove and the cook was kneading bread at the table in the centre of the kitchen.

A couple of other maids and servants sat around the table. They all rose when Johanna came in.

"Sit down, Your Majesty," said the groundsman, still wearing his coat. He indicated the chair he had just vacated, with a sideways look at Li Fai.

"It's not necessary. I'm not staying long. I only came to see the shepherd. Shepherd Carolus came into the church to say that something was wrong with him."

The groundsman and the maid exchanged a dark glance.

"Yes, you may well be staying long," the groundsman said, his voice dark.

"What's going on?"

The groundsman shook his head. "No one is quite sure, Your Majesty, but it's not good."

"Can I see him?" Johanna asked.

They exchanged worried glances.

The groundsman said, "I'm not sure that's either a good idea or safe."

"I've got someone with me."

He glanced suspiciously at Li Fai. "I don't know that it would help much."

"Is he—forgive me for asking—but is the shepherd practising . . . magic?"

A few more uncertain glances.

"Don't know if that's the word, Your Majesty."

"Nah," the cook said. She hadn't yet spoken. She was a stout woman with ample breasts and broad hips. "The word you want is exorcism."

The maid exclaimed, "Anna, you don't say—"

"It's accurate enough," the groundsman said.

"Have you seen any evidence of . . . strange phenomena?" Johanna asked.

"Nah," Anna continued in the same blunt tone. "He just seems to think there are."

The maid protested, "You don't know—"

"Nah, I don't know anything," Anna said. She put flour-covered hands at her sides. "I'm glad I don't know anything about this stuff. And that I don't have to go up there to do any work."

Johanna's heart thudded. She felt that they knew more than they let on. "We're here to help him. I think he's been stubborn and has refused to seek help with this box he received."

At the same time as the groundsman said, "What box?" the maid said, "Greetje said it had been sent to him by the Holy Father of the Belaman Church. She said he wouldn't tell her what was in it."

Anna and the groundsman glared at her. They were, perhaps, under instructions not to mention the box that the shepherd told everyone he didn't have. Why did he think he could handle this alone? "I still want to see him."

"The young master is not in a state to speak reasonably," the groundsman said, his voice dark.

"I still want to see him."

He nodded, gravely. "Come."

He left the room and Johanna and Li Fai followed him. Anton stood in the hallway. He was too tall to stand up straight in this very low corridor.

"We're going upstairs," Johanna said.

"Do you want me to come?"

"Maybe stay close where you can come quickly if I call you."

He nodded, his face grave. Johanna often wondered what her guards knew of magic. It couldn't be much, but they had to know that she possessed it.

The stairs were at the end of the hallway and quite steep compared to the ones in Johanna's house.

About halfway, there was a little landing where the stairs switched back in the other direction. The only thing Johanna could see about the upper floor was that it was dim and dark.

The groundsman gestured. "It's the last room on the left. You will find it easily."

Johanna became aware of an eerie sound: first a slap like that of a wet cloth on stone and then a grunt. "What is that noise?"

"Trust me, you'll be sorry you asked that question."

CHAPTER 21

JOHANNA SLOWLY CREPT up the stairs, trying to be as quiet as possible. A couple of the risers creaked badly, but the noise upstairs didn't stop. In fact, now that she was closer, it became louder.

A slap followed by a grunt, slap, grunt, slap, grunt.

Li Fai followed close behind. His face showed little emotion. He held his hand in the pocket of his jacket where his dragon box would be.

Johanna carried her box in her handbag and wondered if she should take it out, too.

She stopped on the first step after the landing. They were now out of view of the groundsman and Anton but couldn't see much more of the upstairs corridor than a section of wall and the large grandfather clock that stood there.

The noise continued. *Slap, grunt, slap, grunt, slap, grunt.* It was nothing like she had ever heard before. The groundsman's words still echoed in her mind, and with every step she became more convinced that she *would* be sorry for asking what it was.

Li Fai had stopped next to her. He extracted the dragon box from his pocket. The dragon figure on the lid glowed with orange light. He was about to open it—

Johanna put her hand over the top of his hand.

He looked up and met her eyes.

How could she ever have thought that his face was unemotional? The expressions were subtle but that didn't mean they were absent: concern, alertness, determination.

A moment passed in which neither of them moved. Johanna wanted to say what the wood had shown her that *might* happen between them, but she didn't know where to start. She wanted to taste his lips before going to face the evil that might kill her, or him, or both of them. But all she could do was stare at him as his unusual dark eyes looked back at her.

She wanted to touch him, but was too scared that he might get angry. That he would be upset or, scariest of all, would remind her that she was married and that this was most inappropriate. That he didn't feel the same things she did.

Meanwhile that horrible sound continued upstairs.

Slap, grunt, slap, grunt, slap, grunt.

"We must go," Li Fai mouthed.

Johanna nodded, feeling the magic moment slip through her hands.

Li Fai went first, Johanna following close behind. Up the last flight of stairs, into the hallway.

At the very end of the hallway a door stood open. A glow of firelight came from the room, casting a rectangle of orange light on the floor and opposite wall.

Johanna and Li Fai edged down until Li Fai was almost at the rectangle of light and could see into the room. He beckoned Johanna over. She peeked past him.

The room was bathed in firelight. All around the walls, on tables and cabinets that held books and statues and other objects, stood candles with flapping flames. They were all church candles, too, representing a fortune in good quality wax.

The shepherd stood in the middle of the room with his back to the door. He had stripped the shirt off his upper body. It hung around his waist. Unlike Roald, he was quite broad in the shoulders. He held knotted ropes in both hands and took turns flinging each rope over the opposite shoulders and slapping it across his back. The ropes hit his skin with a wet slap, and each time, he let out a grunt.

His entire back was raw and bleeding, his hair loose and

soaked with blood. Each time he flung the rope, a spray of blood flew from the soaked fibres onto the walls and floor.

The smell of it hung in the air.

Johanna raised her hand to her mouth, swallowing hard to keep the bile down.

She didn't think she made a noise, but he must have heard her because he turned around.

His face glistened with sweat. His chest looked no better than his back. Blood ran down his chin, down his neck and over his chest.

"What are you doing here?" His voice sounded raw.

"I . . . I'm sorry. I was going to . . . Why are you doing this?"

He took a few steps to the door. Johanna backed into the opposite wall. He bent over her and bellowed in her face, "What are you doing here?"

Johanna was unable to say anything except utter a tiny squeak. She was fighting to keep her dinner down and to keep the black spots from her vision. She was aware that something warm and glowing orange landed on her shoulder.

The shepherd froze and then backed away, staring at Li Fai's dragon.

"What are you doing?" Johanna asked again.

"It's a church matter."

"Beating yourself raw is a church matter?"

"It's none of your business! Why don't you go back to your nice palace and let me deal with this, huh?"

"Since when has it been all right to speak to your queen like that?"

The shepherd snorted, flung the ropes onto the table in the middle of the room and put on his shirt. Spots of blood soaked into the fabric at his back. His hands trembled while he did up the buttons.

"You received a parcel from the Belaman Church," Johanna said. The dark-coloured crate stood behind him on the table.

He gave her a *what?* look.

"It contains an ancient relic from the church that the Most Holy Father Severino returned to you, now that the Belaman Church has cast our church out."

"You don't have to tell me what it contains. I'm dealing with it."

"It is a thing of dark magic. How do you think you can deal with it by killing yourself like this?"

He said nothing, didn't move, didn't acknowledge her question. By the Triune, she was feeling terrible all of a sudden.

"Why hide it? Why pretend that you don't have it? Why not call for help?"

He just stared, his mouth twitching. Drops of sweat rolled over his forehead.

Johanna looked into the dimness of the room. Now that her eyes were used to the darkness, she could make out the vast collection of objects on the cabinets that stood against the walls.

A shelf contained statues of stone, clay and wood. Some represented various forms of the Triune, others were single figures.

A velvet-lined tray contained jewellery made of silver. There were pendants, medallions and rings for fingers much bigger than hers with the Belaman cross, or skulls. Another tray had teeth and bones, and much-thumbed books that almost fell apart with age.

A soft red glow edged the rim of the open crate. Johanna had first thought that this was from the fire and all the candles, but now she realised that the light radiated from inside the box.

"That's it, isn't it?" she said.

He said nothing so she stepped past him into the room.

"Don't touch it." His voice sounded raw. "Don't look at it, in . . . your condition. Greetje . . ." His voice wavered. "Look at what it made me do! She sneaked in here when I wasn't looking, she let that terrible thing set its magic loose on her and our child."

"Greetje is fine," Johanna said. "Your boy is fine."

"Boy?"

"He was born yesterday. She had a very hard time, but she's much better today. She is wondering why you haven't been to her."

His eyes were wide, the whites shot through with blood. "Because I'm bewitched! Because I will contaminate her!" He was trembling so much that he could barely stand. "I can't see her. I need to destroy this thing first."

"Then accept our help."

The shepherd glanced sideways at Li Fai, whose dragon had returned to his shoulder.

"He's a magician."

"So am I and so are you. We are going to need magic to defeat this thing."

"Magic is forbidden by the church!" His eyes grew wide again. "My great teacher the Shepherd Romulus always said that the world would be a peaceful place without magic. It was magic that killed him, magic that did all this to our town!" He spread his hands.

"Probably, but magic exists, and it's not going away. There is no point in denying it—"

"It is evil!" Spit flew from his mouth. He picked up the ropes and started hitting himself again.

Both Johanna and Li Fai jumped forward. Johanna made for his left arm, Li Fai grabbed his right side. He struggled, uttering a beastly growl.

The rope dripped blood over the front of Johanna's dress. Her hands almost slipped off his arm with his sweat.

She yelled at him, "Stop doing that! There is no point."

"I am evil. I am tainted, not worthy to be the Triune's servant."

Li Fai said, in his soft voice, "Evil is never born. It is made out of despair, poverty and ill treatment."

The shepherd blinked at him. His eyes showed whites on all sides.

Johanna said, "Calm down. It's this evil thing that has made you have these thoughts—"

"It's in the *Book of Verses*! This evil thing is a sign from the Triune, sent to me to demand my repentance." The sweat was dripping off his face. "It's . . . it's . . . a punishment for the times I've used the evil in me to my own advantage."

"So that's what it's all about? You're still denying your own magic?"

"Magic is a force from the Lord of Fire."

"Stop being so stubborn. Some of us are born with it. There is nothing in the *Book of Verses* that says all magic is evil."

"There is! It says in—"

"We'll have that discussion once we've destroyed this relic. We cannot do that unless we use magic." She stepped sideways to pass him. He grabbed her arm. Johanna used the little trick that Kylian had shown her: she grabbed hold of his wrist with her free hand and twisted. Her arm came free.

"You cannot fight evil with evil. It's . . ." His eyes rolled back in his head. His knees buckled. It surprised Johanna so much that she couldn't hold on to him. He crumpled to the floor.

Johanna met Li Fai's eyes in a moment of horror. By the Triune, what now?

She shook the shepherd's shoulder. His hand flopped about. He uttered a low moan.

Well, that wasn't part of the plan. They were likely to need the shepherd's magic. "Come on. Wake up!"

Now she became aware of a low hum that made the floor vibrate. She met Li Fai's eyes. "What's that?"

Li Fai went to the table and looked over the rim of the box. As he did so, a red glow pulsed from inside.

Johanna gasped.

Li Fai jumped back. The little dragon on his shoulder shrieked and jumped into the air. It hovered over the box, hissing at its contents.

Red light pulsed back.

The dragon hissed again.

Red light flashed in response, stronger than the previous time.

"Can you stop it doing that?"

Li Fai snapped his fingers. The dragon snorted a puff of flames and came back to his shoulder.

"What can we do now?" Johanna shivered. She thought of the tentacled blob with the pulsing light inside. Was there even a way they could safely destroy this thing?

She was going to ask Li Fai, but he was staring at the shepherd. A pale mist surrounded his head.

A slight breeze wafted into the door and made the mist swirl in the direction of the table.

"No," Johanna said. That mist was his essence, and the thing in the box was going to suck it up, and become stronger.

She jumped in front of the misty tendrils, but they wound their way around her. Never mind destroying the relic, the first question was: how could she keep it from getting stronger?

Crude measures were needed. Greetje had said something about a lid . . . There it was, leaning against the wall. She ran a few paces across the room and grabbed the lid. Her fingers met with the soft fabric of the lined inside. She turned the lid so that side faced down, kept it between the red glow and her face, and slammed it over the top of the crate.

The red glow vanished from the room.

Phew. That was almost too simple. Li Fai blew out a breath.

"Give me something heavy to put on top." The lid hummed under her hands with the power of the thing inside.

Li Fai picked up the first thing within his reach: a stack of books, which he slammed onto the lid. The pale mist surrounding the shepherd's head had vanished.

Johanna crouched next to him, shaking his shoulder. "Shepherd, shepherd." She shook harder. "Master Willems?"

He groaned.

Thank the Triune, he was still alive.

But now she became aware that something else was happening in the room. The books that Li Fai had put on the lid had caught fire. Flames licked the leather covers and the corners of the pages. One of the titles was an abridged edition of the *Book of Verses,* the other two were also religious titles. Li Fai's dragon danced around, trying to stamp out the flames. Smoke blew from cracks between the lid and the crate. Li Fai had retreated to the door, his mouth open. The glow of the fire turned his face orange.

"What's going on, Your Majesty?" Anton had come up the stairs. He held his sword raised, but one look into the room and he resheathed it. He took off his jacket instead and flung it over the burning books. The dragon jumped on the jacket and it seemed to have put out the flames.

"Careful. Get out of here!" Li Fai called at him.

"Come on, get up." Johanna pulled the shepherd's arm. He was too heavy for her, so she yelled at Anton who was still staring at the dragon. "Help me take him out of the room."

Anton took the shepherd's other arm and they dragged him backwards to the door.

The crate was still blowing smoke from the cracks. The smoke smelled acrid and foul, like the burning of waste.

The little dragon was now trying to fold itself around the crate, closing off the gaps by putting Anton's jacket in front of the openings with its paws or tail. But there were too many gaps, and when something went *poof* inside the crate, the creature scuttled off to its master.

Li Fai held his dragon on the palms of his hands. He blew on its back, as if blowing out a candle. The dragon shivered. It glowed brighter. It *grew*.

A sibilant voice whispered in her mind, *Without wood, there cannot be a fire. Without wind, there cannot be a fire. Without fire, there cannot be dragons.* The voice sounded like Loesie's, but that was impossible, of course.

Johanna understood it now. That was the hierarchy of magics. Wood, wind and water were basic magics without which the others could not exist. In order to reach for the power of dragon magic, there needed to be wood to fuel the fire for the dragon to use. Without wood, fire, water and air, a dragon was nothing.

The crate was made of wood. Johanna had once made broom and shovel handles grow. Could she do that again?

Johanna opened her bag and took the box out. She had touched it so much last night that it barely still showed her possible futures. That future was now in her own hands.

The little tree unfolded itself when she opened the lid. A breeze sprang up and made its branches wave. It brought humid mist that made little droplets on the leaves, which ran down the trunk.

The tree grew a root over the edge of the box, and down over her hands and another one on the other side. Both roots reached the table one after the other. A third root wrapped itself around the crate, with side-roots creeping over the wooden surface. It secured the lid in place. The wood sprang little buds and bunches of pine needles. It grew and grew.

The lid cracked, releasing a gush of thick smoke. Red light pulsed within the depths of the box, two ruby-coloured eyes, accompanied by the *whoop, whoop, whoop* of the soul-sucking heartbeat.

Little flames sprang up around the gap where most of the smoke came out. They crept over the tree's bark in an ever-expanding patch.

The air whirled around, fanning the flames. Johanna had to do her best not to run. The smoke made her cough.

Something large and warm brushed past her. Li Fai's dragon had grown so large that it almost didn't fit into the room. It pawed the gaps between the tree roots where the smoke came. It held its nostril at a gap and exhaled with a gush of air. Flames leapt out the other side of the tangle of roots.

The relic hummed, and a flash of red light blew outwards. The dragon growled. Smoke trailed over the floor. The shepherd lay there, his eyes still closed. The smoke didn't touch him. The wind that whirled through the room kept the smoke away from him. In fact, the breeze was coming *from him*. It was the voice of his wind magic.

The breeze grew stronger and the flames grew bigger. The smoke curled up around the dragon's legs. The wind tugged at the smoke and when it didn't budge, grew stronger, and stronger, and stronger. The tree's branches waved. The roots still grew thicker, crushing the crate into an ever-shrinking space, which caused more smoke to come out. The fire grew and grew.

The dragon nosed it, blowing flames in and out of its nostrils. It inhaled, drawing in flames and exhaled, fanning them. Inhaled and exhaled. The fire roared. It inhaled and exhaled, and inhaled—

And all the flames were gone.

The wind still tore around the room, tugging at the smoke, but by itself, it would never get rid of all of it.

The dragon sat very still. It occasionally blinked an orange eye. When it breathed, a puff of smoke came from its nostrils.

Then it slowly lowered its head. It stuck its snout into a gap between the tree roots. It roared. A gout of fire spewed from its mouth.

Johanna screamed.

She retreated, but the growing tree had not only crushed the box, it had grown twisted and interlaced roots all over the floor. She tripped over one and fell on her backside, losing her grip on the wooden box. She could barely still see what was going on and could barely breathe.

A strong gust of wind tore through in through the door. It whistled in the tree's branches. It blew aside the curtains. The windows blew open. Smoke billowed into the fresh air, and dissipated into the night. The tree had enclosed the entire crate in a mass of twisted roots.

The wooden box lay at Johanna's feet, empty except for a few sparks.

"Close it," Li Fai said in the silence. He still stood at the door and didn't appear to have moved at all.

His dragon gambolled through the air, having shrunk to its former size. It jumped onto his arm. He scratched it under the chin while it held its head up.

ANTON AND THE SERVANTS, as well as some people Johanna didn't recognise who might be neighbours, stood in the hallway, staring into the room. Several people gasped and uttered exclamations of surprise.

"What in the Triune's name is going on here?"

"Look at the tree."

"Oh, the poor shepherd."

"It's the Queen!"

Johanna heaved herself up, brushing dust off her dress.

Her fall didn't seem to have had any effect on her child. Women always said that you shouldn't fall when with child, but like so many of these warnings that old women loved to give people, that was probably a fable. Maybe she should try to ride a horse next.

The shepherd groaned, pushing himself into a sitting position. His shirt was soaked through with blood and stuck to his back. His hair hung down in dirty strings soaked with blood and sweat. But his expression was clear. He frowned at the mass of interlaced tree roots that covered the table and surrounding floor. The tree was a strange thing, made up of part willow, part oak and part pine.

Then he frowned at Johanna.

He inserted his hand under his shirt. It came away wet with

blood. "What have I been doing?" He looked around. "What happened to my spare room? Where is Greetje?"

"She is safe."

His frown deepened. Then his face took on a horrified expression. "I want to see her. I have to apologise."

"Yes, but I have to talk to you first."

Johanna met his eyes. Then he looked down. His cheeks grew red.

"Wind magic," she said. She had strongly suspected for years, but had never heard it out of his mouth.

He nodded, like a little boy caught with his hand in the sweet jar.

"So much wind magic that it burst free of its constraints."

The shepherd said nothing. He had contained more than twenty years' worth of wind magic. That might be why he spent so much time here in this room and he had become so obsessed with dealing with the relic without any help.

"Because it finally broke free, we could encase this evil thing. I don't think it's gone. It's still there under the tree."

"I guess I'll have an interesting spare bedroom."

Johanna shook her head. "I wouldn't stay in the same house with that thing. Who knows when it is going to come back to life. You can come and live in the palace until we know what to do next." There were a good number of people there already. One extra family wouldn't make that much of a difference.

He protested weakly, "But this is my parents' house."

His parents had died in the fires. "It's not to be helped. You can return once the evil has been destroyed completely. Maybe it would have been better not to take the crate home."

"And have this evil thing in the church?"

It was telling that he considered the church, or his standing in the church, to be more important than his family.

"Do you know who sent you the crate?" She thought of what Li Fai had told her about the monk who didn't want to have his name recorded in the ship's log. It now made even more sense than it did when Li Fai said that it was common that senders chose to remain anonymous.

"Someone in the Belaman Church who hates us, who would

be familiar with the power of this thing. I'm not convinced that the Most Holy Father Severino knew anything about it."

"Is it a known, proper church relic?"

"It's a relic of *a* church. The Church of the Triune doesn't hold much value in relics or other holy objects. This clearly demonstrates why. Objects are nothing. At most, they're symbols for the real thing."

Johanna knew differently, but clearly, the shepherd was not ever going to change his mind or his attitude towards magic. And to be honest, he had always been like that.

NOT MUCH LATER, Johanna took the shepherd to the palace in the coach with the white horses. He sat opposite her, where Li Fai had sat before, but the silence between them was cold. It was very late or very early, depending on your point of view, and she felt exhausted. The scent of fire and blood still hung around her.

She thought of all the times she had ached to speak to him about magic, and all the times he had either ignored her remarks or questions or had actively denied them.

With the box—Li Fai had assured her that it would grow a new tree next time she opened it—she understood far more about magic than she ever had.

Not so long ago, she had even considered marrying Master Willems because of his magic. What a miserable marriage that would have been.

More miserable than her own marriage in the last few months? Of course she had not fought with Roald, but he had been unwilling to do anything she asked.

She should be more demanding, not take no for an answer. Same as with the King's Council, she should speak up and tell people how it was going to be done, not wait until they approved, because they never would.

She would write the letters and send them.

She would answer any questions they had, and lead the meeting when the leaders of countries and cities arrived.

If the King's Council had objections, she would address them, and then go ahead and do whatever she planned.

Johanna witnessed an awkward visit of the shepherd to his wife. Greetje still sat in the bed, although she looked healthy and happy. He seemed reluctant to hold his son, as if he was still afraid that he was contaminated, or that he would contaminate the boy.

She didn't think that the problems between them were restricted to what had happened with the crate. According to the servants, they had always fought.

While he went back home to collect some clothes and other items, Johanna went to her office. It was cold and dark in there. Her eyes were gritty with fatigue, but she lit a candle and, by its light, completed the letters she was going to send tomorrow. One to King Leopold of Burovia, to the regent of Lurezia, to Baron Uti, to the Aroden family, to King William, to Li Han, to the mayors of the major towns on both the Rede and Saar Rivers. The pile grew. She was going to face all of Saardam's enemies and make peace with them.

When she was finished with the letters, she wrote out more details about the investment plan. There was a meeting of the King's Council tomorrow, and nothing and no one would keep her from attending.

By the time she finished, the sky on the horizon was starting to turn light blue.

Johanna blew out the candle and walked quietly through the hallway to the royal bedroom.

She had almost reached the door when a dark figure came out of the shadows.

Johanna gasped. "Who goes there?"

A man's voice said, "Forgive me, I cannot sleep."

It was the shepherd.

Johanna blew out a breath.

"I'm sorry to disturb you at this time. Now that . . . I've acknowledged my . . . gift, I keep seeing things wherever I go. When my wife breathes out over my skin, I see her deepest wishes."

Ouch. In his case, that couldn't be anything except painful.

"I promise myself and her that I will do everything to make her happy. But she is asleep, so I can't talk to her yet. So I go and stand in front of the window, but the breeze from outside tells me stories, too."

"Hasn't it always done that?"

"Not like this." His voice was barely a whisper. "I've seen . . . on the wind . . . the Red Baron is coming. King Leopold is coming. King William is coming."

"I know that," Johanna said. "I've invited them."

A Word of Thanks

THANK YOU very much for reading *The Dragon Prince*. The story is not finished here! In book 6, *The Necromancer's Daughter,* all stakeholders to the rebuilding of the port come to Saardam, and Johanna juggles their egos, disagreements and murder attempts.

As author of this book, I would appreciate it very much if you could return to the place where you purchased this book and leave a review. Reviews are important to me, because they help readers decide if the book is for them.

Also be sure to put your name on my mailing list, which I use to notify subscribers of news and new fiction. For everything else, please visit my website at pattyjansen.com.

THE NECROMANCER'S DAUGHTER

Book 6 of the Ghostspeaker Chronicles

PATTY JANSEN

CHAPTER 1

IT WAS AT DUSK on a warm summer evening that Queen Johanna of Saarland walked through the palace hallway accompanied by two guards, each carrying an oil lamp to light her way. She had been sitting in the private sitting room when the guards had come to call her. Apparently a visitor had come to the palace. The guards wouldn't say who it was, only that he waited in the garden room.

As she followed the guards across the hall into the large ballroom, where their footsteps echoed in the empty space and the flapping flames of lamps in sconces did weird things with shadows, several scenarios played in Johanna's mind, none of them pleasant.

It could be a representative of the Belaman Church, unhappy with the accusation that they had been trying to control Saardam through a magical relic. That accusation had proven very hard to kill, even if Johanna herself didn't believe there was much truth in it. Yes, the relic had come from the holy city of Seneza and had been sent to the Shepherd Victor, leader of the Church of the Triune in Saardam by someone dressed as a monk, but Johanna refused to believe that the Most Holy Father Severino of the Belaman Church would sanction such a thing. Or if he did, he could not possibly be terribly holy. Which, in itself, would be a scandal of the first order.

It would be better then, that the visitor was someone from Saardam's nobles, who were still sour over their loss of position when King Roald had taken the throne, and more recently, the death of one of their young men. Young Auguste had *fallen* off the deck of a ship where he wasn't supposed to be, and although the nobles wanted to accuse someone of his murder, all the signs showed it had been an unfortunate accident revealing some of the young man's illegal activities. Johanna didn't think the nobles had any reason to accuse, nor draw attention to the young man's activities.

But maybe the visitor was an envoy from any of the guests about to arrive in the city to negotiate potential investment in Saardam's gutted port. They were kings and barons and princes, as well as a slew of folk with commercial interests who would be tagging along.

But it was the first group—the foreign nobles—that had taken Johanna a disproportionate amount of time to deal with. Heaven knew King William had been difficult enough already, almost to the point where Johanna wished he'd declined involvement in the project—and he hadn't even arrived in the city yet.

The start of that meeting was less than a week away. The men and their entourage were about to arrive in Saardam, to gawk, to bicker, and hopefully to agree on a few things or put down sorely needed deposits on sorely needed facilities.

The palace was being readied for that event. For weeks, the palace servants had been run off their feet, building, painting, fixing, cleaning, furnishing.

Already, they had put tables and chairs in place for the dinners that would be held in the formal ballroom, the hall that Johanna now traversed in the darkness and where the large space echoed her footfalls and those from the guards' hard-heeled boots.

The tablecloths were still in the linen cupboard, safe from the sparrows that lived in the bay window inside the domed roof where no one could reach them and came into the room when the doors were open, and that would leave little reminders of their presence on the pristine white cloth.

The guards led Johanna through the doors to the side of the

hall into the garden room. Looking towards the west, the many windows and glass doors of garden room caught the last of daylight, a mere orange glimmer on the horizon.

Every time she came here, a little shiver went over her. This was where she had seen so many men killed during the first attack on Saardam by Alexandre's bandits, and where she had seen the ghost of Princess Celine crack the stone slab in the ground and rise from the grave. The bodies of the soldiers had long since been removed, the broken glass swept up and the headstone replaced, but the foul magic atmosphere lingered as if something had died here and the decomposing juices had seeped into the stone, and could not be removed by any amount of scrubbing.

A single lamp burned in the room, casting a pale yellow glow over the floor and stone that marked Princess Celine's grave. A bench stood there these days, for Johanna came to sit here in the afternoons when the low sun set beyond the wide expanse of the river, behind the marshy shore on the other side and the sand dunes that sheltered Saardam from the force of the sea. She would sit, pray to the holy Triune and contemplate all they had lost and all that needed to be done. It was not a pleasant thing, to come here, but she felt she owed it to Roald's sister and his parents.

Today, someone else sat on that bench.

As Johanna came in, the dark-haired young man turned around and rose at the same time. The orange glow from the flame showed his olive-skinned face with a pair of clear, alert eyes the colour of the night.

His mouth spread into a smile.

"Oh," was all Johanna could say. Her heart jumped.

She hadn't seen Li Fai for over two months, had been avoiding him because . . . because that subtle, polite smile ignited a warm feeling in her that reminded her of all the reasons why she was avoiding him.

And by the Triune, she understood *why* she was avoiding him: because in his quiet, unassuming way, he was heart-stoppingly handsome.

He wore locally made clothes that were classy because of

their understated simplicity. No excessive frills on the collar, no garish patterns on the trousers. He'd also done away with the jacket and wore only a plain waistcoat. It was warm enough.

"You look . . . different," he said.

"What, this?" She put her hand on her swollen stomach. It had grown very big and round. She would joke that her dress could double as an army tent. At any rate, she had said goodbye to her toes and would not be able to see them until after the child was born. Still a month to go, Helena said. Just enough time to get these meetings with kings and barons and dukes over and done with.

Li Fai said, "I haven't seen you for so long. I wanted to teach some magic, but you are always busy."

"I'm sorry. I have a lot of work to do. The city is in a big mess." She was such a liar.

"I understand." He looked down. The light gilded his face, the skin soft and smooth. He was about as tall as she.

A little uncomfortable silence followed, in which she would have liked to say something about how much she enjoyed learning about magic and hearing the stories about the "art" boxes that children in his country received if they had any magic capability. But she couldn't say that because the guard stood behind her, and she was unsure how much the guards knew about magic, or how much they knew about all the other things that had gone on in the Shepherd's house or before.

And the silence was painful because she didn't *want* it to be so awkward and uncomfortable. She wanted to talk and laugh, and practice magic.

She finally found something to say. "I still . . . have the box." Her cheeks glowed. "I keep it on the shelf in my study."

"Do you open it?"

"Sometimes, when no one is looking. The tree grows in it every time." That tree had saved her life when facing the ancient relic sent by the church.

Li Fai smiled again, and that smile almost made her cry. If life was simple, if she had been ordinary Johanna Brouwer, living with her father and being reminded that she should get married, she might have smiled back, and batted her eyelids. She might have hoped that he would ask her to come and visit his family at the iron ship, or go for a walk along the canals.

But she was the king's wife, even if the king was far more interested in frogs than ruling the country, and life was altogether far more complicated.

And she really had no time for this kind of nonsense. She should stay distant and royal, like a real queen. "Do tell me why you have come to see me."

"I'm very sorry about the time of day. This is a quite disturbing matter, though."

"Please sit down."

He sat on the bench.

Johanna hesitated, but the bench had a soft comfortable cushion. Her legs tended to hurt when standing too long, so she sat carefully, at the very far end of the bench, so as not to give that guard whose name she didn't know—where had he gone anyway?—a reason to raise his eyebrows.

Only then did she notice the plain cloth bag that lay on the seat next to him.

He picked it up and inserted his hand into the cloth.

He extracted an object consisting of a dark wooden handgrip with a metal tube that reflected the light from the lamp.

"Is this. . . ?"

"A gun, yes."

She had seen powder guns before. Johan Delacoeur, a military man, scoffed at guns. He always said that he could do so much more with ten good archers and swordsmen than with twenty men with guns. But clearly, inventors improved the weapons all the time, and this didn't look like any kind of gun she had seen. Those had been awkward things with long barrels that had a little lever at the back that contained a burning match. Johan said that the smell of the burning match gave away the position of a marksman.

This weapon's barrel was quite short. It had a little metal lever on top, but was otherwise smooth.

Li Fai turned it over. Embossed in the wood was a little sign. He held it up to the light and Johanna could make out the dragon symbol that his father, the eastern merchant Li Han, used to mark goods sold through his company.

"Your father's?"

Li Fai shook his head. "There are twelve of these, all of them with our stamp. Or something that looks like our stamp. We didn't put it there. This weapon is not bad, but not of a quality that my father would consider selling."

Only then did she fully comprehend what he was telling her: even after they had unmasked the lame efforts by Auguste LaFontaine, someone was still smuggling.

"How can that be?" The group of Auguste LaFontaine and his friends had been unmasked, their fake stamps taken away, and any goods confiscated. There hadn't been that much to begin with. It had been, Anton of the guards had assured her, a very amateur operation.

She met Li Fai's eyes. "Where did you find this?"

"We didn't. The harbourmaster's diligent staff found it. Since we found those other falsified stamps, they have been looking out for this sort of thing."

"Where did they find it?"

"Packed into crates being unloaded from a Burovian ship that arrived from Florisheim. The captain says he's just carrying stock and doesn't know anything about it."

"Do you believe him?"

Li Fai shrugged. "It's bad form to open cargo that you're contracted to carry." Which wasn't really an answer. It was, however, how the Church relic had made it to Saardam on board Li Han's ship. To a captain, honour was often more important than law. Even if you knew that cargo might be illegal, you did not open crates and look in bags, if you wanted repeat business and if you wanted to keep your good name.

"Yes, but he should have found it suspicious, with this shipment coming from Florisheim with your stamp already on it. The crates would have had your stamp, too."

"They did, and the captain still may not have had any reason to question it." He sounded like *he* would have questioned it. It sounded like he would not have carried the freight without a good explanation. "He *should* have questioned it. I believe that if the captain or the guards had the wood art, they would have seen why they shouldn't have carried it."

Ah. There was the reason that he had come. Li Fai, of course, *didn't* see things in wood. She reached out for the wooden handgrip of the gun.

"Not that one. It has been handled by too many people in the last few days."

He put his hand back into the bag and retrieved a piece of wood. It was a splintered piece the length of her hand. The wood was roughly cut and unpolished.

"I took this from the crate's lid. I had to be quite forceful with the wood to remove it, but I didn't touch it with my hands."

Johanna took it from him. The moment her hands came into contact with the rough wood, her mind filled with images.

Li Fai swinging an axe. It hit the wood with a giant thunk. Ouch.

Then two guards carrying the crate. One of them was complaining about how heavy it was.

The crate sat on a table in the harbourmaster's office. Li Fai stood over it, looking, wide-eyed at its contents.

Then a much vaguer scene. It was dark, and two men were carrying the crate up an incline that was possibly the ladder out of a ship's hold. They spoke in rough, foreign voices. Another man met them on the deck, also speaking in a foreign language, possibly Burovian. The men set the crate at the man's feet. He wore a dark cloak and boots with silver buckles. This man looked like a noble.

He argued with the ship's captain. Johanna had taken some lessons in Burovian, and she thought she heard the word for *payment*. Was the noble taking the crate off the ship? Was he delivering it? Buying it?

Then the arguing men suddenly fell quiet. The two men who had carried the crate hid behind a stack of different crates. The noble scurried down a little set of stairs into the door to the ship's cabin.

On the quay, someone shouted in the darkness, "Halt. Who goes there?"

No one replied.

Then the images faded.

Johanna again faced Li Fai in the darkness of the garden room, the expression on his face eager. She shook her head. "I can't tell. Too much has happened since for the memories to still be clear enough to identify people."

Disappointment showed in his face.

"Sorry. Maybe you could find something from the warehouse where the crate was going? Surely there would have been other cargo."

"I could, except no one knows which one it is. It looks like the rest of the shipment was delivered direct to another part of town. A witness saw a wagon being driven away from the quay that night."

Just a wagon, of course, meant little. Plenty of wagons used the streets at night. Johanna remembered lying in bed in her room at the front of the house and hearing the sound of horse's hooves on the cobblestones. Wagons would come at night to pick up scraps, and sometimes even the peat man would still come after dark.

The memory was like a little stab of homesickness. Up here in the palace, she was so out of touch with those things. The best quality peat just appeared in the basket next to the hearth and she rarely even saw who put it there.

"Thank you for warning me about this," she said to Li Fai. "We will do our best to find out who the owner of this shipment is."

He made to get up, but hesitated.

"Is there anything else?"

"No, but . . ." He sighed. "My father asks that the guards punish those who are so keen to make us look like smugglers. Everyone in town seems to think that we've done some bad thing. When I walk in the street, mothers pull their children out of the way. People won't speak to me and scurry back into their houses."

"I don't think you're smugglers."

"No, but other people do." He took a deep breath and continued, "My father says that if you want his money, you should be more careful with who you let into your town." He looked at her when he said that, and there was an intense expression in his eyes.

"Just your father or do you speak for yourself as well?"

Did she see a flinch? "My father decides about our business. He does not like being accused of things we haven't done."

"But *you* know that this accusation of you is none of our doing?"

"I do." He flinched again and said, "But my father says it is made possible because your husband is a weak king."

Johanna could agree with that.

He took another deep breath and added, "He says you're a weak queen." Now he averted his eyes to the hands he held on his lap. His voice had lowered. "I'm sorry, that's what he says, whether I like it or not. He ordered me to say those things, so I have done right by him and said them."

Then he said in a lower voice, "My father does not understand. My father has no love for the art even if he employs sailors who have wind art for their advice on how to avoid storms and other hazards. He doesn't like the art and doesn't think that kings and emperors should get involved with it."

"Do you think I'm a weak queen?"

He said nothing for a while. His cheeks were red. Johanna's heart was thudding. She *was* a weak queen, dependent on the King's Council as she was. Because the nobles on the council didn't trust her, and because Roald wasn't going to make any decisions himself. And because they wouldn't let her make any decisions because she was a woman and they thought that she was stupid.

Li Fai said, "I prefer not to pass harsh judgement on people who treat us honourably."

In other words: he agreed that she was a weak queen.

"Tell me then, what should I do in your father's eyes? What does he say about me at the dinner table?"

"He says things that would not be wise to repeat." His cheeks grew red. "We are, in our culture, very open. We do not pretend things are better than they are. We do not say a thing to please someone, especially if that person is a friend."

The intense expression in his eyes made her squirm. "I am a weak queen. I would do so much more, but these men control every step I take, every decision that has to be made. I have to ask them to approve everything I want to do. Half the time, they don't. the other half, they dither until it is too late."

"My father says you should get rid of them."

Johanna snorted. "That's a lot easier said than done."

"He didn't say it would be easy either. He likes to work with strong rulers."

And she, clearly, didn't fit the bill.

A cold hand of panic clamped around her heart. Li Han might not even be interested in the investment in Saardam at all. He might simply hang around because King William and other royals were coming. Li Han might want to negotiate with them for better conditions of stay and hire of an office in Anglia or Lurezia.

Li Fai met her eyes and the look in them disturbed her. He reached out, briefly putting his hand on hers. He said, his voice low, "I want to stay. I think you're honourable. I think it is a great asset that you are not part of the royal families of the lowlands who are all related and intermarried, and who are all only interested in their own wealth. I would like to see you succeed."

His father, clearly, did not believe she could.

CHAPTER 2

JOHANNA WASN'T SURE how she made her way out of that room. She walked with Li Fai back to the hallway, with the back of her hand still tingling from his touch. She ached to reach for his hand and tell him that she wanted him to stay, too, that it didn't matter what his or her father said, or the King's Council, and that she didn't believe that he or his father smuggled guns or would do anything else that might cause harm to her position. But there were guards watching and while they could probably not hear the conversation, they would see everything.

Soon the rumours would be flying. *The queen has a lover*. And right now, in her situation, that would not look good.

So she felt very awkward walking next to him, not quite knowing what to do or say, and worrying that *not* saying anything would damage what little personal contact she had with him.

Li Fai's face showed no sign of such inner turmoil. He remained utterly aloof, like the prince she understood him to be.

The uncertainty ached inside.

They arrived in the cavernous foyer, where he bowed to her and left through the big doors that stood open to let in the fresh night air. Johanna stood at the top of the stairs watching him go down the stairs and cross the forecourt and walk out the gates.

She was a weak queen. Why, yes, she was, of course.

He *had* let it shine through that he didn't agree with his father's opinion of her, hadn't he?

That meant *he* didn't agree with his father, but he said the things his father had told him to say out of duty, hadn't he?

"Nice night, Your Majesty," a male voice commented.

Johanna startled. She had not noticed that the guard was so close. "Yes, it is indeed." Her heart thudded.

Where was the time that people didn't follow her around wherever she went? Why had she never appreciated her freedom?

She nodded to the guard, hoping that none of the guards noticed her inner turmoil, and then she cringed because caring what the guards thought of her was what made her weak. She should be ordering, not asking, and she should yell at them when they did something wrong.

With that one visit, Li Fai had brought her entire plan into doubt. She was weak. The kings and barons of the neighbouring countries would never listen to her.

She and Father had assumed, foolishly, that Li Han's support was a given. Father had met him before and they got along well. But clearly Li Han's patience was running out. So much of Johanna's proposal hinged on Li Han's presence with his iron ship, because if he went elsewhere, the reasons for neighbouring countries to care much about Saardam evaporated.

She had been too complacent, too lazy about proving her worth, because she had assumed that Li Han had reasons *not* to want to go to Lurezia. For one, King Benito was a cantankerous old man likely to introduce new taxes if foreigners annoyed him. He was unpredictable and had a reputation for hating any kind of change.

She had assumed that Li Han would *not* want to go to Anglia, because it was quite far away from the other lowland countries and the weather was dreadful for sailing a lot of the time.

But she might have been very, very wrong about those assumptions.

Johanna found Father at his desk in his room, meticulously drawing a building plan on a large piece of paper.

He looked up briefly when she came in, but continued his

work, dipping his pen in the inkpot, drawing a couple of secure handstrokes. His work was slow but his hand still steady despite his age, and his work more ornate than hers because he had lots more patience.

"You should have asked Roald to help you," Johanna said. Roald was always drawing things.

Father snorted. "He would draw flowers in the corners." He kept working. "It's faster to do it myself. I've still got all that to copy."

He gestured at the pile on the corner of his desk, which contained outlines for proposed projects that the visitors could invest in. Once the visitors had all arrived, he and Master Deim would kick off the official part of the gathering with a trip around town to show the visitors the proposed sites for new buildings.

He was working so hard, and she hated disturbing him with unwelcome news.

"Li Fai was here," she began.

Father kept working, drawing precise pen strokes on the paper.

"He says that people have been using his brand to smuggle weapons."

Now he looked up sharply. Johanna told the story as she had heard it from Li Fai, leaving out his assessment of her style, telling of the noble taking delivery of the guns, but leaving out that she had seen the vision through the wood, because Father was still uneasy with the subject of magic.

He listened, his frown deepening. "I thought we had caught the young rascals who were falsifying Li Han's stamps."

Johanna sighed. "Yes, I thought so, too." She had also thought, foolishly, that Li Han was happy about the actions by the guards in punishment of those acts.

Father rubbed his chin. "And we don't know anything about who these smugglers are and where the stock is going?"

"Not yet. The guns are coming from somewhere inland. Burovia maybe." Although most of the Burovian trade came through Lurezia. "Or Montania."

"Florisheim," Father said, a dark expression on his face.

"That's where a lot of illegal trade takes place. It's brought there by forest bandits, mountain bandits and other unsavoury scoundrels, to be distributed in the western regions. The Red Baron is not interested in controlling the illegal trade through his land because he makes money from it, and he probably uses some of those men as spies. If pressed, he argues that smugglers are on the Burovian side of the river anyway. King Leopold will argue that the bandits are not Burovian, so he can't do anything. That silly game has been going on for a long time."

"All the time with Li Han's stamp?"

"I doubt it. It's more likely that they used different disguises. But it's the same thing, even if Li Han's wares are a lot easier to recognise. Also the illegal importers might have latched onto the opportunity Li Han presented. A lot of people *want* Li Han to be guilty. They want to believe that he would do such a thing. Because he's foreign and strange to them, and they're afraid of the iron ship."

Johanna knew enough about that. Even after he'd been here for months, about half the King's Council were still opposed to his presence. Nobles, mostly, those belonging to the old guard of power, those who had controlled King Nicholaos before he became a supporter of the Church of the Triune.

Johanna shivered. Those men had connections much wider and more powerful than hers. "No one got a good description of the man on the deck of that ship taking delivery of those guns, except that he wore boots with silver buckles."

"That would apply to almost all nobles. Silver buckles are very popular."

"Were popular. They're a little bit passé now."

"What do I know about fashion?" Father spread his hands and both of them stared at the popping fire in the hearth. "Still, a good number of people would have shoes with silver buckles in their wardrobes. They would not wear their finest on a dark night on the quay."

That was true.

"This worries me, just before all our important guests are coming to town," Johanna said. "Any of them who arrive by ship will be mooring right there at the quay. Imagine people smuggling guns on the ship right next to King William's."

Johan Delacoeur loved to say that guns were not much good in battle—having poor aim and taking too long to reload—but were excellent for assassinations of important men.

She shuddered, thinking of what a terrible nightmare it would be if something happened to King William or any of the other important guests.

Father nodded, his face serious.

Johanna said, "We need to find as many of these weapons as possible. Other shipments may have already gone out to wherever this was going, or still be in warehouses. We can't have entire shipments of guns lying about right next to where all the important people will be arriving. We need to know where they come from and what they're for."

"There is no way we can find out all those things. The guns will be for rebels, and they will be sold for money without much care about their purpose. There is a lot of talk about impending war, and people want to arm themselves. We don't have time to worry about any guns that have already reached their destination, only the ones that are still here. We will have to search all the warehouses. Johan Delacoeur can order that done."

"Does he have enough time for that?" Johan was always complaining that he didn't have enough men and that he had trouble finding good and trustworthy soldiers. During Alexandre's occupation of Saardam a lot of the younger men had left town to fight elsewhere or had been killed while defending their homes.

"We shouldn't need to check the entire city. Just the warehouses at the quay, and then they can close off the quay when the guests are arriving, and monitor their ships. We ask citizens for assistance. Many have no love for rogues or bandits and are afraid that someone like Alexandre will come back. They will report suspicious activity."

As Father spoke, Johanna knew that her ability could make a substantial difference to the chances of discovering caches of weapons in time. She must check the warehouses herself. Most of the buildings contained structural elements made of wood that could tell her stories of suspicious activity.

It was too late to do it today, but she would do that tomorrow at dusk, after church maybe. Add that to the incredible pile of things that needed to be done before the talks started, preferably before the guests arrived.

In a way, the thought of going into town alone, for the first time in months, excited her. She had been too complacent, too obedient, too tired to bother arguing against her advisers, too tired to even think for herself.

Father said that he was going to bed and Johanna also went to her private rooms. Her back ached, her feet were swollen and she was so tired that she could sleep for days. She'd be glad when this meeting was over and she could prepare herself for the birth of the child.

Roald lay on the couch in the sitting room, fully clothed and fast asleep, by the light of a sputtering lamp on the last of its oil. These past few weeks it had been warm enough to forego the fire, and Johanna quickly grabbed a candle to light it with the flame from the lamp before the room plunged into darkness.

During all this, Roald barely stirred. His face had acquired a healthy tan from all his work in the garden. His arms had become pleasantly muscled and his hair had bleached, which made the fact that his beard was red stand out more.

Johanna was happy that he liked gardening so much, but despaired at the prospect of having to make him appear at the meeting. He had not been to any King's Council meetings since the council was instated. When council member Theo Kloostermans met Roald in the hallways of the palace, he would ask some provocative political question, and then for the next week, the council would have to hear about the silly response, or lack of response, he got. Theo's agenda was pushing for the instatement of a regent, which happened to be Johan Delacoeur, who was of very distant royal blood through a king's illegitimate dalliances.

Theo didn't think Roald was fit to occupy the throne, and he wasn't.

Theo didn't think Johanna should be on the throne either, but that had to do with the lack of standing of her family. Theo was an old guard noble of a family closely associated with the Belaman Church.

On top of that, Theo was a belligerent, unpleasant character.

And Johanna was simply going to have to produce Roald at the very least during the opening dinner of the gathering. He would have to wear finery, and his crown, and would have to behave, give a short speech—which Johanna had written out but he'd so far refused to practice. All of this without laughing, squealing, banging his head on the table, rambling about gardening or about Rinius' theories—by the Triune, these were men of the Belaman Church which had hanged Rinius for being a heretic. And heaven forbid that any of the guests would bring their wives, because Roald *would* comment on the size of their "tits", loudly.

And clearly any failure on his part would be her fault. As it was, apparently, her fault that the king had a tanned skin like a peasant. Never mind that Roald was happy and she could handle all the rest, if only they let her.

She left him asleep on the couch and went back to the hallway, where she found Nellie in the linen room, putting away folded sheets.

She gasped when Johanna came up behind her. "Oh, mistress Johanna. I didn't see you. Look, I've got the bedding for the crib." She held up a small pile of white sheets with a pattern of flowers embroidered at the top.

Johanna tried to imagine a little baby in the bassinet that stood in the corner of the royal bedroom, but she could not. Yet this child was going to appear soon and that would bring even more trouble when the truth—that Roald wasn't the child's father—was immediately obvious.

She pushed away the unease that these days was never far under the surface. "I'm tired. I'm going to bed."

Nellie nodded. "I'll just finish putting these away and then I'll be there."

Johanna went to the bedroom and took off her dress. In only her underdress, she stood in front of the mirror, pulling the fabric tight over her swollen stomach. There was absolutely no hiding it in any way. She feared for the reaction of the important visitors, all of them men, when they saw her and whether they would still take her seriously. The King's Council was still getting over the fact that she didn't sit in her room with her feet up all day; but after destroying the old church relic, she had more or less demanded to be allowed to attend meetings, even if they said she should retire "in her condition".

There was a soft sound at the door and Nellie came in. She pulled back the stool at the dressing table. Johanna sat down. Nellie took the pins out of Johanna's hair, letting down the plait.

"How are you going with the preparations?" Johanna asked.

"We have the guest wing almost ready." King William's lodgings had been ready for a while, but with so many guests coming, the palace staff had worked hard to restore the previous guest wing to a state that visitors could use. It meant fixing up floors, walls and windows and, more recently, curtains, beds and furnishings.

"I'm sorry, Nellie, to cause you so much work."

"That's all right. It's kind of exciting anyway. Never in my wildest dreams would I have thought I'd ever see all these kings. Do you think they'll be bringing their wives?"

"Some will." Johanna thought of Baroness Viktoriya of Gelre and figured that was one wife they could do without. But she would never come. And King William wouldn't bring his wife. Apparently a lot of seamen considered it bad luck to have a woman on a ship.

"I've heard rumours that King Benito will bring his wife," Nellie said.

"Would that be his fourth or fifth?"

Nellie sniffed. "Mistress Johanna, that is an unkind remark."

"Well, apparently he divorced all of them because he still has no heir. One would think that he was the problem."

"Oh, mistress Johanna!" But the rebuke came with a laugh. Nellie had changed recently, become less nervous and happier. Maybe the thought that she would look after the baby princess made her happy. For as long as the princess was little at least, Nellie would have a doll to dress up in pretty clothes. But if omens were anything to go by, the little princess would need her magic sooner rather than later, and Johanna would make sure that she learned how to use it for good, and how to fight the evil coming from the man who was probably her father.

Johanna shivered. She always felt the chill of magic coursing through her when she thought about Kylian. It still upset her that she could not remember what had happened at the farmhouse of the Guentherite order. Some part of her still hoped that the child was Roald's and that all her worries would be for nothing.

Nellie finished combing her hair and retrieved an earthenware jar with a wooden stopper from the drawer. "Do you want me to do this now?"

"Yes, please." Johanna sat on the bed, and Nellie rubbed ointment into the skin of her legs and stomach. It was a concoction given to her by Helena to help with the itchiness of the stretched skin on Johanna's belly. It was an affliction common for women in her situation, Helena had said. The ointment helped a little, but it had a pungent smell.

"You're getting to be so big," Nellie said. "If I didn't know any better I would think you were about to burst."

Johanna felt like that. She'd been having trouble sleeping, and walking any distance was getting difficult. And sometimes when the child wriggled it gave her a painful kick in the ribs. But Helena said the end of August, and Helena knew about these things.

"To be honest, I wouldn't mind if it ended sooner." Johanna shuddered at the thought of what would happen when the child came. Sometimes when she lay awake at night she could still hear Greetje's screams.

Of course Greetje had gone to her husband a long time ago, and looked happy with her fair-haired little boy. She had long since forgotten the ordeal.

"One more week," Johanna said with a sense of determination. "Then I'm going to ask Helena if she has something to make the child come."

She'd heard women talk about a special tea they drank, and some kind of seed that women would shove up their—well, where the child came out—and that the poisons leaked from the coating would bring on the pains.

Nellie rubbed ointment into the firm skin with a gentle movement. Where this used to be relaxing, Nellie's touch now made Johanna's stomach cramp up. Johanna winced and pushed Nellie's hands away.

"But I thought this made you feel better?"

"Not anymore."

In all reality, nothing made much of a difference in her level of comfort anymore. She was tired, bloated and everything she did every day hurt: walking, sitting, lying down, eating too much, eating too little, even pissing and not to mention that pooping had become a major source of anxiety and agony.

By the time Johanna changed into her nightgown, Roald had woken up and shuffled into the bedroom, carrying a book.

Nellie left, after having lit the candles on the bedside table.

Roald climbed into bed and opened his book.

By the Triune, he needed a haircut. His beard was getting unruly, too.

"Maybe you need to see a barber before the guests arrive," she said.

He pulled a face.

"The visitors start arriving tomorrow," Johanna continued. "I would like it if you didn't look like a bandit."

He didn't react. He was leafing through the illustrations of plants. Johanna knew this was not the case, but sometimes she felt like he was ignoring her on purpose.

She tried again. "I will ask the barber to see you tomorrow."

"I have carrots to be harvested."

"Yes, and they're very nice. Did you look at that speech I wrote for you?"

"You can give it."

"No, Roald, I can't." She leaned closer to him. "There are some things I can't do, because people don't accept it when I do them." There were many such things, actually. "You're the king."

"Yes. That means I get to do exactly what I want."

"It doesn't *quite* work like that."

"Oh yes, it does. The garden was my idea. It's very nice and we're giving lots of food to the poor people."

And that was true, too. They had even started giving away

young hens to people with families. "I know what we're doing is good, but I still need you to come. I still need you to visit the barber. I still need you to make that speech. It's short. I would like you to come to at least one of the meetings to make it clear that I have your blessing."

No reaction. He looked at his book.

Johanna put her hand over the page. "Roald, listen." She crouched so that he was forced to look her in the eyes. "This meeting is very important to Saardam. King William is going to arrive. King Leopold will be there, and Baron Uti, and King Benito. We don't want to give them the wrong impression."

"Everyone of those people already knows that I'm an idiot."

"But you can prove that you're not. Because you aren't."

"I'm the idiot king! I don't need to learn the speech. I know it already. Welcome esteemed guests. We welcome to our table the King of Gluttony, the baron and his wife with giant evil tits." And he started laughing.

"Roald! You can't talk about our guests like that."

"I'm right, though. And everyone agrees, but they're all too scared to say so."

"You can't say that. We want to get them to invest their money in our city. We don't want to anger them."

He fixed her with that eerily innocent expression of his. "They talk about me when I'm not listening. They don't like me. I don't like them. I don't want to pretend-like them."

And that was as much as she got out of him. Father had given her the task to prepare Roald for the meeting, but so far that project had been an utter failure. She didn't want him at the dinner because it would be a disaster. Yet he had to be there, at least for the opening, at least to show the guests that he cared.

She remembered Roald giving a speech at his welcome ball, and dancing with girls. She remembered thinking that he was really odd, but now that she knew more, she realised what an incredible achievement it was for him to even have come that far.

How had Queen Cygna managed to get him to cooperate?

CHAPTER 3

BUT JOHANNA couldn't ask anyone how to get Roald to do his kingly duties. None of the people who had prepared him back when he gave a speech at the ball were still alive. She shuddered to think how much work that would have taken, and threats, and how petrified he would have been.

She realised that if she had wanted Roald to be obedient, she should have treated him as one treated a naughty child from the moment they got married. Some of the nobles made whispers in that general direction, that she should be "firm with him", and give him no option but to cooperate. But Roald was not a child, and she didn't like the idea of treating him like one.

She paid the price for that way of thinking now.

After breakfast the next morning, she went into the garden with him to try and talk to him while he worked.

He told her several times that he didn't want to go, but mostly just pottered about the garden beds and talked about his plants. He chased ducks back into their pen, fed the chickens and harvested beans with childish enthusiasm. Anyone would say that he was ignoring her on purpose, but Johanna knew that wasn't true. It was just that when he got into a mindset, he was incapable of listening to anything else.

Even arguments that would work with children had no effect

on him. He was not interested in food. He could not be bribed with trips. He cared little about material things and even less about pleasing people he liked. In fact, she doubted that he cared as much about people, including her, as he cared about the garden or the horses. And things that did interest him, like books or study, weren't hers to promise. In fact, the less said about his obsession with Rinius, the better.

And as she sat there on the bench to take the weight off her sore feet, sipping tea brought by a maid and watching Roald pull weeds out of the carrot beds, she knew that *she* didn't want to force him. He had his plants and his ducks and chickens. He didn't know how to communicate with people and the idea of trying to force him made her ill.

But he *had* to be present at least at the dinner. She'd already had an argument with Father about that. And everyone considered Roald her responsibility, except he was a grown man, and the king to boot, and the one thing he understood about his position was that he could do exactly as he pleased.

As usual, her efforts to talk to him pretty much ended in nothing. He didn't listen, he argued about the smallest bits of trivia and latched onto details that didn't matter.

It got quite warm in the garden, and Johanna went back inside, tired, frustrated and despairing of what to do.

The guests would be here soon. Roald hated most of them and would not hesitate telling them so. And yes, when she was a child, she had also despaired of Father's complaining at the dinner table that he had to deal with so-and-so and then later watched him be perfectly nice to this person. It was odd, when you thought about it.

It was called *growing up*. Learning to lie with a straight face, for the sake of harmony, business or some other grown-up cause.

Roald was very much still a little child.

She sat at her desk, but grew too uncomfortable with her belly pressing against the edge of the table and her upper back sore from trying to bend over so that she could still see what she was writing. She was too tired to concentrate.

Maybe Li Han was right. Maybe she was as weak and inadequate as some in the King's Council said she was. Maybe it was more important that Roald be kept as a puppet, performing his puppetlike duties, than that he be happy.

Maybe she'd done everything wrong for the past year and maybe all her plans were about to unravel.

The desktop blurred before her eyes. She was so tired, so sore, so much still needed to be done and she was too tired to do it.

So instead of working, she lay down on the couch and promptly fell asleep. But not even her naps were pleasant anymore. She dreamed that she was sitting in the Red Room talking to all these important guests and that Roald came in with a gun. He started shooting people, and strange enough everyone stayed in heir seats. When she asked why, an overdressed noble told her that it was a payback for all the times they had laughed at Roald. Then there was a bang and his brains flew everywhere.

Johanna sat up, sweating.

The bang had been caused by Father entering the room. "Johanna?"

Johanna struggled to sit.

"Are you all right?" There was concern on his face.

"Yes, just . . . I fell asleep. I'm so tired."

"You shouldn't try to do everything. We have the situation under control. King Leopold and his entourage have just arrived. They're being taken to their quarters now."

King Leopold and his party would be staying in the beautiful Mayor's house where repairs had just been completed after minor fire damage and more substantial damage from wild parties held by Alexandre's cronies. Joris Decamp himself was still living in his old house so that the restored house could be used as guesthouse for the visiting royals, because even with hasty restorations, the palace did not have enough suitable rooms for that many royal guests.

Father went on, "Johan went to meet King Leopold and his party. He and the king served together in the Border Forest war."

That had been long before Johanna was born, in southern Burovia. Men and their war connections could be a mystifying thing, but she was glad that someone else handled King Leopold.

No doubt he and whoever else arrived before tomorrow night would be at dinner in the palace on the night before the meetings started.

In the afternoon, she managed to get Roald to sit still for long enough for the barber to trim his hair and beard.

Next, Helena came to see her, and completed her examinations with a frown that did not leave her face. Not happy, clearly. To Johanna's complaint about finding it hard to do her business, she suggested eating prunes.

"They're in season, and they will make it soft—very soft if you eat a lot of them. It's very common with women in your condition to have this trouble. The child is sitting very low."

That was not a good thing, apparently. To Johanna's questions about tea or seeds to bring on the birth, Helena made a non-committal reply that she would bring some.

Johanna heard *if you need it* in her words and a wave of panic came over her. "Is the child going to come early?"

"There is a good chance."

"But that's impossible with all these guests here."

Helena chuckled and shook her head. "When a child is ready, it's ready. It waits for no kings or priests or weather."

Johanna met her eyes, a feeling of horror creeping over her. Helena's message added to the constant messages her body was giving her: you don't have as long as you planned. The child decided when it came.

By the Triune.

And yes, she had known that.

All her fatigue was gone in one hit. As soon as Helena left, she went to her office and completed all the work that had seemed impossible to do this morning. Then she went to the bedroom. She dragged the cabinet that held the bedpan and water pitcher to the side so that Helena would be able to put the birthing chair in front of the window. She climbed up the little stool and retrieved some pillows from the top shelf of the wardrobe. She put them against the footrest of the bed so that they were ready.

She took a tiny little singlet and a couple of wrapping cloths from the wardrobe and put those on top of the cabinet next to the bassinet. Nellie had already fixed the bedding. Johanna pushed back the veil so that the child could go straight in.

Then she noticed that where the cabinet had stood in front of the window, the floor was dusty, and she went to the corridor to find a broom.

She swept the rest of the room, too, because there was some dust under the bed.

Father came to have a look what she was doing, and she informed him, "Just making sure everything is ready."

He raised his eyebrows, but left her alone.

After the evening meal, which was the last one they took in relative quiet, Johanna dressed to go out.

She had one night to go out to the warehouses to check on the gun smuggling business. She owed it to Li Fai to try to find out who was taking delivery of those guns.

She asked Anton of the guard to get her a coach.

"I need to get an account book from the office," she told Father when he was curious about it.

"Why not ask one of the boys to get it for you?"

"I just want to go out, see something else, before . . ." She spread her hands and left the matter of whether she meant before the meeting or before the child was born up to him to decide. Both probably. And, also, she fervently hoped that she wasn't giving the impression that she was going to visit Li Fai, because Father was the sort of person who saw through everything. If people were going to gossip about the two of them in that way, she wanted their gossip to be true.

Sitting on the bench in the coach, watching the city streets go by through the little window, she let her imagination run rampant. In the vision she had seen when he first gave her the magical box that she carried in her purse, they had sat in the meadow on the outskirts of the city, and he had kissed her. When she had asked about it, he'd said the box showed *possible* futures, not certain or probable futures. But she could not help wondering why it had showed her that.

Because you wanted it? a little voice inside her said, and by the Triune, she did. Meeting him again after trying to avoid him for two months had made that clear to her. She'd hoped that his absence from her life would make her forget what she felt when she saw him, but if anything she had gone from wanting to feel his mouth on hers to aching to take him inside her, and having him please her in a way that Roald had done only twice, and then by accident.

Lately he had been completely disinterested.

What if she casually dropped in at the iron ship and asked Li Fai a lame question? She could ask him to come with her to inspect the warehouses *just for her safety*. They would be in the dark by themselves, which would give him plenty of opportunities to . . .

Would he do what she so desperately wanted?

Or did she misinterpret his smiles and gentle touches, and would meeting him again leave her heartbroken?

No, she couldn't afford to let herself be distracted. She'd go and see him later. Right now, she desperately needed to check the warehouses for activities that might endanger the influential guests.

But if there was one thing she feared resulting from this meeting of kings and barons and other important people, it was that Li Han would decide to go elsewhere and take his son with him.

Then you've just got to show him why he should stay, that little voice said inside her head told her. Normally her little voices sounded like Master Deim, but she couldn't imagine that he would give her this advice. Father wouldn't, either. Make no mistake, they both would like Li Han to stay, but it was about the iron ships, not about his son's sharp eyes and his muscled shoulders, and the way he looked at her when she spoke about magic.

The coach came to a halt at the quay in front of Father's office. Anton jumped off the driver's seat to open the door and helped Johanna out. Over the past month or so, the little ladder had become so awkward that he almost supported her entire weight.

"Are you sure you don't want me to come?" he asked.

"Just watch from here," Johanna said. "You can casually walk along the quay, but don't follow too closely. I don't want to draw attention to myself."

Judging by the look on his face, he didn't like it, but didn't protest.

Johanna went up the few steps to the front door to Father's office. When she opened it, the familiar smell of spices and tobacco wafted out. It was also mixed with a faint tang of must. These days Father didn't use the office very much anymore.

On a coat stand in the hallway hung a heavy cloak that Father would use to go out onto the boats when it rained. Johanna put it on over her regular clothes. It didn't shut at the front, because her belly was too big, but she pulled the sides as close together as they would go. The hood went over her hair so that it would shade her face. She then snuck out the back entrance that once would have provided entry for servants and minor workers.

It came out into a narrow alley where the looming walls on both sides took away almost all of the light still remaining of the day. Even after almost a full year since the invasion by Alexandre and his bandits, the faint tang of burnt wood still hung in corners where not many people came. The houses behind the office had been damaged, and half-burned beams had been removed from the roofs and dumped in the alley.

Johanna followed the narrow walkway to where it opened out into the street that ran back to the waterfront. A few people came the other way in the street, but it was dark, her hood hid her face, and Saardam was big enough that not everyone immediately knew everyone else by the way they walked.

It was a good feeling to be free again and not recognised. Although it would be even nicer without that big belly.

She glanced over her shoulder at the coach that still stood in front of the office, with Anton standing next to it. No doubt he had seen her, because he idly wandered along the quayside in her direction. Johanna turned away from him, making her way along the quayside to the warehouses. But walking was not as easy as it had once been. Her legs hurt and, with each step, the child bumped into her bladder. That caused the constant sensation that she needed to pee, which she had learned to ignore as much as she could, but by the Triune, it made walking an excruciating agony, especially for any distance. The far side of the quay, normally a short stroll away, became an almost unreachable target.

Coming here might not have been her best idea ever.

But Johanna gritted her teeth and slowly made her way down, stopping frequently to catch her breath or let her poor legs recover, putting her hand or this or that wooden pole or fence or window frame.

She saw images of ships arriving—yes, King Leopold was definitely here. He had arrived in a sleek and ornate river sloop that lay moored at the quay, guarded by two men with lots of shiny metal decorations on their uniforms. The ship's large cabin made it suitable for the transport of passengers only. It had a harness for no less than ten sea cows. She could see King Leopold coming down the gangplank. He was a short rotund man who had so little hair that he wore horsehair wigs, mostly black, because he was known to say that white horsehair made him look old.

The quayside immediately in front of Father's office was still empty. This space was reserved for King William's ship, which would be an ocean-faring vessel with a deep keel that needed the deepest part of the harbour.

Anton followed her at a distance, but she didn't want to make it too clear what she was doing. After having been to Master Willems' house when she and Li Fai dealt with the old church relic, Anton would know about magic, but he had never said anything about what had happened in that house.

Johanna finally arrived at the eastern end of the harbour and stopped for another rest. The buildings here sheltered the quayside and adjacent water from the breeze. The moonlight reflected in the oily surface of the still water, rippling only when something moved underneath.

Fish, she hoped.

This was the spot where Auguste LaFontaine had drowned. It was close to the spot where she and Nellie had fished Roald out of the water on the night that the city was ablaze and all seemed lost.

It was also close to the spot where, a month ago, ships with teams of sea cows and horses had finally removed the wreckage of the *Lady Davida*, burned and too damaged to be salvaged. The deck hand Adrian's body had not yet been found.

There was so much death here.

CHAPTER 4

AFTER A SHORT REST, Johanna kept going.

A string of warehouses along the eastern quay jutted out into the wide expanse of the river. Father's sea cow barn and the *Lady Sara* were right at the very end, but in order to get to them, you needed to walk past all the warehouses. The ships that had been moved from the main quay to make space for the dignitaries lay double-moored along this side. Li Han's ship was a familiar shadow against the moonlit water: solid and stubby, with a single fat chimney protruding from the deck. A storm light hung at the top deck, where there was just enough of a breeze to make the flame flap. Its light produced a pool of yellowish glow that lit the side of the cabin. Someone's washing hung there, and Johanna could also see a part of the cage that she knew contained fat grey and white ducks.

She stared at it, willing Li Fai to come out of the cabin and talk to her. But all remained quiet and she knew it was better that way

She went into the first warehouse on her right. It used to belong to a fabric merchant but now it was being used for the storage of food. As soon as she opened the door, little squeaks in the darkness betrayed the scurrying of mice. She walked along an aisle between two bays of shelves, but away from the door it soon became so dark that it was impossible to see. She touched the wood of the shelving, but saw nothing that indicated a need for further investigation. Just quay workers unloading and loading freight. Chatting to each other. The warehouse manager ordering them around. Where to go, what to bring, where to put it.

She continued to the next warehouse, which contained furniture and carpets. The wood here told stories of couches being moved around. The owner's wife had a fair bit to say in the business. She ran the warehouse and did the accounts while the husband talked to customers. Johanna recognised the couple and was glad that they had survived.

The next warehouse was the timber shed where Nellie had found the chips that told the story of Li Han's stamp being falsified. The owner had been questioned and a web of smuggling unmasked. The owner had then sold the business to an honest man. The wood chips and shavings on the ground and the planks in shelves against the walls told stories of young men working hard.

Johanna sank to her knees and dug in the woodchips, but none of the stories she found there were particularly interesting or relevant.

The next warehouse was a shipyard. The back door of the shed was open, and the reflection from the moonlit river out that way silhouetted the skeletons of boats that stood in the dry docks in the process of being built. The wooden hulls of the boats told stories of men sweating over fires to melt the tar to seal the gaps between the planks in the hull. It fascinated her to see how this was done, but told her nothing about gun smuggling.

Half the shed was also over the water. The sea cows down there snorted and chewed noisily.

It was really dark here, and Johanna didn't want to risk falling in the water, so she made her way back to the entrance.

Well, that was a waste of time. Clearly the weapons weren't being stored in the harbour, as Li Fai had suggested.

She looked again at Li Han's ship. A little voice in her mind kept telling her to come up with excuses to go up that steep gangplank, where she'd been only once before, and where the ducks would start quacking, and where Li Fai would come from the cabin to check out the racket.

She wanted to go up there so badly, but she couldn't. Li Han was one of the guests at the upcoming meeting, by the Triune. He was not a guard to be taken into confidence about the risks posed to visitors by smuggled guns. He was one of the visitors who needed to be protected against the man with the silver-buckled shoes whose identity she was no closer to discovering.

But hey, something was now going on across the harbour.

Between the tall bow of Li Han's ship and the much lower deck of the *Lady Sara*, she noticed movement of people with lights on the deck of a ship on the other side of the harbour, a river sloop that lay moored on the harbour side hiding behind King Leopold's ship.

The vessel was sleek and dark, with a low cabin that had numerous windows with closed curtains. Wasn't that the ship that had brought Roald back before the ball that started all this misery? The Burovian ship that belonged to the Guentherite brotherhood?

Yes, she was almost sure it was.

That could mean only one thing: *Kylian* was here. The ship's position, moored alongside the Burovian king's ship, betrayed the relationship between Baron Uti, his cousin King Leopold and the Guentherite order of the Belaman Church that practiced necromancy and magic.

She should have known there was a good chance that Kylian would turn up with his father, but it was especially galling that he dared walk into *her* city.

She peered into the darkness, but was too far away to recognise any of the people on the deck. She didn't *think* Kylian was one of them, but he would be there.

A chill came over her despite the warm weather. The cold went deep inside her belly, where the child squirmed and kicked. There was magic in the air, and even if she couldn't feel it, the child could. She clamped her arms around herself.

She had best go back to Anton. Kylian would feel it if she used her magic, and she did *not* want to encounter him in the dark alone.

But there was a soft noise closer to where she stood. Her first thought was *a rat*, but the sound came from her right, somewhere in the water.

Johanna took a few steps so that she could see around the bow of Li Han's ship and peered into the darkness.

Something *glowed* underneath the surface of the water.

By the Triune, that looked like . . .

She had seen things like this before . . . in Florisheim, where ghosts emerged from the water and wandered over the surface . . . because at the Guentherite brotherhood's farm, a deep hole dug in the ground to find black rock had disturbed the spirits of the dead. And because Kylian was practicing his necromancy, bringing ghosts back to their bodies.

Johanna watched, her heart thudding.

The underwater glow made a little dome in the water's surface, and then broke the surface. The silvery, glowing blob that came out took a while to acquire a shape. First it grew a bud at the top, and then two smaller buds on each side of the bigger one. Those two grew long and thin, waving at the sky. The top bud grew into a head with long flowing hair. The rest of the shape elongated and became a body in a thin, elfinlike dress.

The ghost of Princess Celine had returned to Saardam.

She walked over the water to the Guentherite brotherhood's ship. The men on the deck had gone below. She put her hands on the bow, looking up at the railing. When no one came, she threw her head back and wailed. It was a sound lighter than the wind, colder than ice, sharper than glass. It chilled Johanna deep inside.

A man climbed to the deck and looked over the railing. She reached out for him with both hands, but he slapped her aside. She fell to her knees, wailing, sitting on the water's surface as if it was solid.

The man threw an object at her. She flew up and threw the object back at him.

His laughter echoed over the water. Magic erupted from his hand, engulfing her. She sank back under the water.

By the Triune. Was that Kylian?

He straightened and looked over the water as if he sensed her.

A chill went through Johanna. Her stomach cramped up. By the Triune, she suddenly needed to pee so badly that it hurt.

The door to Father's sea cow barn was directly behind her. There would be a bucket in there to do her business.

Johanna stumbled to the door, pain lancing through her stomach with each step. The child squirmed inside her, wedging some body part under her ribs. She winced. That hurt, little one.

Johanna pulled the door open—

And she stopped.

A small fire burned on the paved floor in the loading area. Two figures in dark robes crouched by the fire, both small and thin and dressed in rags. Oh by the Triune, why did Father's barn always attract beggars?

She stammered, "I'm sorry. I thought . . ." But she didn't know what she thought or what she could say to a couple of urchins. She didn't look like a fellow beggar. She didn't even look like a fishwife. She hoped they weren't familiar enough with the royal family to know who she was. Come to think of it, she should probably get out of here and let Anton deal with it.

But then one of the two beggars lowered the hood of his tattered old cloak, and it was not a *him* but a *her*.

Johanna recognised the pale, wide-eyed face. She gasped. "Loesie!"

By the Triune, she had changed so much. She looked taller, her eyes more alert, and her expression more vicious. Johanna wanted to hug her, but something stopped her. Loesie looked . . . formidable, and suddenly so much older. Her hair had always been dark, but now it had gone even darker, flecked through with a few white hairs at the temples.

The person with her was also a woman. She looked younger than Loesie, had flaxen blond hair like Nellie and a round face with freckles.

She would have been pretty if it weren't for her eyes. Mist whirled within the milky white irises.

The air grew cold. A chilling breeze ruffled her hair. Johanna didn't have the ability to feel magic in the air, but she was certain that if she could, she would be staggering back from the magic force that radiated from this woman. The child inside her kicked her hard in the ribs.

This had to be Kylian's magic, there was no doubt about it.

Loesie said, "Yes, we came back. We saw on the wind that a lot of fuss be happening. We figured this be where the action is."

"Did you see Kylian? He's on a boat on the other side of the harbour." She put her hand on the curve of her stomach to calm herself down.

"Why do you think we's hiding in here? It's warm enough to sleep outside and if we didn' have to, we sure wouldn' be sleeping in s stinky shed with slobbering and farting animals."

To illustrate Loesie's words, one of the sea cows swam past, leaving a trail of bubbles, while munching noisily on a chunk of cabbage.

"You are certainly welcome back," Johanna said.

Despite the magic in the other woman's eyes, there was something reassuring and familiar about Loesie's words. *This* was her old Loesie. Johanna had never been happy with the Loesie who, after having been cured of her possession by Duke Lothar, lost her country accent. "You and your friend can stay here. It's not like Father is using the barn a lot these days."

"This here be Annette. She were on my granma's farm. She were dead but she came back to life. She be demon-touched so don' get too close to her."

"Thanks for warning me." Johanna had no such intention. Each time she looked at the young woman, she felt a chill.

Loesie said, "And look at you. The babe is close, I can feel it."

Johanna responded automatically, "Another month."

"Hmmm." She clearly didn't believe that.

"What are you doing here?" Johanna asked, pushing away unease. She wanted the child to stay put until after the meeting. "You're not selling cheese?"

"We's sold some. The farm still needs money to pay for clothes and all that."

"Did any other people of your family survive? I thought they were all gone."

"Only the demon-touched survived. We be a whole farm of

bewitched women and children, working the fields through magic. But we still need eatin', so that's why we be selling the cheese. That and we be following the ghosts that have floated down the river."

"Did you notice them when they came past the farm?"

"No. They'd be coming from Gelre. The necromancer brought them. He's been travelling the river for years. He made ghosts everywhere. They's all in the water."

"That long? You never said anything about it?"

"I were bewitched. Even when we came back here, I were not myself. The Duke took part of it away, and then I washed the rest off in the river. Then I helped the girls."

"Girls?"

"Them's the ones he needed. The necromancer journeyed all along the river up and down and up and down, killing and raping. He killed those he could not rape. And he killed the rest after he raped them. Like poor Annette here, they's stuck in between life and death. Except he can't easily kill the ones with magic, and he can't kill the ones who's become with child after he's raped them so those ones came to the farm, often with bleeding wounds from where he's tried to kill them."

By the Triune. Johanna felt sick. "How many of you?"

"We's a group of twenty-one. Other farms, I don't know. The Duke knows how many. There's other places where they hide besides our farm."

Johanna thought of the work farm at the Guentherite brotherhood. "How many of those women are Kylian's minions doing his bidding?"

"We's not minions. He might wish we were. The farm be a safe place where the women can hide from him. We had six babes born just this month. If the mother's been badly touched by him, she dies, and we have an extra mouth to feed a long time before we have a pair of hands to work on the farm and a magician to teach. They's more worry for us."

"You teach magic now?"

"No, I'm no teacher. The teacher be the duke. He comes to visit. We keep the children alive and busy."

"Is the duke here?"

"Not yet, but he be coming, bringing some other girls. The necromancer is up to something."

Didn't Johanna know about that.

But when Johanna asked, Loesie didn't know what Duke Lothar planned or when he would arrive. She didn't know what sort of magic, locations, relics or substances he would be using.

That was the thing that frustrated her most about people with magic: they did not plan, and they did not let others know what they were doing. Or maybe the duke had announced his plans, and Loesie had not paid attention. Loesie was the worst person to ask about these types of things.

Johanna said, "I don't know how often I can come to see you here. We have all the important guests arriving, and I'd be lying if I said I had any time to come and see you, because I don't. This is the last night before they all start coming into town."

"Don't be worried," Loesie said. "You look after the important people. They's all non-magical anyway. They only need to be kept busy, and they won't even see that there's something going on. They think they's important, but they's all so dumb. You look after them. We'll look after the magic."

Johanna wasn't sure it was so simple. For one, Kylian would come for *her* and the child; but for the time being, she could do nothing else.

CHAPTER 5

JOHANNA RETURNED in the coach to that exact same spot on the quay the next morning for a completely different reason. The harbourmaster had sent word to the palace of King William's arrival, and this important guest needed special attention. So she had dressed in a formal but not too flamboyant dress, asked Nellie to do her hair, and clambered into the coach. Father sat on the bench opposite her, wearing the formal Carmine family coat that Mistress Dina had made for him. The weather was rather too warm for it, and beads of sweat pearled on his forehead.

Johanna wasn't feeling the best after her foray the previous night. Her legs were tired, her feet so swollen that they almost wouldn't fit into her shoes, and the chill of magic that had stabbed through her belly had never completely subsided. She *knew* that the child had magic, and that almost certainly meant that it was Kylian's, as she feared—and as, according to Loesie, seemed to have happened to a lot of other girls. What was Kylian's game?

She sat in the coach entertaining dark thoughts while summer turned out one of the most beautiful days this year.

The sky was brilliant blue and the painted houses made a pretty picture that belied the city's damaged state.

There were a lot of people on the quay, most of them

watching from the deck of ships or from the steps or upstairs windows to offices. The mooring in front of Father's office, which had been vacant last night, was now taken up by an impressively large ship.

Because they were both seafaring nations competing to discover new lands, Saarland and Anglia had been at war several times. The countries were currently in a period of stalemate in which both did their best to ignore each other. Not openly hostile, not friendly either. It had been a long time since an Anglian ship was sighted in the harbour. In fact, Johanna could only remember one time, when she was very little. That had been a merchant ship nowhere near as impressive as the king's flagship.

The three-master towered over Saardam's fleet of river sloops and over the buildings that lined the quay, and most of those were over two floors high.

The ship's masthead, the Anglian long-horned bull bowing its head, ready to attack, loomed over the stern of King Leopold's otherwise impressive river sloop. The ship's name was *Targon*, after the Anglian capital, painted in silver letters on the bow. The hull was dark, of sleeker design than the Saarlander seafaring ships. It was said that she could outrun most of the pirate ships that inhabited the southern Lamorian Ocean. Most of the many sails hung loose and deck hands were in the masts and webbing to stow them. A line of uniformed soldiers stood on the poop deck overlooking the harbour with stern faces and lances by their sides.

The gangplank was down, and two rows of armed soldiers stood guard on either side. They wore the typical red jackets of the Anglian guard, complete with their distinctive caps with the dangling fox's tail.

Their trumpets glittered, the sails flapped, the paintwork on the ship's deck shone with bright colours, and brilliant gold and glittering silver.

Father stared at the ship through the little window in the coach's door, like a young boy in a lolly shop.

Compared to the ship, her coach was rather plain, as she had thought appropriate for the fact that most of Saardam still suffered deprivation and hardship. Anton and his colleague on the driver's seat were well-clad and looked dapper, but they weren't a smidgen on these Anglian guards.

The difference was quite unsettling and made Johanna think that she might have made a mistake. Pomp and ceremony intimidated people. It made people believe that a kingdom, a family, an estate, was the best and richest ever. When people were impressed, they were more likely to accept what a person said. She really *should* get more flamboyant dresses, pretty up the coach and furnish the palace with the most extravagant decorations, but it didn't seem fair to her when many people in Saardam barely had roofs over their heads.

Fair: another word that *real* kings and queens never cared about.

Would she ever get over the feeling that one day, someone would come and say "She's only a commoner!" and would put her right where she belonged?

The bugles sounded. The coach stopped. Anton jumped off the driver's seat, walked past the side and opened the door, letting in bright sunlight. Johanna rose, a little awkwardly in that dress.

The herald shouted, "Hail Queen Johanna of Saarland!" People cheered.

He shouted again, "Hail King William of Anglia."

People cheered again.

Johanna used Anton's hand to climb down from the coach and waited until Father was down as well. The Saarlander guard had cleared a path from the coach to the ship. Walking between those rows of people on Father's arm, Johanna felt very small. The weight of a lot of expectations rested on her shoulders.

She and Father waited at the bottom of the gangplank while the visiting party came down in slow steps, a gaggle of ornate hats, rich velvet jackets, shirts with lots of frills, and high-heeled boots. Even though Johanna had never met King William, there was little doubt about which of them was the king.

He was a tall man without being gangly. He had curly ginger-blond hair which he wore in a loose ponytail at the back of his head, a red face and startling blue eyes.

The other companions were all men, and two were guards in uniform. Another one was a scribe of some sort, carrying a leather-bound book and the last one . . . he was of fine build and walked behind the king as a servant, but he wasn't dressed like one. He had grey eyes and soft flaxen hair which hung loose over his shoulders. He wore a blue hat with a big feather, light blue trousers and a shirt with an excessive display of frills. He carried a watch or compass of some sort on a gold chain, and had lots of rings on his fingers. He was far too old to be the king's son, and too different in build to be a brother.

King William stepped off the gangplank onto the quay. He looked around with his thumbs hooked in his belt, and said, "Say, where is the king of this godforsaken place?"

Johanna gritted her teeth. "We welcome you to our city, Your Majesty. I am sure nothing here is new to you. I hope your travels have been favourable. I am Queen Johanna—"

"The lass who invited me?"

Several people took in sharp breaths.

Johanna straightened her back. She had been warned about him. "I invited you, yes. And thank you for coming. This here is my advisor, Dirk Brouwer." She gestured at Father.

King Williams let out a loud laugh that echoed over the water and no doubt could be heard by everyone at the quay. "A merchant? A merchant is the king's chief adviser?"

He was really starting to annoy her. She corrected, "The queen's advisor, and yes, a merchant. We want to become the lowland city where everyone comes to trade, sell and buy. *We* ask the experts."

Another round of gasps. This remark referred to one of the more recent sea battles between the two countries, involving King William's father, that Saardam had won because Anglia had taken strategic advice from a noble who had no interest or knowledge in the matter of sea battles.

But King William let out another very loud burst of laughter. "Ha, ha, ha, you have spunk in you. I like that. You'll get along fine with my court advisor. This is Earl Maximilian Clarendon de Blasisse."

The little man in the light blue outfit bowed. "It is an honour to finally meet you, milady." Even his voice was whiny and foppish.

Johanna met Father's eyes over the earl's head. What a strange character. "Do accompany us to the palace where your accommodation is ready. We will send our servants to collect your necessities."

Johanna preceded him to the coach, again traversing the path in between walls of curious onlookers.

Her coach had room for six, but King William was so tall that he took up two seats—after having almost banged his head on the doorframe. Johanna let the king and his companion have the forward-facing seats while she and Father took the rearward-facing ones. The king sat spread out in the middle seat, pushing the little foppish Earl against the side of the coach. The king's legs were so long that Johanna and Father each had to sit to the side as well, and still his left leg kept brushing her dress, which was distracting. He looked pointedly at her belly, but said nothing about it, which at least was a welcome change from King Leopold, whom she had barely seen but had already managed to inform her, "Your husband should be ashamed that you have to work in this state."

The coach jumped into motion and the harbour slid from view.

No one spoke inside the cabin.

Johanna felt intensely uncomfortable facing this tall, red-bearded, blue-eyed man who was scrutinising her as if she was the latest curiosity. Who was rumoured to have a bad temper. Who was rumoured to always want to have things his way.

Fortunately, Johanna had business to discuss. She had asked the coach driver to return to the palace via a longer route that took them past the areas that were worst affected by the fires. Most severely burned buildings had been demolished and, with summer in full swing, those houses that were going to be rebuilt this year were progressing at a steady clip, though many building lots still lay empty. In one place a group of carpenters were replacing a bridge that had been burnt beyond safe use. Johanna explained how citizens had rallied together to pay the carpenters and how they were sharing houses so that the houses of everyone could be rebuilt. She explained how the shops and warehouses were surviving and how a fleet of canal boats had sprung up to ferry goods around the city that would otherwise be carried by wagons over the city's many bridges.

King William snorted. "It irks me how all that hardship is necessary because that old man gave all your money to that silly church. Did you ever find out what he hoped to achieve except a pile of burnt rubble?"

It was a remark as rude as it was apt.

"We can only guess about the king's motivations. King Nicholaos and Queen Cygna were both killed."

"Yes, I know. But would it be too hard to find out what the church did with all the money? That's what worries us from where we're standing. Because the Carmine family was not poor, and the church could easily have built a pretty stone building with their fortunes. One that didn't burn down." He gestured a large, hairy-fingered hand at the window. "They could have repaired all these things with that money. If the Church indeed got all of it and if the Carmine family truly has so little money left."

Johanna's cheeks flushed. "I'm sorry, but do you mistrust me?"

He laughed. "You have innocence written all over your face, little queen."

By the Triune, the rude boor!

He continued, "Let me give you a little hint. Royal families from as old a lineage as the Carmines have hundreds of years of experience in covering their tracks. The money you find in the coffers is rarely all there is. It is rarely even *most* of what they possess."

His attitude needled her. He was probably doing this on purpose to see how far he could go. She could dispute him and tell him that they had already looked everywhere and found very little. "Does this mean you want to tell me to look for that money before asking for your investment in our port? You're wrong about that. I don't want anyone's investment to solve our financial problems. As you can see, we're managing quite well. I want the money to build something we can all be proud of and to ensure lasting peace in this area."

King William threw his head back and laughed. That loud laugh of his hurt her ears and was getting very irritating, especially in a small space like this. It was as if he treated every question she asked as childish.

Johanna's anger flared. "If you truly believe that I'm stupid, then I can assure you that the meeting will be very short." By the Triune, she was trembling and sweating, and hardly dared look aside to see Father's horrified face, for surely he would be horrified.

King William's face became serious. "Let me be very serious with you. Your spunk amuses me. You're a merchant daughter having wedged herself into a fragile royal family who have made a lot of stupid decisions made worse by a run of rotten luck. But don't, for one moment, believe that you're ever going to be worth more than that child you're carrying. We are here because the concept of investment in dedicated quay space and warehouses interests us. For far too long, that harbourmaster with his exorbitant fees has annoyed our captains, not to mention your ridiculous taxes. The proposal that your men have drawn up is worth discussing. That's why we're here."

Johanna stuck her chin in the air. "For your information: *I* wrote a good deal of that plan. And I prefer if the plan was the main thing we discussed, not my status or my worth. And you're wrong about my worth, by the way. I will prove it to you."

He did not laugh anymore. Those steely blue eyes turned cold. "Do you really think you can be a match for a king in one of the oldest royal lineages in the known world?"

"I obviously don't have your experience . . ." —in being a pompous arse— ". . . but I've saved the crown, I've led my people into Florisheim, I've helped them ward off ghosts, I've freed them from magic, I've defeated a tyrant, so maybe yes, I can."

He nodded. "Challenge accepted."

Johanna returned his gaze, a little seed of triumph growing inside her.

CHAPTER 6

FORTUNATELY THE REST of the ride to the palace was short.

The coach stopped at the bottom of the palace steps where a guard of honour waited for the king. They were all dressed in smart Carmine livery. The marble steps they stood on were neatly swept and the entrance to the foyer with its marble columns had been scrubbed clean.

The herald announced the arrival of the king, and the soldiers lifted their trumpets, glittering in the sunlight. The fanfare echoed over the forecourt.

Hang all of King William's pomp. Those were her men, and they looked good and presented well, and she was proud of them.

A good number of citizens had gathered on the other side of the gilded fence and looked on while the party arrived. Besides their own, there were two other coaches, with the king's entourage and their luggage.

It struck her that, as ordinary Johanna Brouwer, she would have loved to see this. She would have stopped and watched, and told Father all about the extravagant clothing, and he would have sniffed and said that rich people had no sense of what money was really worth, or some such.

Now, she took Father's velvet-coated arm and walked up the stairs, chin held high.

A whole bevy of servants waited in the foyer, ready to take the king and his companions to the guest quarters. Apart from the foppish Earl, the king's entourage had alighted from the second coach and were just coming up the stairs.

As soon as they were in the foyer, Father fled to his study, with the excuse of having work to do, and it was left to Johanna to lead the party to their lodgings.

The guest quarters had gone through a complete cleanup in the last few weeks. The apartment consisted of a large sitting room in which the palace servants had collected a fine selection of furniture, with a bedroom off the main room. There were two large four-poster beds in that room, each with a luxurious bedspread and ornate curtains. Nellie had really worked hard to get the quarters in this state, and Johanna could see the little touches of Nellie's presence everywhere, from the little posy of dried flowers on the bed, to the way the curtains hung. And to think that Alexandre's bandits had used it as their camping room, and had even made fires in the corner.

The Earl immediately crossed to the window of the room. "You have a vegetable garden at the palace? My, you do things differently here." His voice was really annoying and Johanna wasn't sure whether he was interested or whether he wanted to mock her. "My husband is a keen gardener. I'm told it is a very relaxing pastime. Anyway, make yourself comfortable in this room. The maid will come around when the evening meal is ready."

And with that, Johanna could finally leave him.

While King William settled in the guest quarters, Johanna quickly ducked into her private sitting room before the evening's informal meal. Her feet were sore and she needed to lie down for a bit.

Father was also there, reading and writing up the last of his notes.

"That was . . . interesting," Johanna said.

"He'll be a difficult character to work with," Father said without looking up from his work. "He's not here to negotiate or to be cooperative. He's trying to provoke us. And succeeding admirably." He gave her a stern look.

"He was being condescending."

"Dear daughter, 'Condescending' is every king's middle name. Leave it. Ignore those remarks. He wants to poke you."

"Into doing what?"

"Getting angry at him so that he can show how much more superior they are in war?"

Because Anglia was superior, there was no question about it. Johanna sighed. "Let's hope he'll get along very well with King Leopold. They can both try to bluff each other under the table."

"Well, actually, it's King Benito you need to watch, because he seems to think that Lurezia can take on Anglia in the sea trade."

"Lurezia? They hardly have any ships. Not even half as many as we have."

"We don't have that many anymore."

"That's because they were all burned. We can still build ships. The Lurezians can't."

"I guess then you haven't heard the rumours that they bought blueprints off Li Han that show how to make the iron ships."

"I don't believe those rumours." Johanna spread her hands. "You don't need blueprints. Rinius has spelled it all out in his books. Once you can get over the fear of reading the books because they're banned, you can easily find this information. I know. I've seen it. Roald has the books. It's *building* the ships that requires skills that no one has mastered yet. This is what they were trying to do in the Guentherite brotherhood's summer residence. And they failed because they had a large explosion of bad air that, apparently, proves that Rinius is right about another matter of alchemy." She sat down on the couch, kicked her shoes off and put her swollen feet on the footstool. "Lurezia is controlled by the Belaman Church. They would not suddenly become interested in the very things that condemned Rinius to death: heretic sciences and alchemy."

"That's the other rumour: that the Lurezians are here to present the Belaman Church's viewpoint."

"The Belaman Church cast out the Church of the Triune. They have no say over us."

"Don't dismiss the Belaman Church so easily. They are a very old, very powerful and very rich organisation, who never took kindly to this new upstart church in Saardam that declared the Belaman Church's riches obscene and against the spirit of belief. Some will say that they should have been invited to this meeting, and they are probably still represented, though not in an official capacity."

"We're talking about business, not belief."

"The Belaman Church is up to its ears in the business of buying up land and farming and making money for its upper hierarchy. They're extremely powerful and can sink our project in the blink of an eye."

That was right. They could. In fact every single attendant to the meeting could possibly do so single-handedly.

The door opened and Nellie came in, red cheeked. "Oh, mistress Johanna."

"You look shocked, Nellie. Is anything wrong?"

"It's awful," Nellie said. "The king and that . . . foppish little man are staying in the same room. Sleeping in the same bed." Her eyes were wide.

Johanna said, "What do you mean?"

"I heard rumours about that," Father said in a bemused voice.

Nellie nodded. "Isn't it outrageous, master? It's the same room where the shepherd's wife stayed. Imagine what he would have to say about this." She put teacups back into the cupboard and left the room again.

"Rumours about what?" Johanna asked after the door had shut behind her.

Father shook his head. "Sometimes I wonder what you did while you were out travelling with the duke's bandits."

"What does that have to do with it?"

"Well, were there any women there?"

"No. But . . ."

"Did they ever talk about women?"

"I don't get what you're talking about."

"I'm talking about bandits who plundered and could get whatever they wanted yet they were mostly uninterested in the women they found." He lowered his voice. "Because, you know, sodomy."

Oh. She had wondered what that meant and still had no idea what those men actually *did* to each other, and furthermore couldn't see how whatever it was that they did was hurting anyone. "Why does the church make such a big deal out of it?"

Father spread his hands. "Because it's the church?"

He dipped his pen in the inkpot and returned to his work, and Johanna left, feeling uneasy. Unless there was something going on that she didn't know about, she failed to understand why this *sodomy* thing was as worthy of preaching as bad magic. How many people did the practitioners of *sodomy* kill? Did they perform necromancy? Did they turn people into slaves under the very eyes of the church? Did they turn people into ghosts?

But maybe that was why the noble men considered her a weak queen: because she didn't see why certain things excited them so much.

Johanna could not possibly turn up even at the informal dinner in her utilitarian dress, so she heaved herself to her feet and went to the bedroom to get changed. She found Roald in the room. He sat on the bed, with his knees pulled up against his chest like an angry toddler, rocking to and fro. His face was set in a hard expression. A set of fine clothes lay on the bedspread next to him.

"Roald, what's going on?" Johanna sat next to him. He didn't reply, so she put her hand on his shoulder. His muscles were hard with tenseness.

"No," he said, his voice hard. He stared at the bedspread.

"I haven't asked you anything yet."

"No."

"Who asked you to do what?" It would be someone who had told him that he had to come to dinner, Father probably, in the time that Johanna had taken King William to his quarters. Father could be a little set in his ways. Not always very tactful, she had to admit. And yes it would be great if Roald could show his face at dinner, because it would make dealing with pompous men like King William and King Leopold so much easier.

"He said I had to dress up and behave like a real king. I don't like that man. I am the king and I can do exactly what I want." He stuck his chin in the air.

So it was probably not Father because Roald got on reasonably well with him, and Father would not have used those words. Whatever. Someone from the King's Council had told Roald that he should be there and Roald was digging in on the subject. "What if *I* told you that I'd like you to come? I don't really want to go either."

He looked at her, startled. "But you invited them."

"Yes, but that doesn't mean I like them." She was tempted to tell him what King William had said about her, but that would lead to all kinds of tangential discussions the she had no time for.

She said, "It's true. That can be our little secret."

"Hehe." He grinned. "I like secrets."

Yes, success. "But you know: they're only secrets as long as you don't tell anyone."

He looked disappointed. "But that's not exciting."

"No, but there is nothing exciting about this meeting. All these men are very boring and they're only here to see proof that we're poor and not coping with the situation—"

"That's not true at all. We are doing fine. We're fixing everything. We're not going hungry. I've got a garden full of beans that we can give to the poor people. And they get eggs, too. And carrots."

"I know." But the lack of crops being farmed outside the city because whole communities had been killed was something that would come to haunt them later in the year.

"Can I tell the guests about the garden?"

"I guess . . ." She wondered how that was going to go down with men the likes of King William, but it would be preferable to Roald talking about Rinius. "Come now." She pulled his arms loose from the tight grip around his knees. "I'll help you get ready or we'll be late."

She managed to get him dressed and then needed to get

dressed herself. She told Roald to wait in the library for her to collect him. Nellie came to do her hair, red-cheeked and flustered.

"It's so busy, mistress Johanna," she said. "I scarcely know what to do with myself. I've spent all day on my feet organising the girls to do the rooms, and then I have to go and check to see if they did everything properly. Most of the girls . . . they're very keen and pretty, but they have *no* experience and no idea how to do rooms."

"Thank you for doing all that, Nellie."

"Oh, mistress Johanna, I wouldn't want to be doing anything else, but it *is* very busy right now."

Johanna had taken her place at the dressing table, and Nellie came with the jewellery box and combs, brushes and pins.

"Did you know that Loesie is back in town?" Johanna asked her.

Nellie's hands stopped combing. "Is she?"

"I met her at Father's sea cow barn."

"I really don't understand why that girl doesn't behave like everyone else. I'm sure she could come up here and you'd give her a proper room to sleep in. Why, mistress Johanna?"

"Because she's Loesie." And there was no other answer necessary. Because Loesie never did as you wanted or expected her to do. "She's got a friend with her." Johanna shivered at the thought of the girl's white eyes. "Apparently Duke Lothar is coming, too."

"Is he invited to the meeting, too?" Nellie looked slightly horrified. "I don't remember seeing his name on the guest list."

"Not personally, but he'll be welcome when he turns up." If anything, he and his bandits could make or break any agreement that would be made in Saardam in the next few days, either by attacking ships going upriver or leaving them alone.

Nellie replaited Johanna's hair and pinned it up. Johanna sat patiently through her ministrations. It promised to be a beautiful summer night, but one she wouldn't spend in the garden. Instead, they would be in the ballroom, where it got hot and stuffy on days like this, and where the servants would open the doors, which made things a little better, but which also let a lot of insects and sparrows into the room. And she would be tired, keen for it to end, and eating any of the rich food would give her the most dreadful case of heartburn.

She gazed wistfully out the window when she noticed that the water in the river bore several spots which appeared lighter than the surrounding water, *glowing*.

"Wait a moment," she said to Nellie, who had been getting ready with a bottle of perfume.

Johanna went to the window.

No, she had not been mistaken. Parts of the water glowed, and these patches appeared to be moving of their own accord, with the current, sideways, and against the current . . .

Nellie gasped, raising a hand to her mouth. "Oh mistress Johanna, are those. . . ?"

"Ghosts? I'm afraid so." She put a hand on her stomach, where the child was squirming and kicking. It was almost as if the little princess could feel the magic. Johanna could feel it, too.

Instinctively, she put her hand on the windowsill to see if any ghosts had come through this room, but all she saw was herself sitting at the dressing table, and Nellie coming into the room, followed by a young man . . . Frederik from the stables, she thought—and, goodness, Nellie! She snatched her hand off the windowsill.

"What?" Nellie whispered.

"I didn't know you liked Frederik that much."

Nellie exhaled a soft, "Oh." Her cheeks turned red. "Well, I . . . I guess I forgot that the windowsill is also made of wood, mistress Johanna. Sneaking around when someone in the house has a gift of magic is not easy."

"Don't be ashamed. He's a good man. We'll need all the help we can find. He's good with horses, and we may just need horses. No person who has a good heart will receive any scolding from me. Saardam needs to stand united. I'm afraid Kylian did not come alone this time." Nor would he take defeat as an option.

CHAPTER 7

NELLIE CONTINUED doing Johanna's hair. While she pinned down recalcitrant locks and covered her creation with a jewel-studded hair net, Johanna thought that a lot of things suddenly made sense about Nellie's behaviour lately. For example, Nellie insisting on moving the dressing room furniture because it was "much nicer than the spare room stuff". She *knew* Johanna would see what she'd been up to, and had gone to great pains to remove the evidence, but couldn't remove the windowsill of course.

It also made sense how Nellie had been so happy recently. Nellie deserved a nice young man. But if anything, it drove home to Johanna that she and Roald weren't getting any closer to being a normal couple.

He could be silly, and they could laugh together. She would tickle him and sometimes they'd roll over the bed or the floor. It was fun but the times he'd please her were very few in between, and never seemed intentional on his part. Their coming together was a game more than an act of love, and of course he would never understand her.

She cared for him as a member of the family, like a brother. But the relationship was all about him. From his perspective, there *was* no relationship. There was just him and the people who saw to his needs. She was just one of those.

Often, she wondered what it would be like to be dragged into a room, pushed up against the door and kissed silly, like she'd seen Frederik do to Nellie. She wanted to be carried to the bed and jumped on by a lover who knew that the act required two people to be satisfied.

When Nellie finished with her hair, Johanna went into the corridor where she met Father going in the direction of the dining room.

"Roald will be there," she said before he could ask. "I'll get him now."

"You look worried. Is anything wrong?"

Lots, but she couldn't talk about those things now, especially not about the ghosts and Kylian, or Loesie in the barn, or Duke Lothar. "No. Nothing that matters right now anyway. I'll be along soon, with Roald."

She could feel his gaze prick in her neck as she walked down the corridor. Father knew her well enough to know that something was up, and he wouldn't rest until he knew what it was.

Even though darkness had not yet come outside, no light reached the hallway other than from the candles burning in sconces. The light, adequate as it was to see where she walked, didn't reach in all of the doorways and niches. Johanna expected Kylian to come out of the shadows and sneak up behind her. She expected a cold hand over her mouth, and a stench of death and decay, or a stab of magic. Nowhere was safe, not even her own home.

Roald sat in the library, in one of the armchairs, reading his well-thumbed copy of Rinius. He looked so peaceful that she hated to disturb him.

"Come, let's go," she said.

She was sort of hoping that he would throw a tantrum and refuse to go, because once he had his head full of Rinius, he usually kept talking about the theories that had seen the author hanged in Seneza.

But he didn't. He simply put the book down on the little table next to his chair and rose. On the table was a sheet of parchment: the text of the speech she had written out.

Well, *that* was a much better sign.

He said nothing and took her arm as they left the library. Johanna was never sure what he thought of her other than that she was "his" woman and could get very defensive about her and Nellie, but sometimes she felt like he understood that there were certain things he really needed to do—even if he didn't want to do them—or risk people getting very upset with him. And he definitely didn't like that.

When they entered the ballroom, a lot of people were already standing around. They had not yet gone anywhere near the table, because the hosts of the occasion should be the first to be seated.

The herald at the door announced, "All hail King Roald and Queen Johanna of Saarland."

People cheered and clapped.

Johanna felt Roald's muscles tighten under the hand she held on his arm. He was staring ahead, avoiding the gazes of all those people at the table. And there were a lot more of them than she had realised.

Besides King William and his little assistant Earl Maximilian, the Anglian delegation consisted of two advisors and three businessmen. King Leopold had come with two nobles who were prominent Burovian businessmen, and the new Duke of Aroden was accompanied by his wife and three nobles. Baron Uti had also arrived. His son, of course, was not here, and neither was Li Han. But Johanna recognised some other familiar faces at the table. Fleuris LaFontaine had come with the baron, as well as Ignatius Hemeldinck. Both men wore dark velvet trousers and heavily frilled shirts such as Johanna had seen in the baron's castle. Neither of them showed any emotion when meeting her eyes, as if they had never seen her before.

Watched by all the guests, Johanna led Roald around the table to the two high-backed ornate chairs that stood there. He walked stiffly, like a puppet. Johanna had to help Roald pull out his seat, and a courtier rushed forward to help her. Drops of sweat glistened on Roald's forehead.

They sat down, and all the guests could take their positions as well.

"Welcome all," Johanna said into the oppressive silence. "I

am deeply appreciative of your presence here in response to my invitation." She met King Leopold's eyes. He held lips pressed together. Clearly *he* disapproved of her being here or her having sent the invitations.

"The king will now say a few words of welcome."

Roald's face grew red.

He rose from the table, but had trouble standing because he didn't push the chair back far enough and the edge of the seat pushed into the back of his knees.

A courtier rushed over to pull the chair out of his way.

Roald stood frozen, staring at the table in front of him, while everyone was waiting for him to speak.

He stammered, "I . . . I . . ." His face grew even redder than it already was. He wiped sweat off his forehead.

Johanna turned to him and whispered under her breath, "Welcome to our home, distinguished guests."

He repeated her, haltingly and then went on with the text of the speech pretty much as she had written it. Welcoming the guests, hoping the meeting would be productive to cement a lasting peace between the countries in the region. His voice sounded a bit lifeless and rehearsed, but not bad enough to raise eyebrows. The speech touched on the reason why investment was necessary without mentioning the loss of the family's fortune to the Church, without mentioning the carnage and oppression by Alexandre and his men. It was a short speech, and contained little of importance. Ronald managed to get through with only a few minor stumbles.

When Johanna was reasonably confident that he'd get to the end safely—because Roald was much better than any person she had ever met at remembering written words—she studied the behaviour of the guests.

King Leopold would know of Roald's condition. His expression was blank, and he was drumming his fingers on the table, as if he was about to roll his eyes and ask for some "real men" to come and talk to him.

Baron Uti glared at Roald, but then again he always glared at everyone. He would be more than familiar with Roald's condition and looked ready to "ask the idiot to shut up."

Fleuris LaFontaine and Ignatius Hemeldinck looked bored. Ignatius was fiddling with a fork. Both men looked a lot older than when they'd been left behind in Florisheim. The dark velvet, trendy as it was in the baron's court, did not flatter either of them. Both men wore a lot of jewellery, so they must be doing well.

King William held his head cocked, as if he was highly interested in what Roald had to say. It was kind of eerie and strange in a way, as if he was the only one in the room who took Roald seriously.

Polite applause followed the speech, and when Roald sat down, Johanna gestured at the gaggle of servants carrying trays that had built up at the door so as not to interrupt the speech.

They now entered in a procession, depositing their heavenly smelling loads onto the tables. From the food, you would never know that Saardam's food stores were running low.

There were roast ducks and chickens and vegetables, some from Roald's garden. There was venison and an entire roast pig with the head still attached. There were cheeses and thick slices of warm bread, applesauce and butter, fruit and cream. A servant filled the glasses with cider.

Conversations started up around the table. Father had been in charge of seating. He had placed King Leopold next to Baron Uti and King William with his entourage on the other side of the table. He had placed Master Deim and himself next to King William, and the earl directly opposite Roald.

There were two other women at the table: Duke Aroden's wife and another woman who appeared to have come with Baron Uti, but whom Johanna had never seen before. She had ginger blond hair and a broad face. Maybe she was his daughter, although she looked a little old. Both of the women looked bored, and Johanna made a mental note to make an effort to talk to them.

For some reason the discussion turned to gardening, which the earl seemed to like. Roald spoke at length about his efforts. Had there ever been a dinner held in this room where royals discussed the matter of duck poo? The Earl liked roses, and they went on to discuss those. It looked like all potential disasters were temporarily averted.

Johanna leaned back into her chair. She was so incredibly tired and yes, the cook had excelled at producing the best, but the rich food gave her heartburn, as pretty much everything did these days.

She met Master Deim's eyes across the table. He and Father sat with King William and his entourage, talking, from what Johanna could judge, about tobacco and ships.

The king asked about the iron ships, and Father informed him that Li Han was expected to attend the talks. The king knew Li Han, judging by the way he spoke about the eastern trader.

Johanna let the chatter wash over her. There was a lot of polite talk about the weather. Duke Aroden's wife had an annoyingly loud laugh. The woman with Baron Uti said little, and then only spoke to him while keeping her gaze fixed on the table. Occasionally she gave Johanna an angry look. Maybe that angry expression was just the way she normally looked.

Father and Master Deim now found something to talk about with the new Duke of Aroden, who, Johanna understood, was a brother of the old duke who had been killed by bandits. The new duke had lived in many towns in many countries, some of which Father or Master Deim had visited, and some they had not.

Somewhere after much of the food had been consumed, there was a big to-do in the foyer.

Another group of noble guests came into the hall, with, in their midst, a dusty-looking, darkhaired, dark-eyed man on the wrong side of middle age.

There were cheers and hullos all around the table.

The newcomer was King Benito of Lurezia, dressed in a travel cloak and sturdy riding gear. He was a hawkish character with a large nose and slicked-back hair. He came around the table where he greeted Johanna by kissing her hand. His moustache tickled her fingers. He smelled of horse.

Servants rushed in with extra chairs, and the newcomers found places next to King William. That was *not* where Johanna would have put him. Not Father, either, judging by the look on his face.

"Look at you, old codger," King William said. "Didn't think you'd make it."

"Deciding to take the road was an interesting choice," King Benito said. "The road is so badly rutted that we had to pull the coach out of the mire no less than three times. But the river is not safe anymore."

"What are you talking about?" King Leopold scoffed. "We came down the river without the slightest problem in the world."

"That's because you own all the bandit troops that make passage unsafe, my friend."

"I most decidedly do not!"

"Either you or that cousin of yours."

"Do you have a problem with me?" Baron Uti said, placing both his hands on the table, as if ready to get up to teach someone a lesson.

Everyone had gone very quiet.

In the silence, the blond, broad-faced woman said, "Do shut up, pa. He's just poking you with a sharp stick to see if you will jump. You don't have to perform on his command."

King William let out a long bellowing laugh. Earl Maximilian giggled like a girl.

Then the others started laughing as well, including Baron Uti, even if he cast his daughter a furious glance.

Neither Fleuris LaFontaine nor Ignatius Hemeldinck laughed.

Discussions around the table went on where they had left off.

Johanna felt like she was losing control over the meeting. All these important men knew each other much better than she knew any of them. Moreover, they didn't speak much to her, referring instead to Roald, who gave them silly replies. His cheeks were red and his eyes bright from the wine.

Any time he started speaking, he waved his hands and strained his legs as if about to climb on his chair and do a little dance.

Maybe she should just let them talk and go to bed early. Let Father and Master Deim handle matters on her behalf. She probably worried far too much. Not only that, worrying achieved nothing, because it was not as if any of these men would change their behaviour because of her.

She was looking for a way to escape when King William said, in a loud voice. "Say, I've brought all of you a fine drop of gin. It would be nice if we could find a nice spot where were we can talk as men amongst each other."

A lot of the men made noises of approval.

"Yes! Let's go into the garden room," Roald said.

"There are no seats in there," Johanna said. Certainly, he couldn't be serious about having a drinking party over his sister's grave?

"Who needs seats?" King William bellowed. His cheeks were even redder than Roald's.

"I would," Johanna said. "But I get that I'm not invited."

"Pah, the women can retire to some dressing room and talk about women's things. Seems to me that you have a lot to discuss." He looked pointedly at her belly.

CHAPTER 8

OHANNA BIT HER TONGUE.

By the Triune, that man made her angry. Somehow, he had managed to turn a civilised meal into a drinking party. She hated it that they were dragging Roald along. He did not normally drink, and they would have him under the table in no time. Who knew what damage he would do to her plans while he was drunk?

The men all got up and filed out of the room into the open doors of the garden room, where servants were hastily lighting lamps and dragging in a few chairs for those men for whom standing was going to be a problem.

Johanna remained at the table with the Duchess of Aroden and Baron Uti's daughter. Duchess Aroden gave Baron Uti's daughter a suspicious look and was rewarded with a scowl.

What a pair. Johanna couldn't possibly have picked two less compatible women had she tried. What in the Triune's name was she going to say and where would she take them? Idle women's chatter about clothes, children and artistic pursuits was not her thing. She couldn't imagine it was the baron's daughter's thing either.

Then she had an idea. Her old house used to have a smoking room where Father would sometimes take valued customers or friends. He would have tea brought up there while the men smoked pipes and pondered about life and other things not related to business. At her house, it was a little sunroom, jutting into the garden, with large windows, a table and a couch or two.

The palace had a similar room, even if it had not yet been included in the latest repair schedules. The room was, in fact, not too badly damaged. It was a little shabby but, since it was almost completely dark, no one would notice that.

A stream of servants moved into the ballroom to clean up the remains of dinner. Johanna stopped one of them and asked for tea and cakes to be brought to that little sunroom.

The woman said she would, and so Johanna asked her two female companions to come with her. She led them out of the hall into the foyer and then across the hallway of the unrestored office wing to this little room.

The windows were open and the soft night air that came in was laced with the scents of summer. An owl or some other bird of the night wailed in the distance.

Johanna bade the two women to sit.

"I am awfully sorry, but I don't remember your names," she said.

"I'm Carlotta Aroden," said the duke's wife.

Johanna said, "My mother was an Aroden. Her name was Sara."

"Oh, yes, I remember her. She was from the other side of the family."

A wealth of emotions hid under that slightly cool response.

Growing up in Saardam, Johanna had only ever seen glimpses of the intrigue and rivalry between the two halves of that family and it was probably best not to delve into it.

She shifted her attention to the baron's daughter. "And your name is?"

"Natalya." She sounded peevish, but that could be a product of her heavy accent.

"I understand you are Baron Uti's daughter?"

She seemed to find that funny. "Ah, no. Baron would want that he has daughter. But he does not. I am daughter of Baroness Viktoriya."

"But I thought you called him 'pa'?"

"I did. Everyone calls him pa. But I am not his daughter." The expression in those widely spaced eyes was confrontational, as if challenging Johanna to ask who her father was. Johanna wasn't sure that she needed the complication of knowing this.

The servant woman entered with a tray from which she unloaded a plate of cakes and dainty biscuits, a teapot and cups onto the little table in the middle. She poured the tea and gave each of the women, starting with Johanna, a cup and a plate with one biscuit and one little cake.

Then she bowed and left.

"How long?" asked Duchess Carlotta, with a nod at Johanna's stomach.

"About another month."

"Oh, I remember how terrible it was with mine. I could barely move. It's admirable that you are here hosting us all."

The duchess, as she was happy to volunteer, had three children, all of them quite small, currently being looked after by her sister. She gave their names and ages, named their tutors—apparently having tutors was important—and outlined who would inherit which part of their land.

Johanna tried to listen, but found her attention waning. Natalya rolled her eyes several times.

Johanna tried asking *her* questions but she kept her answers short and clipped, and Duchess Carlotta would jump in with a flood of trivial matters that were not always related to the question.

Johanna tried steering the conversation away from the subject of children to the reasons the women had come.

Duchess Carlotta seemed to have come purely for reasons of entertainment. The children were too noisy, she needed time away from them, and oh did they know how much more pleasant the climate in Saardam was compared to the stifling humid summers in Aroden?

Natalya said very little. While Carlotta produced a flood of chatter, Natalya studied the room, eying the ceiling with its patches of peeling paint and the comfortable chairs that had seen better days but that had somehow survived treatments by Alexandre's bandits.

There was something chilling about that cold gaze from her strangely wide-spaced eyes.

Eventually Johanna could no longer contain her curiosity. When Duchess Carlotta fell silent because she was sipping her tea, she asked, "Can you tell me, then, Natalya, what your father's family is and how you came to live at the baron's castle?"

"My father is Count Hector."

Duchess Carlotta gasped. She put her cup down so suddenly that it almost fell off the table. "But that is . . . the magician of the Black Mountains." She turned sideways, leaning away from Natalya. Then she met Johanna's eyes. "He is said to kill his rivals with a single look, and kill sheep so he can drink their blood."

Johanna had heard some of the stories. One she remembered in particular was that the count stood up for people in a village who were the subject of mistreatment by landowners. He wasn't, by all existing evidence, a real count, since that required being of noble birth. He did, however, seem to be a real magician.

Natalya stuck her chin in the air. "Whatever is said of my father, he is not a peddler of evil. The same cannot be said for some other visitors to this palace."

Duchess Carlotta snorted. "Whatever are you talking about, child?"

"I am not a child. I am many times older than you, although you probably won't believe me."

Duchess Carlotta stuck her chin in the air. "You are one of those . . ." She spread her hands.

"Yes, one of those. The world is divided into those with magic and those without. Magic comes from the east and seeps through the land. Magic wants to insert itself into powerful families and powerful institutions. My mother and I went to the baron's castle when the signs came that the baron's newborn son was showing strong signs of magic. But the boy was already spoilt and the baron would not let us near him at important times."

All of a sudden, something else became clear to Johanna: the same division ran through the Aroden family. Her mother had never spoken of her home much. According to Father, she never even went home for the major celebrations, like weddings. Duchess Carlotta—married into the Aroden family—had casually dismissed her mother as being *from another part of the family* that she was unfamiliar with, probably unaware of the reasons why.

Magic. Because Sara Aroden had magic, she had been stripped of her noble title and entitlements and she had been allowed to marry a well-off but not noble Saarlander merchant. It had probably been a relief to the Aroden family when she died young.

She met Natalya's eyes, and saw in them that Natalya knew, and that she spoke the truth about being much older than either of them.

"So," she said, hesitating. "Why did you come?" Her heart was thudding. She had expected this to be a boring discussion about children, tea and artistic pursuits.

Natalya turned her hand palm up. A little spray of sparks leapt from her hand.

Duchess Carlotta gasped and rose from her chair. "You have come here to sow evil amongst good people. Like that father of yours, and your stepfather and stepbrother. I would be done here and ask my husband to come home with me right now, if it weren't for poor Johanna, who has unwittingly unleashed this flood of evil on her city that has barely recovered from that last attack."

Natalya laughed loudly, in a way that reminded Johanna of King William. "Dear Duchess, I can assure you that *poor* does not describe this cunning little queen. Her machinations are why we are here. They are why we will sort out this magic in the next few days, even if the men think they've come here to talk about business and money." She laughed again. "All the forces of magic are gathering and won't leave until some of us have won, some of us are defeated, some badly wounded and some of us are dead."

"Don't talk like that. You sound like a man-wife."

"Whatever I sound like, it makes no difference when you're dead."

"This is scandalous. Are you making threats?"

"No, although you will not believe me. But petty concerns about what a woman *looks like* or *sounds like* are not important."

The Duchess huffed. "They should ban this filthy magic."

Johanna said, "Banning does not make it go away."

"Ban the people with magic. Put them in a fort and close the doors. Then we can go on with our peaceful lives."

Johanna rose.

"What?" Duchess Carlotta frowned at her.

"Show me your fort, because I'll only live in it if there is a good place for me and my child."

The duchess' cheeks coloured. She sat back down.

Johanna continued, "Magic goes where we have no control over it. Neither the king, nor the church nor any shepherd or holy father. People are born with magic like they are born with blond hair or with freckles. They can't help it."

Natalya nodded sagely. She was going to say something but at that moment a shout echoed from somewhere else in the building, accompanied by the sound of breaking glass.

"Oh, those men," Duchess Carlotta said. "They always drink too much and lumber about like idiots. Should we check to see what they're doing?"

"It is not drink," Natalya said. She was looking out the window and Johanna followed her gaze. A telltale pale glow hung in the garden.

The Duchess gasped, and raised her hand over her mouth. "But that's . . . that's . . ."

A ghost.

CHAPTER 9

JOHANNA MET NATALYA'S EYES.

"Ghosts are not common here?" Natalya asked.

Johanna shook her head. "I think your stepbrother has brought them. He is here. I haven't seen him yet, but I've seen his ship."

Natalya nodded. "He has brought all his unused souls and other ghoulish creations. They wander around feeling lost and trying to trick people into giving them more power."

"It's worse than that," Johanna said. "King Nicholaos hired the necromancer to resurrect his daughter. He was only partially successful and the princess' ghost hovers around, attacking unsuspecting citizens. She must be looking for her place of rest. The men are now having a drinking party over her grave."

Duchess Carlotta gave a little gasp. Her face looked very pale.

Johanna said to her, "If you're uncomfortable, feel free to retire to your quarters."

"Then what are you going to do?"

Natalya replied. "We'll see if any ghosts need warding off. It's not something I recommend for nice ladies."

The duchess straightened her back. "What do you think I am? You may think that I'm dumb and I'll need smelling salts at the sight of the merest little ghost, but I am the Duchess of

Aroden and I protect good against evil. You may call our host Johanna cunning, but she is about to become a mother, and I'll protect her dignity and her child from the likes of you."

A man brandishing a sword now ran through the garden, and further shouts came from the garden room.

Johanna led the way back into the hallway, through the foyer, through the ballroom, where a couple of guards stood huddled in a group just inside the garden room door, looking frightened.

"Oh, Your Majesty," one of them, a young man, gasped. He was barely old enough to have a few hairs sprouting from his chin.

"What happened?"

"We didn't see all of it because we were guarding this door here, but all of a sudden there was this terrible scream and something smashed through the window."

"Did you check?"

He shook his head. "Our orders are to guard *this* door, Your Majesty. It could be a trick to draw us away."

His companion's eyes were wide. "I never go into that room unless ordered. You shouldn't go in there either, Your Majesty. It's haunted. I wouldn't want anything to happen to the little one."

"Our husbands and fathers are in there, so I'm going anyway." Johanna sidestepped them to the double doors that provided entry to the garden room. She was fuming. That was all they cared about: the heir to the throne.

King William's words came back to her. *You will never be worth more than the child you carry.*

Duchess Carlotta said behind her, "It strikes me that you may want to dismiss some of your guards, if they're as weak as that. If any of our guards said that to me, they'd be dismissed on the spot."

That comment hit Johanna in the gut. She hesitated with her hand on the door handle.

She was a weak queen indeed, one who allowed men with ulterior motives to run her life. Of course Duchess Carlotta was right.

But the guards were Johan Delacoeur's responsibility.

Then dismiss him, too.

Roald could do this. He had the power.

But wrecking people's livelihoods and making enemies out of reluctant friends was not her style. She appreciated Johan's experience, and believed that he would select better men if only he could find them. He was very old-fashioned and still needed to fully come around to the idea of having her in charge.

Dear Johanna, you are much too nice, Master Deim had said on many occasions. Usually, he was talking about the church, but it was something that he would say about Johan Delacoeur, because as a seasoned merchant, he never trusted anyone.

Not trusting anyone was something she had a lot of trouble with.

She opened the door to the garden room a crack.

A stifling waft of liquor-laced air came out.

Johanna peered into the darkness. The lights had gone out, and the only thing she could see were rectangles of moonlit garden through the windows directly opposite the door. A patch of light hovered in the garden, an ethereal figure in a dress, holding what appeared to be a lance at someone's head.

By the Triune, how badly had these stupid men provoked this ghost?

Johanna pushed into the room, ignoring groans and other sounds in the darkness. She nearly tripped over someone's arm, then slipped on a wet patch—she hated to think what that was. It stank of liquor in the room, laced with a distinctive tang of vomit.

"Here let me help," Natalya said. She held her hand up. The shower of sparks that came from it cast an ever-so-faint glow by which Johanna could avoid the legs of another man passed out on the floor. She didn't try to see who it was, didn't want to know.

Weren't these nobles just disgusting? How long had she and the two women been drinking tea? And they had managed to get this drunk in that short period?

She reached the door to the garden.

A couple of people also stood looking outside, but she couldn't see who they were.

The ghost was slowly circling the man who lay huddled on the lawn.

"Who is that?" she asked.

A dry voice replied, "You shouldn't be here, Your Majesty. It would be harmful to the heir of the throne."

That sounded like Theo Kloostermans. Whenever had he snuck into this meeting? He definitely hadn't been at the dinner.

"Thank you for your concern, but I asked who that is. I can look after my own wellbeing."

"It is Shepherd Victor." Johanna recognised Master Deim's voice. And Shepherd Victor also hadn't been at the dinner. What was going on?

"What happened?" *Like, what are they doing here?*

"We were just minding our own business, and this . . . apparition came out of the ground while we were all talking and drinking—"

"Drinking mainly, by the look of things." Johanna said, and if she sounded peevish, then fine.

"It is what men do, Your Majesty," Theo Kloostermans said. "With all due respect. This is when deals are made."

"When everyone has passed out on the floor? Then it's no wonder that these men and their deals are all so stupid. Us women, cast aside for being *no more than the child you bear* were discussing real power." By the Triune, she was angry all of a sudden at all these stupid attitudes. "Anyway . . ." She undid the latch to the door.

Theo Kloostermans held his arm in front of her. "Don't go out there, Your Majesty. Think about the heir—"

"The heir is fine with this. Stop trying to control me, because you don't and you can't." Johanna sidestepped him. "I've dealt with this ghost before." Not that it had always ended happily. But she knew that she could control the ghost with her wood magic. The box that Li Fai had given her was in her study, but she happened to know that there was rake with a wooden handle leaning against the wall just outside the window, because she had seen Roald leave it there.

Johanna stepped onto the paved area outside the door. She

found the rake, and went down the stairs into the old rose garden.

Once she had moved away from the palace, away from the talk of the men, she could hear the Shepherd's wailing voice in prayer.

Someone walked on the gravel path behind her. It was Natalya, of course, following her as a silent shadow. Duchess Carlotta came as well, following a bit behind Natalya. If nothing else, Johanna admired her determination. She must be frightened to death.

The ghost of Celine circled the figure on the ground.

The Shepherd was face down, on his knees, backside up, his hands clasped in prayer. He was crying, the words muffled in the grass.

Johanna remembered the vision she had seen when Li Fai had given her the box. It had shown her the Shepherd breaking down when trying to control the relic that was still trapped under the tree in the house where he and his wife used to live. The relic had been calling evil beings and foul forces into the church, and the Shepherd had been powerless to control them.

When she asked, Li Fai had said that the visions showed *possible futures*.

She shivered.

Johanna held the rake in front of her. Natalya stood next to her, holding out her hands. Duchess Carlotta had wrapped her shawl around her head, leaving just a small opening for her eyes, nose and mouth. The whites of her eyes showed with fear, but she didn't back down.

The ghost stopped moving, and cast her ice-cold gaze in Johanna's direction. She laughed, her mouth wide open.

The air she exhaled turned to ice, burning against the bare skin on Johanna's face and hands.

The lance in her hand fused with her arm and grew into a long tendril.

The ghost's other arm grew longer, too. Celine's hair fused into moving tentacles that looked like writhing snakes.

The Shepherd lifted himself on his knees. He balled his fists at the sky. "By the Holy Triune, Bearer of Evil, begone with you!"

The ghost ignored him, having found someone new to play with. She floated closer to Johanna, walking about a hand's width above the ground without touching it. She wore the yellow dress that used to be the favourite of Celine's. Her feet were bare.

A feeling of cold magic went through Johanna's stomach. She raised the rake, willing the wood to start growing, but the rake's handle remained a rake handle, showing her distracting images of the garden in full daylight and Roald on his knees weeding the carrot beds.

Why didn't this wood grow in the same way it had grown when trapping Alexandre? That twisted tree had grown from a broom handle.

Because there had been many other people. Maybe there had been other people with magic who didn't know they had magic, or maybe the magic just needed other people to work, or—

The ghost was coming closer. The tentacles reached out for Johanna. She stumbled back, and almost tripped over the edge of a garden bed. She was so heavy and awkward, and a fall could be much nastier for the heir to throne than anything the ghost could manage to do.

Johanna's backside hit the hedge and she could retreat no further.

The Shepherd was yelling at the top of his voice. "Begone you devil, begone! The holy Triune with smite you to the seven hells."

The cold exhaled breath of the ghost bit into Johanna's skin. She squinted her eyes against it, continuing to wave the rake.

She willed it to sprout buds. She imagined the vines as they had grown from the broom handle. She imagined the tree as it had grown from Li Fai's wooden box, but the rake refused to obey.

Celine's ghost reached for Johanna's hand with tendrils of glowing ether. This close up, the ghost's face didn't resemble Celine at all. The face was skull-like, the eye sockets were empty, the nose two elongated slits, as if the flesh had rotted off. The hair writhed and twisted into knots. The mouth had no lips and pointed teeth. It opened, emitting a low hiss that made the hair on the back of Johanna's arms stand up.

Johanna was holed up against the hedge, which was too tall for her to step over. She had nowhere to go. She had tempted this ghost too often. This time, the ghost would win. The mouth opened further—

Then a female voice hissed foreign words that sounded like shards of glass slicing through fabric. A breeze whirled around the ghost, whipping up leaves and dirt. Johanna's skin stung with the warmth of it, after the icy cold of the ghost's magic.

The ghost froze.

The woman's words filled the night. Reverberant, sibilant, sonorous, the tone of her voice was everything at once. She stood with her hands stretched out. The woman was Natalya, of course.

The ghost let out a hiss of cold air that pushed against the warm breeze, but it couldn't manage to drive it away.

The ghost retreated past Natalya and the Shepherd. It floated backwards across the lawn and the garden beds, and before it reached the wall, it winked out and was gone.

Johanna lowered the rake.

Duchess Carlotta was staring at her.

Johanna wiped sweat off her face. She asked Natalya, "What was the thing you just said?"

"It is a simple spell for repelling ghosts. Ghosts are afraid if they have never heard it before. After a while, they get used to the spell and it won't work anymore. It was a gamble that it would still work on this ghost."

"Well . . . thank you."

"You should not go fight this ghost anymore. This is not a simple ghost. This is something more evil."

"It is the ghost of princess Celine, resurrected years after her death. It's Kylian's attempt at necromancy."

Natalya hissed. "We do not speak his name."

CHAPTER 10

SHAKEN AND FEELING SHIVERY, Johanna led the women back to the garden room, where a number of the men were standing at the top of the stairs, talking in groups. In the dark, it was hard to see who they were except for the tall one, who was probably King William. She recognised Master Deim's voice in amongst their chatter. He was saying, "The danger has gone now. We can all safely go to our beds . . ."

"Where is Father?" Johanna asked him.

A slightly stooped figure detached from one of the groups and enveloped her in a hug. "Please, Johanna, will you never do that again? I thought it would kill you."

"I'm all right," Johanna said. She shrugged off his concern, because admitting that she had thought the same would bring all sorts of unwelcome thoughts. "Where is Roald?"

"Inside. He didn't see the ghost of his sister."

"Did you shelter him from the sight?" That was surprising. Roald tended to be curious.

"He's . . ." Father hesitated. "He'll be all right."

Johanna wasn't sure she wanted to know what was behind that evasive reply. The air that wafted out of the open doors into the room stank of liquor. Roald never drank. That was probably as much as she needed to know.

Someone had lit a lamp inside the room, and by its light

431

Johanna and the two other women picked their way between glass, a fallen chair and messy patches on unmentionable substances across the room. She spotted at least three men asleep on the floor. No one she recognised.

The little Earl was at the table that the men had dragged in from the ballroom, pouring himself another drink. He hefted his glass when Johanna passed, and giggled. "Cheers." His cheeks were bright red. "I will . . . will drink to . . . the van—vanquishing of the goat—er, ghoaf—ghost! Hic."

"Disgusting," Duchess Carlotta said in a low voice behind Johanna, and for once, Johanna agreed wholeheartedly with her. She also noted that Duchess Carlotta made no attempt to find her husband.

"They're happy now, but they won't feel so good in the morning," Natalya said.

Duchess Carlotta snapped, "And they won't want to get out of bed, and they'll be complaining about their heads all day."

There was clearly some backstory to this remark, and Johanna thought it wise not to ask any further. Duchess Carlotta was right, and it was annoying.

Tomorrow morning was the day that Father and Master Deim had planned to take the visitors around the city to show them the possible sites for building new quays and warehouses. It was an important day in the program and she'd wanted the men to be alert and asking questions, not worrying about their heads.

And then a thought: King William thought that she was just a little woman, worth only as much as the heir she could produce. Was he deliberately trying to distract all the guests?

By the Triune, he wouldn't do that, would he?

In the ballroom, she found the group of terrified guards in the same position as they had been when she came through. Seeing them there made her angry, too. Had they done anything to prove their worth?

One of the men gasped. "Your Majesty! You're back."

"Yes, I am. You can now go in there. The ghost is gone so you don't have to be afraid anymore. It is quite safe. While I've been doing your job, I wonder why I pay for you when you're standing out here being scared, like a bunch of adolescent girls. Go inside and help clean up the mess. Put a halt to this raucous party. Drag these men to their beds where they belong. Take away their liquor."

The guard flinched. "Yes, yes, Your Majesty." He bowed.

"Then don't just stand there. Do it!"

The men scurried off.

"Idiots," Johanna said in a low voice. She really must talk to Johan Delacoeur about it. She knew what he would say: that it was hard to get good men, and no doubt it was. But better training cost nothing. He'd better explain to her why he hadn't yet started that training.

"Sometimes you need to scare the men," Natalya said. "Otherwise they will just do whatever they want. Men are stupid. They do not think."

Johanna could definitely agree with that. "This makes me angry. These men called up Celine's ghost by having the party over her grave. It was their fault."

"They will always do what they want, because you're a woman and they won't listen to you. But we rule the world of magic and ghosts. You wanted to know the reason why I came with the baron. I didn't tell you because I first wanted to see if I can trust you. Now I think I can. Come. It is high time that we talk about this." And she took off across the foyer.

Johanna followed Natalya down the stairs that led to the old servants' quarters, with Duchess Carlotta close behind.

On the way down, Natalya told her, "The pull of magic is very strong in this city. Everyone who has even the smallest gift of magic will want to travel here. They will make up an excuse to go, but their mind is pulled here and they cannot say why they suddenly have to visit relatives they haven't cared about for years. They are drawn here because the magic lines have broken to the surface. They are virgin lines that have never been seen before. Everyone wants to draw from their power."

Johanna remembered Duke Lothar talking about magic lines in his estate. She remembered the living tunnel of trees.

"We never had magic in Saardam."

"No, that's right. The lines must have shifted. Magic things must have happened that have brought the lines to the surface. Or maybe the magic discovered this virgin, empty place, and all the types magic are fighting to own it."

"Magic events . . . We trapped Alexandre's spirit in a tree, and we did the same with a relic from the Church."

"Those are evil things. I can feel them, and I have been around a lot of bad magic. Those vessels of evil have not been defeated. They're struggling against their tree prisons. Give them half a chance and they will escape. I can think of several people who would love to give them a hand."

She didn't need to name names. Kylian, Baron Uti, maybe even King William would be happy to have his greatest rivals in the sea trade occupied with something other than seafaring. Then he would pounce, snag Li Han's business and the iron ships.

They arrived at the bottom of the stairs.

This was another part of the palace that had been relatively unaffected by the carnage upstairs, but that was also in need of repairs and freshening up. Originally, these were servant quarters. At the moment, there were not enough servants in the palace to fill up all the rooms, and this was where the extra influx of less important visitors had been put up: any of the travel companions who had no ship to sleep on, and who would not stay in their master's rooms.

So far, the Lurezian party was the main one that had come overland, and Lurezian was the main language spoken in the passage, by the men in the livery of King Benito who stood talking in groups and who greeted Johanna with bows when she came past.

Like many basement corridors, including the one in her familiar old house, the basement had a low ceiling barely high enough for the tallest of men. The kitchens were here—on the other end of the hallway, as well as the servants' bedrooms.

The hallway was quite wide and well-appointed, with little benches along the sides, as well as some statues and ornamental vases that had probably been received as presents by King Nicholaos and Queen Cygna and had been deemed not good enough to be displayed upstairs. Johanna remembered walking through the storeroom containing all this material, dusty and soot stained but strangely untouched by the bandits who had occupied and plundered the palace. They must not have known anything about art because they had left many priceless items: paintings and vases, gold-rimmed plates and carved statues.

Natalya knocked on a closed door at the end of the passage.

A young woman in a maid's dress opened and spoke to Natalya in a language that Johanna didn't recognise. She looked at Johanna and dropped into a curtsy, then she stepped back, opening the door further.

Johanna went inside. It was dark in the room, which was a typical servant's room, with enough space for a bed, a chair and small table and a clothes rack.

A nun rose from the chair, in a habit that covered her arms and went all the way to the ground. Her cap and veil were white and blue, her habit dark blue. Johanna had no idea what order that represented.

She curtsied. "It is good to see you, Your Majesty." She spoke with a southern accent.

The woman's face was unfamiliar, if perhaps a little too well-fed to be in a monastery.

The woman went on, "Thanks so much for seeing me at this time of the day in your condition. Do take my seat, Your Majesty."

Johanna wanted to protest. She got a little sick of situations when people treated pregnancy as a debilitating disease. Farmers' wives worked in the field right up to the moment their children were born. But this game of being the most polite in the room was going to go on forever, so she sat, and let the nun take place on the bed. Natalya shut the door, cutting off the view of the corridor and a couple of curious maids standing there.

Then there was a small sound, and Johanna saw that the nun hadn't been the only one in the room.

At her foot of the bed stood a bassinet with an infant.

That was . . . odd. Nuns didn't marry, they were married to the church. Any "fallen" nun who had a child wouldn't be allowed to stay in the order, let alone travel with a royal party of any kind dressed in a habit, while bringing her infant.

Unless . . .

The nun gave another little bow. "My name is Francina. You might have heard about me. I have joined the Sisterhood of Forgiveness recently."

"There is only one Francina I've heard of." But certainly this woman couldn't be the same person as King Benito's latest wife?

She nodded, her eyes glittering. "He chose me, because I was a widow and I had two children by my first husband."

King Benito had succession problems, Johanna remembered, and that might have been the reason for such an odd choice as a wife. But why the nunnery and why wasn't she upstairs with her husband?

Francina reached out for the infant in the bassinet, who was fast asleep. The prince or princess was wearing a little bonnet, which Francina pushed down. The infant's hair was fox-red.

Not the king's obviously.

Johanna felt cold. The child inside her squirmed. She looked from Natalya to Francina to Duchess Carlotta, who was frowning and didn't appear to understand the implications.

Johanna whispered, "Is this. . . ?"

Natalya nodded. "The necromancer is spreading magic through all of the western lowlands by means of his children. It doesn't matter if the woman is a princess or a farmer's daughter, if she is married or not, if she is young or old, if she comes to his bed because she wants it, or if he has to rape her. Many infants are born that are his."

"Yours, too?" Francina asked, meeting Johanna's eyes.

Johanna looked down. "I'm not sure."

"Yes," Natalya said. "I can feel it. Here." She put her hand on her chest.

Johanna's cheeks burned.

"There are others. Princess Maribelle of Burovia has little girl. There is no father. Queen Margit of Montania has little boy, the heir to the throne. He is eight years old and quite possibly the oldest of all the necromancer's children. They are everywhere."

By the Triune, this was also what Loesie had been talking about, but from the perspective of the poor farmers' daughters who, cast out and frightened by magic, ended up on her farm. "What is he trying to do?"

Duchess Carlotta was looking on, her face pale.

"Are any of your children the necromancer's too?" Francina asked her.

Duchess Carlotta gasped. "Heavens, no." Her cheeks went red.

"He bewitched a lot of us, so there's no shame."

"Well," the duchess huffed. "That would not be an excuse in the eyes of my husband. If I said anything of the sort to him, he'd accuse me of seducing another man and being unfaithful."

"Pah," Francina said. "While being unfaithful themselves?"

"Husbands are useless," Natalya said. "They sleep, they get drunk, they act like they are important. They are not."

Francina nodded sagely. "My husband kicked me out. He allowed me to come here, because he is still hoping that the boy will turn out to be his son. He's not. Husbands try to control our lives, but they can't."

Duchess Carlotta didn't look too sure but eventually nodded as well, her face set. She repeated, "Husbands are useless."

"I cannot blame my husband for anything," Johanna added. "But his condition means that he does not help me at all. He is not interested in anything other than gardening and horses."

Francina asked, "Does he even . . . you know how to do it?"

"He does. He's not terribly interested anymore."

"If I were you, I would take a lover. Do you have one? Or more than one?"

"I don't," Johanna said.

"Well, that's a pity. As long as you're with child, there can't be any unfortunate consequences."

"Oh!" Duchess Carlotta exclaimed. "Your talk is really quite scandalous, for a nun. What sort of order is the Sisterhood of Forgiveness?"

Johanna had a feeling what was going on. "This isn't a real order of the Belaman Church, isn't it? I have never heard of the Sisterhood of Forgiveness."

"Oh, it's a real order, but not one that the Belaman Church agrees with. The order helps the women who have been unfortunate, who have fled from their husbands, whose husbands have cast them out or have run away, leaving the wife with the children and without money. The mothers take the habit as protection, and the children live in the convent."

What an excellent idea.

Francina continued, "Magic is very often the reason that the women were cast out. I started to notice a lot of children with red hair, all born of noble women. Their stories were all similar: they were seduced by a handsome red-haired stranger who did not mention anything except his name. Few know that he is the son of Baron Uti. For myself, I'm not ashamed of what I did. My parents brokered the marriage, but King Benito is a smelly old man, much more interested in horses than in people. He never gets violent when he's drunk, but he drinks so much that he doesn't get it up, if you get what I mean. I wasn't like some innocent noble girl. I know what's required to make an heir, and he can't do it, simple as that. He'll never have an heir. He knows that, and he wants the little boy to become his heir anyway, because otherwise the throne would go to his nephew, and King Benito hates his brother. So that's why I'm here. He wants me to take off the habit and pretend the boy is his son. I'll look after the boy, but I'm not going to pretend to be his wife and deal with his filthy habits anymore. But he is so afraid that something will happen to his heir that we had to come on this trip."

Magic. This was the thing that Natalya had been speaking about. Making up excuses to visit Saardam. That would have been Loesie's excuse as well.

A chill made the hair on the back of Johanna's arms stand up. All these people were here because of the magic she had unleashed.

CHAPTER 11

JOHANNA WOKE UP, her heart thudding.

It was dark in the room. Pale moonlight slanted in through the window, silvering the cabinet with the water jug and the bedpan.

Johanna lay back on the pillow, waiting for her breath to calm, wondering what it was that had woken her and given her such a fright.

She remembered leaving Francina's room in the servants' corridor quite late. Upstairs, it looked like the raucous drinking party had continued as if Celine's ghost had never been there. Clearly the two young guards had been unsuccessful at putting a stop to it. She had peeked into the room, but the stench of liquor and vomit had been even stronger than before, and she had simply decided to go to bed alone.

There had been a dream, she remembered vaguely. Something in which the gnarled tree in the market place came to life and started strangling people.

In the dream, she'd been leaning into the wind, gazing at the tree, while people rushed past in the market place.

Johanna was the only one who appeared to have noticed the mangled and bloody body of Johan Delacoeur in the branches.

As the tree had dropped Johan's lifeless body at her feet, a throbbing red light had risen over the roofs of the city, coming from the Shepherd's house . . .

A stab of magic had gone through her, knotting into a hard ball in her stomach, making it glow from within. It wasn't painful exactly, but gave rise to a sensation of pressure of something that needed to get out.

She sat on her straight-backed chair in the ballroom, and all the men were looking at her.

Helena was in the room, yelling at her, "Push like you've got to shit really badly and you've been waiting for days to get it out."

Johanna wanted to say, "Not here," but she had no voice.

The child was coming and she was not ready for it. The meeting hadn't finished, they hadn't agreed on anything, and—

Then she woke up, gasping for air.

Her heart had calmed somewhat. She reached next to her, and found that the bed was empty. By the Triune, where was Roald? She sat up, but it was too dark to see if he had been in the room at all.

Johanna pushed herself from the bed to use the bedpan. It took a long time these days, and the cold edge of the metal bit into her legs.

The window stood open a crack, but she couldn't hear any sounds that indicated that the drinking party was still going.

Johanna found her slippers, pulled on the only dressing gown that still fit her—it was Father's—and waddled to the corridor. Ouch, her feet were so sore these days.

It was quiet in the hallway as well. The door to King William's guest quarters was closed, and when she listened at the door, she could make out the sound of snoring.

Now she was getting really worried. Where *was* Roald?

A young guard called Dirk—like Father—stood in the guard station in the foyer. He bowed when Johanna approached. The light from the oil lamp showed his surprised expression.

"The king?" he asked, his eyes wide when Johanna asked. "I wasn't on duty. I haven't seen anyone come this way since I started. It was all quiet, the other men said."

Seriously, what had those young guards been drinking? "Let's go and check it out."

The garden room was deserted. The floor had been cleaned —at least the part that Johanna could see in the pool of light from Dirk's torch—the glass removed and bottles and cups taken away.

There was no sign of Roald.

"When did you last see him?" Dirk asked.

Johanna had to think about that. It had been at dinner, because even when she came in here, after the Shepherd had broken the window, Father had told her that Roald was fine but that it was probably best if she didn't see him.

Probably he'd been blind drunk. Probably he had felt ill. Likely he had realised that she or Father would not be impressed.

What did Roald do when he thought she would be angry with him? He hid somewhere. In the garden usually.

"Come with me," she said, and crossed to the doors that opened onto the terrace.

The Moon had moved to bathe the western side of the palace in a pale glow that was bright enough to make out paths and hedges. Johanna grabbed the rake, just to be sure, and set off for the little gate that connected the old rose garden with the private garden where Roald grew his vegetables.

And there, something was definitely happening. A dark-clad figure was climbing out the window of her study. Now she realised what had woken her up: the breaking of glass.

Dirk yelled, "Stop, intruder!"

The man dropped himself out the window and ran through the garden. Dirk went after him.

When he had vanished, Johanna realised there was a second figure in the garden, on the path between the beanstalks and the carrots. He sat on his hands and knees, coughing. No, retching.

Johanna knew who that was. "Roald!"

She ran to him.

He coughed and coughed.

"Stop it. Calm down." He stank of stale liquor.

"He was . . . trying to break . . . into your workroom." He slurred his words. "I tried to . . . stop him."

She bent over, putting her hand on his shoulder. He felt cold and was shivering. Who had left him alone so that he could have wandered into the garden? Why had no one seen to it that he went to bed?

He coughed, bringing up nothing more than slime. He rocked from side to side on his hands and knees.

Dirk came back into the garden. "He was too fast."

"Did you see who it was?"

"Unfortunately not."

Johanna didn't think it could have been Kylian. She would have felt it.

"Take him inside." She nodded at Roald who still sat on his hands and knees, and let out a large wet burp. By the Triune, if she could play a trick on King William, she would. This was disgusting. "Make sure that someone washes him and puts him in bed."

Dirk nodded.

Johanna hoped that he wouldn't ask Nellie, but he'd go to one of the maids instead. Nellie didn't deserve to have to deal with this.

Johanna needed to check her study. She lit a lamp from the firebox in the grate and walked around holding the light aloft.

The place was a mess. Glass and other rubbish crunched underfoot. Books and papers lay strewn everywhere. The ink had fallen over, leaking onto the rug.

Was anything missing?

The drawers that contained money were closed, and indeed the money was still there.

Then she lifted the lamp to the shelf where she kept Li Fai's box.

It had sprouted roots that covered most of the shelf.

Johanna gasped.

She reached out for the box. A spray of magic enveloped her hand. As she touched the wood, the roots evaporated, the box came loose from the shelf and it returned to its usual appearance.

The wood showed her a flash of magic too bright for her to see anything else. When she opened the lid, the little tree unfurled itself as it usually did. But the leaves seemed unusually bright and it was as if they *trembled*.

CHAPTER 12

JOHANNA'S HEART THUDDED like crazy. Someone had tried to attack the box.

That box was the symbol of her developing magic. She needed it. The box connected her with Li Fai. Apart from the tree, it contained memories.

She knew for certain: Kylian was stalking her and waiting to make his move. He was not interested in talk and civilised meetings. He would use magic. He probably wanted the box to cripple her ability to fight against him, maybe even to free Alexandre's spirit and the Church relic's magic from the tree. Kylian did not have wood magic, but he had brought all the magical tools that he had. He had brought Celine's ghost and a flood of other ghosts that would frighten the citizens—who were unused to magic—so much that they would either run or hide.

Last time, he had sent Alexandre with men and animals. Alexandre had been defeated, so this time, he had brought a magical army. Saardam had no ability to fight this invasion.

There was no time to waste. She should see Li Fai—rumours be damned—and also Loesie, to warn them. She should ask Loesie to call whatever assistance she could muster into the city. She should find Duke Lothar. He would not want to be found, but she could use her magic to track him down. The longer she waited to do this, the more time Kylian had to set up his plans.

But, first, she needed him to check if her box had been damaged or compromised, make sure it was still all right to use it.

Johanna went to change into her clothes. The dressing room looked out over the east, and a faint glimmer of daylight coloured the sky over the roofs of the city.

She had taken her dress out of the wardrobe and was wondering how to do up the lace when Nellie came in. Her eyes widened. "You're not going out right now, mistress Johanna?"

"Sadly, I am. Help me get changed."

Nellie started tying up the lace at Johanna's back. "But why, mistress Johanna? What could you possibly want to do at this time of the day?"

"I could tell, but you'd be horrified, so I won't."

"Well, *that* is certainly reassuring."

"I think there is a plot being cooked up for another occupation of the city."

Nellie gasped. "Why ever would you think that? The kings are all here to talk to you."

"A *magical* occupation."

Nellie took in a sharp breath. "But Kylian is not even here."

"He is in Saardam. I can feel him. I've seen his boat."

Nellie's face showed an expression of horror. Nellie knew all too well about the persuasive powers Kylian possessed. Johanna had always wondered what had happened between him and Nellie in Duke Lothar's garden, and now knew what *would* have happened had she not looked out the window and seen the two in a very friendly chat. It seemed that Nellie was lucky to have escaped the fate of so many girls.

She put on her cloak and left the room. It might be getting light outside, but it was still very dark in the corridor. A group of people, one of them with a torch, was coming into the end of the hallway. She presumed that these were the guards and servants with Roald. She felt guilty for not looking after him. Poor Roald. He really couldn't help that King William had enticed him into drinking far too much. Roald couldn't make those kinds of decisions for himself.

"Your Majesty?" Anton was on duty in the foyer, and he was surprised to see her.

"I have to go out," Johanna said. "I will need the coach and horses."

He nodded. "I will see to it." And he went out the main doors to the stables to rouse the coach driver.

Good old Anton. *He* did as he was ordered without questioning. He offered to help her, protect her, and was always there for her.

Johanna waited on the little bench in the foyer. The soft noises that echoed through the hallway indicated that somewhere in the palace people were getting up, ready to cook and clean. Soon enough someone would come up here to ready the table for breakfast, although the distinguished visitors would probably not be in the mood for it for several hours. She pulled the hood of the cloak over her head, unwilling to be recognised, just in case.

Anton came back. "The coach is ready."

Johanna followed him outside, where it had gotten significantly lighter. The coach stood at the bottom of the stairs with the two white horses.

After days of nice weather, storm clouds were rolling in and squally gusts of wind exposed the silvery underside of the leaves on the willow trees. Somewhere in the distance lightning flashed in the clouds. The air smelled humid.

"Where to, Your Majesty?" the coach driver asked. He held the horses' reins tightly. The animals were tossing their heads, manes flying in the gusty wind.

"The eastern trader's ship."

He nodded. Like Anton's, his face remained blank.

Anton helped her into the coach and while she settled on the familiar bench, he climbed up on the driver's seat. The driver whistled and the coach jumped into motion.

Not questioning their orders, that was how guards and servants were supposed to react. Not to argue, or let their own feelings or curiosity come through. She really should raise the subject of training with Johan Delacoeur. She had so much to learn about how to be a successful ruler that people would respect. Sadly, being kind or gentle wasn't one of those things. People took advantage of rulers who were too nice. Girls were always taught to be nice, so they were more susceptible to being taken advantage of.

The coach made its way through the city by the grey light of the early dawn. The only people on the streets were servants and merchants, hidden in the collars of their cloaks against the squally wind. They turned right onto the quay. The ships in the harbour bobbed on the choppy water, rigging and flags flapping. At King William's ship, a couple of deck hands were securing a couple of barrels around the foremast to stop them rolling around the deck.

The coach stopped at the mooring position of Li Han's iron ship.

Anton jumped off the driver's seat and came around to open the door. "Your Majesty, are you sure this is the place where you wanted to go? There is no one here."

"I'm sure, thanks." She took his hand to climb down the awkward ladder.

The wind made a lot of noise. Rigging flapped, hulls creaked. Unspecified things banged and squeaked. Most of the ships were visibly moving on their moorings. Except Li Han's ship. It lay as still as ever. Johanna glanced up at the smooth, dark metal side that loomed over the quay.

Johanna stopped at the bottom of the gangplank. "Li Fai!"

Her words were lost in the wind, so she called louder, "Li Fai, I need to talk to you."

She listened.

Maybe they were all asleep and would not wake up.

But then the sound of footsteps rang through the hull, followed by the unmistakable quacking of ducks. At least someone was awake.

"Johanna!" Li Fai stood at the top of the steep gangplank. "What are you doing here?"

"I need to talk to you." Johanna's voice was almost blown away by the wind. A lock of hair came undone from the bun and swept over her forehead.

Li Fai came down. He held out his hand. "Come inside. It's going to rain."

Johanna put her hand into his. His grip was warm and strong, and he pulled her easily up on the deck. She had only been here once before. Father and Master Deim had mostly dealt with Li Han, but Johanna had always kept herself a little distant, for fear of rumours.

How silly that seemed now. She should have come much earlier, to set up lessons for children with magic.

The ducks all bunched together in the corner of their cage, quacking, poking their beaks through lattice that was made out of some kind of twig.

"They're hungry," Li Fai said when he noticed her looking at them. "The deck hand will come soon to feed them."

Johanna followed him across the deck to the side of the main cabin. A burly guard in leather armour watched them from above.

Li Fai opened a door and gestured Johanna into a spacious cabin that looked like a study, with a table in the middle, silk paintings strung on frames, shelves around the walls that contained jars of samples.

A couple of lights burned around the cabin, spreading a warm glow.

Li Fai indicated a little bench for her to sit on, and she did, enveloped in the nutty scent of spices.

He sat on another. "What is the matter?"

"I have come to warn you. Tonight, someone broke into the palace. I think he tried to steal my magic box."

"I know," he said. "I could feel a disturbance through my art. Show me the box."

She took it out of her purse. Held up in the palm of her hand, it looked very much like it usually did. Li Fai reached, touched with the tips of his fingers and withdrew his hand like he'd been stung. He took in a sharp breath. "The art is very strong."

"What does that mean?"

He shook his head. "I don't know. It feels like . . . the box defended itself when someone tried to imbue it with evil."

"Did he succeed at all?"

"I can't be sure. I'm but a small peddler."

"What about that large dragon of yours?"

"The dragon is not that brave. He wants to stay in his box. He doesn't like the feel of this man's art. The dragon can be a real coward."

Johanna couldn't help but laugh at that.

His face remained serious. "I'm speaking the truth. I'm not all that you hope me to be. I hate to disappoint you."

"You helped me defeat the relic."

"Your tree did most of that, and the relic was but an object."

"A strong magical object."

"Yes, but I fear that you give me too much credit."

The expression in his eyes was sad and very serious. What did Johan Delacoeur usually tell her? *The best generals are highly aware of their own shortcomings.*

She let a silence lapse. It would be handy if he had all the answers, but then again, if he did, this situation wouldn't exit, because someone would have dealt with Kylian long ago.

"I'm sorry," she said in a low voice.

"There is no need for you to be sorry."

"There is. I assumed that you knew everything. I hoped that you could tell me how to defeat this evil, but it's not a thing one person can do. I just saw that in the garden with Celine's ghost. I should not have assumed that you are the answer to all my problems." Some problems, maybe, but those were probably best not mentioned.

"Can I still use the box, or do you have another box I could use?"

He shook his head. "Sadly, it doesn't work like that. The box is not easily replaceable. You will have to cleanse it."

"Do you know how to do that?"

"No. Except I know it's not easy."

"Can you help me?"

"Helping is always a good thing."

She went on to tell him all she knew about magic, including about Kylian's magical children and the women downstairs.

A deep silence followed her words. His throat worked as he

swallowed. His gaze wandered from her eyes to her stomach and back again. "You shouldn't trust me blindly. How do you know what machinations my father has in place?"

"Your father, yes, I realise that. He has a business to run and will make decisions accordingly. Trust doesn't come into it in the same way it exists between, say, friends or relatives."

He met her eyes. Blinked. Said nothing. Johanna's heart thudded. Any moment now he was going to tell her that she acted inappropriately, or he was going to say something that put her down as a stupid woman or shattered her wish.

He licked his lips. "Well . . ." And a moment later again, "Well . . . I could try to help you. I don't know how much good it would do, but—"

"Thank you." Johanna almost choked up inside. She had spent so long looking for a court magician without the slightest success. She might not want to give Li Fai that title, but his assistance was so much better than anything she had before.

A ghost of a smile went over his face. "With my little knowledge, I would say we would first need to . . . secure the spirits in the trees to make sure that no one can easily set them free."

Johanna frowned. "Shouldn't we should protect the kings first?"

"They can look after themselves."

"But the ghost is already in the palace."

"If they don't have the art and don't disturb the ghost, it won't harm them."

"That's easy to say. The Shepherd was trying to chase it off with prayer. It took exception to that." When ghosts wanted to start throwing things, there was a need to do something.

"If the shepherd left the ghost alone, it would not harm him. The palace and the stupidity of those men is not our main concern."

"It is mine, because if anything happens to any of my guests . . ."

"It will be many times worse when the spirits escape from their tree prisons. I suspect that the necromancer is here to free his creations. By tampering with your box, he hampers your powers. He could probably sense the presence of the box, and wanted to render the power harmless before he makes his move."

"Can we stop him from reaching the trees?" One was in the market place, the other hidden in a house that was now abandoned. Both were easy localities to visit in a disguise and have no one notice it.

"We could try to put a ward around the trees so that we are warned when someone comes in—"

Johanna rose. "That sounds like a good idea. Let's do it now." She remembered Sylvan putting wards around the campsite at night when they were in the forest. "Do you know how to put wards?"

"Yes, but . . . I haven't done that for a long time. The spirits here are different. I may need someone else—"

"I'll come. We'll need to hurry, though."

He frowned. "There will be people in the marketplace already. Nothing will happen during the day. Spirits are active at night. We can come back after dark."

"Yes, but I need to go back to the palace because of the meeting. I don't want anything like last night to happen again." He would understand the importance of protecting the guests. His father would attend the meeting. Maybe he would be there as well.

"I'm really not sure, though. I'd like to have someone there who has done this before. I can help, but I don't know how good it will be."

"Please, you are all we have." There was no one in Saardam who knew that much about magic, barring Duke Lothar, if he was indeed in Saardam; but if he was, Johanna had seen no sign of him. Or maybe Natalya, but Johanna wasn't sure what she knew or how much to trust her.

CHAPTER 13

L I FAI AGREED to come with her to check out the trees and put wards on them if possible. They left the cabin and its wonderful nutty scent for the fresh morning air.

On the deck, one of Li Han's domestic staff, a middle-aged woman dressed in a dark tunic, stood with a bowl casting handfuls of grain into the duck pen. The birds went head-down in a frenzy, gobbling up as much of the grain as quickly as they could. The woman shouted and waved the bucket when the ducks became too eager. Then she noticed Li Fai and bowed to him, and also to Johanna.

Li Fai helped Johanna down the steep gangplank, where the coach still waited, with Anton and the driver watching without the slightest expressions of puzzlement on their faces.

Johanna told Anton that she wanted to go to the tree in the marketplace.

It was only a short ride from the quay. As Li Fai had rightly noted, stallholders were already arriving with their produce. A bit further down the canal, cheeses were being unloaded from punts and carried up to the market house to be weighed and registered.

The tree that held Alexandre's spirit stood lonely and forlorn. The trunk was twisted, the branches grew stunted and gnarled, and the leaves were marked with ugly white patterns. It was a sickly looking thing that a gardener or farmer would have chopped up for firewood long ago.

Li Fai climbed from the coach first and did Anton's job of helping Johanna down the awkward ladder. A gust of wind blew his jacket and shirt open, showing a bit of his soft-skinned chest. Johanna debated telling him that one of his shirt buttons wasn't done up properly, but she might embarrass him. And maybe, if there was another gust of wind, she might see his skin again.

"That thing makes me very uncomfortable," he said.

"Yes, me, too."

She approached the tree slowly. It was such a weird and twisted thing, with bunches of closely spaced branches growing out of the trunk at random places, with a bark whose grain resembled the patterns made by swirls of ink dropped into water. A couple of people had stopped to look. Johanna had heard only a fraction of the rumours that went around the city about her involvement with the tree: that the tree looked like this because she knitted it together from a couple of brooms, that she used it to spy on everyone and that she could talk to the trapped spirit and it would reply.

She reached out for the trunk, but Li Fai grabbed her arm. "Don't touch it."

"I have to. It is how I can tell if anyone has been here and tried to interfere with the tree."

"I can feel the evil in this tree. Have you touched it before?"

"I have." Not very often, and not since Kylian had come to town. Last time, she had been transported to the previous day, when scores of people walked past getting their daily groceries, ordering supplies for their households, bringing cheeses.

"Did it ever show you a working of the art?"

"No. Not at all. It just shows me the usual things that wood shows me: the things that have happened in this place previously."

He retreated, but the expression on his face showed that he didn't like it.

Johanna touched the tree's trunk and was transported to yesterday afternoon, when the summer evening had turned golden and the stallholders had already closed their businesses and were packing up their wares.

A little boy pulled his mother's hand to get closer to the tree. His mother gave it one look with a horrified expression on her face. "Come. Don't look at that dreadful thing. You'll turn into a ghost if you do."

The boy turned to her and asked in a perfectly serious voice, "What is it like to be a ghost?"

"Don't ask such things!" his mother scolded.

"But I want to know!"

"No one knows, because everyone who becomes a ghost is dead."

The boy frowned. "You mean like grandma?"

"By the Triune, what is wrong with you today? Let's go home straight away."

"I only asked a question!" the boy cried.

"It's been enough of that now. I don't understand why you're always so fascinated by this dreadful thing. We're going home."

The boy kept looking at the tree while his mother dragged him away.

Johanna shivered. That look in his eyes chilled her. She didn't know the woman or the boy, but there was no doubt that the boy had magic.

"Johanna, Johanna." Li Fai pulled her hand away from the trunk.

Johanna looked at him. "Yes, what's going on?"

"Didn't you hear me at all?"

"What did you say?" She frowned at him.

"I was getting worried about you. Come away from that twisted thing."

"Can you put a ward around it? I don't think anyone has tried to free the spirit yet."

Li Fai pulled a face. He had his hand in his pocket where he probably hid his dragon box. The dragon was a coward, huh? That was not how she had seen it. "It's hard doing it while there are so many people around. I'll come back tonight and try to do it."

Johanna let her gaze roam the marketplace, the quay and the cheese sellers waiting at the weigh house. He was right.

"Come." He drew her away from the tree and led her back to the coach.

"To the palace, Your Majesty?" Anton asked.

"Not yet. I want to check the Shepherd's old house."

He nodded and jumped up on the bench with the driver, while Li Fai helped Johanna up the little ladder.

"I hope I will be able to put up the wards. That tree has bad art," he said, when they sat opposite each other in the coach.

"I know."

"I don't think you know even half of what's going on. The tree puts thoughts into people's minds. It makes people think that it's just an ugly tree—"

"It is an ugly tree."

"Yes, it is, but it's much more."

"It's a prison for an evil spirit. We trapped the tyrant Alexandre in there. If you cut open the tree, you would find his bones ground to dust."

"There is a lot more than ground bones inside. Can't you see the evil straining against the bark?"

She frowned at him and then looked out the little window as the coach jolted into motion. "Do you see that now?" She had never seen anything of the sort. The trunk was just covered with bark. It was a kind of twisted bark, and she suspected that the wood underneath was also twisted, but there was nothing else remarkable about it. Trees grew like that sometimes. She understood trees.

"I could see it. The trunk glows with evil magic. When you touched it, the glow spread over your hand. I told you to get away from it, but you didn't hear me."

"Well, that's . . ." She frowned at him, disturbed. She didn't remember him having said anything.

"That's why I said not to touch it."

"But I did, and it did no harm to me. I saw nothing remarkable except people from the town going about their normal business." But that little boy had magic. He had known that the tree was special.

There was something she was missing, some clue. Something that Kylian knew and that she would know if only she knew the signs.

"You should go home," Li Fai said. "You don't want to risk yourself and the child by exposing yourself to bad magic."

Johanna laughed. "Most of the bad magic is inside the child. It's why a lot of these things are happening. I want to check out the other tree as well. You can tell me what you see there. If this is Kylian's doing, it's very different from last time he tried to capture the city." *And succeeded.* "He came to the ball and danced with all the girls. Alexandre and his men were hiding in the baron's ships and Kylian disappeared from the palace as soon as the barbarians started setting fire to the houses. This time, I haven't even seen Kylian yet. All the magic is hidden, so that no one suspects anything and there is no reason for anyone to be alert. We don't even know how to organise ourselves to try and fight it."

"You can't fight magic except with magic."

Johanna had heard that before. "I'm afraid, because we're unprepared, I'm alone, and I'm not at my best. I have to take care of the meeting and can't be where I want to go."

"You're not alone. You have me and your daughter."

"But I'm reasonably sure that she is Kylian's."

"She will belong to whomever teaches her first."

"How do you teach infants? They don't listen."

"May I?" Li Fai moved to the bench next to her. He placed his hand on her stomach. A warm glow spread out from the spot where he touched her.

"What is that? How do you do that?"

He withdrew his hand. The glow vanished. "Does it hurt?"

"No, it feels . . . good."

"Every night when you go to bed, put your hands there, and then think about good and happy things. When a child is born with the art, its art is neither good nor evil. It is the men that make it one way or the other. If you train her to have good thoughts then she will more easily understand the value of using her art for good when the time comes to teach. When she is born, stroke her bare head a few times a day. I've heard old midwives say that when the infant is born, the mother must be the first to touch the child's skin, even before it has fully emerged. That way, the child feels that there are others with the art. Those are the things that should be done."

Johanna nodded. She would do them. Soon.

"It surprises me that there are not more people in this town with evil art."

"There was never much magic here. Any people with any ability came from outside, like my mother."

But there were other children with magic in town. They must be taught or the neglect of their ability might well lead to these children becoming disciples of men like Alexandre, which, she suddenly realised, could hold for Octavio Nieland as well. Almost all noble families had links to other towns. The advice about newborn infants must be made known to all the midwives and the mothers. They must find someone wise and experienced to teach older children.

"Thank you," she said softly. "You're helping me a lot."

"I don't know. The work must be done by you. It is not easy or quick, but will be rewarding. It is when the art is neglected that it turns dark and makes people evil."

"Many of us are afraid of magic. Most of us don't know anything about it. Can you teach us?"

"I could, if my father decides to stay. That depends on the negotiations."

"Would he really go to Anglia?"

Li Fai shrugged. He averted his eyes.

"You want to stay, right?"

He nodded, slowly, and let a deep silence lapse. The coach's wheel rattled on the cobblestones. The driver and Anton were laughing.

"I want you to stay, too."

Li Fai met her eyes with an intense look. Johanna's heart was thudding so loud that she could barely hear anything else. He leaned with his elbows on his knees, clasping his hands together so tightly that the knuckles were white.

She lifted her hand, and placed it on top of his.

He shook his head. "Maybe it would be better if we left. This is not right. I . . ." He pulled his hands out from underneath hers. "You have better things to do than worry about me. I am only a merchant's son and I'm—I'm sorry. Forget I said all of this."

He met her eyes, breathing through widened nostrils.

Johanna's cheeks burned. "Li Fai, I—"

The coach came to a halt. Li Fai gasped and jumped back to the bench opposite her, his cheeks bright red.

CHAPTER 14

ANTON WALKED around the coach and opened the door. He helped Johanna down the steps, with Li Fai following close behind. The wind had picked up and the grey clouds released the occasional spitting drops of rain.

"Wow." Li Fai looked up at the house, long since abandoned by the Shepherd and his young family. The tree on the second floor had mangled the house. It had broken through the roof. Its branches spread over the house and part of the neighbours' roofs. Roots as thick as a man's thigh had come out the broken upstairs bedroom window and grown down the façade of the house, between the windows, down the side of the steps to the front door and forced open the door into the servants' entry downstairs.

It was a type of tree Johanna was unfamiliar with and no one had ever seen in Saardam, probably because the box it had grown from was made of foreign wood brought by Li Fai. How the tree survived was anyone's guess, because no one watered it.

"It's grown so much bigger," Li Fai said, his voice low.

"Haven't you been back here since we defeated the relic?"

He shook his head. "This place has bad art. I don't like it."

No, Johanna didn't like it either. Whenever she came past the house, a chill ran over her back, and that same chill now made the hairs on the back of her arms stand up.

Johanna didn't want to go into that house. Evil rolled from it in waves. But if Kylian or someone else had returned and was trying to free the evil from the tree, this would be the place that he did it: the marketplace was much too exposed to too many curious gazes.

Slowly, she climbed the steps to the front door. It stood open, having been wrenched from its frame by fat tree roots. A scent of must and dead leaves wafted from the dark maw. In the months since she and Li Fai had defeated the relic, tree roots had grown across every room, pushing up carpets and floorboards. Animals had moved in.

At some point, the family's servants had been in to remove whatever of the family's furniture had survived the struggle with the relic, but hadn't been back since. It was a sign of the level of evil that reigned here that none of the city's many poor had been in to clear out the items left behind. A table stood, in the middle of what might once have been a sitting room, attached to the floor through thick roots that descended from the ceiling, encasing the table in their stranglehold and disappearing again through the floor.

Johanna clamped her arms around herself. The warmth of summer had not yet penetrated the inside of the house. It was very dark here, despite the fact that it was fully light outside. Mice and rats scurried in the darkness out of her field of vision and from somewhere upstairs came the chirping of little nestling birds.

The last time she had come here, the stairwell had been dark, but tidy, with a dark red runner on the steps and a big clock against the upstairs wall. The runner now lay at the bottom of the stairs. Johanna had to climb over it. The carpet was wet and made squishy sounds under her feet. Rats had chewed holes in the carpet and left their smelly mess in the corners. The clock in the upstairs hallway . . . had sprouted branches.

It was the oddest sight ever. The clock face was stuck at a quarter to twelve, wrenched out of place by sprouting buds. They were oak leaves, because the clock was made from oak wood.

Li Fai stopped to look at it. He rolled one of the leaves between his fingertips. "Interesting."

The clock had grown roots, too, and because the large tree in the spare bedroom—the one that trapped the relic—had shattered the roof, dark stripes from rain water had stained the walls and caused the paint to peel and grow mould.

The upstairs hallway was like a humid, lush cave, with moss-covered tree roots crossing the walls and floor. It reminded her uncomfortably of the ice cellar that she had inadvertently stumbled into when running from the bandits on Duke Lothar's estate.

Johanna hesitated.

Li Fai was at her back—she could feel the warmth of his presence—and though she could never sense magic in the air, the pulse of it was so strong that she could feel *something* there, even if it was not the same sensation as someone with wind magic would feel.

That pulsing sensation wafted out of the door to the spare bedroom.

The room itself was little changed since she had last left it. The tree that grew through the roof had behaved like a normal tree in that its crazy rate of growth had slowed. It was a strange type of tree, unknown to her, with smooth bark and tiny leaves.

The Shepherd's tables and cabinets still stood around the walls, mostly with their macabre contents intact. Daggers, skulls, knives, teeth, beads carved from bone. All these items lay as when she had last come here, albeit now covered in a layer of dust.

The roots of the tree had crushed the box that had contained the relic, and fragments of it lay on the floor, some of them having sprouted branches and roots of their own. It was like an eerie dark forest in here.

She took a deep breath and reached out for the trunk of the tree. Li Fai wanted to stop her, but she insisted, "I have to do this."

As soon as a hands touched the smooth tree bark, her vision faded.

The anger of the magic pulsed within the wood. It was much clearer than the magic in the tree in the market place.

The relic was trapped, not defeated.

A vision now came to her. It was dark in the room and someone was coming closer with a storm light that bobbed up and down with the bearer's footsteps. A pale face glowed in the candlelight, and another one. Two boys snuck in from the hallway. The one carrying the storm light put it down on one of the cabinets. He looked around the room.

"Oh, wow, you are right, this is so amazing!"

"Don't touch anything, though. Some of these things are bewitched." The second boy wore a coat that was far too big for him and a cap that shaded his face. He carried a box under his arm that he set on the floor and removed the lid from. On a bed of cloth that looked like it had been cut from an old curtain lay an assortment of the kind of things boys typically collected from the shores of the river and the beach: empty mussel shells, bird skulls, dried sea weed, bits of gnarled wood and polished rocks.

"I want that one," the first boy said, still looking at the cabinets in the room. He pointed at a dagger that lay by itself in a glass cabinet. It was an old, dirty and crooked thing, and had a dark heft with inlaid silver and a stained blade. The only thing that looked clean was the ruby set at the pommel.

"No, you can't. That's an evil thing."

"You're just saying that so you can have it."

"If I wanted to have it, wouldn't I already have taken it before bringing you here?"

The boy turned to his friend, comprehension dawning on his face. "But . . . how do you know that it's evil?"

"The heft is made of silver and bone. The jewel in the top is a ruby. Those are the things that magicians use."

"You know you scare me sometimes? How do you know all these things?"

The other boy didn't answer that question. He had picked up a little glass jar and rolled the contents—some kind of seeds— around by the light of the lamp.

Johanna recognised him as the boy who had wanted to go to the tree in the market place. The boy with magic. He studied the seeds in the same chilling, calculating way that the tone of his voice had displayed. Too mature for his age.

"What are you doing?" the other boy wanted to know.

The magic boy unstoppered the jar and shook out some of the seeds into the palm of his hand.

"They're just seeds," his friend said, but his voice sounded dubious. "What are you going to do with those?"

The magic boy let the seeds drop on the ground. "If you were a tree, how would you feel about growing all alone on the top floor of a house?"

"Well, I . . ." His friend gave the magic boy a strange look. "That's rubbish, Rue. Trees don't feel, at least not like people do."

"How do you know that?" He put the jar back into his pocket and studied the cabinets. "This is a thing that you can have." He opened one of the glass doors and took a dusty piece of pottery from the shelf, a little statue of a naked troll.

His friend was still fascinated by the dagger with the ruby on top. The magic boy collected a few other things: a roll of parchment, a handful of old silver coins, and a skull of a bird with a long crooked beak.

He put these in the box with the rest of his collection, pointing out how each of these things was special. Then he said, "Will you stop looking at that dagger!"

"But I want it," the other boy said.

"You can't have it. Come, that thing is going to bewitch you. I shouldn't have brought you here." He put the lid back on the box.

"And so you were going to keep all this for yourself?"

"Will you stop it? This is the Shepherd's house. It's not yours, and it's not mine either."

He more or less pushed the other boy out of the room.

When they were gone, a faint glow lit up on the floor, as the seeds that the boy had dropped sprouted and grew little plants. And then nothing more happened, because there were no more visions.

Johanna shivered.

She remembered Li Fai saying *It is when the art is neglected that it turns dark and makes people evil.*

"What did you see?" Li Fai asked behind her.

"The only people who have been in here were two boys collecting bits of curiosa. One of them has magic, but he's far too young to have anything to do with Kylian."

Still, something about the vision didn't sit well with her. Why had he thrown out the seeds? Who was this boy?

She clamped her arms around herself.

Li Fai studied the cabinets around the room, bending over in the semidarkness to look at this or that object, but not touching anything.

She touched his arm, disturbed by how warm he felt and how very cold she felt. "Come on, let's go. This place scares me."

"It is not a comfortable place." He continued looking at the objects on the shelf, squinting in the low light.

"What are you doing?" she asked.

"I'm not sure. Something in here still feels . . . alive."

"The dagger," she said, before she could stop herself.

He let his gaze roam over the shelves. "Which dagger?"

"The one with the—" The spot where it had lain in her vision was empty. That was . . . odd. The vision had not shown her that anyone else had been in here after the boys left. She told Li Fai about what she had seen. He knelt on the ground where the boy had dropped the seeds. Only a few desiccated stalks remained, which he picked up and held on the outstretched palm of his hand. "Do you recognise this plant?"

"From just those stalks? It seems like some sort of garden weed to me. Give them. I might ask Roald."

He handed the stalks to her, and she opened the little powder box in her purse and dropped them in.

"The art is even stronger in this house," Li Fai said. "If I wanted to lay a ward, I could perhaps do it for the tree in the markets, at night when no one is watching. I'd have no chance with this construct of evil. It would require a capable master."

"You're more capable than you think. I've seen your dragon."

"It's nice of you to say so, but no, I don't believe that."

A short silence followed his words, in which Johanna's frustration at her own inability to fully comprehend magic boiled over. In fact, did *anyone* understand it?

"We better go now anyway," Johanna said. "Or I'll be late for the meeting."

"Yes. I was going to go to the palace with my father. I better make sure he doesn't spend too much time worrying about where I am."

They went outside into the light and the gentle warmth of a cloudy summer morning in Saardam.

The coach was waiting and Anton stood on the steps of the house. The relief on his face when he saw her was disturbing. "Oh, Your Majesty, there you are. I was getting worried, because we need to go back to the palace—"

"I know. We can return home now."

Anton held open the door for her and helped her in. "Quick, Your Majesty. We are going to be quite late already."

Johanna looked around, but Li Fai wasn't following her into the coach.

He said, "I can walk from here. You go home quickly before your father gets worried."

Johanna nodded. Father *would* be worried.

She waved to Li Fai. Anton shut the door and jumped up on the driver's seat. The coach jolted and then Li Fai was gone from view, and Johanna was left alone with her worries. She had two tasks: she should bring the negotiations to a success and she should stop Kylian or his minions from reviving the evil relic or Alexandre's spirit.

There might not be time to do both of them properly. There might not even be time to complete one of the tasks within the short time she had.

A T THE PALACE Johanna found most of the men already at the table, surprised that she was late. She crossed the room in quick strides and sat down to polite nods. A young girl came to bring her breakfast.

There were cheeses and bread and jams and cooked eggs, everything the foreign guests might want. Johanna ate as much as she could, which wasn't much these days. She knew that she'd be hungry later.

For the number of people at the table, the gathering was surprisingly quiet. Duke Aroden sat bent over, staring at his plate. The duchess glanced at Johanna a dark expression on her face. Earl Maximilian was not eating at all. Baron Uti was eating, but doing so quietly. His face and bald head shone with sweat. Ignatius Hemeldinck and Fleuris LaFontaine sat by his side, both pale-faced.

Only King William was being his loud self, but several of the members of King Benito's party cast him dagger looks across the table. King Benito himself sat scowling at his plate.

Roald had not yet turned up. She should go and check on him if she had a little time, but it was probably just as well if he didn't come on the trip, with all potential for disasters that would entail.

Father had come to breakfast with all his notes and papers,

and as soon as the servants started to clear away the plates, he folded out his plans and explained what they would do for the rest of the day. More than a few of the guests looked unimpressed.

Johanna glanced at King William, who looked pretty pleased with himself. Just what was his game? Making sure this meeting didn't succeed?

To be honest, she couldn't muster much enthusiasm for leading an excursion into the fields and all over town. She could have easily gone to bed and slept all day. And she hadn't even attended the drinking party.

Father and Master Deim had devised a very full program. First they would look at all the warehouses in the harbour, and then they would cross the little creek outside the city to have a look at the farms that would have to be cleared in order for new warehouses to be built. One of the guests asked what they would do for lunch. Father informed him that a few people from farms were going to bring food to an old farmhouse shed that was empty but in a good enough condition to stop for the midday meal and be dry if it rained.

Then breakfast was done and everyone went to dress for their expedition.

Johanna saw Nellie in the dressing room. After the initial gloominess, the day promised to become sunny again and most of her dresses were quite warm.

"I hate it how I spend all my days feeling hot," Johanna said.

"It will soon be over," Nellie said. She put Johanna's hair up in a bun and pinned down the stray strands.

Johanna was already sweating. It was so incredibly tempting to claim sickness.

Before leaving the room, she looked at herself in the mirror. "I look like a fat cow. An overcooked fat cow. How can anyone take me seriously?"

"I don't think you do. You look very pretty and motherly."

That was just the problem. Why had she ever thought this was a good idea? She had enough of being like this. She didn't care how much it hurt and what people would say. She wanted the child out.

Johanna met Father and all the other guests in the foyer. This time, local businessmen had also turned up, including Li Han with Li Fai, who met her eyes with an intense look. The harbour master had come with a couple of merchants, including, she noticed with dread, Octavio Nieland, who stood talking to Fleuris LaFontaine and Ignatius Hemeldinck. When his cold gaze met hers, he stuck his chin up. Johanna turned away from him, but could still feel his stare prick her neck.

Father led the group outside.

Smartly dressed guards and coachmen waited at the doors, ready to take the guests to their coaches.

Johanna's coach with the white horses stood in front. Johanna rode alone this time, because it would simply not do to show preference to one of the guests over the others.

The caravan set off through the palace gates. People in the street stopped to watch the spectacle of coaches and horses and dapper-looking coachmen. They cheered and waved to Johanna. She sat stiffly in front of the little window in the coach's door to wave back. Her attention was drawn to a man with a little girl at a street corner. Years ago, that might have been her. When that girl was older, she might say, "Do you remember the time that all the kings came to town?" And it would be a defining moment that everyone remembered.

She, ordinary Johanna Brouwer, of merchant, not noble, descent, would have to make sure there would be something else to add to the memories of those people, so they would say, "Yes, dear, that was when the agreement was signed and we've never had a war since."

So much hinged on these few days that she could not allow herself to be distracted. Even magic would have to be dealt with later.

The first stop was the harbour. The coaches stopped in front of the ruined ammunitions depot and the party gathered at the point where the eastern arm split off from the main quay. From this position, you could see King William's ship side-on. It towered over the other ships in the harbour.

The focus of this stop was the ruined ammunitions depot.

Father explained that the harbourmaster had applied to have

it moved out of this position, so that the site would come free for development. He suggested that offices and warehouses should be built for the biggest investors.

"Mooring space is going to be a problem here," King Leopold said.

To this, Father explained that there was a canal along the back, and that the plan was to widen it. Here, the harbourmaster took over and detailed some of the necessary buildings. He hinted at the fact that Saardam might be a future base for iron ships, which needed fuel, and that needed to be stored somewhere; and the making of those ships would require more and bigger halls.

"I'm guessing all this is just a way of softening us up for a doubling of mooring fees?" King William stood with his hands behind his back.

Oh, the terrible boor. Was he always like this? Johanna said, "No one who cannot afford the fees and who has helped invest in these developments will pay any."

The men turned around and stared at her. King William let out a bellow of a laugh that echoed over the harbour.

"Would you mind keeping it down a little?" Duke Aroden asked.

It was time to go to the next stop. Johanna dragged herself to the coach. All of a sudden, she was so incredibly tired. She met Li Fai's eyes while Anton helped her up the ladder. He waited next to his father to board one of the other coaches. He acted very proper: not a nod, not a smile. But he had been looking at her a lot today, and she wondered about what he had been trying to tell her this morning in the coach to the Shepherd's house, and she wondered what would have happened had the coach not stopped at that moment.

It was not right, he'd said.

Of course she knew what wasn't right, or at least she thought she did. Or she *hoped.*

It could only mean that he felt for her in the same way she felt for him, right? That a glimpse of soft skin sent her heart racing, that his smile made her cheeks glow.

The coach started moving with a jolt, but went at a slow pace to allow the others to keep up. Johanna squinted into the bright sunlight, struggling to keep her eyes open.

The next stop was East Harbour, where the fire damage had been limited to a few spot fires. Several of the warehouses were empty here, because the owners had moved elsewhere after the fires. Only the very far end of the harbour was deep enough for seafaring vessels, and this was where the Nieland family's *Josephine* lay. The ship had sustained some damage when a neighbouring ship on fire—rumour went that it had been the *Lady Davida*—had bumped into the hull and made deep scorch marks on the otherwise pristine vessel.

As to why, a year after the fires, the damaged ship had still not been fixed, well, people said that the ship builders had refused to deal with the Nieland family because of Octavio's support for Alexandre. It was a wonder that he hadn't left town yet, but additional rumours said that he would leave immediately once his father died.

Nothing escaped King William's sharp gaze. "Why has no one put that worm-ridden old barge over there out of its misery? Was it so bad that not even the bandits wanted it?"

Several men—visitors and clueless ones—laughed.

Octavio hissed. "What makes *you* think that you can come here and insult us?"

King William laughed again. "Boy, they do have feisty merchants in this place."

Octavio rushed forward. Johanna saw what was happening and managed to step into his path. He almost crashed into her. "Get out of my way, woman." Spit flew from his mouth.

She put her hands on her hips.

Master Deim joined her. He stared at Octavio. Octavio glared back.

"Learn to control your temper, man," Master Deim said, his voice low.

"Did you hear what he said?"

"He's here to provoke, and succeeding admirably. Ignore him."

"When you're courting him to *buy land* in *our* town?"

"Buying the rights to use warehouse space," Johanna corrected.

"And whose stupid idea was that?" His gaze bored into hers. "By the holy god, stupid woman, do you even know what you're playing with?"

"Yes," Johanna said. "Grown men who behave like toddlers."

His nostrils flared. His muscles in his shoulders strained. For a moment, she was afraid that he would hit her, but he came to his senses, stuck his chin in the air and turned around.

King William laughed again. By the Triune, that man was annoying.

"That's not a good enemy to have," Master Deim said to Johanna in a low voice.

"He was never going to be a proponent," Johanna said. "Better that we know where he stands in the open so that everyone else can see it, too." But she was trembling and sweating in her hot dress.

Father continued with his presentation unperturbed.

Even if Octavio Nieland was not interested, King Leopold seemed to warm to the idea of having dedicated warehouse space. He asked about prices and how taxes and harbour fees would be handled. Father and Master Deim dealt with his questions.

King Benito looked on with a scowl, but she understood that this was a normal expression for him. He asked a few questions, most of them practical, which indicated to Johanna that he was interested, too. Seeing that, King William couldn't afford to stay behind, and he out-questioned everyone else, except Johanna wasn't sure that he was completely serious.

Towards midday, the caravan of coaches left the city through the old gates. The fields were lush and green and full of flowers, cows grazed and the scene would have been utterly peaceful if it weren't for the burnt-out shell of the farmhouse that stood on a hillock surrounded by willow trees. A shed a bit further down appeared to have survived the fires. The coaches stopped at the creek crossing, where a couple of young men waited to punt them across the sluggishly flowing water.

From there, the party waded through the thigh-high grass the short distance to the burnt-out house up the riverbank. Two carthorses stood in the yard, tied to a tree. The farm cart waited in the shelter of the barn, which had both doors open. A farmer and a woman young enough to be his daughter sat in the driver's seat. The flat tray on the cart, scrubbed to within and inch of its life, bore a selection of serving trays, each with plates of local produce. There was roast duck, chicken and pork, pickled mussels, cheeses, pâtés, smoked sausages and plenty of fresh bread. The farmer's daughter handed out plates, and a woman who was probably the girl's mother brought cider, and water for finger bowls.

The cider, especially, met with a lot of approval.

Once everyone had a plate, the group dispersed around the barn.

Johanna's feet ached, and she had to sit down on the dusty haystack in the corner of the barn. Many of the men remained standing. She ended up close to a group that contained Li Han, his son and a couple of Estlander merchants. Li Han appeared to know these men, judging by the way they were laughing and talking. Johanna would look at Li Fai, at the way he moved his hands when he spoke, and how utterly serious his face looked. He glanced in between his father's acquaintances a few times, meeting her eyes squarely.

She then averted her gaze, studying the walls and ceiling instead, while her heart thudded audibly and her cheeks glowed.

This farm had lain abandoned for quite a while and the barn was full of cobwebs. The farming family had left long before the fires. The land belonged to one of the noble families and they had never been more than caretakers. This area had a tendency to flood and, after losing all their cattle in a flood, the family was forced to set up elsewhere. Alexandre's bandits had set fire to the house last year.

The walls still stood, but the roof had fallen in. The scent of burned wood was gone, and weeds grew in the corners of the house's rooms. The overgrown yard was surrounded by willow trees, and the land sloped down to the river shore and marshy ground where a riot of plants flowered.

This area was the masterpiece of Father and Master Deim's

plans and when most of the men had eaten their fill, Father started his talk.

Master Deim hung up the map on the inside of the farm door and explained how they would build a wall around the tongue of land, and how they would use windmills to makes sure the land remained dry. He gave all his calculations of how many stones would be needed to build seawalls, how much sand would have to be carried in to make the ground safe from flooding in the future, and where bridges would be built to connect the area to the rest of the city without the need for a punt. Also, the creek would have to be dug out so that bigger vessels could come in, not to speak of the warehouses and shipyards that would be built once all those things had been done.

The men were now definitely intrigued.

"Turn this useless piece of land into market space?" Baron Uti scoffed. "Why not use another piece of land?"

But some of the others were asking questions about the techniques. The idea of pumping water out with windmills was nothing new, just the thought of applying it over such a big area.

Master Deim answered all the questions without once mentioning the name of Rinius, who was the originator of many of the ideas.

Even King William appeared intrigued. At the very least, he had stopped laughing. His face bore a small frown, and occasionally he would speak to the earl in a low voice. Johanna understood that flooding could be a problem in parts of the Anglian capital, Targon, as well.

Johanna had heard about the ideas so often the she knew them by heart, and she trusted Father and Master Deim to deliver the ideas in a way that businessmen understood. That seemed to be her lot: stay in the background and let the men carry out her plans. A sad thing, but it was the only way the kings would accept it.

She studied the faces of the guests. King William appeared intrigued. The man was annoyingly awake after that late night. Some of the other men were yawning and looked as wilted as she felt. Duke Aroden's face was positively grey. She had already spotted him dashing off into the bushes twice.

Li Han and his son were also unusually bright and alert, not having attended the party last night, and the early morning trip didn't seem to have affected Li Fai in the slightest. She understood he usually rose very early.

Johanna picked bits of hay out of her dress. Nellie would probably complain about getting dust and sticks on her clothes, but she didn't care. Hopefully, soon after all these men left, she would be able to put this dress in the wardrobe and never touch it again.

Unless she had another child. Roald's this time, although she doubted that would be possible.

The farmer's daughter brought another round of cider. The men made toasts. Some of them were getting entirely too cheerful again. Duke Aroden was arguing, red-cheeked, with Ignatius Hemeldinck. He slurred his words and his movements were jerky. Johanna felt sorry for Duchess Carlotta.

More cider was served. This time, even Father and Master Deim were drinking, although not nearly as much as some of the others.

Then Baron Uti asked in a loud voice, "These building plans are all very well, but there is the remaining issue with the Church. I'm afraid that most of us would be unwilling to condone investment in this city when it is ruled by a church that forbids *our* church and that actively campaigns against our morals."

Father said, "Saardam is not ruled by the church. We also have a Belaman Church for those who wish to attend it. Most of the nobles do, in fact."

"But the king comes from a strong background of support for the Church of the Triune."

Now Johanna felt pressured to speak up. "The king is not his father. We—the king, myself and the King's Council—see the problems caused by King Nicholaos and his over-generous donations to the church."

The Baron blinked, as if he wanted to say, *What's that woman doing here?* "Where does the king stand in this matter?" His cheeks were red from the cider.

"The king is well-educated in various branches of the church.

You will know that he spent some time at the farm of the Guentherite brotherhood—"

King William sucked in a breath. "Are those bandits still around?"

"Watch it," King Leopold said. "They are honest, law-abiding citizens. A religious order. It's ludicrous to use the word bandits for them. Bandits are the rogues that live in the woods and make passage of the rivers hazardous."

Baron Uti protested. "Hey, what are you looking at me for?"

"It's your brother who's doing that."

"I have no brother." The Baron tightened his arms over his chest.

Johanna stepped in. "Gentlemen, I can assure you that the Church of the Triune will have nothing to do with this project, at least not in any way that limits your business concerns."

Baron Uti glared at her.

Then someone else said, "Well, I don't really want to spoil the pretty queen's party but that silly church has a pretty good grip on this town these days."

Johanna looked in the direction of the voice. It was Octavio Nieland. He gave her a hard, emotionless look.

"I agree," Fleuris LaFontaine said. "That church has got its tendrils everywhere."

Johanna glared at him. *And the Belaman Church doesn't? They even try to control us from Seneza.* "I assure everyone that the Church of the Triune will *not* interfere with any of your businesses or any of the people you bring into our city. I cannot see any representatives of the church here and they will not sign any of the agreements. They are not involved."

An uncomfortable silence followed her words. Then the farmer's daughter came in again with another barrel of cider, and some of the men cheered.

Johanna couldn't bear the tension anymore. These men were going to get horribly drunk yet again, and they were going to come to fisticuffs soon. And she did not want to be present when that happened.

She got up and left the barn. Father looked at her, but didn't say anything. Li Fai looked at her, too, but didn't say anything either.

The fatigue and aching overwhelmed her. She felt powerless, she wanted to go home and sleep, she couldn't do this anymore.

The overgrown garden blurred before her eyes.

This had been a bad idea. These men had come here only to hold drinking parties, and to fight with each other. Her project never had a chance. They had come here to steal her ideas, and then use them to lure Li Han to *their* towns. And then she would lose Li Fai, and all his knowledge about magic.

She would lose what had never been hers.

JOHANNA PUSHED through the tall grass. She had to get out of here, had to go somewhere to compose herself, to gather her frayed nerves and push away that all-pervading feeling that she had failed at everything she had attempted. They didn't need her at the meeting, she wasn't wanted there and most of the kings and dukes didn't take her seriously. It was *her* idea, and now Father and Master Deim were taking all the credit and answering all the questions.

But at least it was happening. She shouldn't behave like a child. Life wasn't fair, especially if you were a commoner woman.

She reached the water's edge and continued along the river-bank. The grass was tall here, and full of buttercups and caraway. A couple of coots skittered from the reeds that lined the river and flew low over the water. Roald would love it here.

"Johanna."

She turned around. It was Li Fai. Something in her had known that it would be him. She had seen this situation in her vision. Possible futures he'd said, and now she understood. She had a choice. She could lead him back to the barn where the men were drinking and arguing, or she could walk with him . . . until the next choice presented itself.

He caught up with her, wading through the long grass, and she led him up the little rise. From the other side, you could look over the wide expanse of the Saar delta. Saardam lay to the left: rows of brightly painted houses that looked a bit strange without the tower of the main church. None of the sounds from the city penetrated here. In fact, the only sounds were the soft lapping of the water against the shore, the sighing of the summer breeze through the weeping willow branches and the warbling of a lark overhead.

Johanna picked her way through the long grass to the little beach at the end. A tree trunk lay half on the sand, half in the water. Johanna sat down on it. She undid the restricting buckles to her shoes, slipped her feet out and stuck them in the water. It was lovely and cool. A few tadpoles skittered out of the way.

Li Fai sat down next to her, without saying a word. He pulled an apple from his pocket, put both his thumbs next to the stem and pulled it apart, neatly splitting the apple in half. He held one half out to her.

Johanna shook her head. "I'm sorry, but apples give me a terrible heartburn."

He bit into the flesh with a great crunch.

"I hate it when they drink so much," Johanna said. "They don't listen, they talk about all these stupid things, like parties they've attended. I feel like I've wasted my time." The river blurred in front of her eyes. She fought away the tears.

"Men are not good when they have been drinking. They say things they would never say otherwise."

They *did* things they would never do otherwise, too, like fight; and if a bunch of kings came to blows over some trivial issue because they seemed to *want* to fight, she would be blamed.

This meeting was going to be a disaster.

She angrily wiped her eyes with the back of her hand. She didn't want to cry. It was so annoying that she tended to burst out into tears with every little thing. Helena had told her that this was common for women with child.

Li Fai was quiet, looking at the water.

"So, what does your father think?" she asked, breaking the uneasy silence. Her voice felt choked.

"He keeps asking me why we should stay when so many

people in town keep committing crimes in our name. He says none of our hosts have addressed that."

That was true. She'd had no time to look into the weapons smuggling issue, beyond going to the warehouses and not finding anything of note. Having been too busy guarding the important guests, the guards didn't appear to have made any progress either.

"My father has been talking to King William." There was sadness in his eyes.

Johanna's heart jumped. "You don't want to go to Anglia."

He shook his head. "It is a bleak place where the streets are shrouded in mist half the time and it rains the other half. Everything is grey. There are no people from anywhere else except Anglia and they don't understand different habits. As soon as people see you're from another land, they try to raise their prices so they can make more money from you. It is very hard to know who to trust enough to call a friend. I really don't like that place."

"Do any people there have magic?"

"Not that I've seen, but my father wouldn't care. He doesn't have the art."

"But you could tell him that we would like you to teach and that if you stay, you could have a school of magic. I know there are children in town with magic. They must be taught. *I* could use your teaching."

She met his eyes.

Johanna's heart was thudding. This was the part she had seen in her vision, where . . .

"You do need teaching. Wood art is a special thing. It is powerful and dangerous. There is much to learn about it."

Clearly, he was the best person to do that.

"I'm trying to get your father to stay with our plan, but I don't think it's working. *I* want you to stay. I think we could both greatly benefit from cooperation." She slipped into more formal wording than she wanted. She so desperately wanted this *not* to be about business, and even after all this, she still feared he misunderstood her, and she was afraid to be hurt because of it.

He nodded. And then he whispered, "On the other hand, it could be that you give me a reason to stay."

Johanna met his eyes, seeing herself reflected in his perfectly black irises. This was the part where she made a choice and her life took another turn. She could be proper and lose him, or she could find some happiness.

She didn't know what to do. Even if kings and queens had lovers, the thought made her uncomfortable. Roald was a nice man, in his own way, and she hated to betray him. He needed care and someone to guide him. Being married to him hadn't, overall, turned out as badly as she'd thought.

But did all that mean that she couldn't ever find someone who made her heart beat faster?

The riverbank, reeds and the churning water blurred before her eyes. She blinked hard, but a tear ran across her cheek anyway.

A hand moved into the field of her vision and wiped it off. "You're a strong-willed woman. You can make anything work. Crying doesn't suit you."

"I know," Johanna sobbed. The tears were unstoppable. "I'm just so . . . tired, and I feel stupid—"

"You're not stupid."

"And I feel irrelevant."

"Those men will only be important until they realise that those who matter in today's world, are those with money *and* a wish to make the future better."

"But they pretend I don't exist." Johanna wiped at her face.

"Don't." He held her hand. "You'll smear dirt all over yourself."

"It's powder, not dirt."

"It doesn't look good." He bent down and scooped some water up into his hands. "May I?"

She leaned back and he splashed cool water over her face. The touch of his fingertips was a very pleasant sensation. She lifted her chin.

He massaged her shoulders and the sides of her neck, which were very tense. She wriggled behind her back for the laces of her bodice and pulled them loose, draping the dress' top loosely over her shoulders. He massaged the top of her arms and her back, her skin pale in the sunlight.

She closed her eyes, but peeped between her eyelashes at his oh so serious face while he did this.

He took off his vest, and when he bent over her at a particular angle, she could see right into his shirt. He had no hair on his chest at all. He had none on his chin either.

His face was so close now that she could feel his breath on her skin. His hands had gone from making firm movements to a soft caress. He bent over her shoulder and traced the outline of her shoulder with his lips.

Johanna gasped.

"It upsets you? I'm sorry, I won't do it anymore. I won't—"

"Be quiet and use your tongue for something else."

His eyes widened. He smiled, and then he closed the gap between them and kissed her.

His mouth was soft and tasted of foreign spices. For a long time they sat there, lost in the moment. She leaned into him, replying to his kiss. His hands stroked her shoulders and back and pulled her dress further off her shoulders.

She was going to protest that the others might come, but they were all drunk in the barn, and wouldn't lower themselves by going for a stroll along the river. They would be asleep, badly hung over from the previous day. And she could see or hear them coming from a good distance anyway.

She lowered herself to the sand next to the washed-up tree trunk. When she touched the wood, it showed her that a couple of ducks often slept here, their beaks tucked under their wings.

She pulled her dress over her head. The sunlight was extremely bright on her underdress. It felt warm on her swollen breasts and her round stomach. Li Fai stroked the stretched skin, which was redder and more blotchy than it had ever been.

"That's from being hot all the time. I'm ugly. I look like something bloated and dead."

"You're beautiful." He slid his hand up to her breasts, bunching the dress up.

His touch made her shiver. Her breasts perked up, the nipples dark and firm. He took one in his mouth and rolled it with his tongue. Johanna let her head hang back, breathing deeply. She wanted him so badly. No harm could be done now. To be frank she didn't even care if anyone saw them. Her body screamed out for him.

He teased her, inserting his fingers in the wetness between her legs. With all the pressure of the child in that area, she was so sensitive there.

"Please, do it," she whispered. "Before someone comes. Please."

He loosened his belt and pulled down the front of his trousers. Oh my, he was ready. She reached up and pulled him closer.

"Isn't it going to hurt you?"

"I'll tell you if it does." She wasn't sure that she cared anymore anyway. Could it possibly hurt any more than every-thing hurt already?

She rolled on her side and pulled the back of her underdress up. "Quick. Do it."

He didn't need telling twice.

CHAPTER 17

WHEN IT WAS DONE, she dozed in his arms. Happy, tired, satisfied. For a moment, she didn't want to think about the implications of what she had just done, and of all the other difficulties facing her.

She could have lain there forever, but the sun was sinking alarmingly, and the others would wonder where she was and would even come looking for her.

So she eased herself from his arms. He smiled at her, and that smile made her heart weep. She pulled down her underdress. The overdress, that horrible stiff thing made by mistress Dina, still lay draped over the tree trunk. She pulled it over her head. Li Fai helped her do up the laces at the back while she tried to brush all the sticks off the skirt.

She jammed her swollen feet back into her shoes. Slowly, they made their way back towards the barn. Butterflies fluttered low over the grass, stopping occasionally to sit on flowers. Bees buzzed and a family of quails ran squawking into a thicket.

It was so beautiful and so warm. She wanted to hold Li Fai's hand, but didn't dare do so. There would be plenty of talk already.

Her judgement that the men were all asleep turned out to have been right. By the time they entered the farmyard and came back to the barn, King Leopold and Baron Uti were just coming outside, stretching and rubbing their eyes.

King Leopold exclaimed, "Oh! There you are."

"I went for a walk by the river while you were sleeping."

The Baron laughed, but was looking at Li Fai, one eyebrow raised.

Johanna broke the uneasy silence. "We should go back now. The evening meal will be served in the hall."

The barn doors opened and more people came out. King William, with straw in his hair, Earl Maximilian, looking slightly rumpled.

Father and Master Deim sat in the corner in deep discussion with two Anglian merchants. Johanna gathered that they were talking about the building of ships. Were they talking about having the *Lady Davida* rebuilt in Anglia?

Father met Johanna's eyes. She hoped she didn't blush, because Father always had a pretty good idea of what she had been up to.

Li Fai joined his father, who had also taken the opportunity to have a nap.

Walking back to the creek where the punt waited, the group was a lot more subdued than on the way here. Most of the men were quietly talking. The snatches of conversations that she caught indicated friendly discussions, reminiscences and tall tales. The group had sorted into people who got on with each other and hopefully this might mean that there would be no more fights, at least not until the negotiations started tomorrow morning.

Maybe she could get a decent night's sleep tonight.

Li Fai's face was a bit sunburnt. She suspected hers was, as well. Thinking about him still made her glow.

At the other side of the creek, the coaches still waited. Anton helped her into hers. Through the little windows she could see Li Fai and his father climbing into another coach. She remembered the soft feel of his skin. She remembered his hands at her sides. She remembered how he laughed when she found her pleasure, and then went and did it again. Pleasure was meant to be like that. It wasn't just a thing for the man. It was meant to be enjoyed by both.

If his father decided to stay in Saardam, and if she could negotiate a good enough deal so that this was an attractive proposition, and Li Fai taught her magic, he could give her a lesson in the art of loving, too.

By the time they came back to the palace, the long shadows of the poplar trees were creeping over the forecourt. The row of coaches stopped, the order reversed ,from when they had left, with Johanna coming last, so that she didn't have to wait.

As soon as Anton had helped her out, a guard came to talk to him. He nodded, his face serious, and then came to Johanna.

"What is going on?" Johanna asked.

"He says they found more of those smuggled weapons, Your Majesty."

Johanna's heart jumped.

Father was waiting to guide her up the stairs, but she gestured for him to continue.

He protested. "But what about the evening meal?"

"I'll be along later. Go ahead, keep position for me." She wasn't hungry anyway. For the last few days, she'd had a feeling that everything she ate or drank got stuck inside her and refused to come out.

Father did as she said, and she watched him go slowly up the stairs with the group.

"Where did you find them?" she asked Anton in a low voice when the last of the guests were out of earshot.

"In an office that belongs to the Hemeldinck family."

Johanna knew the place. Ignatius' brother owned an accounting firm there.

"Did you arrest anyone in conjunction with it?"

"No. We are following them from a distance to see what they will do now. There seems to be a group of men involved selling weapons in Florisheim."

Master Deim had said that he suspected as much.

"Where are these weapons now?"

"They're in the harbourmaster's office."

"Can you possibly bring them here so I can have a look?"

He bowed. "I can do that, Your Majesty."

He retreated and Johanna continued further up the stairs. By the Triune, she did not want to deal with this now as well as everything else. She went briefly to her private quarters to get changed. At least Roald had managed to get out of bed; that was something.

She met Nellie in the dressing room.

"Oh, goodness, mistress Johanna, your face is sunburnt."

Johanna looked in the mirror. Nellie was right: her cheeks glowed and felt hot. It had been such a long time ago that she had spent any amount of time outside. She stood in front of the mirror for Nellie to help her out of the dress.

"Whatever have you done while you were there?"

"What do you mean?"

"The laces are all tangled up."

"I loosened the dress because it was too tight. And then I couldn't see to do them back up." Her cheeks burned.

Nellie helped her get changed, did her hair. Johanna sat patiently through her ministrations when her attention fell on the powder boxes on the dressing table. By the Triune, she still had the stalks of that plant that had grown in the Shepherd's house in the powder box in her purse. She should show them to Roald to ask him if he knew what sort of plant it was.

When Nellie had finished, she found the box and went into the library.

Roald sat in his usual chair with his nose in a book. Johanna stopped at the door, suddenly overwhelmed by the terrible act of betrayal that she had committed in her very selfish needs.

He didn't notice her, but kept reading, sliding his finger over the page and moving his lips.

Johanna crossed the room, feeling heavy. Should she confess? Would he understand? Would he get angry or start banging his head against the wall?

He lives in his own world. I can look after him, but he won't ever satisfy me in that way. The coming together of a man and a woman required two people to act.

"The evening meal is ready," she said. Her voice sounded high to her ears.

Now he looked up as if it were the first time he had noticed her. He said nothing about her burnt face.

She opened the powder box and carefully extracted the stalk that Li Fai had picked up. "Do you know which plant this is?"

He took the stalk from her and rolled it between his fingers.

Then he sniffed it and studied the leaf fragments that had broken off and that lay in the bottom of that box.

Then he said, "Forget-me-nots."

Johanna knew the pretty blue flowers that often grew in damp pieces of land. "What is the point of forget-me-nots?"

"Don't you know? You give them to a girl you like, and then the girl forgets everything except you. The forget-me-nots make you forget things."

"Forget. . . ?" She could still see the boy dropping the seeds on the ground in the Shepherd's spare bedroom. He had to have done that on purpose or by order of someone else. And what would have been the reason for him to have dropped the seeds if it wasn't to steal the dagger with the bone and silver hilt and the ruby in the pommel?

What was the relevance? Who was that boy? He did *not* look like an innocent child. He was a child with magic who knew exactly what he was doing. A boy with magic, desperately in need of magical schooling or he would become a miniature version of . . . his father? Was this another one of Kylian's children?

Johanna felt sick. She thought of Li Fai's words about "children with the art". It was a sad thing that when children were born that weren't entirely normal, people would shun them, and even the parents would hide them and attempt to erase them from their lives, like Roald's parents had done to him.

He was still sitting there looking up at her, dependent on her like a child. The room blurred before her eyes. She dropped to her knees in front of him, eased the book out of his hands and enclosed him in a hug. He made a surprised noise.

"Roald, whatever happens, I will look out for you. I will be there to assist you. I may have . . . other needs sometimes, but that doesn't mean that I love you less. You're my family, my brother."

He said nothing for a long time, as he was wont to do in situations like this, and then he said, "Does this mean that you want me to do something like go to dinner?"

"No. You can do what you want."

"Good, because my head hurts and I don't want to go to dinner. Those men only want me there so that they can laugh at me."

"I know. They laugh at me, too. But they won't be laughing much longer."

Johanna really needed to go to the dining hall, so she wrestled herself to her feet—it was disturbing how hard that was when you were as heavy and unbalanced as she was—and left him sitting peacefully alone in his favourite chair in the middle of the library.

He wasn't sad and he wasn't in need of pity. He loved his garden, his knowledge of plants and the stars; he was utterly unsuitable for the throne, and there was no way she'd force him to do things that, in the end, people would laugh about.

Despite the way their relationship had started, she loved him as a brother, not as a husband. If it was too obvious that the infant girl was not his daughter . . . she'd deal with that later, but she couldn't see how that could ever be a certainty.

If he ever asked her about Li Fai, she would tell him the truth. No, she would not give him the opportunity to hear about it before she told him about Li Fai: that she needed to learn certain things about magic and that it might involve intimacy and that it didn't mean that she cared any less about looking after him.

Johanna shut the door with a soft snick, enclosing herself in the darkness of the hallway. The sound of raucous laughter drifted down the hall.

Back to the barbarians.

Johanna was late to the table. The food had already been brought, and the drinking had started. Faces were red from having been out in the open air all day, and it seemed that, in their way, the men were having a good time. King Benito had even enticed a serving maid to sit on his lap.

Duchess Carlotta met Johanna's gaze across the table, rolling her eyes. Johanna made a mental note to go down to Francina when she could, and tell her about the things Li Fai had said about bringing up a child with magic.

Johanna was looking for a way to retire gracefully to her room when Anton came up from behind.

"Excuse me, Your Majesty. The guards have brought those weapons and arrested a man in relation to it. I'm sorry to disturb you."

"No, not at all. Where are the weapons?"

"In the Red Room. The prisoner is there, too. He has been asking for you, unsavoury character that he is."

"I'll see him now."

Johanna rose from the table. Father met her eyes across the room. He would know that something was up. Once again, she relied on him and Master Deim to keep the kings and dukes from attacking each other, although admittedly, most were far too drunk to do that.

She followed Anton into the foyer and into the corridor. Their footsteps echoed in the empty space.

There were two guards at the Red Room. One of them opened the door for her and Anton.

It was always very dark in this room, which reminded her of Baron Uti's castle: spooky and stale, imbued with the scent of long-gone history. Such rooms were whispered about in terms of who had been murdered there.

Another guard waited inside the room, next to the table on which stood a wooden crate. On the rug in front of the dark hearth lay a young man bound by his hands and feet. He wore dark but neat clothing, and she recognised the silver buckles on his boots. He lifted his head when Johanna came in, and she recognised that sleek ponytail and dark eyebrows. It was Sylvan, Duke Lothar's bandit son.

CHAPTER 18

JOHANNA SAT DOWN on the slightly musty couch.

The guards faced her across the table where the crate stood. She noticed that one man had a bleeding scratch over his face and bruising around his eye. Apparently, Sylvan had put up a bit of a fight. She found the thought strangely amusing. Out of all the bandits that had captured her, she had respected Sylvan the most of all. He had not been like Sigvald, paying for his men to have their way with poor peasant girls.

"Tell me where and how you apprehended this man." And where was his bear?

"This bandit turned up at the Hemeldinck office, speaking in some foul language. We assumed he came to take delivery of the haul. We asked him why he was there and he said he had business with the Hemeldinck family. We asked him, did he know that they now consort with the enemy? And he said that anyone who fights against evil is no enemy of his. We asked him did he know that the Hemeldinck business was associated with the smuggling of arms, and he said that arms smuggling was better than peddling foul magic."

"Undo his bonds."

"But . . . Your Majesty . . ."

"Do as I say. I know this man. He is Sylvan, son of Duke

Lothar of Gelre, and he's a strange character but no enemy of ours."

The guard did as Johanna ordered, still giving her uncertain looks.

That was the trouble with her. They didn't understand her because they didn't expect these sorts of commands. The Red Room was an audience chamber used for formal meetings, designed to keep the guests from getting too comfortable. It was also where, in the past, traitors were questioned and sometimes tortured, and where the king would have given orders to kill, raid and plunder.

Those practices had already stopped with King Nicholaos, since he had professed little interest in warfare and conquering. The conquering had, instead, been done in faraway lands by sea traders like the Nielands, and even most of that had been the conquering of trade.

Sylvan sat on the rug rubbing his wrists, rubbed raw by the rope. His face shone with sweat, and his cheeks were hollow, his eyes strangely bright.

"Have you had anything to eat?" Johanna asked.

His eyes widened, and she guessed not, so she ordered one of the guards to go to the kitchens and get a plate of food.

"Nothing too fancy?" the guard wanted to know.

"Whatever is left over. No one will miss it. And do hurry."

The man bowed and left the room.

Johanna shifted in the chair. The child was kicking her in the ribs.

"I heard that you and your husband took the throne," Sylvan said.

"After you delivered us to your father's castle, we were reunited with our countrymen, escaped Florisheim and ousted Alexandre. It is a very long story."

"I'm sure equally long ballads will be written about it." Was that a tone of sarcasm?

It struck her how, while she trusted Sylvan more than the others, he had always been a loner and a character she completely failed to understand.

"What were you doing in Saardam?"

"My father tells me what to do."

"Picking up a delivery of illegal weapons from Florisheim? Does he tell you to do that? To be distributed where?"

"You don't understand anything."

"Try me."

He eyed one guard and then the other one. His lips twitched. Then he jerked his head. Despite the bad memories of that time that they were taken through the forest, Johanna still reacted to it. She understood his silent language. "Leave me alone with him."

"But, Your Majesty . . ."

"I know this man. He presents no danger." She hoped. Where *was* his bear?

The guards left the room, with reluctant expressions on their faces.

"I wish you'd listen to us," Anton said at the door. "This man is dangerous."

"I have listened. This is my decision."

He looked down. "I will be just outside the door."

"Understood."

Then Anton left, too, and the door shut.

Sylvan crawled backwards and pushed himself up on a chair. He was all knees and elbows to the point of being emaciated.

"I can see that life has not been good to you."

He snorted. "Somebody released a great number of ghosts in our forest. We've been fighting the encroaching magic. We've lost most of the ground. It's coming this way."

Johanna nodded.

"You can fight magic with guns?"

"You can kill a magician with a lead bullet. You can't kill a magician with magic if that magician is stronger than you. That's where we went wrong previously."

"You mean the attempt to kill the baron at a dinner at his castle?"

"It was poison meant for my nephew."

"But someone told him it was there?"

He shook his head. "That glutton of an uncle of mine ate

from the food and became ill. Then he assumed that it had been an attempt to kill him."

"That's why he jokes about it?"

Sylvan nodded. "My uncle knows what his son is up to. My uncle allowed that . . . shifter woman to marry him, with her strange daughter, because he thought she might be able to stop him."

By the Triune. "And what about Ignatius Hemeldinck?"

"He supports the baron. None of them were sure where you stood, because of your . . . child. I think the evil of the child does not twist the woman's mind."

"You're not sure then where *any* of the women stand."

"None that have children of the age of eight and younger."

In the shock of the revelations, she found some sanity in Li Fai's words. "Evil magic is not born. It is made through neglect and lack of schooling of children with magic."

He gave her a sharp look.

She continued, on very thin ice now, "You have a lot of magic, but your father loved you and taught you and you didn't turn bad. I have some magic, but my parents loved me. My mother knew what it was like to be an outcast, so she made sure I wasn't, even if she didn't know how to teach magic. Kylian was a child of an unfortunate union. He was probably hated from the day he was born."

"He was left on my uncle's doorstep. The Baron never seemed sure what to do with him, especially when he had tempers."

"There is a different kind of teaching." Johanna took her wooden box out of the purse. As soon as she opened the lid, the air whirled around it, became bright and formed into a tree.

Sylvan's eyes widened.

She told him what Li Fai had said about children with magic in the east, about teaching, about the mother touching them when they were born. "If we don't do this, we are going to have children go bad. I have already seen a boy who could easily take Kylian's place when he gets older. We need to get to him before his evil becomes irreversible."

Sylvan snorted. "That is all very well for later, but first we need to stop Kylian, and I very much doubt that he can be stopped with love and trinkets."

Blunt, but true.

"My father says that the magic lines have risen to the surface in Saardam, and that magic is fighting to sort out who will hold power over them and what the nature of this power will be."

She was going to say something, but the door opened and a servant maid came in with a tray. "You wanted this, Your Highness?"

"It's for him," Johanna said.

The maid put the tray on the table and backed away, wide eyed.

Sylvan grabbed a duck leg and tore at it with his teeth like a wild animal. Within a few short moments, it was reduced to bones.

It was kind of disturbing to watch. Feral. "How long since you've eaten?"

"Too long," he growled and stuffed half a sausage in his mouth and then wiped off the grease that ran down his chin.

"Where is your bear?"

An expression of pain went over his face and Johanna wished she hadn't asked. "He killed it. The monster killed it! I will not rest until I've killed him. This has been going on far too long. Waking ghosts, trying to raise people from the grave. I will kill him, if I have to do it with my bare hands!" He brought his fist down on the table with such force that the plate danced and the cider trembled in the glass.

Johanna shied away, reminded that he was not *quite* as harmless as she had pretended him to be. "So what about the guns? I have people here very upset because smugglers used their marks to illegally ship the weapons."

"Can't be helped. We need them."

"Who is *we*? The bandits?"

He laughed, not in a happy way. "Sigvald and his men are a bunch of idiots. They're only in it for the money. I needed them, they needed money, so that's where they stand. They do jobs for us, like bringing the guns. But lately they've been finding the overland route hard."

"But who in Saardam needs the guns and what for?"

"You're kidding? There will be a magical war the likes of which you have never seen before."

"A war? A fight, I believe that, but a war? You mean Kylian against the rest of us?"

"And his ghosts, and his *children.*"

He looked at Johanna's stomach and a cold chill took hold of her.

Kylian's children.

"You have to get out of here, because it's that child he wants to complete his work."

Johanna was going to ask, "What work?" but she could put the facts together. She had seen Celine's ghost. She knew what he'd been trying to do. Despite what Sylvan said, she had a very strong suspicion that the bodies in the ice cellar were Kylian's victims waiting to be resurrected. Celine's body, having lain under the gravestone for two years before the king contacted Kylian, might not have been in any state to receive a ghost. He only needed another girl in the same family.

Bile rose in Johanna's throat. She desperately swallowed it away.

Sylvan sat back, having cleaned everything off his plate.

"Stay here in the palace," Johanna said. "You'll be protected by my guards and the presence of all my guests."

"Can't." And then, a bit later, "Can I have my guns back?"

Johanna reached for the crate. This one did not bear Li Han's stamp. It had a heavy lid with a metal latch. She undid it without touching the wood. Inside the crate, in a bed of straw, lay three powder guns with shining barrels and wooden handgrips. They were works of art, with little embellishing engravings in the metal and wood. The wooden handgrip had last been touched by an old man with a moustache, who had placed the guns next to each other as they still lay in a workshop that looked foreign to her.

True to Sylvan's word, it seemed that these guns had come from Florisheim.

"What are you going to do with them?"

He gave her a sideways look. "Friends are coming." It sounded evasive.

"I will leave the crate here," she said. "I will keep a guard on the door. If you can convince my arms advisor that you should have the guns, you can have them." She almost wished that she could be present at a meeting between Sylvan and Johan Delacoeur.

She called Anton in and told him to put Sylvan in a room where he could be watched but that was not a prison cell. She told Sylvan that he needed to stay inside to avoid being arrested again. She figured he would find a way to get out anyway.

Johanna then went downstairs to see Francina and Natalya.

She found both women talking in the kitchen, where a fire burned in the hearth for heating water for bathing.

"Where is the infant?" she asked.

"He was asleep in the room," Francina said, her eyebrows raised.

"Don't leave him alone."

"He's not alone."

"Is there anyone else in the room?"

"No, but we're just next door."

"That's leaving him alone. Kylian is in town and he will be using his children. I don't know how and I don't know when. You have to hold your son and stroke him every day, and tell him that you love him, so that he can get used to your voice."

"But I already do that." She gave Johanna a deep frown. "What in the heaven's name is going on?"

"I wish I could tell you for certain."

JOHANNA LEFT THE TWO after having received assurances from Francina that she would do as Johanna asked.

In the foyer, she checked with Anton that Sylvan had been given a room, and was informed that he had.

The sound of raucous laughter drifted out the double doors into the hall. That was King William, arrogant and blissfully unaware that anything was happening.

Johanna couldn't bear the thought of having to go back inside that room. She hesitated in the foyer. Her belly ached and her back ached. She was tired enough to sleep, but couldn't bear the thought of lying flat in bed.

She went into the study and sat down in her chair. She was still not comfortable. The child squirmed, heartburn never ceased to bother her these days and her back was sore.

In the darkness, she eyed the piles of documents that she would have to deal with at the meeting tomorrow. This was the serious part of the meeting, where they got firm commitments from attendants and negotiated prices, locations and special considerations. That was where the attendants would put their money on the table. Did they want a cooperative facility in Saardam? That questions would be answered tomorrow.

Uncomfortable as she was, she must have dozed for a bit,

because all of a sudden she woke up. It was pitch dark in the room, and she swore there had been a sound.

"Nellie?" Johanna attempted to say, but her tongue wouldn't cooperate.

There was no reply. But there had been a sound, she was sure of that.

Johanna stuffed her feet into her shoes and waddled to the door. The light was out in the hallway, and the window. The Moon peeked out between large clouds. The wan light silvered the lawn and Roald's vegetable garden, and the few hedges that had survived the fires and subsequent neglect and that Johanna insisted should be kept as mementos of Queen Cygna's old palace garden.

Beyond the garden wall, the water of the delta spread out. A slightly lighter strip on the horizon indicated where the moonlight reflected on the sand dunes.

A cloud slid in front of the Moon, casting palace garden in darkness, but patches of silvery light still tracked over the marshland on the other side of the river. There were also lighter patches in the water close by from the ghosts hanging around, waiting to pounce. Johanna counted at least eleven. An army of ghosts, waiting under the surface of the water.

She shivered. Maybe she should ask Li Fai to stay in the palace. What about Natalya? Maybe she should sleep upstairs? Just in case these ghosts came and attacked the palace. What had she said about spells? That the ghosts became used to their repelling power and that they lost effectiveness.

Johanna went to the bedroom where Roald was fast asleep. She gave him a shove so that he stopped snoring, but she couldn't get comfortable. Everything ached. She was too hot and when she threw the blankets off, she was cold. She lay awake until the first glimmer of daylight came into the room, when she couldn't stay in bed any longer.

Ow, ow, ow. Walking hurt her back. She awkwardly used the chamber pot, and even that hurt. Everything was stuck down there.

She wrestled herself into her dress and went in search of

Nellie. She found her at the table with Frederik, chatting and laughing.

"Oh, mistress Johanna!" Nellie got up, abandoning her tea.

"Sit down." Johanna stumbled across the kitchen and dropped unceremoniously into a chair. She leaned back, closing her eyes. "Everything hurts, Nellie. I can't sleep anymore. I'm not ready to talk petty disagreements between self-important men."

Nellie put a cup of tea in front of her. "Oh, you can do everything. You've done worse things than this."

"Yes, but not while looking like a bloated pig's carcass."

"I do think your comparisons have become a little morbid, mistress Johanna."

"I *feel* morbid. I want this thing out of me."

"Well, your wish will soon come true." She put a plate with bread and jam in front of Johanna. "The meeting will be over, we'll ask Helena to come and give you some of her ointments and teas, you'll put your feet up, and wait."

"I'm through with waiting." And besides, there was a magical war left to fight. "Have you seen Sylvan?"

"What? He's here?" Nellie's eyes grew wide.

"He doesn't look very healthy, but yes. He says Kylian killed his bear and he's out for revenge."

"I don't like that man at all. Those were scary times."

Johanna nodded. They were.

Frederik rose and bowed. "I will be ready to protect you, Your Majesty. I don't have much and I have no weapons training, but if necessary, I will fight."

"Thank you."

That was the story of Saardam: no shortage of people willing to act, but no one with the knowledge to do so.

Nellie got to work. A young girl came in, and Nellie ordered preparations for breakfast.

Johanna nibbled at the bread, but she felt ill and left half of it on the plate, certain that if she ate any more, she would throw up, and that would be embarrassing in the meeting.

She heaved herself to her feet and trundled off to her dressing room to get ready for the day. Nellie came in and helped her, informing her that the men were having breakfast, that all of them were there, and that most of them were in a talkative mood.

"That King Benito really is a piece of dirt," she said. "You know I don't like saying bad things about people, but do you know what he said to me?"

"I can guess the gist of it. Try to keep out of reach of his hands, and do your work. It will soon be quiet again." She met Nellie's eyes and burst into laughter. And Nellie laughed, too.

"You know, Nellie. I've told you this before, but you are my only and best friend. I don't know what I'd do without you."

"Don't say things like that, mistress Johanna. Look, you're making me cry." She wiped at her eyes.

Nellie left the room to check the laundry, and Johanna went into her study. She spread all her notes over the desk and sat down for a last-minute read-through, but she had trouble concentrating. The child was squirming and her insides were being battered.

Eventually, she gathered up her notes without having read anything and made her way to the meeting room sweaty, trembling and hoping that Father and Master Deim had their wits together, because she was certain her future held throwing up and having to retire to her room with a fever.

The meeting was held in the Red Room, where the servants had moved out the couches and chairs that normally stood there, and had replaced them with a table and straight-backed chairs. And, she was glad to see, the crate of smuggled guns was also gone.

Baron Uti and his party were already in the room. Johanna greeted them, seeing the baron in a new light. She was highly tempted to ask him some questions. From the moment of the fires, she had thought of the baron as supporting Kylian, but Sylvan had indicated that this might not be the case.

Fancy that. Even though they came from different angles, she and Baron Uti had been on the same side all along. The baron had just been too afraid of his son to let her know.

It was a good thing for the future of this agreement that

would be negotiated today, but the entire agreement would be worthless if they couldn't also rein in Kylian's magic.

Johanna took her place at the table, gesturing for the baron and his party to do the same.

King Benito and his entourage came in, followed by King Leopold. Li Han entered with his wife. Johanna's heart jumped. Was there a reason Li Fai was not there? One by one, the others entered in quick succession.

Johanna opened the meeting with a brief welcome and handed it over to Father, who outlined the proposals and made it clear that this was the time for nations, families and businesses to make their commitments.

He ended with, "We are going ahead with this scheme. How big it will be will depend on the level of commitment we can get from your nations. It is our view that by implementing this plan, we can forestall future conflicts and enhance our region to place it on a competitive advantage in comparison with other trading regions. Let the discussions begin."

King William was the first to speak up. He put his elbows on the table and joined his fingers in a thoughtful gesture.

"How do we know that this plan, this plea for investment, is in fact not a grab for power in this region?"

King Benito was nodding and Duke Aroden sat with his arms crossed over his chest, looking belligerent.

Master Deim went on to explain that the developments and investments would deliver joint profits, and that a grab for power would look very different, with the benefits all channelled to one party.

King William argued, twisting arguments his way.

Baron Uti sat twiddling his thumbs, and his face grew redder and redder, until he slammed his hands on the table and said, "This is all very well, my friend, but if you're not interested, can you at least shut up and let those of us who do want to talk get a word in?"

King William whirled to him. "Who says I'm not interested?"

"Well. Are you? Because you might shut your trap for a moment if you are."

King William put both his hands on the table. "What did you say?"

"Gentlemen!" Johanna called out. Too loud and too angry, but she just couldn't stand it anymore.

King William gave one of his loud bellowing laughs. If it was possible, that irritated Johanna even more. It was as if something broke inside her.

"If you are not interested in this plan then there is the door. If the only response you can make when I, a woman of common birth, say something is to laugh, then there is the door. We are here as friends and colleagues, and we have the best interests of this region in mind. If you don't share that view, please, by all that's dear and by the Triune God whom you all profess to hate so much, get out of this room and leave!"

A stunned silence followed her words.

King William began, "Well, I—"

"You can go out there and face our real enemies. Out there is an army of magic, waiting for us to fail, waiting for us to become weak. They're cowards and hide. They use ghosts and apparitions that are incomplete resurrections. Their leader fancies himself a necromancer—" Someone gasped.

Johanna met Baron Uti's eyes.

"This man should have been stopped a long time ago. It suited most of you well enough that Alexandre occupied Saardam, because he would get rid of that hated church. The Church of the Triune is much older than you think and much stronger. They are not going to go away because the Belaman Church wants them gone. The harder you try to suppress them, the more they will resist. And it's irrelevant, because we're all on the same side. The Church of the Triune forbids magic, the Belaman Church allows some of it, but doesn't support magic used for evil either. None of us want to be overrun by evil magic. Magic manipulates royal houses. It penetrates their decisions and influences kings when they decide to go to war. Magic benefits by selling and making weapons. It benefits by creating discontent. We have seen this in all of your countries. It is now starting to happen in Saardam. We have to fight evil magic by standing together. We have to defeat the necromancer."

Another deep silence.

King William said again, "Well, I . . ." He spread his hands.

"Are you interested in contributing and helping us fight?"

"I don't know about that magic. I don't know that I would call it real—"

"Oh, it's real," the baron said.

"The necromancer is his son," King Leopold said.

"Thanks, cousin."

But King Leopold was far too serious to react to the snark. "It is serious. Magic spreads. It feeds on discontent and conflict. Can you imagine the ways it will use us to destroy each other once we figure out how to make iron ships?"

There were nods all around the table. Master Deim spread the pages of the agreement document over the smooth wooden surface. "Let's talk money."

Johanna leaned back. She was sweating and her stomach churned like crazy. Bile rose in her throat. By the Triune, this was not ending well. She rose.

All eyes were on her.

"I'm sorry, I have to . . . have a brief stop."

She rushed out of the room, through the hallway, and only just made the outhouse in time. Her stomach had been empty, and produced nothing more than a bit of slimy froth. Disgusting. Whoever had told her that the vomiting was restricted to the time before a woman knew she was with child was a huge liar.

She stood there, gulping air. She so desperately wanted to lie down and sleep, but she simply had to go back. But crossing the Red Room back to her seat, a hot pain stabbed through her lower belly. It wasn't bad enough to cry out, but by the Triune.

Johanna sat down, keeping her face straight, and drank some water while pretending to listen to the discussion between Master Deim and King Leopold. Pretending only. She heard nothing. The blood was roaring in her ears. The water went straight through her and she now needed to pee. When she wriggled on the seat, it felt like she had already had an accident. Her underdress felt wet. But the prospect of getting up to leave the room again was too embarrassing, so she stared at the documents, ignored all the conversation and concentrated on just breathing calmly.

Finally the men finished talking, and everyone was getting up from the table to move to the ballroom for the midday meal.

"Are you all right?" Father asked in a low voice when Johanna was the last to get up.

"I think so," she said, but by the Triune, she was not all right. Her dress was soaked and stuck to her backside. Even the chair seat felt damp. Luckily the heavy velvet overdress didn't show wetness.

"I just need to . . . I'll be along soon."

CHAPTER 20

THE HALLWAY APPEARED to have grown ten-fold in length, but she managed to make it to the bedroom. Nellie had been in to make the bed and open the curtains. Light streamed in through the window and she could see the chickens in the yard scratching for food. Roald would be out there somewhere. Some part of her wanted to call him. She wanted to admit that she wasn't well, that there was something wrong. But once she went down that path, the "weak woman" judgement was usually not far behind. And she absolutely had to be ready to get that agreement signed, and she had to fight Kylian.

First she needed to get rid of that wet dress. Standing in front of the mirror, she wrestled to undo the laces. The ends hung on her back and she could barely reach them. Where was Nellie?

She went to the corridor but didn't see her, but walking really hurt and she didn't dare venture down to the kitchens. She would leave a trail of puddles over the floor. She had just lost all control down there. A constant stream of drops trickled down her legs.

She twisted her arms around her back in front of the mirror and managed to reach the laces and pull them loose.

The back of the dress was wet. Her underdress was soaked.

Even her stockings were wet. She wanted them off. She undid the tie at the top, but couldn't reach any further down, so she pulled the first one off by stepping on the toe and wriggling her foot out.

A breeze came into the open window and made her shiver. She felt ill and crampy. She had hardly eaten anything, but the meal appeared to have disagreed with her badly. She wriggled to other stocking off.

Ow, ow, ow.

She put the bedpan on the cabinet and sat on it. The touch of the cold rim to her skin made her shiver. But now matter how much effort she did, everything was so badly stuck down there, she couldn't even pee more than a few drops. Oh, this was terrible.

A cramp tore through her. Her jaws chattered. She badly needed to do a big one. The men were all at the midday meal talking about her but—oh, at least a big gush of fluid hit the pan.

Strangely, she felt nothing. It was impossible to see into the bedpan, she didn't think anything else had come out. The need increased.

She shivered and pushed. More fluid hit the pan.

Pushed again.

Oh. That actually hurt. Really badly. That's what you got when you couldn't go for so long. She should have eaten those plums that Nellie had mentioned.

Come on, come on.

Pushed again.

Her backside was so numb, she couldn't feel anything coming out.

It hurt. The pressure didn't let up. She needed to go. She needed to get rid of this now. It had bothered her for days, and—

Ow.

Ow, ow. She couldn't stop pushing.

Oh, it hurt so much that it scared her. And somehow this seemed no ordinary business.

Wait—

She pushed herself off the bedpan. Her legs were trembling so much that they almost wouldn't support her weight. She grabbed the edge of the cabinet, hit the edge of the bedpan with her hand and sent it flying. It hit the ground with a big clang and bounced over the floor, spilling its contents everywhere.

Oh, by the Triune. She couldn't expect Nellie to clean that up. But she could barely move.

Johanna stood there, sweating and her legs trembling. Fluid ran down her legs. She looped her hand around her side and felt underneath. Her fingertips met tightly stretched slimy skin. There was something big and hard underneath.

"Oh, by the Triune, Nellie! Roald!"

The door remained closed.

"Anyone, help!"

She stood there with her legs wide, unable to move. The child's head pushed against the skin between her legs. Some fluid dribbled onto the floor. "Please, please Nellie! Get Helena!"

But it was far too late for all that.

A hot stab of pain went through Johanna's stomach. She couldn't restrain a cry. There was no way to stop it, no way to wait for Helena, or even to wait for anyone to turn up.

The underdress irritated her and she yanked it over her head and dropped it on the tiles. She held onto the cabinet to drop herself to one knee, and another knee, onto the fabric of the underdress. Moving was hard. Her breath came in shallow gasps.

She waited with her eyes closed until the pain and the need to push crested.

Johanna pushed, hunched over, her hand between her legs. The skin stretched.

It hurt, but it felt so good. She gasped a deep breath and pushed again. The skin parted under her hand and her fingertips met the slime-covered, hairy top of the infant's head. A flush of warmth went through her arm.

Magic.

She gasped for air again and pushed, groaning. Sweat ran down her forehead into her eyes.

The head was almost out. Oh, by the Triune, that hurt.

She was vaguely aware that the door to the room opened.

"Johanna!" Roald ran across the room and dropped to his knees next to her.

Another pain washed over her. Johanna pushed until she saw purple spots in her vision. Ow, ow, ow. She howled, and pushed. The child's head came out, waxy and covered in bloody slime. And the top of the body came out. Roald held his hand under the head so she wouldn't drop to the floor. And the rest of the body shot out with a gush of fluid. Roald caught her. A shrill cry filled the room.

"Oh!" Johanna cried, and she burst into tears.

Roald awkwardly cradled the screaming child in his arms. The fleshy cord was still attached to the disgusting mess of blood and tissue that lay on Johanna's underdress.

"Oh, mistress Johanna!" Nellie exclaimed from near the door. She ran across the room and threw a blanket over Johanna. "Let me help you into bed."

Nellie grabbed Johanna under the arms and hauled her up. Johanna almost fainted and then let herself be guided by Nellie to the bed. "I'll call Helena immediately." And then she was gone.

Roald came to sit on the bed. He had grabbed the first thing out of the wardrobe—which happened to be a shirt—and wrapped it around the child. "It's a girl. See? It's a girl." He lifted up a corner of the fabric and pointed at the girl bits.

"Yes, Roald."

"Another of my women."

Johanna looked at the little face, scrunched up and covered in blood-streaked slime. The bottom lip trembled.

She felt dizzy. She felt . . . good. That had been surprisingly easy, nothing like the ordeal Greetje had gone through.

"Where did you even learn to help like that?"

"On the farm."

She held his hand. "I love you, Roald."

Nellie came back into the room, followed by Helena, who put her bag on the bed. "Oh, you didn't even wait for me."

She went on to tie the child's cord, and wash her, and wash Johanna.

Then someone knocked on the door. Nellie went to open. It was Father. His mouth was open. "I . . . I was going to say that the meeting was starting again. I guess you won't be able to make it."

"I'll be along later," Johanna said.

"Don't be silly," Nellie said.

"It's extremely important."

"You will take ten days' rest, as Helena will tell you."

Helena was nodding fervently.

"But farming women keep working straight away. I feel fine."

"You are no farmer's wife. I will make sure that the princess feeds properly before I leave."

Arguing with Helena seemed pointless. She did feel weak, though, so she let Father take care of the meeting and let Nellie tuck her into bed.

Nellie took the little one from Johanna and cradled her in her arms. "What are you going to call her?"

"Celine," Roald said, and Johanna wanted to protest, because of that name. Because Celine's ghost was around, looking for a body to possess and because she didn't want the little infant girl with the dark eyes and the scrunched-up face to be that body.

A breeze went through the room and ruffled the curtains. It made the hair on Johanna's arms stand up. That was some construct of magic for sure. Kylian knew that the princess had been born.

She needed Loesie to come. She needed Natalya, Li Fai and Duke Lothar to ward off the ghosts.

But she couldn't make any valid arguments against using the name. To many people in Saardam, Celine was a saint, a beautiful young princess taken away from them by an illness.

Celine it was. She said softly, "Celine Sara Cygna."

As she watched, magic flared around the child. Already the light was turning golden. Kylian would come for her in the night. She needed to protect the little one by then.

Time was ticking.

Roald went back to the library, and Helena gave Johanna the child to feed. Her breasts were hard as stones, and as soon as the little one latched on, milk squirted out.

When the child was satisfied, Helena left, with a promise to come back later in the day.

"Please, Nellie, look after her well." Johanna slipped from the bed.

"Mistress, what are you doing?"

"I need to warn the kings. I need to find all the magicians in Saardam."

"You need to rest, mistress."

"Come on, Nellie, help me." She was bleeding, so she grabbed a towel, wadded it up and tied it between her legs with a strip of fabric. Her belly was floppy, the skin wrinkled. She put on her underdress.

Johanna went to the wardrobe. Eyed the corset. Guess now she didn't need to wear the special dress anymore. "Help me get this on."

"Mistress . . . Helena said . . ."

"I don't care what she said. This is more important than anything. Stay here with the child. Let no one into the room. Wait for me to come back."

JOHANNA WALKED through the hallway to the Red Room not much later. She felt a little light-headed and the pad in her underwear already felt quite wet, but those were minor inconveniences. Oh, to be able to walk normally without feeling like a sea cow on land!

When she entered the room, she caught a snatch of discussion—it seemed to be about money—before everyone fell quiet. "I'm sorry for the delay."

King William sat opposite the door and was one of the first to see her. His mouth fell open while he stared at Johanna's normal dress. He called out, "Scandalous! You should be resting."

"There will be plenty of time to rest." Johanna gingerly sat on her chair. Ow, her backside was uncomfortable. She looked around the table. All of the faces were astonished except that of Li Fai's mother, who nodded, her lips pressed together.

Johanna went on. "Have you signed anything yet?"

"We were about to," Master Deim said.

"Well, we were talking about the payment terms," King William said. "I'm not going to sign any document that includes unspecified terms that can be changed after signing to suit the provider of the service, in this case the Saardam Harbour Authority. I think—"

Johanna pulled a sheet of vellum out from the folder in front of her. "Why don't we sign first that we commit to the project, with terms to be hashed out later."

"Why?"

Father gave her a sharp look.

"If we sign this now, we have a commitment. We may need a second meeting. I hope we'll be able to hold that meeting tomorrow. For now, I'd like to get your commitment signed, and then I'd like you to return to your travel parties if they're in the palace. If they're not in the palace, I'd like you to bring those people into the palace for the night."

Several of the attendants made surprised noises.

"Why don't we finish the negotiations instead?" Duke Aroden asked.

"There is evil afoot in the city. Forces of magic are gathering in secret places and planning a move against us."

Baron Uti looked at her. He knew what this was about. He didn't protest, a sign of how badly she had misunderstood his position.

Johanna explained as quickly as possible all the things that had been going on.

King Benito banged his fist on the table when he spoke of Francina and the little red-haired boy. She even spoke about little Celine, not meeting Father's eyes while she did so.

She spoke of Loesie and her friend, Sylvan, and Duke Lothar whom she hadn't seen but who was said to be in town—and Baron Uti didn't once speak up. Then she explained about the ghosts, and for once the important men listened, because they had all seen Celine's ghost.

When she finished talking, they all protested at once. King Leopold said that it couldn't be so bad, and that ghosts had never harmed anyone in Burovia, Estland and Gelre, where they were common. Several nobles of the King's Council still maintained that ghosts weren't real.

Johanna said, "This has been possible because none of us recognised the danger of magic. Instead of learning about it, we ignored it. We said it was part of the Belaman Church and sanctioned it. We made it the domain of priests, while most priests have absolutely no understanding of it. In Saardam, we ignored the issue of magic altogether."

"It must be forbidden forever!" Theo Kloostermans called out.

"No. We tried that, and it doesn't work. Children with magic are born every day. We must teach our children magic so that they can tell the proper ways of using it and the bad ways of using it. If we use magic for good, we will have our iron ships. Without using magic, we will forever be on the lookout for attacks by people who use magic, because there will always be more magicians than we can kill. We can trap them inside trees, and there will always be people who will free the evil because they believe it suits their aims."

Mayor of Saardam Joris DeCamp said, "But the spirit has been trapped in strong healthy wood. The tyrant had his soul crushed out of him when the tree grew."

"Yes, and someone has stolen a dagger from the Shepherd's house that may well be able to free the spirits from both trees."

"Stolen? Who still enters the Shepherd's house these days?"

"People who consort with evil. It was a young boy, possibly used by the necromancer to carry out his orders. No one suspects child magicians, and that is why he uses them, especially when the children already have magic and are unschooled in how to deal with it. All an evil man needs to do is offer them a treat or a trinket."

Baron Uti nodded, crossing his arms over his chest.

A deep silence followed Johanna's words.

Duke Aroden looked at her, wide-eyed. "So it's a war between spirits and ghosts, but what does all this have to do with us?"

Haven't you listened to a word I said? "It affects everyone. The necromancer wants to rule these lands through fear and magic. He's brought an army of ghosts. When we make agreements, it puts us in a stronger position. He doesn't want us to be strong. He wants us cowering from him and his magic. He wants the iron ships."

Li Han snorted. "We will never sell any of them."

Several people looked alarmed. It was the first time that Li Han had even commented on the existence of the ship.

He continued, "I will not get involved in fights. We are here to trade. We can easily go a place where all these troubles don't exist."

"But the lowlands are one of your biggest markets for silks and spices."

Li Han didn't reply to that. They both knew it was true. Li Han *could* go elsewhere, but apart from some of the towns around the Golden Sea, some of which would be hostile to him, no place had as many people with money living as close together as in the lowlands.

"We are now at an advantage. Last time, the necromancer burned the town and brought an army of lackeys with bears. We were unprepared and taken by surprise. This time we can see him coming. We have a number of people who can help us and all of us are on the same side."

"Well, I . . ." King William began in his usual belligerent tone.

"You are not on our side? Does Anglia have any magic?"

He snorted. Apparently not.

"Magic is spreading from the east. It will take us before it will take Anglia. It attempts to take control over our centres of trade, our churches and our places and means of travel. We know what they can do, if Alexandre's reign of terror is anything to go by. The palace is a safe zone. Call all your staff inside the palace if they aren't already here."

King William gave her a furtive, disturbed look. "You think so, huh?"

"I don't *think* so, I *know*. I can see the ghosts, I know what's going on east of here, I can see what they tried to do to our church, and what they're now doing to our children." She looked around the table to the collection of royal and noble faces.

Baron Uti sat nodding. His cousin King Leopold looked uneasy. King Benito glared at the baron. Duke Aroden's face was prim. Belonging to "the right side" of the Aroden family, he would have a profound dislike for magic and would consider anyone with magic "dirty".

Johanna took their silence as agreement.

Father quickly drafted up a statement that the kings and

barons agreed on investing in the port facilities. Everyone signed it, including Johanna. Then the meeting dispersed. Johanna didn't know for sure that all the guests would indeed bring their travel parties into the palace, but at least she had tried.

She was extremely tired, her backside hurt, and she needed to get back to her little daughter. Altogether, the meeting had taken longer than she had expected, and her breasts were so hard with milk that even the press of the fabric of her dress on them was painful.

The sunlight came in low through the windows, but the light brought no warmth. By the Triune, it was as if all the joy had been sucked out of the air. She had better go back quickly— What were all these people doing there?

A veritable crowd had gathered in the hallway. They were servants of the palace and minor nobles of Saardam, those who had gathered in the foyer for the scraps of information that came out of the meeting.

They were all looking away from Johanna, to the end of the corridor where Nellie stood, holding Celine. Looking terrified.

Johanna could not normally see magic in the air, but the pulsing glow that radiated from Celine was so strong that even Johanna could see it. She bet even the nonmagical people could see it.

"Nellie!" Johanna pushed through the onlookers, who parted for her. She hesitated. There was an utterly evil look in Celine's little eyes, far too mature for a child of less than a day old.

"I don't know what to do, mistress Johanna." Nellie's eyes were wide with fear.

"Give her to me."

Johanna held out her hands. When Nellie put the bundle in Johanna's arms, magic swirled all around her. It crackled and stung her skin.

A woman gasped.

Someone whispered, "Sorcery!"

The magic found the wooden box in her purse. A strand of fire wound itself around the handles of the purse in ever-increasing speed. It whistled a high, screeching musical tone.

Johanna cradled the child against her chest, and put her hand over the box. The magic now swirled up her arm. She wriggled the box out of her purse with her free hand. She couldn't manage to open it with one hand, so she held the box out to Nellie. "Open it."

Nellie's terrified look fixed on the strands of magic. She took the box.

Johanna patted the child's back. The angry glow of magic vanished. But before Nellie could open the box, a man yelled, "Oh, look, look!" He pointed at the end of the corridor.

Johanna didn't want to look. She already knew that there were ghosts coming into the window, white ethereal presences oozing through the glass, shapeless patches of glowing ether that swirled and boiled. The window blew open, shattering glass. A larger, darker presence came in.

Johanna knew who this was, wearing his cloak of ghostly ether.

Several of the people behind her ran.

Johanna whispered, "Nellie, the box!"

Nellie whispered back, "It won't open!"

"Give it to me!"

But it was too late.

"Little Queen," said a male voice that sounded cultured and pleasant without being syrupy and strong without being over-bearing.

She hadn't heard that voice since the fateful night on the Guentherite farm when . . . She tightened her arms about the child. Little Celine had calmed down. She was warm and sleepy. Not evil. *When a child is born with the art, it is neither good nor evil.*

Li Fai had said that. Where was he? Where was Roald? Where were Loesie and her friend, and Master Deim and Duke Lothar and Natalya and all the people who could help her? How could she get her box back?

The male voice went on, "You know why I am here."

"I don't recall inviting you."

"You invited all important persons in the lowlands. You didn't think to send a personal invitation to the most important one of all?"

He walked around her. Since she had seen him last, he'd

grown a goatee. His red curls hung loose over his shoulders. The shimmering cloak made from ghost ether exuded a faint glow. Underneath, he wore black and his leather jerkin. He trailed a hand over her shoulder.

The chill that went through her body made her gasp. "Go away, Kylian."

He laughed. "Are you afraid of me?"

"No. I've just had enough of your games."

"You're not even a little bit afraid?" He leaned over her shoulder from behind, breathing cold air into her neck.

Johanna held her breath, determined not to flinch.

Celine squirmed in her arms, her little hands groping at Johanna's dress.

"Oh, look, the little one is hungry." He extended one finger to the child.

Johanna batted his hand away. "Keep your hands off her."

He laughed.

Celine started crying.

"I think she needs mother's milk, don't you?"

Johanna stroked Celine's head, desperate to show her love, desperate to protect her from Kylian. *What* was he up to?

"I think you'd like to feed her, wouldn't you? Answer me."

"I have no idea what you want. If you're so convinced that she needs feeding, then let me go so that I can feed her."

"Yes, she needs feeding. You need a quiet place to do that." His strong hand closed around her upper arm.

"Kylian, stop it!" Johanna tried to wrench herself loose, but the trick he'd taught her during their first meeting required two hands, and she only had one free hand.

He laughed. "You haven't forgotten anything."

He started off in the direction where the onlookers stood, dragging her with him. The servants and minor nobles and everyone else who had gathered there scurried out of the way.

A servant yelled out, "Leave our queen alone." He tried to pull Kylian's arm, but Kylian batted him away without even looking at the man.

In large strides, he dragged her through the hallway. Johanna had trouble keeping up with him, having given birth only at midday. He went into the ballroom, where the tables were ready for the evening meal, and out the double doors on the other side into the garden room.

Indeed, he took her to the place she feared: the bench that stood next to Celine's gravestone.

He pushed her down roughly. Celine was screaming, her toothless mouth wide open.

"Feed her."

"With you watching?"

"You think I don't know what a woman looks like?" But he turned around anyway, with the swish of his cloak.

Johanna undid the buttons at the front of her dress, opened it and pushed down her underdress. The fabric was wet with milk and her breast was so swollen that Celine found it hard to take the nipple. She screamed hysterically and nosed about, and the milk squirted in her face.

Kylian cleared his throat.

"Just go away!" Johanna shouted at him, feeling hot with frustration. "This is none of your business."

Celine found the nipple and latched onto her breast. Ouch. Quiet.

"But it is my business." He turned around. In his hand, palm up, he held the dagger with the bone and silver heft and the ruby pommel.

Johanna's heart jumped. "What are you doing with that thing?"

"You recognise it?" He smiled, not in a friendly way.

"Why should I recognise such a terrible ugly thing? It's a weapon. Put it away."

"As you wish, Your Majesty." His voice was mocking. He slipped the dagger in a sheath he carried on his belt. "You're a very bad liar, do you know that?"

Johanna did not respond. She covered Celine's little down-covered head with her hand. She thought of Li Fai's words, desperate to show Celine love before he could use her, because that was the reason he had come here, right?

She finished feeding on one breast and Johanna wriggled her

around for the other one. She was so little, so vulnerable, so peaceful, now falling asleep in Johanna's arms.

Kylian came back within the pool of light cast by the lamp. He knelt on the gravestone, pulled that dreadful dagger out again, and traced the engraved letters in the headstone with the tip of the blade. "Come over here."

"Why?"

"Don't ask. Do as I say." He grabbed her upper arm and pulled her up. Celine woke up with a cry.

"See what you just did?"

"You can always give her to me."

"No way." Johanna cradled Celine against her chest. Her dress still hung open.

Kylian pulled her with him. She tried to resist, but his grip on her arm was like a vice. His nails dug into the soft skin under her arm.

He pulled her until she stood on top of the slab of stone that covered Princess Celine's grave.

"Stand here."

"No." She shifted aside and ducked his grasping hands, holding Celine close to her chest.

He grabbed her by the arm, squeezing the soft flesh in his hand. "Stupid woman, do as I say." He looked down the front of her dress, which she hadn't been able to close yet.

"No." She tried to twist her arm out of his grip, but he pulled her against him. He smelled of horse and leather. His breath was hot in her neck.

"Let's get this over and done with. You're getting to be very annoying. Give me the child."

"No. You're not having her for your foul tricks."

He laughed.

Then there was a sound at the door. Kylian look up sharply.

A male voice said. "Hey, you. Let go of *my* women."

Oh no, Roald.

CHAPTER 22

KYLIAN TURNED AROUND and laughed.

"Look who we have here. It's the lame prince."

"Watch what you're saying." Roald strode into the room.

Johanna shook her head, for all the effect that would have on him. He was in his formal clothes and had probably been getting ready for dinner.

He waved his hand at Kylian. "Come on, come on, let her go. I'm the king and you have to do as I say, or I will call the guards."

Kylian chuckled. "Do you know what I'll do to your guards?"

"They're my guards and they're the best. They will kill you."

Johanna continued shaking her head. If Roald annoyed him enough, Kylian would kill him without a thought, with that terrible magical dagger or simply with magic.

Roald took no notice of her. Kylian took no notice. They faced each other on top of the gravestone in the pool of light cast by the single oil lamp that always burned.

Roald was taller than Kylian, and all the work in the garden had done pleasing things to his physique.

"Look at you," Kylian sneered. "Do you really think you are someone? Do you think that you and your pathetic commoner fishwife can change the course of history and stop the march of real power across the land?"

"What are you talking about? You are here by yourself. I can see no power."

"Do you really think that I'm here alone?"

He snapped his fingers. The glass of one of the doors burst inwards. A slight figure carrying a pickaxe stepped into the room. Johanna recognised the young boy whom she had also seen in her visions.

She exclaimed, "Rue? Ruben?"

He turned to her with an ice-cold, detached look in his eyes. His face was pale as a ghost's. He was dressed in rags that were intended for a much bigger man, with the sleeves and legs rolled up.

"Rue, what has this evil man promised you in return for your help?"

The boy turned away, his face unemotional.

"I am your queen, this is your king. Answer me."

But he kept staring into the distance, white-knuckled hands holding onto the handle of his pickaxe.

Several other people had followed him into the room, stepping through the broken glass: a farmer whom Johanna had seen at the markets, two men in the uniforms of the city guards, and Octavio Nieland.

It was the sight of the latter that disturbed Johanna most. His face looked blank, his eyes empty, and he walked in a strange, jerky way. His chin, at least a few days unshaven, was wet and the drool ran down the front of his shirt . . . the same one he had worn to the dinner on the first night.

Behind those people came other . . . beings. A bear-like animal that walked on its hind legs like a person, a tall and emaciated man with hollow eyes, scabbed lips and yellow teeth, who looked like he'd been dead yesterday and had been dug up from the grave.

Then there were the ghosts: so many of them, slipping in and out of human shapes, whirling, floating, oozing. All these people and beings gathered around where Kylian stood on the gravestone, a mass of magical, terrible creatures.

Kylian let go of Johanna's arm. She shuffled backwards off the gravestone, taking Roald with her. Maybe if Kylian was distracted, she would be able to reach the door to the ball room, but his terrible army spread around the room and covered all the exits. They were trapped.

Kylian raised his arms. His minions gathered around him and knelt on the ground, including Octavio Nieland, who, in his right mind, would never kneel to anybody. What had the necromancer done to him?

The ghosts formed the outer circle of the crowd, casting a broad ring of silver light.

Kylian started speaking. His words were harsh, sibilant, vibrating. They cut like shards of glass and hummed like a nest of angry hornets. His voice rasped like grating millstones and spat like demons.

The chant, this spell turned the air cold and radiated fear in rolling waves.

Johanna wanted to run, but the fear paralysed her. There was nowhere to run. This evil would take the entire city and all its citizens would be turned into jerky, mindless puppets like Octavio Nieland.

Roald had closed his arms around her and the child. Amazingly, Celine was fast asleep, her little fists balled against her cheeks.

Kylian's chanting grew louder and more frantic. The light from the oil lamp showed showers of spit flying from his mouth. Somewhere at the back of the crowd of beings, a voice started humming.

And then a female ghost floated in through the broken window, over the heads of the beings. It was Celine, in her yellow dress, barefoot, with snake-like tendrils of hair floating behind her as if she were underwater.

The humming grew louder until the air vibrated with it.

Roald tightened his grip around to Johanna's shoulders. His face was pale and sheened with sweat, his eyes wide.

The ghost came to a halt in front of Kylian. She held out her hands, opened her mouth and let out a low keening wail.

Kylian gestured to Johanna. "Bring her here."

Johanna held the child closer to her chest. Kylian's magic

probed at her mind. She turned away, looking at the door, away from his demanding gaze.

Kylian repeated, "Bring her here."

"No," Johanna said. "She is only an infant. She has no fault and no business in your evil plans."

"She is mine!" Roald said.

Kylian laughed, not a pleasant sound. "This child has as much Carmine blood as your dear wife." His nostrils flared. A strand of magic flared out from him. It circled around Roald and pushed him aside. "Bring. Her. Here."

The magic spread to Johanna, swirling around her, binding her legs. She was forced to take a step forward, and another one. She couldn't stop and couldn't turn around. Her arms were frozen around the child, unable to release her, put her down or give her to Roald. He shouted at her, but she heard only Kylian's voice ordering her to come.

She came to him, the man whose seed had quickened in her stomach and who now demanded the fruit.

Celine's ghost stood before him, head bowed.

Kylian held his hands on top of each other against his chest, holding the dagger with the bone and silver handle. The blade shimmered in the ghostly light.

Octavio Nieland rose from his subservient crouch and held out his hands. "Give her to me."

There was no way Johanna could disobey the command. She fought it with all her mind, but lost. Kylian's magic was too strong. Octavio took the swaddled child from her, and held the tiny infant out to Kylian—

Who raised the dagger—

Something inside Johanna's mind broke free of Kylian's magical stranglehold.

She screamed.

And there was a loud crash somewhere in the room, and the sound of many people running in, and the clashing of swords and whooshing of arrows.

The magical bonds fell away from Johanna's limbs.

A group of men had burst in through the door from the ball-room. Johanna spotted Johan Delacoeur, swinging his sword. He cut the head clean off one of Kylian's minions, but the man shambled after his head and put it back where it belonged.

"Sorcery, sorcery!" Another group of soldiers ran into the room, swinging burning torches through the ghosts, scattering shards of ether.

"Johanna, get out of here!" That was Father's voice.

But she couldn't run, not without Celine.

But Kylian and Octavio had disappeared in the chaos. The room was filled with a mixture of soldiers in glittering armour swinging swords or torches. The air was thick with smoke and ghost ether, punctured with moving spots of light from the torches. Swords clanged, men shouted. Beings wailed and growled.

Johanna screamed, "Octavio! Come here and give me the princess if you dare." Her words got lost in the sounds of battle.

A shrill female voice cut through the noise, shouting harsh and guttural words.

That was Natalya, standing as a somewhat squat and dumpy silhouette against deep red light coming from the ballroom behind her. In response to Natalya's spell, many ghosts cleared the area around her. Johanna made her way to the door.

"He has Celine," she cried.

Duchess Carlotta was with Natalya, looking pale and wide-eyed.

Before Johanna could ask what the red light was, the source of it became visible through the smoke and mist: it was Li Fai's dragon, crouched on its haunches, radiating red light and breathing fire from its nostrils. It had grown to monstrous size, towering halfway to the ceiling of the ballroom.

Its owner stood next to it, with Master Deim.

They were accompanied by the shepherd, who protested loudly, "But I can't do that!"

"Enough," Master Deim said. "Our kingdom is in danger, our people, our very freedom. Are you going to be sanctimonious and still maintain that you know nothing about magic? We've all been hiding it, but none have been so stupid as you."

The shepherd was going to protest, but Master Deim spotted

Johanna coming out of the garden room. He crossed the floor and enveloped her in a hug. "Oh, child, I thought you were lost."

"Please, he's got Celine!" Johanna's voice spilled over.

"Who has Celine? Where is Roald?"

"Kylian has her. He has Octavio Nieland and a whole lot of evil beings with him. Roald is in there as well. I couldn't see him anymore. Please we must do something or he will kill her."

A couple of the soldiers ran out of the room. They leaned, panting, against the wall next to the door, and unwound cloths and shirts from their faces.

They were not soldiers at all, but young women, farming women with strong arms and manlike physiques. These had to be the women from Loesie's farm. One of them carried a sword that was both rusty and blunt and looked far too heavy for her. Flashes of ghostly ether shimmered along the blade. She wore a man's clothing, and her face was dirty. Johanna met her eyes.

"Please, Your Majesty, don't go in there. It's a massacre in there," she said. "We can't fight them. There are too many and they're too strong. He has the dagger."

"He hasn't . . . used it yet?" Johanna felt sick.

"Oh no, the first thing he needs to do with it is cut the tree open that holds Alexandre's spirit. Then can perform his completely necromancy."

He was going join Celine's ghost with the infant Celine's body.

Johanna felt sick.

"The only way to fight him is to join the forces of nature," Li Fai said.

"You can't beat him," the woman said. "Believe me, many have tried."

"Have they tried at the same time?" Li Fai asked.

"What do you mean?"

"If we join all our magic together, we can each be one of the elements." He pointed at Master Deim and Johanna. "You can be water, you can be wood."

"But I don't have my box! Nellie has it." Panic washed over her.

"You will have the art of wood regardless of the box. You

have defended yourself with your art before you had the box, right?"

Yes, he was right, she had, but it was so long ago.

Li Fai went on, "I will have to be fire although it would be better to have a real fire artist here." Then he pointed at the shepherd. "And you must be air."

The shepherd gasped and protested, "I don't know how to—"

"Do you think any of us know?" said Master Deim. "We will do our best together. We get one chance at this, or we will all die. We need you. Rest assured we would gladly do without your whining if we could."

The shepherd stared at him, his face pale. Master Deim was one of the least excitable people Johanna knew, and for him to call the shepherd out for whining meant he had to be very angry.

The shepherd knew this. He let his shoulders sink. "I will try." He cast a suspicious look at the dragon.

Johanna would have loved to have Natalya and Loesie to draw on, but she had no idea where either of them were. Surely they would feel the magic in the air? What was Natalya's magic? What else did Loesie have other than wood magic?

Li Fai held out both his hands. She put her hand in his. His skin was warm and reminded her too uncomfortably of different time. One corner of his mouth moved up.

Master Deim took his other hand and then took hold of the shepherd, who still looked uncertain. The women soldiers followed close behind. Like this, they went into the garden room.

The oil light next to the grave had gone out. People and beasts struggled in the darkness, under a cloak of mist and smoke. The only thing Johanna could see was the moving light from torches and the pale glow from ghost ether. Weapons clanged, men screamed, ghosts keened.

They advanced into the room. The smell of steel, leather and burning flesh was strong. Johanna's foot hit something soft—it was the arm of a mangled body in a pool of blood.

Bile rose in her throat. If she survived this, she would raze this dreadful room of death to the ground.

Then: the shrill cry of an infant.

"Celine!"

Johanna wrenched her hand out of Li Fai's. She needed to save the child first, give her to someone to take her deep within the palace where Kylian could not reach her.

Kylian stood on top of the gravestone, holding Celine. Her shrill cry cut through the other noises: the groaning and whistling and hissing of sibilant voices. Shards of ghostly ether floated on the floor around his feet. The ground was covered in bodies and blood.

Johanna desperately wanted a weapon. She spotted the hilt of a sword sticking out from underneath a man's body. Was that Octavio Nieland? She felt sick.

No, a metal sword would be no good. Then she found something else: the pick axe that Rue had used to break the door. She picked it up, and wooden handle felt *alive* in her hands.

The glow from Li Fai's dragon lit the room from behind. So many dead bodies, not all of them human.

Kylian faced her, his eyes burning with anger. "You think you're an adept at magic now? You think you can defeat me?"

"Wood magic is stronger than fire magic and stronger than bear magic." Her hands gripped the handle of the pickaxe. She was so tired. She hoped that there would be no more walking or running involved, because she would surely faint.

"Maybe. But I've got the dagger of bone that can cut the spirits from the wood. I'll open the two ugly trees that you have wrought and free my disciples. Then I'll resurrect the princess' soul inside this little child and she will be mine."

"Why, Kylian? Whatever you do, you will never rule through fear. You can spread your seed all through the lowlands, but all that will achieve is that you will produce lots of other magicians, all of whom have different wishes and philosophies."

"The future lies in machines that can make things for us, using iron magic."

Li Han said, "If you want to be my father's partner in trade, spreading death is not the way to do it. We don't need you. There is a large mass of land across the Lamorian Ocean. We don't need to stay here or deal with you."

Then Master Deim asked in a mild voice, "I know that King

Nicholaos paid you to resurrect Celine. But he's dead, you already have his money. Why are you so obsessed with her?"

Kylian stiffened. He stared at Master Deim, who came forward and pulled a roll of parchment out of his pocket. "Our dear queen wanted to know if there was any money left of the royal family's considerable fortunes, and I went to look for any investments and land ownership of assets that we could possibly sell. I came across this interesting piece of correspondence." He unrolled the parchment. "It says, 'Your eyes are as blue as the summer sky. Your hair fair as gold'—"

"Stop it!" Kylian shouted. His eyes bulged.

Master Deim coolly rolled the parchment back up and stuck it back in his pocket. "You get the idea. It's a letter from a love-struck adolescent to a young princess who was at the age of flowering into a woman, and who was struck by disease and died a little later. I couldn't find any evidence that the letter was ever responded to."

"Stop. It!" Kylian's nostrils flared.

"Master Deim, be careful," Johanna said. But, oh by the Triune, did he make a lot of sense.

Kylian had been love-struck with Celine when both were youngsters. She might have been promised to him and when she died unexpectedly, he'd been so bereft that he wanted to do everything to bring her back to life, to the point of turning into something too evil for words.

A child with the art is not born good or evil. It is the actions of men that make it so.

Those actions of men might have been nothing more than the baron scoffing at his son and telling him to get over it. She could totally see the baron doing that.

Kylian stared at Master Deim, trembling, his face shined with sweat, nostrils wide.

Master Deim held out his hands. "Give the child to me before worse things happen. This child is innocent, and true necromancy is probably impossible."

Johanna held her breath. Kylian closed his eyes and blew out a breath. Slowly, he handed the child to Master Deim.

"Now put down that dagger and come with me."

For a moment, it looked like Kylian would obey. Then he flinched.

"No. Never! I'll free my spirits and we'll rule the world with fear!"

He turned on his heel and made for the terrace doors.

"Call your power now!" Li Fai shouted. He took off after Kylian, who was already almost outside.

No, no. "Do something. Stop him." Johanna's voice broke into a squeal. She tried to run, but it felt like her insides would come out through her backside. She was unsteady on her feet. The wadded up towel felt wet with sticky blood. She was going to faint.

Master Deim ran to her and gave her the crying child. "Get to safety!"

Then he followed the shepherd and Li Fai into the garden, followed by the dragon in big bounding leaps.

A wall of water rose from the river and crashed into the garden. A whirlwind whipped it into a waterspout. The dragon breathed fire to boil the water. The steam formed into a giant whirlwind.

Kylian stopped at the empty spot where once there had been the fountain with the statue of the Triune. He flicked his hand. All the ghostly beings, the empty-faced people and other ghosts, bears and spirits shattered into thousands of pieces. He flicked his hand again, and the shards reformed into a cloak that grew over his body. He was drawing the magical power of all those beings inside him.

A male voice shouted, "Look over here you foul creature!"

Kylian looked. Everyone else in the garden looked, too.

Duke Lothar stood at the top of the stairs into the garden room. In his hands, he held a powder gun.

Kylian started laughing. "You think you can harm me with that thing?"

Duke Lothar lifted the gun. His hand tightened around the trigger. *Click.* Fire flashed.

Johanna covered her ears against the bang.

An unearthly voice rose from the apparition that Kylian had become. The terrible shrieking noise became louder and louder until her ears hurt. The magical being grew and grew until it had bloated to many times its size. Duke Lothar was busy with his gun, tamping in the powder, setting the trigger, putting in a bullet. . . . He held it up to Johanna. His lips moved. "Silver."

He aimed and fired at the bloated monstrosity. At this size, it was impossible for him to miss.

It exploded with a roar that shook the ground. Shards of magic flew outwards, into the sky, into the river, into the garden beds. They blew aside everyone in their way.

Johanna ducked behind a pillar.

Ghosts wailed and hissed as they sank into the river. The last Johanna saw was the ghost with the yellow dress and the flowing locks of hair. It lost shape as it hit the surface of the water, as the adolescent wishes of its owner died.

There was nothing left in the garden except a pile of smouldering ash.

CHAPTER 23

SILENCE.

Johanna came out from behind the pillar. The moon had risen and showed a scene of complete destruction. The entire side of the garden room was gone, even part of the roof of the ballroom had been blown off.

"Master Deim? Father? Li Fai?" Where was everyone?

A groan sounded behind her and someone said, "Keep your hands off *my* women."

Johanna whirled around. "Roald?"

He sat on his knees behind the next pillar. Johanna went to check on him. He said he had fallen and hurt his wrist, but he was otherwise fine.

Duke Lothar had gone to the remains of the fountain to check out his handiwork, poking the pile of ash with his feet. He found something on the ground and showed it to his son who had also come into the garden. It was the dagger with the bone hilt.

More people were coming out of the palace, stepping around the mess and carnage.

Johanna called, "Father?"

"Yes, I'm here." He was at the top of the stairs, just leaving the garden room.

"Thank the heavens you're fine."

Master Deim and the shepherd came stumbling out of the garden, both wet and covered in mud.

"Where is Li Fai?" She asked.

Master Deim shook his head. "I haven't seen him."

"Here, hold her." Johanna gave Celine to Father and went down the stairs into the garden. She stayed clear of the rubble and ash in the empty and broken fountain basin. She didn't want to see the awful sight of what was left of Kylian. When daylight came, the destruction would be clear enough.

The moonlight glittered on something in the garden bed. A large object lay there that was big enough to be a man.

"Li Fai?"

Yes, she was right, it was a body, but it was one of the palace guards. "Li Fai?" She found another body and another one further into the garden.

Then she recognised his boots on a body that lay face down in the grass.

No. Johanna crouched next to him.

"Li Fai!" Please, no. "Li Fai!" She shook his shoulder.

His box lay next to him, open, empty.

No. Where was the dragon? He *needed* his dragon.

She spotted a piece of tail from underneath a fallen section of roof to the side of the old fountain.

Johanna ran across the rubble-strewn lawn. She heaved off the beams and planks with all the strength she had. Roald joined to help her.

The dragon lay on its side. It had shrunk to the size of a dog and was fast fading. The red glow inside its body had almost disappeared.

She knelt, carefully slid her hands underneath and picked it up. "Please, get better. Please." The tears streamed over her cheeks.

Johanna carried the dragon to Li Fai and put it on the grass next to the box. It opened an orange eye.

She took Li Fai's hand, which felt slack and cold, and nudged the dragon with her toes.

"Come on. Stop playing silly games with us. Get back in the box."

It lifted the tip of its tail, but didn't move.

Johanna picked up the box. She held it under the dragon's nose. It sniffed. Shivered. Then lay down its head and closed its eyes.

No, no, no.

Johanna clutched Li Fai's hand against her chest. With all her might, she thought about her happiness when she was with him. She thought about his kiss and how he had gently made love to her.

"Look, it's gone," Roald said.

The dragon had almost dissolved in the air. Johanna could barely see it through the haze of tears.

Johanna gathered the last wisps of ether in the box. She shut the lid and put it next to Li Fai's body.

"He's a good friend," Roald said.

You wouldn't know. Tears streamed over Johanna's face.

"Come." Master Deim pulled her up. "You've done far too much today. There is a lot of fixing up to be done tomorrow."

"I can't just leave him. Where are his parents?"

"I will tell them."

"Tell them that their only son is dead?"

"Johanna . . ."

"No, I will tell them. He is dead because of me."

"Please, calm down."

"I don't want to calm down. He died because he wanted to protect me."

Master Deim grabbed hold of both Johanna's wrists and looked her in the eyes. "Calm down. Remember, before you do anything silly, why Kylian upset all of the lowlands."

Because he'd fallen in love with Celine.

Because he didn't accept that she died.

Because he was a powerful untrained magician.

She understood the danger. She nodded, and pressed her lips together.

Master Deim breathed out.

Then there was a small sound behind them, a sharp intake of breath.

Johanna looked over her shoulder.

Li Fai's chest . . . was moving. She yanked herself out of Master Deim's grip and dropped to her knees. He was definitely breathing, coughing.

"Li Fai, Li Fai. Oh, help me get him inside!"

Together with Master Deim, she helped him up. He was quite a sight, completely soaked, his shirt sticking to his chest.

Li Fai coughed and Master Deim thumped his back.

Then he opened his eyes and looked at Johanna. He couldn't speak for the coughing, but the gratitude in his expression was enough.

A couple of guards moved Li Fai to the guest room. Johanna and Roald went to bed, and Johanna finally slept, interrupted only when Nellie came to bring Celine for feeding.

The next day showed the destruction of the ballroom and the garden room.

"We'll build another ball room on the other side of the palace," Johanna said. "The garden room can be a memorial garden." She would have memorials for Queen Cygna and King Nicholaos installed there.

The historic trade and investment agreement was signed in the Red Room two days later and all around town, the town crier announced the news to cheers for Johanna and her father.

There would now be money for rebuilding the harbour and warehouses. Of course the kings, dukes and barons still bickered a lot before they signed it, and of course they didn't agree on everything, and of course the negotiations had been full of silly compromises and men behaving like toddlers.

Loesie and her girls left the next day. She wasn't interested in talk, she said when Johanna saw her, and there was work to be done. In winter when the children of the city couldn't play outdoors, Loesie would provide the first teachers of magic Saardam had ever seen.

The shepherd still didn't like it, but he knew better than to protest.

King William left two days later in his huge ship with billowing sails. Johanna stood by the window of her nursery in the palace, holding Celine, and watched the ship sail out the delta and out to sea.

Celine's little body glowed with magic. She would need a lot of training, but she would have a good teacher in Li Fai. She would be surrounded by loving people, and hopefully that would ward her off any bad paths that she might consider. As a magician, when she was grown and took the throne, she would protect Saardam.

Li Fai took a few months to recover fully, during which he moved to a small house with an office in East Harbour. His father and mother resumed the sea trade and came back with strange artefacts and stories of the large landmass on the other side of the Lamorian Ocean. They saw some strange people there, but most of all they spoke about the strange birds. Li Fai's mother's collection of drawings grew.

Life in Saardam became as close as it would ever be to normal.

Roald pottered in the garden, forgot to eat, hated meetings and never once wore his crown.

Houses were rebuilt, the harbour project started and flourished. Ships came in. Father took delivery of a new ship, appointed new crew, a new accountant and resumed the river trade.

Johanna continued to struggle with the King's Council and the old-fashioned men in it who grew only slightly less old-fashioned.

Celine learned to walk and run and kept Nellie busy. Her hair was straw-coloured and curly. She had freckles on her nose, and everyone commented how much she looked like Roald. Her magic made Johanna sure she *wasn't* Roald's, but it mattered little. Kylian was gone forever. The people of Saardam adored the princess.

In autumn of the next year, Johanna finally got to use the birthing chair for a very normal, hard and painful delivery where Helena could be present, water could be boiled and fires stoked in plenty of time.

But the story of the little black-haired, dark-eyed prince is one that might be told another day.

A Word of Thanks

THANK YOU for reading the Ghostspeaker Chronicles.

The story of Johanna's son is told in the Dragonspeaker Chronicles. You can find out more about these books on Patty Jansen's website.

ABOUT THE AUTHOR

Patty Jansen lives in Sydney, Australia, where she spends most of her time writing Science Fiction and Fantasy.

Her story *This Peaceful State of War* placed first in the second quarter of the Writers of the Future contest and was published in their 27th anthology. She has also sold fiction to genre magazines such as Analog Science Fiction and Fact, Redstone SF and Aurealis.

Patty has written over twenty novels in both Science Fiction and Fantasy, including the *Icefire Trilogy* and the *Ambassador* series.

pattyjansen.com

BOOKS BY PATTY JANSEN

More information:

PATTYJANSEN.COM